FOR GIRLS WHO WALK THROUGH FIRE

FOR GIRLS WHO WALK THROUGH FIRE

KIM DEROSE

U

UNION
SQUARE
& CO.

NEW YORK

UNION SQUARE & CO.

NEW YORK

UNION SQUARE & CO. and the distinctive Union Square & Co. logo are trademarks of Sterling Publishing Co., Inc.

Union Square & Co., LLC, is a subsidiary of Sterling Publishing Co., Inc.

Text © 2023 Kim DeRose

ISBN 978-1-4549-4887-2 (hardcover)
ISBN 978-1-4549-4888-9 (e-book)
ISBN 978-1-4549-4889-6 (paperback)

Library of Congress Cataloging-in-Publication Data

Names: DeRose, Kim, author.
Title: For girls who walk through fire / by Kim DeRose.
Description: New York : Union Square and Co., 2023. | Audience: Ages 14 and up | Summary: "Four high school girls take justice for their sexual assaults into their own hands by forming a secret witch coven and casting revenge spells on their attackers"—Provided by publisher.
Identifiers: LCCN 2022059132 (print) | LCCN 2022059133 (ebook) | ISBN 9781454948872 (hardcover) | ISBN 9781454948896 (paperback) | ISBN 9781454948889 (epub)
Subjects: CYAC: Witchcraft—Fiction. | Rape—Fiction. | Revenge—Fiction. | Friendship—Fiction. | High schools—Fiction. | Schools—Fiction. | BISAC: YOUNG ADULT FICTION / Paranormal, Occult & Supernatural | YOUNG ADULT FICTION / Girls & Women | LCGFT: Witch fiction. | Novels.
Classification: LCC PZ7.1.D4754 Fo 2023 (print) | LCC PZ7.1.D4754 (ebook) |DDC [Fic]—dc23
LC record available at https://lccn.loc.gov/2022059132
LC ebook record available at https://lccn.loc.gov/2022059133

For information about custom editions, special sales, and premium purchases, please contact specialsales@unionsquareandco.com.

Printed in the United States of America

2 4 6 8 10 9 7 5 3 1

unionsquareandco.com

Interior match image by Popov Nikolay/Shutterstock.com
Interior smoke image by KDdesignphoto/Shutterstock.com
Cover art by Katt Phatt
Cover and interior design by Marcie Lawrence

For Graham and Frankie

&

For anyone who has walked through fire

1

Elliott couldn't imagine anything more depressing than attending a sexual abuse and assault support group for Santa Barbara County teen girls housed in a kindergarten classroom.

No, that wasn't true; she could easily name half a dozen things *way* more depressing, and that was sourcing from her own life alone.

But that wasn't the point.

The point was that sitting in a miniature chair, listening to other girls detail all the ways their lives had been ruined by douchebag boyfriends and random assholes, abusive babysitters, and creepy neighbors (not to mention *family members*), all while Crayola stick figure families and five-year-old-sized handprint butterflies smiled down on you was goddamn *tragic*.

Elementary schoolteacher Mary Yoshida, fearless leader of said Tragic Kindergarten Kingdom, was nodding as Emma, a new girl with curly red hair and pale freckled skin, detailed how the scummy college freshman she'd met at her best friend's Fourth of July party got her drunk and then forced himself on her behind the garden shed. As Emma spoke, Elliott picked at her black nail polish, the flakes collecting on her vintage Smashing Pumpkins T-shirt.

"...and I just, I don't know," Emma concluded, pulling her shirt sleeves down over her hands. "I feel like I should be angry? But instead, I just feel... numb? Or maybe... I don't know. I don't even know *how* to feel." Emma wrapped her arms around her stomach and let out a shuddering sigh. "So that's it. That's me. I've never really said any of that out loud before."

"*Thank you*, Emma." Mary smiled warmly, leaning toward the girl. "We're so glad you shared with us. And it's okay not to know. These things take time to process. That's why we're all here. To share, to listen, to process. Thank you for being so honest and brave."

Emma gave a quick nod, staring at her scuffed-up Converse.

Mary cupped her hands in her lap and looked out at the group, which changed in size week to week. Most of the time they numbered about a dozen, but today there were closer to twenty-five. The start of the school year had everyone triggered.

Mary had perfect posture and this preternatural Zen quality that Elliott couldn't decide if she detested or admired. (Is that what came of being a rape survivor for over two decades, Elliott wondered. Or had Mary gone to some weird, serene place just to survive? And was it racist to call her Zen? Or was it fine since she was, in fact, a Buddhist?) Mary had been a counselor before becoming a kindergarten teacher, and once upon a time she'd apparently known Elliott's mom when they were both college students at UCSB. Which intrigued Elliott . . . but not enough to speak.

Mary calmly surveyed the girls. "So? Who else would like to share?"

Silence fell upon the circle. There was the squeak of people shifting in their chairs.

Mary's eyes moved clockwise and landed on Elliott. Elliott stared back. No fucking way.

"Well," Mary offered gently, adjusting her cat eyeglasses. "I think it's worth discussing what I know we're all thinking about. And, Kaylie." She looked toward the blond girl seated three seats to Elliott's left. "I'm so glad you decided to attend group today. I can only imagine how difficult this past week has been for you."

Kaylie was slunk down in her chair, mouth clamped shut, arms crossed over her chest, wearing a hoodie and rumpled pajama bottoms. She and Elliott were both seniors at Santa Barbara High and had gone to school together since elementary—though it's not like they were actually *friends*. Kaylie had always been your classic girlygirl; showing off her gymnastic moves at recess and collecting American Girl dolls back in the day, breezing through the halls of Santa Barbara High with her vast array of friends, and cheering at all the games. Not exactly Elliott's vibe.

Not that Kaylie wasn't *nice*—she *was*. She was cheerful. And sparkly. And basically, the poster child for well-adjusted adolescence and All-American high school life.

Which was why it had been such a shock the first time Elliott came to group and spotted her, of all people.

"If you want to process things together," Mary offered. "We're here to listen."

Kaylie remained silent, eyes fixed on the rainbow rug their chairs were circled around.

"Well, I just wanted to say that I feel *horrible* about it," Chatty Charlotte leapt in, her eyes brimming with tears. "And I am so, so sorry, Kaylie."

Chatty Charlotte was *always* feeling. If Elliott had a nickel for every time Charlotte emoted all over somebody else's problems, she'd ship Charlotte off to a remote desert island. *Definitely* not a candidate for the List.

"It's just so messed up," Charlotte continued. "I can't get over it. How could he . . . I mean, how could *that* be the verdict?" She covered her mouth with both hands like she might cry.

A few girls murmured their agreement.

Never Have I Ever Raya, who just could *never* believe the reactions of outside people (Raya was second only to Charlotte when it came to sharing in group, and therefore a hard no for the List), cleared their throat. "When I heard the verdict . . . I just *couldn't* believe it. It just made me feel like nobody even cares. Like, all this bad stuff can happen to us, and no matter how much we speak up, the world just keeps *going*. You were so brave, Kaylie. You deserved better."

"Yeah," agreed Church-Mouse Maritza, who was *waaayyy* too meek for the List. She always spoke like she was sitting in the first pew at mass. "You did. And it sucks."

"It totally sucks, and I'm so sorry," added Miss Prima Ballerina Madeline, a straitlaced senior at private Catholic school Bishop Garcia Diego. Madeline was new to group, but from the little Elliott had seen, she was in *zero way* List material.

Girl after girl jumped in with their heartfelt condolences, assuring Kaylie that the verdict was totally unfair and reminding her that she was so awesome and brave.

Elliott stayed silent, finding each girl more irritating than the last. The thing is, they weren't *wrong*. Kaylie *was* brave. And it *was* unfair. Start of junior year, Kaylie gets raped by a senior while drunk at a party, has the whole thing filmed and shared with the varsity baseball team, is brave enough to go to the police and press charges, takes the stand as "Emily Doe," and the judge decides he doesn't want the *guy* to have his entire life ruined "by one mistake" just because he "has potential" and "a future ahead of him"? What about *Kaylie's* potential? What about *Kaylie's* future? Did *she* get a vote on having *her* life ruined? Did *any* of them?

It was kind of amazing to Elliott that after everything Kaylie had been through, she kept showing up to school every day acting bubbly and totally *normal*. Especially given the trial's recent blowback: supporters of Kaylie's rapist had taken to social media and were buzzing in the halls about how #MeToo had gone too far and how that "slut" was just trying to take some poor guy down. Maybe *they* didn't know that "slut" was Kaylie—the video didn't show her face, and she'd managed to remain anonymous, except to her immediate family and two of her closest friends—but *she* knew. She still had to hear all that crap.

But the Kaylie in group was always a stark contrast to the Kaylie at school. In *group* she let her cheerful persona drop, her face relaxing into a serious expression so that her outsides more closely matched her insides (or so Elliott assumed).

And yet *this* dead-eyed version of Kaylie was something else entirely. Was this the *new* Kaylie, Elliott wondered. The Kaylie who'd given up? The Kaylie *after*?

Chatty Charlotte was launching into round two of her condolences, and it was more than Elliott could bear. "This," she burst out, "is *bull*shit."

The girls flinched and looked over at her, like they hadn't realized she could even *speak*. A marble statue come to life. Charlotte glanced at Mary, wondering if this outburst would be sanctioned or scolded.

"Elliott," Mary said proudly, as if Elliott had just waltzed in and announced she was running for Tragic Kindergarten Kingdom president. "Tell me more. Let's talk about what you're—"

"*No.*" Elliott shook her head. "You see, that's the whole point. All this *talking* gets us absolutely nowhere. And I'm sick of it."

From the corner of her eye, Elliott saw Kaylie turn her head. Elliott glanced at her and for a moment their eyes met. Kaylie looked away.

Mary nodded slowly, a solemn expression on her face. "Yes. I hear you, Elliott. I really do. It's normal to have a lot of strong feelings when triggered."

Elliott rolled her eyes. This wasn't *triggered*; this was fed the hell up.

"Is anyone else feeling this way?" Mary asked the group. "Let's talk about our feelings of powerlessness and frustration."

Unsurprisingly, Chatty Charlotte piped up. *"I'm* feeling super powerless and—"

Elliott groaned as she got to her feet. "Screw"—she snatched up her backpack—"this."

And with that, she strode out of the room.

Outside, leaning against one of the waist-high brick posts at the edge of the school parking lot, earbuds firmly in place, Elliott blasted Joy Division and shoved her hands into the pockets of her vintage leather jacket, eyes trained on busy Las Positas Street for her grandma's Honda Accord.

Elliott had attended group every Thursday evening for over three months, and so far, as expected, it had gotten her squat. Well, that wasn't *entirely* true. It *had* provided a few potential names for her List. But it hadn't, like, *improved* her life. The truth was, if it weren't for her grandmother's insistence that she go somewhere for "girls like her"—a contentious bargain made from pure desperation and the need to shut her grandmother up—there's no way she'd *ever* attend group on her own.

Girls like her. God. Such a classic judgy Prudence statement.

Not that Prudence D'Angelo's judiness was anything new. Whenever Elliott was with her, Elliott could feel the disapproval rolling off her grandmother, who, based on her many hushed comments to Elliott's father, seemed to object to everything about Elliott. There was Elliott's nose ring ("I just worry that hoop is going to get in*fected,* Daniel. That's all."), her constantly changing hair ("It's just such a *bright* shade of *pink.* Does it always have to be so *abnormal*?"), not to mention every single thing Elliott wore ("Couldn't those ugly boots and flannel shirts *stay* where they *belong*, in the *nineties*? It was bad enough when Veronica wore outfits like that, God bless her soul.").

But the thing Prudence most objected to was the thing she and Elliott never discussed. The thing Elliott's father didn't know about. The thing that prompted Prudence to show up every Thursday evening at Adams Elementary School to pick up Elliott.

Soon enough the other girls began to trickle out, heads down as they hurried along the covered outdoor corridor that led to the parking lot, quickly angling toward their parked cars or rushing toward idling vehicles. Elliott searched for Kaylie in her peripheral vision and spotted her making a beeline for her mom's SUV.

Elliott became aware that one of the girls was walking directly toward her. When she looked, she was surprised to find it was Miss Prima Ballerina Madeline. Elliott had to wonder what had happened to *her.* Like Elliott, and only a couple of the other girls, Madeline had yet to share her story.

Madeline stopped in front of Elliott, arms folded over her long-sleeved ruffly pink blouse.

Elliott lowered the volume on "She's Lost Control" and pulled out one earbud. She could hear the cars rushing by on Las Positas and the flagpole clinking in the wind as she raised her eyebrows in a question. *Yes?*

"It *is* bullshit," Madeline said evenly.

Elliott eyed her, in her expensive leather riding boots and designer jeans, her long glossy chestnut hair carefully arranged over one shoulder, her pale skin accented with just a hint of tasteful makeup. Was she for *real?*

At that moment a silver Honda Accord pulled into the parking lot and flashed its lights at Elliott. Elliott pulled out her other earbud and picked up the backpack at her Doc Martens–clad feet. She gave Madeline one last assessing glance before heading to the car.

"Make a salad, will you?" Prudence instructed Elliott as she slid a casserole dish from the oven.

"Yes, master," Elliott muttered as she set the final napkin on the table and then went to the cabinet to pull out a large glass bowl.

Ever since Elliott's mom's death seven years ago, Prudence had become a fixture in their house. Cooking up meals to put in the freezer, doing all the ironing, cleaning out and organizing the cupboards. Tasks that no one had asked her to do or even cared about but that she took upon herself for the sake of her poor widowed son-in-law and her wayward granddaughter.

"Hey, El," her dad greeted her as he came into the kitchen from his home office. Daniel Brandt had been so handsome when Elliott's mom was still alive, with his shock of black hair and twinkly eyes set behind Buddy Holly glasses. And he still was, just an unshaven, wounded sort of handsome. He placed a kiss on the top of her head. "Sorry, I got a call from a client right when you—" He stopped short, eyeing the casserole dish on the counter. "Prudence, what is that?"

"What?" Prudence asked innocently, wiping her manicured hands on the KISS ME, I'M SICILIAN apron she always insisted on wearing. "It's lasagna."

"I *told* her," Elliott warned as she chopped up a carrot.

"Prudence, we talked about this. El and I are going vegetarian. We can't eat this." He motioned at the lasagna.

"Well, I *used* ground turkey, Daniel," Prudence defended, managing to sound like both a martyr and a matriarch. Characteristics, Elliott noticed, that often went hand in hand.

Elliott's dad shook his head as he walked to the fridge. "I'm ordering us Thai," he informed Elliott, pulling out his phone as he grabbed a beer. "Hey, how was your SAT prep course? Boring as always?"

"Pretty much," Elliott lied as she abandoned her salad making, aware of her grandmother quietly Saran Wrapping her precious lasagna just a few feet away.

It was both a blessing and a curse that Prudence, of all people, had been the one home that morning when Elliott came in after . . . after what had happened to her. Just seeing someone familiar had caused Elliott to burst into tears.

"Ellie?" her grandma had asked in concern, pulling her into an embrace.

"Something happened," Elliott had sobbed. "This guy . . ." She couldn't even complete the sentence.

Prudence had suddenly held Elliott at arm's length. "Did he hurt you?" she'd asked in concern.

Elliott had nodded, mascara streaking down her cheeks.

"Well, did you *do* something?" her grandmother had asked softly. Her voice was gentle, but her words were an accusation as she gripped Elliott a little too tight.

Elliott had sobered a bit. "No . . . it wasn't my fault," she'd managed.

Prudence had pressed her lips together, like she had her doubts.

Elliott had anticipated the lecture that was sure to come—she was positive her grandmother had *a lot* of ideas and assumptions about her, even before this crisis—but to Elliott's great surprise and relief, Prudence had remained silent.

"Just . . . please don't say anything to Dad," Elliott had begged, wiping her eyes. "He's dealt with enough already."

"Of *course* I won't," Prudence had agreed, as if doing so was completely out of the question. Which had only made Elliott feel worse.

It was an acknowledgment of what she'd already known: she was a burden, something from which her father must be protected.

Lying faceup on her bed that night, Elliott listened to Bjork's "Army of Me" while staring idly at the vintage movie posters on her wall—Agnès Varda's *Cléo from 5 to 7*, Leos Carax's *Mauvais Sang*, Jacque Rivette's *Céline and Julie Go Boating*, some of her mom's favorites. Her mother, Veronica—Ronnie to her close friends—majored in film studies, writing her thesis on the representation of women in late twentieth-century French cinema. She'd gone on to become a film editor, mostly editing commercials, but she'd done a few documentaries, too.

If her mom were still alive, Elliott often wondered, would Elliott be brave enough to tell her about what had happened to her? And if she did, what would her mother think? On the one hand, her mom had been an artist and a free thinker, so maybe she'd be open and understanding. On the other hand, she'd had a strict upbringing under Prudence's iron thumb, and her Catholic roots ran deep.

It is bullshit.

Madeline's words rang through Elliott's head. Something about her had seemed surprisingly . . . resolute.

Rolling onto her stomach, Elliott opened her nightstand drawer, pulled out a battered leather journal, and flipped to the most recent entry. At the top of the page was the heading POSSIBILITIES and listed below were three different initials.

Clicking on her pen, Elliott added one more—M for Madeline—which she circled in bold.

2

The following Thursday at five forty-five, Elliott paced the edge of the Adam's Elementary School parking lot, clutching the straps of her backpack. Her shoulder-length pink hair was tucked behind her ears, and her earbuds were firmly in place lest one of the Tragic Kindergarten Kingdom citizens, who were already trickling in and heading down the covered corridor, took it upon themselves to brave a greeting. Not that she expected them to. No one was particularly eager to associate with anyone else in group, except Chatty Charlotte, who was desperate enough to talk to just about anyone.

Would Kaylie show up to group this week, Elliott wondered. She'd been back at school as of Monday and, shockingly, seemed entirely back to normal. Elliott had spotted her that very afternoon, laughing with Breanna Hernandez as they walked down to the field house for cheer practice.

How Kaylie could haul her ass out of bed after all she'd endured was a marvel to Elliott. It was like she had a full-time job publicly being varsity cheer captain, a competitive gymnast, and a member of both the National Honor Society and Associated Student Body and a side hustle privately dealing with the trauma around her rape and the subsequent court case. Elliott decided she either must be totally dissociating or actually tough as shit.

At two minutes to six, a sea-green Prius pulled into the lot and parked in a spot at the far end, near the edge of the stucco cafeteria building. Madeline climbed out, adjusting the hem of her J.Crew cardigan before carefully pulling her mane over one shoulder and beeping her car locked.

Elliott popped out her earbuds, pausing PJ Harvey in the midst of crooning to Thom Yorke about the mess they were in, and strode across the lot.

"Hey," she called out.

Madeline glanced around before realizing Elliott was addressing *her*. "Hey," she said in surprise, adjusting the strap of her purse as she surreptitiously assessed Elliott's outfit: Nirvana T-shirt and oversized grandpa cardigan, black tights under cutoffs, black fedora, and well-worn burgundy Docs. Not exactly Bishop Garcia Diego attire.

Elliott stopped before her and glanced back at the buildings to ensure Mary wasn't snooping around. When she looked again at Madeline, she was sure to keep her voice low. "How'd you like to skip group and actually *do* something about shit for once?"

Ten minutes and a short drive later, Elliott led Madeline to the back room of Anastasia's Asylum, a small café on upper State Street, where they settled into oversized velvet chairs straight out of *Friends'* coffee shop, Central Perk. A decaf sugar-free vanilla chai latte with almond milk for Madeline; a double Americano for Elliott. The music, which was way too loud, was all '90s all the time—the Cranberries' "Dreams" at the moment—but both the volume and the era suited Elliott just fine.

"You ever been here?" Elliott asked Madeline, who was taking in the décor: white Christmas lights strung across the ceiling, bohemian tapestries, posters for '90s indie films like *The Doom Generation* and *The Virgin Suicides*, a framed black-and-white photo of Kurt Cobain and Courtney Love.

"Actually, no. But it seems . . . cool," Madeline replied, her gaze landing on *An American Girl in Italy*, a famous '50s-era black-and-white photograph of a young woman walking down an Italian street clogged with men. She frowned a little.

"You know"—Elliott leaned toward Madeline over the small mosaic-tiled table so she'd be heard—"I used to like that photo. I used to think that girl was so sophisticated and cool, catching all the guys' attention. But now I look at it and she just seems *disturbed*. Trying to escape all those leering creeps."

Madeline gazed at the photo, taking a sip of her chai latte. "I watched that old eighties movie *Say Anything* with my parents the other day? And all I could think was, yeah, it's romantic if it's Lloyd Dobler standing outside your window with a boom box, but ninety-nine percent of the time it's some jerk who can't take no for an answer and is now officially stalking you."

Elliott snorted in appreciation.

"Here's your chocolate cake," said the waitress, coming up to their table and handing a chipped plate to Elliott. "You two need anything else?"

"Nope, but thanks," Elliott replied. She waited until the waitress disappeared into the café's front room.

"So, listen," Elliott whispered confidentially, hands wrapped around her coffee mug. Her nails were painted deep indigo blue today and she had a silver ring on every finger. "I don't know about you, but I'm sick of watching all these assholes just waltz away from the damage they've done, completely unpunished or unfazed. I've been thinking about this *a lot*, and I think it's time we take matters into our own hands."

Madeline's eyes lit up like someone had set her insides on fire, a wide grin slowly spreading across her face. For the first time, Elliott sensed there might be something a little wicked buried underneath that prissy, type-A surface. She was also highly aware of the dark purple circles under Madeline's eyes, as if she hadn't slept in weeks. Which she probably hadn't. Elliott herself had bolted awake in a cold sweat every night at 3 a.m. for three months straight.

"I one hundred percent agree. And I have *a lot* of ideas," Madeline whispered back. "I've been brainstorming ways to get back at my ex and— Here, let me just . . ." She pulled out her phone and punched in the code one-handed.

Ex, Elliott noted. So that's who was responsible for the lack of sleep and general admission ticket to Tragic Kindergarten Kingdom. She took a bite of her chocolate cake as Madeline rattled off her list of ideas.

". . . alternatively, if we pooled our money and anonymously took over a few billboards," Madeline was saying, "like in that one movie with what's her name, that would be *a lot* more public. Or maybe we combine that with—what? You think that's going too far?"

Elliott was shaking her head. "I think it's not going far *enough*. Look, everything you've listed is way too conventional, not to mention risky. And by the way, you should delete that list. Like, now."

Madeline looked crestfallen as she tapped the screen and then clicked off her phone.

"The money for the billboards could easily be traced back to us," Elliott explained. "Ditto the social media campaign, which would likely get stopped before it even began. And even if you could manage to find a way of breaking into their schools without getting caught on a security camera, which is highly doubtful, papering the school with embarrassing photos isn't likely to bring these guys down."

"Okay." Madeline slowly crossed one leg over the other and settled her phone facedown on her thigh. "All fair points. So, what did you have in mind?"

"Well . . ." Elliott leaned forward, elbows on her knees, and twisted a ring around her pointer finger. "We need something powerful. Something one hundred percent effective. But *completely* untraceable."

"Sure," Madeline agreed. "That sounds great. And if you could come up with a plan like *that*, I'd be all in. But realistically? It's not that easy."

Elliott assessed Madeline from under the brim of her fedora and then grabbed her cup, downed the last of her Americano, and abruptly rose to her feet. "Come with me."

"What?" Madeline grabbed her purse. "But we just got here."

"I know." Elliott strode toward the back door. "I want to show you something."

Back inside Madeline's car, lit only by the dashboard lights and the sodium streetlamp outside, Elliott zipped open her backpack. She pulled out a wooden box roughly the shape of an iPad but about three inches thick, its lid patterned with an intricate, geometric wood mosaic.

"Who's Ronnie?" Madeline asked, eyeing the name inscribed along the box's length.

"Don't worry about it," Elliott dismissed. She proceeded to incrementally slide several hidden panels in various directions, sometimes returning to panels she'd already opened only to partially slide them in the opposite direction. It had taken her nearly six weeks of constant prodding and discovery to figure out how to open the puzzle box, but now she could do it blindfolded. Literally. She'd practiced.

Finally, the last panel clicked into place and the entire lid slid open. Inside was a slim book bound in bloodred leather, which Elliott carefully extracted. Sometimes she felt like she should handle it with gloves.

"What is that?" Madeline asked.

Elliott handed it over. "Open it."

Madeline examined the title—*The Book of Reflection*—and the emblem on its cover—two cupped hands above and below a flaming heart with an eye in the center—and then flipped to the first page. She scanned the introductory text, her expression settling into one of skepticism. "'You, dear Seeker,'" she read aloud, "'hold within your hands a most special device. A means to control your path, a resolution to your darkest tribulations. For when brought together with a coven'— Okay," she cut off, looking up at Elliott. "You're setting me up, aren't you? This is clearly a joke."

"Just keep reading," Elliott insisted.

Madeline sighed. "'For when brought together with a coven—and only with a coven—will the spell most suited to the conjuring witch be summoned. Those who would suppress and destroy you stand not a chance when confronted with the power that lies within these pages.'"

For when brought together with a coven—and only with a coven. Elliott must have read that line a million times, equal parts frustrated and fascinated that she couldn't reveal the book's spells on her own.

Madeline scanned the rest of the page, then looked up at Elliott blankly.

"*Witchcraft?*" she scoffed. "This isn't real."

"Turn the page," Elliott directed.

Madeline pursed her lips to one side, debating, then flipped the page. "'A Note to Skeptics,'" she continued reading aloud. "'To prove this book's power, light a purple candle and follow the spell below. That which you treasure most will appear before you.'" Madeline scanned the spell and then closed the book and handed it back to Elliott. "Okay, this is all insane. Also, didn't we get past this kind of stuff in middle school, along with séances and Ouija boards?"

"Try it," Elliott urged.

"Oh sure, like I carry a purple candle and—what was it again? Fire quartz and white oak ashes?—around with me wherever I go."

Elliott reached into her backpack and produced a handful of quarter-sized pinkish-orange quartz chunks, a stoppered glass bottle full of ashes, a thick purple candle, and a Zippo lighter.

Madeline watched in astonishment as Elliott arranged the fire quartz into a circle right there on the little leather armrest compartment, then used the ashes to make an interior circle.

"Don't worry, I'll clean it up," Elliott said before Madeline could protest.

Once the candle was lit, Elliott set it within the circle's center.

"Now place your hand, palm up, above the book," Elliott instructed, holding the book in front of Madeline. "And chant *Bring forth my heart's desire* three times."

Madeline blinked slowly, sighed, and then placed her hand a few inches above the book. "*Bring forth my heart's desire, bring forth my heart's desire, bring forth my heart's desire,*" she recited perfunctorily before looking up at Elliott. "Is something supposed to actually happen?"

"Well, it's *obviously* not going to work if you don't take it seriously," Elliott chided. "Spells are all about intention. You have to actually focus yourself and *want* it to work. Now, come on, suspend your disbelief for just thirty seconds."

Madeline smoothed a hand over her hair.

"Do it just this once," Elliott challenged. "Come on, there's no one else here to see this and judge you except me, and I'm the crazy one who actually believes this shit, so . . . what do you have to lose?"

Madeline stared at the book, then straightened her spine and rolled her shoulder blades back and down, like someone with the muscle memory of lifelong ballet classes. And then, to Elliott's great relief, she placed her hand back over the book.

"This time take a deep breath and close your eyes," Elliott instructed.

Madeline inhaled, more out of irritation than anything else, and closed her eyes.

"Now take a moment to clear your mind. And think about why you're sitting here. Think about how much you want things to change and how much he deserves payback. And then when you recite the spell, focus yourself and say the words like you actually mean them."

Madeline was very still, her posture perfectly erect. When she finally spoke, her voice was low and even, the words a hush in the back of her throat. "*Bring forth my heart's desire . . . ,*" she chanted, her expression one of steady concentration. "*Bring forth my heart's desire . . . Bring forth my heart's desire . . .*" She concluded the chant, a bite of venom in the final word.

"Okay," Elliott whispered. "Now open your eyes."

When Madeline did, she let out a gasp.

Hovering a few inches above her cupped hand was a hologram image of herself—herself but *older*. She was wearing a cap and gown, which was unzipped to reveal a Harvard T-shirt, and the look on her face was one of pure radiance.

Startled, Madeline pulled her hand away and the image dissipated like a puff of smoke.

"How'd you do that?" she asked, equal parts incredulous and creeped out.

"*I* didn't do anything," Elliott assured her.

Madeline reached for the book and examined it, searching for . . . what? A plug of some kind? A projector? When she handed it back to Elliott, her hand was shaking.

"Holy crap," she breathed. "That thing . . . That was *real.*"

"Yes," Elliott agreed, carefully replacing the book inside the puzzle box and sliding the lid closed. "So." She raised an eyebrow, meeting Madeline's gaze. "What do you say? Do you want to join my coven?"

3

"Dad, I'm going out," Elliott called from the foyer that Saturday evening as she pulled her leather jacket on over the baby doll dress she'd paired with torn black jeans.

"Oh, you are." He sat up from his reclined position on the couch. He was reading book #343 in the detective series he loved, a cup of Earl Grey tea within reach. His usual Saturday-night routine. "Are you meeting up with Vi?"

"Nope," Elliott said evenly, sliding on her Docs.

"You two still on the outs, huh?"

Elliott remained silent as she pulled on her backpack.

"Hey, El." Her dad set his splayed book on his lap. "I was thinking, maybe tomorrow if you're not busy we could do something together. Hit up the batting cages like old times? Or go to a movie?"

"Oh. Yeah. I don't know," she hedged. "I kind of have some homework to tackle. Plus, I'll probably just want to lie low."

"Sure, sure." He nodded, picking up his book. "Totally get it. It was just a thought."

Elliott felt a pang of guilt and went over to give him a kiss on his stubble-covered cheek. "But thanks anyway. And I promise not to be out too late."

"Sounds good. I'll just be here with my cozy mystery, waiting for amateur sleuth Miss Lydia Stillwell to once again crack the case." He smiled at her, a wistful, slightly pained expression crossing his face. "You really do look a lot like her with those bangs."

Elliott had stayed up late cutting Bettie Page–style bangs, a look her mom sported most of her young adult life. She'd made no secret of wanting to dress like her mom, asking her dad's permission to raid her boxes of vintage clothes. And he'd been happy to comply. But sometimes she wondered if it was too much for him, being confronted with this ghost of his dead wife in the form of his only daughter.

"Don't do anything I wouldn't do," he called after her as she crossed to the front door. It was his standard Dad-comment. *But God*, Elliott thought, *if he only knew*.

Stepping outside, Elliott ran through the routine that had become standard procedure for the past three months: Mace in pocket? Check. Knife in backpack? Check. Personal safety alarm in hand? Check. Only then did she allow herself to start down the street.

The evening sky was a deep cobalt blue, stars twinkling behind the silhouettes of palm trees as she headed down Olive Street, passing Craftsman bungalows much like her own. Houses that were once affordable way back when her dad was a latchkey kid living with his working-class parents but now went for well over a million dollars. The only reason they lived on the Upper East side at all—or *any*where in Santa Barbara, for that matter—was because their house had been in her dad's family for decades and her grandparents deeded it to her mom and dad when they got married.

Long ago, Santa Barbara was beachy and funky—an artist's community, or so her dad said. Now it was a weekend getaway for LA hipsters and a place celebrities and billionaires had enormous second (third? Fourth?) homes. They'd taken down the JCPenney and replaced it with a Saks Fifth Avenue, which, her mom had often lamented, was really all you needed to know about the town's overall trajectory.

The American Riviera—that's what Santa Barbara had nicknamed itself, which Elliott found entirely eye-roll-inducing. Though it was better than the alternative tagline, which fortunately never really took off: *Where life itself is an art form.* I mean, who was the self-involved, elitist asshole who came up with *that*?

Not that the American Riviera thing was entirely off base, what with the Spanish-style houses studding the hillside that ran along Santa Barbara's length—houses that looked out over the picture-perfect Spanish-style town and glistening ocean below. The town was charming as *hell*: not too big and not too small, with a top-notch art museum, a picturesque downtown, and an annual film festival. Plus, once a year it threw a weeklong party called Fiesta, a celebration of "Old Spanish Days" and Latino heritage and . . . well, come on, let's be honest: margaritas. Santa Barbara was the kind of place where you could surf in the morning, hike in the mountains in the afternoon, and then dine under the stars at one of the numerous upscale restaurants. It was the kind of place you'd set foot in and then wonder aloud why anyone in their right mind would *ever* want to leave.

That is, of course, unless you grew up there.

If you grew up there, you might look around and note that the vast majority of wealthy people were white, and the people cleaning their homes and mowing their lawns and making their lives easier were *not*. And you might find this divide deeply disturbing. You might wonder: Whose life was allowed to be an art form and whose was expected to be *in service* of that art form?

Elliott stopped just a few blocks from her house, at the corner of Olive and Valerio, and checked her phone. Her Uber was three minutes away. Turning up the volume on Fiona Apple's "Criminal," she could feel the anticipation building in the pit of her stomach. Something akin to that childhood Christmas-morning feeling. Or maybe more like that can't-wait-to-go-to-school-and-see-my-crush feeling (something she'd theoretically felt once upon a time). Or maybe it was more of a shit's-about-to-get-real-and-you'll-never-see-me-coming feeling. Maybe *that* was it.

According to the book, a minimum of three souls were needed to form a coven—but no more than five souls were recommended, and anything past seven was strictly verboten. *Secrecy is of vital importance*, the book advised. *An increased number of witches only jeopardizes the coven, putting all involved at risk.*

That Friday afternoon, Elliott had sent out four separate texts to the phone numbers she'd carefully sourced from—well, okay, *stolen* from—the group contact sheet in Mary's address book, which she'd slipped in and out of Mary's NPR tote bag one evening when she wasn't looking. (Also, who in this day and age kept an actual physical *address book*?)

Elliott made sure to include a selfie so the receivers would know it was legit. A random text from an anonymous number was a total red flag after the crap they'd all endured.

Hey—this is Elliott, the text read. If you're as fed up as I am, meet me tomorrow night at Franceschi Park. 7 p.m. All will be revealed.

If she was honest, that last part felt a bit dramatic and unnecessary. But she was forming a coven here—didn't she deserve to be a little goddamn dramatic?

Franceschi Park was a lookout point and public park up on the Riviera's hillside, with a historic dilapidated mansion on its premises and a panoramic view of downtown, the Pacific Ocean, and the Channel Islands beyond. As a kid, Elliott often picnicked there with her parents. Sometimes, on random school nights, her mom would make a giant sandwich on a loaf of French bread, which she'd slice up into individual portions, and they'd all hop into the car and drive up there to dine during the golden hour, the low sun making everything look all syrupy. That time in Elliott's life seemed perpetually tinged with golden light. A memory trapped in amber.

When Elliott's Uber pulled up, an older couple was idling near their car, the remnants of their picnic atop the engine's hood as they admired the view. Far below, boat lights twinkled from the harbor as the sun sank into the ocean, streaking the sky lilac and pink and tangerine.

Fall and winter sunsets were always gorgeous in Santa Barbara. They used to be one of Elliott's favorite things. Once upon a time she would sit at the top of the Mesa Lane steps at sunset, drinking mint tea and laughing with Vi as the waves crashed upon the sands below. Once upon a time she used to have a best friend named Violet. But that time was long gone, and like so many other things in Elliott's life—her mother, her best friend, her optimism, her innocence—she'd lost her love of sunsets.

Madeline, of course, was the first to show.

Her Prius pulled into the narrow strip of parking lot precisely on time, passing the older couple who were pulling out. After taking the lone spot at the farthest end—because why? Someone might scratch her stupid *car?*—she calmly strode over to meet Elliott, who was leaning against one of the two high-backed wooden benches.

Madeline took a seat on the opposite bench, her spine perfectly erect as she pulled her hair over one shoulder. Elliott could just picture her as a child, always coloring within the lines, first to raise her hand in class, never spilling a thing on her plaid uniform.

Madeline glanced around. "Are you sure about this location? It seems kind of . . . open."

"I'm sure," Elliott replied, arms crossed against her chest.

"People come here to hook up, you know."

"Yeah," Elliott replied. "I'm aware."

Madeline seemed ready to say more but instead crossed one leg over the other and placed her folded hands on her knees. They sat in silence, Madeline facing the sunset, Elliott facing the lot.

Chloe arrived next.

Her Beemer sped into the parking area—windows down, some nameless pop song blaring—and pulled into the spot in front of the benches, her headlights nearly blinding Elliott and Madeline, who turned to look. She hopped out, pulling a Louis Vuitton bag over one spaghetti-strapped shoulder, and sashayed toward them in her boho kimono, denim cutoffs, and ankle boots, raising a hand up to beep her car locked.

Chloe had been on Elliott's list ever since Chloe's first day in group. She'd introduced herself, informing them that she was a junior at Laguna Blanca (an uber-rich private school, which meant she probably lived in Hope Ranch or Montecito) and had originally been adopted from South Korea—quickly adding that, no, she could not speak Korean, and no, she'd never actually been back to South Korea, and no, she did not, in fact, like kimchi. As if providing a short backstory and some up-front answers might ward off the annoying questions she'd undoubtedly heard her entire life.

"Oh, and," she'd added casually, "the guy I was hooking up with took advantage of me when I was drunk."

And that had been that. No *real* details about her admission ticket into Tragic Kindergarten Kingdom. Not even a hint of what brand of post-trauma she was suffering. Just a shrug and a flip of her shoulder-length black hair.

26

"Would you like to share anything else with the group? Maybe how you've been feeling?" Mary had asked.

Chloe had smiled brightly, but Elliott could see pain and anger simmering behind her eyes. When she spoke, her tone was the perfect blend of condescension and cheer. "Nope!"

Yes, Elliott thought. That kind of unconflicted lack of disclosure was something she could get behind. Chloe's reticence along with her pent-up anger were the very things that put her name on Elliott's List.

"Hey," Elliott greeted. "We're still waiting for a few people, so . . ."

"O-*kay*," Chloe said tentatively, looking from Elliott to Madeline. She had to be confused about what the three of them were doing there, but she just shrugged and then perched herself on the arm of the bench Madeline was seated on, legs outstretched, ankles crossed before her as she pulled out her phone.

Bea was the next one to show. Her minivan slowly rolled into the lot and parked a few spots down from Chloe's BMW. When she climbed out, she hesitated a moment near the driver's-side door before coming over to join them.

"Hey," she greeted quietly.

"Hey, come sit," Elliott welcomed as the other girls nodded their hellos. "We're just waiting on one more."

Bea, who was also a junior, ran cross-country and track for Dos Pueblos High and played the oboe in the school's orchestra, which Elliott only knew from the bumper stickers on Bea's family's minivan. She had a twin brother named Otis—who sometimes drove Bea to group in said minivan, waiting in the parking lot the entire ninety minutes—and a penchant for brightly colored Nikes. Other than that, Elliott knew zero about her. She only attended group intermittently, and when she *did*, she never talked—not to share, not to react, nothing. But the fact that she so regularly blew off group seemed like a very good sign to Elliott. And, much like Chloe, Bea had a simmering anger that Elliott recognized all too well.

Bea sat down on the bench Elliott was leaning against, legs spread wide, hands on her knees. She was gorgeous in that super-played-down kind of way Elliott always admired, like a young Janelle Monáe sans makeup or any fashion sense—no offense to Bea's constant rotation of jeans, V-necks, and track jackets—her rich brown skin constantly glowy, her hair woven into two braids that ran down either side of her head.

A breeze picked up, rustling the branches of the eucalyptus trees above. In the distance, the Mission bells rang half past seven. Elliott had her First Communion in that church back in second grade. How long ago that seemed now.

Lights were slowly twinkling on in the city below. As Elliott looked out at Santa Barbara spread before her, she had a straight view down to the sprawling campus of her loathed high school, the football field brightly lit and standing out like a beacon of mediocrity and heteronormative values.

Bea glanced around and began bouncing one leg. Chloe was still scrolling, her face lit by her phone's glow. Madeline sat calmly, carefully pushing back her cuticles. Despite being in group together once a week, they'd never actually socialized outside of Tragic Kindergarten Kingdom, and they certainly weren't *friends*.

"I have to train early tomorrow," Bea informed Elliott. "So I can't be out late."

"Yeah," Chloe agreed, glancing up from her phone. "I have volleyball practice, too. So, are you gonna, like, tell us why we're here?"

At that moment an SUV pulled into the parking lot and stopped beside Bea's minivan. When the driver's-side door swung open, out stepped Kaylie.

Kaylie was far more put together than she'd been in group right after the verdict, but her tie-dyed pink sweatshirt, leggings tucked into Uggs, and hair swept into a high, messy bun suggested a general lack of trying to impress. Maybe, Elliott thought, Kaylie felt comfortable letting her guard down because they already knew the truth.

Registering Kaylie's presence, Chloe, Bea, and Madeline sat up a little straighter, like they were in the presence of a celebrity.

"Hey." Elliott smiled.

Kaylie stopped before Chloe's car, a few feet shy of the benches.

"I'm really glad you made it," Elliott added. She hadn't been 100 percent sure Kaylie would show.

Kaylie was on the List for all the obvious reasons—the travesty of her court case and total lack of justice, the simmering rage Kaylie only let show in group—but also for something else. The year Elliott's mom died, Kaylie invited Elliott to her tenth birthday party. Elliott figured it was just a pity invite from Kaylie's parents, but no: Kaylie insisted Elliott sit next to her when they ate pizza, picked her as her partner for the three-legged race, gave her the slice of cake with the giant frosting flower. It didn't make them friends after that, but Elliott also never forgot.

And now here was something she could do to return Kaylie's kindness.

"So, what's up?" Kaylie asked plainly, zero sparkle or cheer. "Why am I here?"

"Good question," Elliott replied. "But we shouldn't talk here. Let's go down behind the mansion."

Darkness was quickly falling, so Elliott turned on her phone's flashlight as she led the group single file down the asphalt path that extended out of the parking lot. They continued past the open picnic area and followed the steep, tree-shrouded path as it wound farther down the hillside toward where the mansion stood.

"Oh my God, what was that?" Chloe whispered as something scampered across the path and disappeared into the bushes.

"Just a possum," Elliott assured her as they neared the bottom of the path.

They came around a thick, low-hanging fig tree, and the path opened up to a flagstone turnaround, which was half surrounded by a stone retaining wall and was located just to the side of the decrepit mansion.

Around a hundred years ago the mansion had been built by an Italian botanist or something—a dude named Francesco Franceschi. A dude clearly obsessed with giant medallions, if the outside of the stucco house was any indication; it was absolutely *plastered* in them, round busts paying tribute to activists, artists, and philanthropists he'd admired, including poet Emily Dickinson, "prison reformer" Florence Maybrick, and suffragette Mary Wollstonecraft—all of whom, Elliott was confident, would be into a little witchcraft.

For *years* the city planned to tear down the mansion, but the public outcry for preservation always won out. Of course, there wasn't any actual *money* for the preservation (really? In a wealthy enclave like *Santa Barbara*?), apparently just a fanciful notion that *hey, wouldn't that be nice?!* So here the mansion still stood, considered awesome and important but completely unsupported and ultimately left to fend for itself. Basically, the house was them. Or they were the house. Or they were all equally screwed.

Elliott strode to the left-hand edge of the turnaround, which abutted the retaining wall and was perfectly hidden from the park above—she'd checked from every possible angle—and motioned for the other girls to sit. Which they did, but tentatively, forming a reluctant half ring: Chloe and then Bea, followed by Kaylie, and then Madeline.

When Elliott had scouted this location, she'd immediately known it was the spot. The turnaround was remote, open to the stars but surrounded by trees and therefore mostly hidden from the park above. And this circle was practically *begging* for a coven. It was perfect. Well, almost perfect. There *was* the fact that the only fully hidden spot against the retaining wall was next to an annoying stone statue of a little boy holding a placard about peace among nations or some shit (because apparently you could *never* escape the male gaze), but whatever, screw it, *this* was where they were meeting.

Elliott remained standing and opened her backpack to pull out a small camping lantern, which she lit and placed at her feet.

"So, here's the thing," she said, tucking her pink hair behind her ears and slowly pacing before them. "I don't know how you all feel, but I am done with being complacent. I'm sick of the talking and the processing and the sharing of feelings, because as far as I can tell, that hasn't gotten anyone *anywhere*. We sit in that group week after week, listening to girls cry and spill out their guts, and at the end of that hour we walk away and the world is still the same. The assholes who wronged us still roam the earth, wild and free, able to live their lives and do whatever the fuck they want, nobody holding them accountable, nobody standing there reminding them, *hey, asshole, you suck*. Has a single one of them apologized or reckoned with their actions or been truly and properly *punished*, for God's sake?" At this, Elliott looked at Kaylie, who remained stone-faced.

"And I'm sick of hearing things like *living well is the best revenge*," Elliott continued. "Or worse, *forgive and forget*. All that does is enable sadistic behavior. What I want is some actual change. What I want is for these assholes to finally get what they deserve. What I want is *justice*. But no one's going to swoop in on a white horse and do that shit for us—not the police, not the court system, not even our parents. If it's going to happen, it has to be *us*. And I say it's high fucking time we got revenge."

"Hell *yeah*," exclaimed Chloe.

Kaylie's expression remained completely unreadable.

"And exactly *how* do you propose we do this?" questioned Bea.

Elliott reached into her backpack and pulled out the puzzle box, which she proceeded to open, feeling slightly vulnerable with all of them watching—though if they were going to join her coven, best to start trusting them now. "With this," she announced, extracting the book and holding it up for all to see. "Historically, justice through traditional means has only been available to a select few with the social and financial position to obtain it. But for decades, marginalized people—many of whom are women—have had a means of taking matters into their own hands, a method for overcoming their marginalization. And it's all right here." Elliott pointed toward the book.

"But what *is* that?" Bea asked.

Elliott handed her the book.

Bea frowned, flipping through the pages. "It's blank."

"Go to the first page," Elliott instructed.

Bea flipped to the front and scanned the page. "*Witchcraft?*" she scoffed.

"Wow, for real?" Chloe said excitedly, scooching closer to Bea. "My mom and I did this retreat in Tulum once with her spiritual advisor, and we talked *all* about accessing the feminine divine."

Which wasn't exactly the same as what Elliott was proposing, but she decided to let it go.

"You actually expect us to buy into this?" Bea said, handing the book over to Chloe, who was eager to examine it.

"No," Elliott responded. "Not until I prove it to you."

Leaning over, she flipped the page to "A Note to Skeptics" so Bea and Chloe could read. Kaylie stood and came closer, reading over their shoulders.

When Bea was done, she straightened and looked up at Elliott like she thought Elliott was insane. "There's no way this is real."

"It's real," Madeline said from where she was seated a few feet away.

The other girls looked over at her.

"You tried this already?" Bea asked, her skepticism waning.

"Yeah," Madeline breathed. "And it's . . . Elliott's not joking."

Bea glanced back down at the book with trepidation.

Chloe squealed. "This is *so* cool. I want to go first. Can I go first?"

Elliott looked at Bea and Kaylie—*you cool with that?*

"Go for it," Bea said, still not entirely won over.

"*I'm* not going first," Kaylie replied, her gaze on the book.

"Awesome," Chloe exclaimed.

Kneeling on the flagstones, Elliott pulled the spell's ingredients from her backpack and arranged everything in front of Chloe, lighting the purple candle and setting it inside the ring of fire quartz and ashes.

"Okay." Elliott took the book back from Chloe. "So, you're going to hold your hand above the book, palm up."

The other girls watched as Chloe did as Elliott instructed.

"And then you're going to chant *Bring forth my heart's desire* three times," Elliott said. "It helps if you focus yourself by closing—"

"Don't worry, I meditate," Chloe said confidently. "I got this."

Chloe closed her eyes and took three deep breaths, holding each one a few beats before slowly exhaling. And then, quietly but steadily, she chanted the spell's incantation.

"*Bring forth my heart's desire,*" she whispered solemnly, her expression placid. "*Bring forth my heart's desire . . . Bring forth my heart's desire.*"

There was a collective inhalation as the hologram-like image appeared above Chloe's hand. Even though Elliott had seen the book's power before, it still took her breath away, just as it had the first time she'd conjured the image of her mother.

Chloe's eyes flew open, and she inhaled as well. "Oh my God," she breathed, covering her mouth with her free hand.

The hologram was of a fortysomething white man with sandy brown hair. He wore one of those ventilated running shirts, his brow glistening with sweat like he'd just finished a run, and he was drinking a glass of orange juice.

"That's—that's my dad . . . ," Chloe whispered. "Back when he still lived with us. I can't . . . Holy shit . . ."

Bea's lips parted in awe. "How is this happening?"

Chloe pulled her hand away and the image dissolved like a puff of smoke. She looked at Elliott, both shaken and buzzing with excitement. "Where did you even *get* this thing?"

Elliott ignored the question. "Do you want to go next?" she asked Bea, laser-beam-focused.

Bea looked hesitant. "Does it always work?"

"If you have the *intention* for it to work, then yes," Elliott answered.

Bea chewed on her lip a moment, considering. And then she gave a quick nod.

Her hand was steady as she raised it above the book, but when she whispered the incantation, her voice trembled just slightly. "*Bring forth my heart's desire,*" she recited, her voice barely audible. "*Bring forth my heart's desire . . . Bring forth my heart's desire.*"

This time, it was an image of a little girl in braids and a soccer jersey that appeared above Bea's cupped hand, laughing with complete abandon as she ran. The little girl looked so much like Bea that there was no question it was her as a child.

Bea's eyes welled up with tears and she quickly pulled her hand away as if stung. She wrapped her arms around her knees, her gaze on where the hologram had been.

"You okay?" Elliott asked.

Bea nodded, but it was clear that the image had rattled her, as if facing her younger self was more than she could bear.

Elliott looked up at Kaylie, who remained standing. "Kaylie? Do you want to go next?"

Kaylie shook her head almost imperceptibly, still staring at the book. "I don't think so."

"We could look away if you want?" Elliott offered. "If you're worried about what we might see, we don't have to—"

"No." Kaylie took a step back, her gaze moving from the book to Elliott. "Whatever this is, I don't need it."

"Wait." Elliott stood up as Kaylie strode off. "Kaylie, wait!" she called after her.

But Kaylie didn't stop, hurrying up the curved path and disappearing into the dark.

Kaylie's reaction wasn't one Elliott had been prepared for. She'd assumed that Kaylie, of all people, would be the *most* on board with a coven, the *most* desiring of revenge. She'd never imagined that she might say no.

When Elliott looked back at the other three girls, it was clear they were equally surprised.

"That's totally fine," Elliott said, throwing off Kaylie's rejection as she knelt and gathered up the fire quartz. "It's good, actually," she reasoned, dumping it into her backpack. "She *should* exercise her right to choose. I don't want anyone to feel at all pressured into doing this. Besides"—she unnecessarily adjusted the candle—"five was probably too many people anyway. Four's way better. So . . ." She swept a hand through her pink hair. "What do you think? Are the three of you in?"

"I'm in." Madeline nodded firmly.

Which wasn't a surprise. Madeline had had the longest to think about it, and she'd seemed dedicated from the start.

"Totally," Chloe agreed. "I'm one hundred percent in."

Which also wasn't a surprise, given her attraction to meditation and—what had she called it again? The *feminine divine*?

Bea was the only question mark. She remained silent, her chin resting on her knees.

"What about you?" Elliott asked her, saying a silent prayer to a god she didn't rely on because she no longer totally believed in that kind of thing.

"I don't know," Bea fretted aloud. "Between cross-country and orchestra, not to mention homework . . . I mean, I can't even attend *group* regularly, let alone add something else."

Which worried Elliott. She'd assumed Bea's absence was due to her ambivalence, not overscheduling.

Bea gazed off into the middle distance, mulling something over in her mind. When she finally looked back at Elliott, her eyes seemed haunted. "Do you think this is *really* gonna take them down?"

"Yeah," Elliott replied. "I really do."

Bea thought a moment and then nodded. "Then yeah, okay. I'm in, too."

"All right." Elliott nodded, regaining her confidence. This was *happening*. Some part of her, she realized, hadn't been totally sure it would. But now it really was. "*Okay.* Let's make things official and do the binding spell."

Reaching into her bag, Elliott pulled out the binding spell's ingredients: a brass bowl, a vial of salt water, four sprigs of lavender, five raven feathers—one of which she discarded, a feather for each girl—a handful of grave dirt, and her pocketknife.

"Wait, what's the knife for?" Bea asked.

Elliott opened the book. "For the blood bond," she explained. Which did nothing to alleviate Bea's concern. Elliott was beginning to gather that Bea would be the cautious one. "Not *a lot* of blood,"

Elliott assured her. "Just three drops each. Hey, can you read me the binding spell's instructions?" she asked, extending the book toward Bea. She'd memorized it by now, but she didn't want to risk messing it up—and best to keep the cautious one busy.

Bea hesitated before taking the book, holding it gingerly. "'A Spell for Binding Your Coven,'" she read aloud. "'When forming your coven, be certain to select like-minded souls, for you may only join one coven. Once the coven is bound, it can be abandoned but never broken, and the book's powers will only be granted once all coven members are gathered together.'" Bea glanced up at the group.

"Speak now or forever hold your peace," Elliott joked. "Any final misgivings?"

"Nope," Chloe stated, playing with a strand of her black hair.

"None," Madeline agreed, straightening her spine, palms on her knees.

Elliott glanced at Bea, who shook her head.

Once the saltwater, grave dirt, and lavender were mixed together in the brass bowl, Elliott burned the four raven feathers.

"*Take these four and make them one,*" she recited. The girls watched as the feathers shriveled and melted together, filling the air with the stench of burning hair. Elliott added the dark bubbling blob to the bowl.

The final step was the blood bond.

"'Pierce the pointer finger on your right hand,'" Bea read aloud. "'Place your left hand on your coven-mate's shoulder, and then, in unison, drip three drops of blood directly onto the binding spell circle.'"

Bea set the open book on the ground before them so they could all see the three-inch-wide circle inked onto the binding spell's ivory page. Elliott doused the knife with alcohol and then handed it to Chloe, who made a squeamish face.

"So, I'm just gonna, like, *stab* myself with this?" Chloe asked. "Ugh. *Okay.*" She lightly pressed the tip of the blade to her fingertip, without success.

"You have to angle the knife, use more force, and be quicker than that," Madeline advised. Which made Elliott wonder what sort of experience *Madeline* had with blades.

Finally, Chloe succeeded in piercing her finger, cringing as she handed the knife back to Elliott, who doused it with alcohol again.

Bea went next, cautious but precise, following the instructions Madeline had outlined. She handed the knife back to Elliott, holding her finger away from her body and not looking at the blood.

When Madeline went, she pierced her finger proficiently and without hesitation, as if she'd done this sort of thing before.

Elliott went last, the sharp pain of the blade mixed with the sting of the alcohol almost welcome as she watched a bead of dark crimson well up on her pale skin.

Keeping their wounded fingers facing the sky, they each placed their left hand on their neighbor's shoulder so that their bodies formed a circle.

"Okay, on the count of three," Elliott instructed in a hush. "One . . . two . . . three."

The four girls extended their arms and let their blood drip onto the binding spell's circle.

The result was instantaneous; the pages began to shimmer and ripple like the surface of a pond as a fine red mist arose, swirling around the girls like a miniature tornado before rising above them and dissipating into the night air.

"Holy shit," Elliott breathed.

When she looked back at the book, what she saw was even stranger: their blood was slowly disappearing, as if being absorbed into the book.

"Are you seeing this?" Bea whispered to the others, her tone a mix of awe and fear.

"*Yes,*" they answered in unison.

And then the blood was just . . . *gone*—no stains, no markings. Almost as if it had never been there.

The book began to transform, clouding over and changing color, spreading from the center of the circle outward, like a drop of ink blooming in a glass of water, until the pages of the book were a uniform dark blue black.

Simultaneously, Elliott felt a tingling in the center of her right palm. When she looked, she saw a mark had mysteriously appeared there. It was quarter-sized and circular, resembling a strange flower or maybe a sea anemone, and was made up of thin, swirling, faint lavender lines, which called to mind tossing waves or curls of smoke, or maybe cosmic energy.

"Oh my God," Chloe whispered, looking at her own palm.

"What *is* this?" Bea worried aloud, inspecting her right hand.

"I don't know," Elliott remarked, tracing the lines.

"The mark of the coven," guessed Madeline. Which sounded so official.

The binding spell had now been swallowed in darkness, and in its place were several lines of silver text. Elliott leaned over and read them aloud: "'The coven is born, your souls forever bound together. Each witch may now conjure their spell—'"

"Witch," Chloe whispered in excitement, the candle's flame dancing in her eyes.

"'To do so,'" Elliott continued, "'hold your right hand above an empty page and recite the following three times: *Bring forth that which will satisfy my intentions. The spell most suited to the conjuring witch will thus be revealed.'*"

"Wait, so we don't get to *choose* our own spell?" Madeline asked in slight indignation.

"You just watched your blood disappear into a magical, color-changing spell book that also happens to produce personalized holograms," Elliott pointed out. "Are you seriously going to question its power?" Though in truth, Elliott had hoped to have a say in her *own* spell, too.

Madeline quirked her mouth to one side but didn't argue.

"'Only one spell may be conjured at a time,'" Elliott continued reading. "'And a quarter moon cycle must pass between conjuring. However, in due time some of you will discover that these pages are no longer necessary; your magic, now unlocked, will radiate from your skin and spark from your fingertips. Your feet will no longer touch the ground.

"'But before moving forward, a word of guidance and caution: that which you seek is also seeking you.'"

4

Elliott looked around at the other girls.

Her coven-mates.

Holy shit, she *actually* had a *coven*. Moments ago, they'd just been four random girls from totally different walks of life with only one thing in common: being screwed over by boys and men. But now? *Now* they were goddamn witches.

"Wait, so a quarter moon cycle between conjuring," said Chloe. "How long is that?"

"Well, I'm pretty sure a full moon cycle is about twenty-nine days," Elliott replied. "So, about seven days?"

"Okay." Chloe nodded.

"But what does that mean, '*that which you seek is also seeking you*'?" Bea frowned, tracing the mark on her hand.

"I'm pretty sure it's a famous spiritual quote," Chloe informed her. "It's like the Universe wants you to have whatever you seek. You know, like destiny, or the law of attraction or whatever. It's a *good* thing."

"Then why does it say *caution*?" Bea pointed out.

Chloe shrugged, not terribly concerned as she pulled out her phone.

"I think," Madeline added confidently, "that much like forming the coven, the book wants us to be certain before we conjure our spells. We should be clear on our intentions."

"I agree," Elliott added, slightly irritated with Madeline's confidence. "That's how I interpreted it, too. I mean, I *know* what I'm seeking: justice; feeling better; not having the world be such a messed-up, unfair place. And we don't have to worry about what's seeking us if what we're seeking is good, right?"

Bea nodded in consideration, her right hand clenched as she gazed at the book's silver text.

"Well, I for one am loving this—whatever *this* is," Chloe said, holding up her phone to take a picture of her mark. "It's like a fine-line tat—holy *shit*. You guys." She turned her phone around so they could see the photo she'd taken: the center of Chloe's palm was blank.

"*What.*" Elliott pulled out her own phone and snapped a pic. Sure enough, the mark on her hand didn't appear.

"Okay, that's . . . weird," said Bea, as if this made their marks all the more troubling.

"I wonder if only *we* can see them," Madeline considered, inspecting her own hand. "Since we're bound together?"

"Okay, *secret* witch markings? Could this *be* any cooler?" Chloe said, looking around them. "Also, can we get back to that part about, '*your feet will no longer touch the ground*'? Do you think the book means that literally?" she asked in excitement.

"I'm guessing that's a metaphor," Madeline responded, as if she knew these things.

"Maybe," Elliott replied. "Or maybe we'll all end up riding broomsticks," she cracked, though she was only half joking. I mean, they *were* talking magic. Anything was possible. "Anyway, that wasn't even the best part—what I heard was that we could become skilled enough to not even *need* the book to conjure spells." The prospect of which filled her with a new kind of thrill.

The other girls were quiet as this possibility sank in.

"Speaking of conjuring"—Elliott searched the inside of her backpack for a pen and paper—"I think we should draw numbers to determine the order in which we conjure."

"Shouldn't it be the order in which we agreed to join the coven?" Madeline suggested, which would certainly suit *her*.

"No," Elliott argued. "Operating as a coven means we all need to be on the same level. Drawing numbers feels most equitable and coven-like."

"Yeah, that seems fair." Chloe nodded.

"Works for me," Bea agreed as Elliott tore the paper into fourths.

"All right," Madeline conceded.

Once Elliott had written numbers on each piece of paper and then folded them into squares, she placed them inside the empty puzzle box and shook them up. One by one, the girls took a square.

Chloe opened hers and turned it to face the group. "Looks like I'm up first," she announced, her cheerful voice tinged with anxiety.

"I'm second," Bea said, revealing her number two.

"Third," Madeline added.

Which left Elliott dead last. *Really?* she thought in exasperation.

"Oh." Chloe cringed. "Do you want to switch? I mean, this whole thing was your idea. I don't mind."

"Nope." Elliott shook her head, pocketing her square. "I'm a big girl, I can wait my turn." She picked up the book. "All right, Chloe, looks like you're up."

"Wait, we're not conjuring *right now*, are we?" asked Bea.

"Why not?" Elliott replied, turning to a blank page.

"Well . . . I can't be out that late, for starters," Bea hedged.

Elliott glanced at her phone. "It's barely even eight thirty. On a *Saturday*."

"Yeah, but . . . we don't know what's going to happen when we do it," Bea whispered, almost as if she didn't want the book to hear.

"We're not necessarily *casting* the spell," Elliott pointed out. "It just says we're conjuring."

"Do we know that for sure?" Chloe asked. "I mean, what if it's the same thing? What if the spell takes hold the moment it's conjured?"

"Wouldn't that be a good thing?" Madeline countered.

"I don't know." Chloe fiddled with the strap on her ankle boot. "I mean, I wasn't exactly emotionally prepared for the possibility of casting spells when I left the house tonight. I feel like I want to mentally prep myself ahead of time."

Which was maddening for Elliott; here she'd been anticipating this very moment for weeks—she was *finally* going to see the book's full power—and now that moment was being *delayed*? And who cared if the spell took hold the moment it was conjured? The assholes in their sight lines had already gone unpunished for way too long.

But. Operating as a coven *did* mean everyone needed to have a say. Elliott knew it wasn't just about her. So, if Chloe wasn't ready, Elliott wasn't about to be pushy and start things off on the wrong foot.

"Okay," she agreed, replacing the book in the box all calm and cool. "There's no rush. We'll conjure the first spell the next time we meet." And that was that. Totally mature. "But in that case, let's talk logistics."

After a brief discussion, it was agreed that they would gather every Thursday night at 6 p.m., the same day and time as group so that they didn't disrupt their current schedules and draw suspicion or questions from their families. And as far as location, they agreed to keep meeting in that same spot. Franceschi Park was almost always empty during weekday evenings, save for the occasional annoying couple making out in the parking lot, and if the weather turned bad—fairly unlikely, given Southern California's ongoing droughts—the abandoned mansion would be the perfect meeting spot for a coven.

"And how much do we have to tell each other?" Bea asked, looking worried. "I mean, are we committing to telling each other *why* we want revenge?"

"No way." Elliott shook her head. "That's what group tried to get us to do, and look how much good that did. This is about working together to make things *happen*. We don't need to dwell, and nobody needs to justify their actions."

"Good," Chloe and Madeline said in unison.

"Also, if we're going to do this," Elliott continued, "we have to agree to be completely off the grid. No talking about this to others, no emailing one another, no texting, no communication of any kind. And no writing anything down in a journal," she added. She'd already destroyed the list of initials inside her own journal, just to be safe. "We don't want a digital or paper trail so things can be traced back to us."

"Obviously not," Bea agreed.

"Though we should come up with a plan in case of emergencies," Madeline pointed out like the Girl Scout she'd probably been.

Elliott furrowed her brow. "What kind of emergencies do you have in mind?"

"I don't know," Madeline admitted. "I just think we should have a safe way of contacting one another should the need arise. Just out of caution."

"That's a fair point," Bea agreed, apparently always on the side of caution.

"Why don't we come up with a code of some kind?" Chloe offered. "Something clever that only we'll know."

"I don't think we need to get too cutesy with it," Madeline countered. "It just needs to be vague but clear. How about we text *FP* to one another, for Franceschi Park, if we need the group to meet that night?

And if it's really urgent, we can text *Now* and all convene at the park within an hour."

"I guess that works," Elliott agreed, even though Madeline's codes were kind of lame. She couldn't imagine they'd ever have a need for such a thing, but no harm in being prepared.

"Also, should we give our coven a *name?*" Chloe asked, one eyebrow arched.

The other girls seemed unsure about this.

"Oh, come on, we *have* to have a name."

"I think it's too early," Madeline countered. "From what I've read, the coven should get its bearings and solidify its identity before picking a name."

Elliott glanced at Madeline, both surprised and yet not that she was already reading up on covens. "I agree with Madeline. Besides, coven names are kind of passé. Let's just focus on what we're here to do and get some motherfucking revenge."

At school that Monday, Elliott couldn't concentrate. And her gaze kept drifting toward the mark on her right hand, which was resting palm up on her knee.

It's all actually happening, she thought as Mr. Reinhart droned on and on during History. She was *making* it happen. She'd formed a coven and would finally unlock the book's potential.

How would the spells manifest, she wondered as she walked over to the Santa Barbara Bowl during lunch, careful to avoid the droves of seniors exiting via the senior lot. She'd taken to strolling over to the nearby concert venue during lunch each day, hiking up into the hillside to sit in the empty amphitheater and listen to her music. The staff never bothered her, always waving her through as she walked past.

As Bea had pointed out, most of the book was blank. There was the introduction, and "A Note to Skeptics", but besides the binding spell, which had been replaced with the conjuring instructions, that was *it*. No hint of what might occur once a coven came together. Just page after empty page.

Elliott could still remember her confusion when she'd first stumbled upon the book and flipped through its blank pages. In truth, finding the book had been a happy accident, though in hindsight Elliott sometimes felt like the book had found *her*.

She'd been up in their attic one dreary summer day—one of those classic Santa Barbara June Gloom days where the ocean mist blanketing the town didn't burn off until after two—rummaging around through boxes of her mom's old stuff. The boxes were a mix of items her dad couldn't bear to part with and items Prudence couldn't bear to keep: high school photo albums and yearbooks; tickets from every concert Elliott's mom had ever attended; paperback novels and college textbooks; collections of vintage cookbooks and kitschy salt and pepper shakers. Elliott wasn't sure what she was seeking; she just knew she wanted to feel connected to her mom. In the wake of what she'd come to think of as the *second* worst day of her fucking life, she'd spent a lot of time thinking about her mom, wishing her mom were there to comfort her, wondering what sorts of wisdom she might impart. But mostly Elliott just *missed* her.

And it was there, among her mom's notorious collection of morbid oddities—bizarre antique photos, a stuffed owl, dice made from real bone (which always creeped Elliott out as a kid)—that she came upon a slim wooden puzzle box.

Later, Elliott would often wonder how her mom had even *found* the book. On one of her many flea market or estate sale expeditions, most likely. And had *she* ever attempted to use it? If so, how far had she gotten? Not very far, Elliott guessed; if her mom had been in a *coven*, of all things, Elliott would have had *some* inkling. And if her mom had access to magic, surely she'd have used it on herself and would still be alive. Though Elliott had to wonder if her mom had at least managed to manifest *her* heart's desire and, if so, what she'd seen.

What spells would the book reveal, Elliott pondered as she lay flat on her back, watching clouds drift by as Kate Bush sang about making a deal with God. Much like Madeline, she had *a lot* of ideas about how she'd like to exact revenge, but most of them involved various forms of protracted torture. She could only hope that the book delivered on her wildest dreams.

The following Thursday, Elliott headed to group just like clockwork.

"And you're sure this new friend of yours can drive you home?" her grandmother triple-checked as they neared the elementary school.

"*Yes*, Grandma," Elliott assured her. "I told you, it's on her way."

Prudence pursed her lips like she wasn't sure if it was a good thing that Elliott was making friends with other "girls like her."

"She goes to Bishop Garcia Diego," Elliott added, which had its intended effect. *A Catholic schoolgirl*, she could see Prudence thinking. *Well . . . maybe she isn't half bad.*

In the parking lot, Elliott climbed out of her grandmother's Honda Accord and then headed down the covered corridor, passing the girls' bathroom and stopping between two children's murals of the Chumash tribe and the California Gold Rush, waiting until the coast was clear.

She was halfway to counting down sixty seconds when a voice called out behind her.

"Elliott."

When she turned, Mary was headed directly toward her. *Crap.*

"Oh, hey, Mary," she greeted, silently strategizing how best to get away. Mary stopped in front of Elliott with a wide, warm smile. "I'm so glad you decided to come back."

Elliott pressed her lips together and nodded, deciding that in about thirty seconds, she was going to get a fake urgent text from her dad.

"And I like your new bangs." Mary nodded at Elliott's hair. "Ronnie's signature look."

"Yep." Elliott was surprised Mary had used her mom's nickname. Apparently, they'd been closer back in the day than Elliott realized.

"I'm really glad that we ran into one another out here," Mary added, pushing up the sleeves of her jade green sweater. Elliott noticed the edge of a pink burn scar on Mary's arm and absently wondered how she got it. "I've been meaning to talk to you and say—"

"Hi, Mary!"

Elliott glanced over her shoulder and saw Chatty Charlotte coming down the corridor toward them.

Charlotte looked at Elliott uncertainly. "Hey, Elliott."

Elliott gave her a faint nod.

"Hi, Charlotte." Mary patted Charlotte's shoulder as she passed. "See you in there, sweetheart."

Charlotte nodded, quickly continuing toward Tragic Kindergarten Kingdom, clearly aware that a private discussion was underway.

Mary looked back at Elliott. "So, listen," she said softly, tilting her head to one side.

Oh great, thought Elliott. The head tilt was Mary's tell that she was about to impart some sort of insight or wisdom. Neither of which Elliott needed.

"I've been meaning to speak with you again," Mary informed her.

"Oh yeah?" Elliott casually slid her hand into her back pocket where she'd put her phone. She'd give Mary another ten seconds.

"I know you're not a fan of group, but I just wanted to say that I think your mom would be *really* proud of you. For taking care of yourself like this and centering on your healing. I know it isn't easy."

For some reason, the mention of her mom knowing about *this* threw Elliott off and made her weirdly self-conscious. She looked down at her Docs and tucked her hair behind her ears.

"And I meant what I said the first time you came to group," Mary continued. "There is absolutely no pressure to share. But showing up for yourself like this? It's important. And if you keep coming back, I promise it *will* start to feel different."

Elliott nodded, as if she actually believed that crap.

"Also, if you ever want to talk privately, the offer still stands. We can meet for coffee or stay late after group. Whatever you'd like."

"Cool. I'll think about it," Elliott replied. Did Mary make this offer to all the girls in group? What, did she go around having coffee with traumatized teenagers on the reg—zero life of her own? Or was she treating Elliott special just because she once knew her mom?

Mary gave Elliott's shoulder a gentle squeeze. "Okay," she breathed. "That's enough out of me. I'm going to duck into the restroom, but I'll see you inside."

"Yeah, see ya," Elliott replied as Mary pushed through the bathroom door.

But the second the door swung shut, Elliott strode down the corridor toward the parking lot. Did she feel guilty for bailing on group after Mary had gone out of her way to be so understanding and nice? Nah, not really. Besides, what did *Mary* know about Elliott's mom? Her mom had never once mentioned Mary.

"Sorry," Elliott apologized as she climbed into Madeline's waiting Prius. "I got cornered by Mary."

"Oh jeez, *really*? Did she say anything about any of us? Like, was she suspicious that we all dropped out?"

"Nah."

"Okay, phew," Madeline breathed as she backed her car out of the parking space.

"By the way, thanks for the ride," Elliott added as Madeline turned onto Las Positas. "You don't have to do this for me every week, I just needed to keep my grandma off my ass."

"It's no problem. And believe me," Madeline replied as she checked the rearview mirror, "I'm familiar with overbearing maternal types."

When they arrived at Franceschi Park, long wisps of clouds were stretched along the sky, lit gold by the sunset. Chloe was waiting in the parking lot beside her car, dressed all in black like she was playing the part of Teen Witch Number Three. Her boho sundress was more fitting for Coachella than a coven, but whatever. As long as she was taking things seriously, Elliott didn't really care.

"Hey," Elliott greeted her, climbing out the passenger-side door. She'd thrown her hair into a messy, spiky bun and was wearing a pair of her mom's old waist-high plaid red pants; a torn-up, cropped Guns N' Roses T-shirt; her vintage leather jacket; and, as always, her Docs.

Madeline stepped out of the driver's-side door, looking Elliott's complete polar opposite: carefully groomed sideswept hair, designer jeans, gray V-neck cashmere sweater, and a pair of flats that, due to their brass monogram, cost more than Elliott's entire outfit.

Bea arrived just a few minutes later, in her usual jeans and track jacket, and came over to join the others near the benches. My God, Elliott thought, as the four of them assembled, what a weird motley crew they all made.

Once they were ensconced down beside the mansion and seated on the cracked flagstones near the wall, Elliott turned on her lantern, set it in the center of their ring, then pulled out the book and flipped it to the first empty page. She set it in front of Chloe.

"Okay." Chloe tucked her hair behind her ears, a somber expression on her face. "So . . . I just place my right hand above the book and . . . ask? We don't need *anything*?"

"That's what it says," Elliott informed her.

Chloe nodded and then extended her hand over the book, but at the last minute she pulled back in hesitation. "I don't know. Maybe I should take a moment to focus myself. Like I did with that skeptics spell."

"I don't think that's *necessary*, since it doesn't *say* that," Madeline pointed out.

Elliott glanced at her. Since when was *Madeline* a witchcraft expert? "Sure," she agreed slowly. "But if that makes Chloe feel more centered, I don't think it'll hurt."

Chloe nodded quickly and then closed her eyes, her silver eye shadow glimmering in the twilight. She took several deep breaths in through her nose, holding the air for a few seconds before slowly exhaling. And then she opened her eyes and reextended her right hand over the book.

"*Bring forth that which will*— Wait, what am I supposed to say again?" she double-checked, lowering her hand.

"*Bring forth that which will satisfy my intentions*," Elliott instructed. "You have to say it three times."

"Right. Okay. Got it." Chloe nodded, taking a long, deep breath, then extending her hand over the book once more. "*Bring forth that which will satisfy my intentions*," she chanted softly. "*Bring forth that which will satisfy my intentions. Bring forth that which will satisfy my intentions.*"

For a moment nothing happened.

And then, as if rising to the surface from a murky depth, silver script began to appear upon the page.

"It's *working*," Bea breathed.

An electric charge ran through Elliott's body as she watched the spell slowly appear.

"What does it say?" Madeline asked, unable to read the script from her position.

Chloe picked up the book, and a wide grin spread across her face. "'Incantation of Debilitation.'"

"Whoa," Elliott responded. Already the book was delivering on her expectations.

"It's got a pretty detailed list of instructions." Chloe scanned the spell.

"Wait, read it to us," Elliott urged. "I want to hear."

Chloe sat up straighter and cleared her throat. "'To perform the Incantation of Debilitation,'" she read, "'first gather together the following items: three stalks of English sundew, two pinches of bee venom, one pinch of shark fin, a handful of sea salt, two stinging nettles, one ounce of spoiled milk, one ounce of fox urine, and an Eye of Morgan.'"

"What is *that*?" Bea asked, sounding a little weirded out.

"I don't know," Elliott admitted, already liking the sound of this spell. "But does he drink the fox urine? Tell me he drinks the fox urine."

Chloe laughed, then continued reading. "'To cast the spell, gather your coven together under a starry sky within one hundred yards of your victim and place all ingredients inside a pewter bowl. Once the ingredients are folded together, use thorns and coffin nails to create three unbroken concentric circles surrounding the bowl. Then light a purple candle and add to the pewter bowl a personal effect from your victim'— Wait." Chloe looked up at the group. "What's a personal effect?"

"Something imbued with your victim's essence," Elliott explained. "Hair, nail clippings, tears, blood."

"Shit." Chloe sat back. "So I'm going to have to get something like *that* from my *victim*?" She let out a breath.

"Do we think the spells will always call for something like that?" Bea asked, the anxiety written all over her tensed frame.

"I don't know," Elliott replied. She sure as hell didn't want to gather a personal effect from *her* target. Just the idea of seeing him again made her feel small and useless. Like garbage to be tossed away. In fact, she actively went out of her way *not* to see him, altering her path to school, since he sometimes drove along that route, and avoiding Dune Coffee Roasters, since it was his favorite, even though it was *her* favorite, too. She thought a moment. "Well, we don't have to gather them ourselves," she pointed out. "We can take turns gathering them for one another."

"But we should do it in teams," Madeline offered. "Just to be safe."

"Right." Chloe nodded, letting out a shaky breath. It was clear that even though they'd settled on a solution, the mere idea of facing her target had rattled her to her core.

"Hey." Elliott put a hand on her shoulder. "We're in this together, okay? That's what a coven is for."

Chloe nodded again, a bit of confidence returning as she turned her gaze back to the book. "'Add to the pewter bowl a personal effect from your victim,'" she continued reading. "'And then close your eyes and clear your mind. Focus intently and precisely on how the victim has harmed you, and silently gather your rage, recalling every detail of every wrong—'"

Elliott didn't love that part about recalling every detail—that was the very thing they were all trying to *forget*—but at least the spell wasn't asking Chloe to recite her story aloud or some bullshit.

"'As you channel that rage,'" Chloe went on, "'clench your fist over these pages and have your coven chant the following invocation: *Bring forth the outcome this witch seeks.* Once you are ready to cast, recite the following: *Take this pain, take this rage, and cast it back on its creator.* As you release your hand, your spell will be cast and will immediately take hold.'"

Chloe studied the page a moment and then looked up at the group.

"Wait," Madeline said in confusion. "That's it?"

"Yeah." Chloe turned the book so they could all see it. "That's all it says."

"But what does the spell actually *do*?" Bea asked.

"Can I see that?" Elliott asked, reaching for the book.

"I mean . . . some kind of debilitation," Chloe said as she handed the book to Elliott. "Which is kind of vague, but I'm open to the Universe manifesting things the way they need to be manifested."

"It's *incredibly* vague," Madeline said in frustration. "We can't pick our own spells, *and* we don't get to know what they do?"

"Hey," Elliott interjected. "If it says this is the spell most suited to the conjuring witch, then I'm sure the consequences will be exactly what Chloe wants. And to find out what that means, we're just going to have to cast the spell."

5

Chloe

The spell's ingredients, Chloe was pleased to discover, turned out to be pretty easy to gather despite the megalong list.

Sure, a few things were obscure—tracking down the Eye of Morgan took more than a little effort—but after a weekend of online shopping, she managed to procure nearly everything on the list, express shipping all items to her house.

Before parting ways with her coven (*her coven*—it just sounded so cool!), she'd happily volunteered to purchase *all* ingredients moving forward, given that she had a credit card limit of $10K and a dad who paid it off each month without ever checking. One small perk of being a child of divorce and having a father who was totally wrapped up in his new wife and eighteen-month-old twins.

Chloe's mom had been livid when her dad went on to have biological children with his new wife, something the two of them could never achieve—ergo, Chloe's adoption. Of course, her mom never *said* any of this, but Chloe could tell how much it irritated her. Every time Chloe's dad called to talk to her (which was barely ever these days, but whatevs), her mom poured a glass of rosé and then booked an all-day spa visit. Which Chloe tried not to take personally, but it was hard not to feel like maybe she wasn't enough.

Sitting in front of her laptop at the long glass kitchen table, which looked out over the sculpture garden, which was on the terrace just above the infinity pool, Chloe ate a bowl of fruit and nonfat Greek yogurt and searched for English sundew—a rare carnivorous plant. Some of these sites were so rando and weird—what would drive someone to set up a shop *exclusively* selling coffin nails? Ew. She just hoped the ingredients were legit and she wasn't falling prey to some bizarro phishing scam. Though if she was, it was her dad's info, so *ohhhh welllll.*

"Morning, Clo," her stepdad greeted her, grabbing a mug from the cupboard and striding over to the German espresso machine built into the wall.

"Hey, Richard," she said, casually adjusting her laptop so he couldn't see the screen.

He punched in a few buttons and three seconds later she heard the hiss and brew of his cappuccino. "Oh, hey. I saw Arts & Letters is doing a screening of Bong Joon-ho's early short films next weekend. I was wondering if you'd like to go."

"Maybe." Chloe shrugged, not lifting her gaze from the screen. Chloe's mom had always done her best to ensure Chloe felt connected to her heritage—celebrating Lunar New Year, binging K-dramas, shopping at H Mart and failing spectacularly at cooking Korean meals together. And yeah, maybe her mom's best was *kinda* superficial; I mean, it's not like they ever had deep and meaningful conversations about Korean heritage or identity and race. But she knew her mom had good *intentions.* And once upon a time, back when Chloe's dad still lived with them, they'd even talked about taking a family trip to South Korea someday . . . though her mom hadn't mentioned it since the divorce.

But there was something about Richard suggesting museum exhibits and random documentaries and trying to chat her up over boring "literary works" by Korean authors that was so totally *awk-ward*. It was cringe-inducing to watch this middle-aged white man try to be so woke.

Besides, just because she happened to be *born* in South Korea didn't make Chloe, like, *Korean* Korean. She was Korean *American*. She'd lived basically her whole life in Southern California and had non-Korean interests, too.

So, did she want to watch some artsy short films by an anti-capitalist South Korean filmmaker in some stuffy UCSB auditorium with her fiftysomething stepdad and a bunch of other middle-aged cinema weirdos? *No.* No, she did not.

"Hey, baby," her mom called, striding into the kitchen in head-to-toe Lululemon, her ivory skin all dewy and her blond hair pulled into a perfect ponytail. Her mom was perpetually in yoga gear, and did, by Chloe's conservative estimation, precisely eighteen hours of exercise a day.

Chloe quickly changed tabs as her mom came over to give her a kiss on the cheek. "Hi, Mom."

"Oooo, cuuuuute," her mom commented, looking at the outfit she had up on the screen. "You should get that. Wait, what sizes do they have left? Maybe *I* should get that. Oh, hey, before I forget," she added, striding over to the subzero fridge that housed beverages. "We're having the Pearsons over next Thursday for dinner. I know that's the night you have study group, but any chance you can reschedge for just that week?"

"Not really," Chloe replied, flipping back to the spell ingredient she was looking at.

"You're only two weeks into school, Clo, how much work can you have?" her mom teased, grabbing a pressed juice.

"*Mom.* It's junior year, it's not like they're cutting us any slack."

"Pretty please?" her mom begged. "I'll ask Esmerelda to make her tamales."

"I really can't. We have a big group project due soon." Chloe clicked *Buy*, selected overnight shipping, and typed in her credit card number.

"Okay, *fine*," her mom pouted, going over to lean against the white marble island. "Hey, where are you off to so soon, Mister?" she asked Richard, who was screwing a lid onto his travel mug.

"Big meeting with the investors, remember?"

"Oh, that's right."

He went over and gave Chloe's mom one of his super-mushy, drawn-out kisses.

"Mmm," her mom giggled.

Ugh. *Gag.* The second Chloe's payment went through, she flipped her laptop closed. "Gotta go!"

"Okay, babe." Her mom glanced over from inside Richard's embrace. "Don't forget I have my girls' night tonight, so I won't be home for dinner."

"Have fun!" Chloe replied, giving her mom one of her patented *Life's absolutely great!* smiles as she grabbed her bag.

It wasn't that Chloe felt like she had to take care of her mom, exactly. It was more that she just had to protect her from certain things.

After all, she'd *seen* how depressed her mom was after the divorce—the late-night crying, the early-morning crying, the sitting-with-her-girlfriends-drinking-a-bottle-of-wine crying—and while she was better now that she was married to Richard, Chloe didn't want to do anything that might jeopardize her mom's fragile mental state.

So if Chloe needed to hide how much her dad's absence actually bothered her? That was fine. She could handle it on her own. And if she needed to keep quiet about the incident from late last spring? Well, that's just the way it was. She could secretly attend a support group (though definitely not one in Montecito) to check the self-care box, and truthfully *that* was fine, too. I mean, wasn't she going to be out of the house soon enough anyway? Wasn't this good practice at being a grown-up?

"Hey, Clo?" Madison asked as they exited the gym after volleyball practice that Friday, fanning her face. Her pale skin was beet red from practice, and her strawberry blond hair was soaked. "You're coming to Arman's tonight with us, yes?" Madison, whose parents were British, loved leaning into her Britishness by making all her questions statements, amended with either the word *yes* or *no.*

Chloe resisted the urge to flinch at just the sound of Arman's name. At least he was a senior, which meant they had totally different classes. And if she was vigilant, she could carefully orchestrate her day so they never crossed paths. "Ugh, no," she groaned, mopping at her forehead. Like Madison, she was uber sweaty. "I'm still grounded."

"That *sucks,*" moaned Madison as they crossed the parking lot.

"Jesus, when did *your* mom decide to be such the disciplinarian?" asked Brooklyn, beeping her Mercedes unlocked. Somehow Brooklyn's tanned skin always remained sweat-free during practice, ditto her wavy brown hair. "Also, you're going to miss out on Lulu's psychotic break because *I* heard Jasper's bringing that skank *Mina* to the party." Brooklyn, who'd known Chloe since they were three, was the group's self-imposed ringleader / events coordinator / gossip liaison. And she took her job very seriously.

"Didn't Jasper and Lulu break up, like, two seconds ago?" Chloe rolled her eyes, pulling out her car keys. "Typical."

"But we're on for the Club tomorrow, yes?" Madison asked, throwing her bag into the trunk of her Land Rover. The girls met every weekend at the Montecito Club, a private golf and social club their families belonged to, where they took Pilates and hung poolside.

"Yeah, totally," Chloe agreed. "You *know* my mom would never deny me my self-care."

Much like Laguna Blanca, the Montecito Club was almost entirely white. Well, that wasn't true—the people with *memberships* were almost entirely white; the people who worked there were not. Then again, that was true of Montecito as a whole. But being one of only a handful of Asian kids didn't bother Chloe *that* much.

I mean, sure, sometimes kids made dumb comments, like that time at Mikey B's party last year when Becca Housman laughed at a snarky comment Chloe made and then added, *God, you're so funny and chill, Clo, you don't even seem Asian!* Which, WTF? Did she think Asian people weren't *funny* or *chill*? Or that time in ninth grade when Petra Richardson asked Chloe if she knew how much her parents had paid for her. Which, *excuse me*? How was that an even *remotely* acceptable question? As if Chloe were a *pet* or something. And how was *she* supposed to know how much the adoption agency fees and paperwork and travel expenses cost?

But it's not as if stuff like that happened *every day*. For the most part, Chloe just went to school, played volleyball and lacrosse, hung out at the Club, and attended parties, and was basically like everyone else.

Or at least she was *before* the incident.

Now, she had to admit, she wasn't *exactly* like everyone else. Not everyone had to train themselves to remain placid at the sound of certain people's names. Or lie about why they couldn't go out to certain parties. Not everyone kept a flask hidden under their pillow to help them sleep at night or found themselves cuddling with their child-hood teddy bear.

Because not everyone had an incident they were striving to forget.

Then again, not everyone had a secret witch mark or belonged to a *coven*, either.

Elliott

That Friday evening, Elliott informed her dad she was hanging with some new friends—not a lie, exactly, but it was painful to see how happy this made him as he put down his book, all perked up.

"You need any money, El?" he asked, pulling out his wallet.

"Nah, I'm good," she assured him as she pulled on her Docs near the front door. Besides, on their strict budget, it's not like her dad should be handing her extra cash.

"Come on, at least take a twenty," he insisted, holding out a bill.

She rolled her eyes and doubled back to give his shoulders a squeeze. "Dad, I swear, I'm good," she insisted as she kissed his head and then strode toward the door.

Outside, Elliott did her standard Mace, knife, safety alarm check and then waited down the street, earbuds in place, the Red Hot Chili Peppers' "Give It Away" blasting to get herself in the right mood. Five minutes later, Chloe pulled up in an unfamiliar Lexus SUV, one arm out the window. Madeline was already in the passenger seat. Bea was in back. The others had agreed to meet at Franceschi Park, where they'd leave their cars, and then pick up Elliott on the way.

"Hey!" Chloe called over the sound of annoying pop music. She was dressed all in black, including a floppy boho hat, sunglasses, and a trench coat, like a movie star going incognito—albeit a witchy movie star. Once again, Elliott noted, she seemed to be playing a part.

"Hey," Elliott greeted as she climbed into the back.

"Hey," Madeline and Bea each acknowledged, voices raised over the music. They were more subdued than Chloe, though Elliott didn't know them well enough to gauge their precise moods.

The song playing was way too upbeat, more befitting a night of clubbing than one of witchcraft. Not exactly the vibe Elliott had imagined. But if this was the music Chloe needed to get in the right mindset, who was she to judge? After all, it was Chloe's night.

When the coven had met the previous day for their weekly gathering, Chloe was pleased to report that nearly all the ingredients were procured. The only thing she still needed was the personal effect—she'd cringed while saying *personal effect*, like she still couldn't get over having to collect something imbued with her victim's essence. But she had a plan to gather it: that Friday her target was throwing a party at his house, which seemed like a good opportunity.

"Perfect," Elliott had agreed. "And we could perform the spell while we're there."

"At the *party*?" Bea had asked uncertainly.

"Not *at* the party," Elliott clarified. "From somewhere nearby. Just as long as we're within one hundred yards of the victim."

"We could probably do it from inside someone's car," Madeline suggested. Which wasn't the most atmospheric option—Elliott had been envisioning a dark grove of trees somewhere—but she supposed it *was* the easiest.

Wind whipped through the open sunroof as they sped down Mission Street, flying over the street's big dips and taking a right onto the 101 freeway heading north.

"Where are we going?" Elliott called over the music.

"What?" Chloe shouted back.

"WHERE'S THE PARTY?"

"Some estate in Hope Ranch," Bea answered, gazing out the window.

Elliott nodded, one foot up on the Lexus's soft leather seat. Chloe was singing along to the horrendous pop song. Madeline was doing her best impersonation of a robot ballerina up front. Bea's eyes were closed as she leaned her head against the window. Elliott mindlessly played with one of her pink Princess Leia–style buns.

"Isn't it so awesome to be doing this all together?" Chloe asked with forced enthusiasm, looking at Elliott and Bea in the rear-view mirror.

"Mmm." Elliott nodded, eyebrows raised.

"Isn't that our exit?" Madeline pointed out.

"Oh—shit." Chloe quickly veered over to the far-right lane and took the exit for Modoc Road.

Elliott had always imagined a coven being this awesome, pro-gressive, bonding feminist thing, but the truth was she didn't feel at all close to these girls. They barely knew one another. In real life, she never would have chosen to make them her friends.

Which made her think of Vi and how the two of them had always fit together like two missing jigsaw pieces run off to have their own adventures. A familiar hollow ache opened up inside Elliott's chest—an ache she did her best to fill by forging her sorrow into rage.

As they passed through the stone and wrought-iron arch that led into Hope Ranch—a wealthy enclave of mansions tucked up against the ocean bluffs—Elliott could just make out the tall palm trees lining either side of the entry road. Like many of the rich neighborhoods in Santa Barbara, Hope Ranch was pitch-black, with zero streetlamps; the only source of light was Chloe's headlights, which, as they drove along the dark, curving, tree-shrouded roads, created a full-on Lyn-chian *Mulholland Drive* vibe. Elliott also noted that while there was a bridle path along one side of the road, there were zero sidewalks; so basically, you could canter your Thoroughbred in, but if you were an outsider on foot? Stay the fuck out.

Chloe

As they neared the Mahdavi estate—which was only a short distance from where Chloe's dad now lived (with his own private beach and equestrian trail, BTW, never mind the fact that she'd begged for a horse her *entire* life)—Chloe began to get that all-too-familiar panicked feeling in the pit of her stomach. *You're not even going in,* she reminded herself for the hundredth time. *And no one's going to recognize you in Richard's Lexus. Just chill.*

Turning onto La Ladera Road, Chloe drove past the long line of BMWs and Mercedes and luxury SUVs that were parked blocking the opposite lane—though no one drove through this secluded neighborhood at night, so not like it mattered—then turned around at the end of the block and pulled up behind a Jaguar she vaguely recognized.

"Okay," she said, opening up an app on her phone. "So . . . there are actually *two* targets," she admitted, something she'd never disclosed before. It felt vulnerable and a little embarrassing to admit such a thing; she was revealing more of her story than she'd intended *and* the fact that she'd told a half-lie in group. It wasn't a guy, singular, who'd taken advantage of her.

But to Chloe's great relief, the other girls didn't react. Elliott just nodded and said, "Okay, so two personal effects needed."

In that moment, she loved them, these girls who believed her without question and didn't make her explain. She half turned in her seat and showed the screen to Madeline and Elliott, who'd volunteered to go in. Chloe did her best not to look at the photo directly. "Arman's on the left—he's the one throwing the party, it's his house—and Trevor's on the right."

On-screen was a photo Brooklyn had posted to her social media account of Arman and Trevor sitting on the hood of Trevor's dad's Ferrari. They were smoking cigars and throwing wannabe gang signs. Arman's black faux-hawk was perfectly gelled, and he was flashing his stupidly disarming smile. Trevor's blond hair was swooped over one eye and he was scowling at the camera.

Elliott narrowed her eyes, studying the photo. "What a couple of assholes," she muttered, which made Chloe wonder if her assessment was based on the photo alone or the knowledge that they both deserved to be punished.

"The front gates will be open," Chloe said, quickly flicking the image away, wishing she could flick her memories away just as easily. "When you go in, tell them Adam invited you. He invites, like, basically *any* girl he comes in contact with, so no one will question you. I mean, I don't think anyone would question *you*, Madeline, but they might wonder about you, Elliott." And then she quickly added, "It's just, I mean, you're not exactly . . . well, you know what I mean. No offense."

"Well, I *wasn't* offended until you said *that*," Elliott snorted as she unbuckled her seat belt.

Chloe hadn't meant to insult Elliott—though had she? It was hard to tell how much Elliott actually cared. But also? Elliott *wasn't* the kind of kid who showed up to Arman's parties. Couldn't they all just be honest about that? It wasn't the fact that Elliott's style was less conventionally attractive, with her retro outfits, nose ring, and bright pink hair; it was just . . . she was a *public school* kid. And not to be all classist or whatever, but they just ran in *very* different crowds.

"Also, if they're serving any kind of special drink," Chloe added, "I'd be careful. Don't drink anything you don't open yourself."

"What's the layout of the house?" Madeline asked pragmatically, running a hand over her hair.

Chloe *really* didn't want to think about that house too much; she'd spent a lot of time there, but the last time, things had *not* gone well.

She scrunched her mouth to one side. "So, the living room, dining room, kitchen, library, movie theater, and guest suite are all downstairs. Arman's room is upstairs at the far end." She waved dismissively, not wanting to think about *that*. "There's five bedrooms total upstairs, plus Arman's dad's art gallery—but that room's always locked. There'll probably be a lot of people hanging out in the west and east loggias and swimming in the pool. Sometimes people chill in the grotto outside the gym—that's on the lower terrace down past the bocce ball court—"

Elliott muttered something unintelligible as she climbed out of the car.

"Got it." Madeline nodded, pulling on the shoulders of her floral blouse so the neckline sat a little higher before opening her door.

A car drove by as she got out, sending a wave of anxiety through Chloe, who scrunched down in her seat. She watched as Madeline and Elliott strode toward the estate, looking totally mismatched but also surprisingly . . . confident. Like two agents on a secret mission.

Cold flooded her body as they disappeared down the driveway. For some reason she was suddenly shaky. "Is it cold in here?" She shivered, turning on the heat.

Bea leaned forward from the back, arms resting on the middle console. "Are you doing okay?"

"Yeah." Chloe nodded and then shook her head. She wiped at her eyes underneath her sunglasses. "Ugh." She shook out her hands. "Why do *I* feel so nervous?"

Elliott

"So," Elliott whispered to Madeline as they made their way toward the mansion—a mix of minimalist design and typical Santa Barbara

Spanish style. Much like the road Chloe had parked along, the driveway was lined with expensive cars, all of them shiny and new. "Which guy do you want to take?"

"I'll take the one with the surfer hair," Madeline answered, applying a final coat of lipstick before tucking the tube away in her dainty purse. "Trevor, or whatever."

"Sweet, I'll take the faux-hawk," Elliott answered in a jokey fratboy voice. But Madeline didn't react. Elliott could see she was visibly anxious but also trying to remain calm. "Do you know people here or something?"

"What?" Madeline glanced over at her. "At the party? No. I mean, I don't think so." She ran a hand over her hair. "I don't know."

"Well, are you sure you're cool with doing this? Because we could always get—"

"I'm fine," Madeline assured her crisply, tossing back her hair.

"Hey." Elliott put a hand on Madeline's shoulder to make her stop. "Those people in there? Whatever you're worried they're thinking? Fuck them."

Madeline rolled her eyes, like, *Oh sure, because it's that easy.*

"No, seriously," insisted Elliott, looking Madeline dead in the eye. "You are a goddamn *witch* now." She held up her right palm as a reminder. "So. Fuck. Them."

This time Madeline took in her words. She nodded, then shook herself out a little. "Okay. Let's just get this over with as fast as possible."

A sentiment Elliott fully agreed with; she had zero interest in sticking around at some lame-ass rich kid's high school party.

Though if she was honest with herself? She was also a little nervous. And her pep talk hadn't been solely for Madeline. Chloe was right: this *wasn't* Elliott's scene. Being around private school kids always made her self-conscious, like she wasn't as good or as smart as them. *But you're not here to party,* she reminded herself as she rang the doorbell. *You're here on a mission.*

As fate would have it, Arman was the one who answered the front door. His black hair was wet, like he'd been in the pool, and he was wearing swim trunks and an open Hawaiian-style shirt that revealed his muscled olive chest.

"What up?" He grinned, lazing against the oversized wooden doorframe as he appraised Madeline and then Elliott. He probably relied on that crooked smile to charm most people, but the way he was scanning Elliott's vintage black velvet dress and torn fishnets made her want to shove a Doc Martens up his preppy ass. "Okay." He nodded at her. "I see you, Wednesday Addams."

Elliott wasn't sure what he'd done to Chloe, but Elliott didn't *need* to know. His smarmy face was enough to make her blood boil.

"Hey," Madeline greeted him, cocking her head to one side and turning on a social persona Elliott had yet to see from her. Half cheerleader, half chill. "Adam invited us?"

"Cool." Arman nodded, opening the door a little wider. "Signature drinks are in the great room. The taco truck's out back. What up, Zoey," he called out as a skinny, pale redhead in a gold bikini sauntered over to him from a side hallway.

Taco truck, Elliott thought in exasperation and disgust as she followed Madeline through the sleek stucco-and-ivory-marbled foyer, which had that indoor/outdoor feel, what with the lush agave plants rooted in pebble-filled trenches.

Walking into such an enormous estate was kind of shocking for Elliott—sure, she lived in a town *filled* with wealthy people, but it was one thing to *know* about the extravagance of the 1 percent and quite another to enter their arena.

I mean, relatively speaking, she wasn't *that* far off from the 1 percent, given that she had the privilege of living in the United

States, in Southern California, in posh Santa Barbara, with a free-lance graphic designer father who owned his own million-dollar (hand-me-down) home. Maybe they were middle class as far as Santa Barbara was concerned, but in comparison to the rest of the world, they were rich.

But there was rich, as in someone could afford to house you and sometimes order takeout and occasionally rent a cabin in Big Bear. And then there was *Rich*, as in your parents could afford a live-in staff, a pool house the size of a normal house, and quick weekend getaways to Majorca and the Maldives.

These people were definitely *Rich*.

After passing twin hallways branching off to either side, a chrome-filled kitchen, where some elaborate drinking game was getting out of control, and an airy dining room, where a cluster of girls was sitting atop the long modern dining table smoking weed and painting their nails to Kanye West (which, were they *serious*? After everything he'd done?), Elliott and Madeline finally arrived at what Elliott surmised was the great room.

Aptly named, too, because it was fucking *huge*. Easily three times as long as her entire house, all lofted ceiling and oversized fireplaces, mid-century modern furniture, and low sectional sofas. Rich kids were sprawled everywhere, drinking some kind of blue cocktail that involved dry ice, playing poker with hundred-dollar bills, taking selfies with someone's fluffy puppy. The far wall was made entirely of enormous iron-and-glass pivoting doors so that the great room opened onto the pool deck and the long turquoise pool and, Elliott noted with loathing, the *taco truck* just beyond. Which probably housed the only non-rich people at this party, Elliott thought in irritation.

"I'm gonna search upstairs," she murmured to Madeline, knowing that's where Arman's room was located. Plus, she was already done with these people.

Madeline nodded, scanning the party. "I'll meet you back in the foyer."

Elliott backtracked through the house, avoiding two bros stumbling out of the kitchen wearing matching sombreros. *Racist idiots*, she thought in disgust.

At the twin hallways Elliott turned right, passing a library and a door that led to an outdoor dining space, where a cluster of kids was laughing at a video on someone's phone that she highly suspected was of one of them on drugs, before finally locating a floating staircase.

Upstairs, which was quiet and empty, Elliott found herself at one end of a long stucco-and-marble corridor lined with oversized black-and-white photos that probably cost millions. Chloe had said there were five bedrooms and that Arman's was at the far end, but she hadn't clarified *which* far end, and to Elliott's eye there were at least a dozen closed doors. Wonderful.

She picked the first door on her right, which was locked—probably the dad's art gallery, which, speaking of, *what?*—but the second one was fortunately open. Elliott stepped into a massive bedroom with a canopy bed, a pink egg chair, and a wall of stuffed animals that rivaled any toy store. Part of Elliott ached at seeing this little girl's bedroom, wondering how soon she'd get thrust out of childhood and into the real world. Granted, she was undoubtedly a spoiled brat, but still. Elliott closed the door.

Back in the corridor she glanced around, making sure no one else had come upstairs, before continuing onward.

The next door she tried, which was still technically at the far end given the size of the house, was also unlocked and led to what was clearly the primary suite: king-sized bed, giant fireplace, expansive ocean-view terrace. Sprawled on the white fur rug before the fireplace was a half-naked couple making out.

"Hey!" the guy growled. "Get out of here!"

The girl looked over at Elliott, her skirt hiked up to her waist. She seemed pretty wasted.

Elliott hesitated. "Are you—are you okay?" she asked the girl.

"What?" The girl laughed. "Who the fuck *is* this, Aaron?"

"GET OUT!" he yelled.

Jesus, okay, Elliott thought as she darted out of the room and closed the door. So maybe the girl was into it. Fine. But could *she* help it if her instinct was one of suspicion and doubt? After the hell she'd been through, she didn't trust *any* situation.

God. The last thing she needed was to get yelled at by some asshole. The whole thing just made her want to speed up the endeavor.

Madeline

Back downstairs, Madeline had grabbed a blue-liquid-filled crystal martini glass from the bar and was pretending to sip to blend in.

She'd never liked parties. Sure, she always went to them, telling herself ahead of time that she'd be relaxed and chill. But inevitably she'd arrive and feel stiff and awkward and then make up some excuse to leave before everyone else.

"You want a hit?" some guy asked from a low sofa, holding up a bong.

"No, I'm good." she smiled, taking another fake sip as she walked toward an open glass door. She stepped through it and out into the warm night air, the turquoise pool water glowing before her.

There were at least a dozen people in the water, a few in the nearby hammocks, a handful sitting near an outdoor fireplace, half a dozen grabbing tacos from the food truck—which was literally just parked right there on the grass. In the middle of the pristine backyard. *Her* parents would have killed her if she ruined their lawn.

Then again, they'd never let her throw a party in the first place—the mere idea of minors drinking on their premises was enough to give her divorce-attorney mother a splitting headache.

But *this* kid's parents, she was guessing, had probably hired the food truck, signed off on the signature drinks, and already had gardeners lined up to come in and replace the sod.

A high-pitched scream filled the night air as a fully clothed girl was pushed into the pool. When Madeline looked, she saw the pusher was a six-foot-something white dude with a basketball vibe, which made her think of her ex, which in turn filled her mouth with bile. *Don't think about him*, she told herself.

The pusher high-fived his blond friend who, Madeline noted with great interest, happened to be her target, Trevor. He was tall and lean, with sharp cheekbones and a cocky air. She fake-sipped her drink, keeping a careful eye on him as he helped the girl climb from the pool, only to push her back in.

"Hey," a voice greeted.

Madeline looked over to see a cute guy in dark jeans and a gray button-down approaching. "Hey."

"Don't I know you?" He smiled.

Madeline's heart sped up as alarm bells went off in her head. She was absolutely positive she did not know him. "I don't think so," she said casually, looking back across the pool. Her target was picking up a drink from one of the poolside tables.

"Yeah, you're Derrick's girlfriend."

Madeline glanced back at the guy, adrenaline now coursing through her body. "How do you know Derrick?" she replied coolly. And who *was* this guy? Had he messaged her? Was he one of the many random creeps she'd had to block across all social media? She'd assumed they were all older dudes, based on their profile pics, but maybe not.

"We did league together a few years back," he explained, which caused Madeline to relax—but just barely. So, this guy played basketball with her ex. "I used to go to Christian Valley," he added. "Now I'm at Cate."

"Oh." She nodded politely.

"How is D?" he asked, sliding his hands into his pockets. "I haven't seen him since, God, last season, I guess."

"I wouldn't know," she replied stiffly, taking a fake sip of her drink.

"Oh man." He raised his eyebrows. "You guys broke up? Jeez." He shook his head. "His loss." He looked around the party. "So . . . you friends with these guys?"

"No," Madeline replied, tracking her target in her peripheral vision as he rounded the pool and high-fived a friend.

"Yeah, me neither. I mean, not *really*." He shrugged. "I know a friend of a friend. I'm Nate, by the way."

Madeline hesitated, anxiety spiking within her at the idea of revealing her name. That happened anytime she introduced herself these days. What if they decided to look her up later? "Madeline," she forced out.

"Cool." Nate nodded. "So . . . have you decided where you're applying to—"

"Sorry, will you excuse me?" she cut him off. Her target was strolling into the house.

"Oh—yeah, sorry," she heard him say behind her as she trailed her target through one of the open glass doors.

Madeline's old self never would have blown off a seemingly nice guy like that; she would have felt way too guilty. In fact, she still felt a little guilty. But these days Madeline was skeptical of nice.

Furthermore, if he really *was* nice, she was saving them both a lot of time: there was no way he'd want anything to do with her once he learned the truth.

Elliott

Upstairs, Elliott had *finally* located her target's bedroom at the *other* far end, past the office and the craft room and the playroom and the game room, and for shit's sake, this house had a lot of rooms. Also, could Chloe not have been a *wee* bit more specific in her description? *Far end.* Awesome. *Note to self,* Elliott thought as she knocked on the door and then carefully cracked it open, *never ask Chloe for directions.*

Like everything else in the house, Arman's room was both enormous and dripping with privilege: huge flat-screen TV above the fireplace; a signed and framed Steph Curry jersey; Stanford and Yale pennants; a giant tank filled with tropical fish; a modern book-case stacked with trophies and video games and elaborate, completed LEGO sets. The room was perfectly kept, too, which almost certainly had nothing to do with him and everything to do with the housekeeper. *Ugh,* Elliott thought, *what an undeserving prick.*

She stomped across the bedroom toward the spa-like bathroom— a toothbrush or comb should more than suffice—but halfway there, something caught her eye. She paused and crossed to the book-case. Nestled between a LEGO Millennium Falcon and a stack of shoot-'em-dead video games was a small ceramic container that looked a lot like one Elliott had at home.

She peeked inside and a wide grin spread across her face. Score.

Elliott was just slipping back out of the bedroom and closing the door when she saw a couple coming down the corridor headed her way. With a jolt, she realized the guy was Arman, walking backward as he led the bikini-clad redhead, who was giggling and stumbling and clearly wasted. Elliott casually angled toward the nearby staircase.

"It's just in here," she heard him tell the girl as Elliott hurried down the staircase. Part of her felt she had an obligation to storm back up there and protect that girl, make sure she didn't get taken advantage of. But she didn't want to do anything to draw attention and blow things for Chloe. Besides, she reminded herself as she battled her guilt, Arman had a big-time punishment headed his way.

When Elliott got back down to the foyer, Madeline was already waiting at the bottom of the stairs. She was clutching her purse weirdly and had an anxious expression like she wanted to get the hell out of there.

"You good?" she whispered to Elliott.

Elliott nodded, and they made a beeline for the door.

In the driveway, they fast-walked past the row of cars, then practically ran down the street back to Chloe's parked Lexus ... which wasn't there.

A pair of headlights flashed at them from farther down the block.

"What the hell?" Elliott said when she and Madeline climbed inside.

"Sorry," Bea apologized from behind the wheel. "Chloe wasn't feeling great and wanted to park farther away."

Chloe was in the passenger seat, repetitively tapping herself on the indentation between her nose and lip, then on her chin, followed by her collarbone. The music had been changed to something calming and instrumental.

"What's she doing?" Elliott asked Bea as Chloe tapped her rib cage under her left arm.

"Something for anxiety," Bea replied.

"It's EFT tapping to calm my central nervous system," Chloe explained without looking over as she tapped the crown of her head.

"Did it go okay?" Bea asked them.

"It was fine," Madeline said stiffly.

Chloe finally turned to face them, apparently done with her tapping. "Did you get the stuff?"

Madeline unzipped her tiny purse and pulled out a stoppered glass test tube filled with a bright blue liquid. Elliott wondered if she'd special ordered that tube or if she was just the kind of girl who readily kept test tubes on hand.

"I swiped Trevor's drink and poured some in here," Madeline explained. "It's bound to have his saliva."

"And I found this." Elliott fished the ceramic container out of the pocket of her leather jacket and held it up for all to see.

"What *is* that?" Chloe frowned, eyeing the molar-shaped container.

"A tooth fairy box," Elliott clarified, cracking it open so they could all see its contents.

Chloe wrinkled her nose. "Gross."

Inside was one of Arman's milky white baby teeth.

6

Chloe

Casting a revenge spell on the guy she'd once obsessed over wasn't exactly something Chloe'd ever imagined doing from inside her stepdad's car. Then again, there were a lot of things she'd never once imagined. Like *having* a stepdad (and barely ever seeing her actual dad). Or needing to cast a revenge spell in the first place.

The Incantation of Debilitation stated that they needed to cast under the stars, but they certainly weren't casting *outside*, so they'd opened the sunroof to reveal the night sky. It was a little cramped inside the car and difficult to form a circle, but they did their best, Bea and Chloe sitting backward in the front seats to face Madeline and Elliott in back.

Chloe had stolen an oversized silver serving tray from her mom's absurdly large entertainment set, which Madeline was currently holding on her lap, and Elliott was pulling out the ingredients from Chloe's mom's farmer's market tote bag. Elliott had asked Chloe if *she* wanted to be the one to prepare things, but Chloe absolutely did not. She needed to keep herself grounded and calm. And so, as Elliott added the ingredients to the pewter bowl—starting with the stinging nettle, and then adding the spoiled milk, which filled the car with a rancid smell—Chloe launched into another round of EFT tapping.

"Even though I'm anxious and scared," she whispered to herself as she tapped, "I still know that my body is safe."

"Wait, does it say what order the ingredients should be added?" Madeline asked as Elliott dumped the dried fox urine into the bowl.

Bea looked down at the book in her hands and scanned the silver text. "No, it just says to add all items to the pewter bowl."

"Okay," Madeline replied, watching as Elliott dropped in the Eye of Morgan—which had turned out to be a rare purple gemstone with a creepy eyelike center that had cost Chloe more than her iPhone.

"Okay—there, that's all of it," Elliott said once she'd added the last few items. "Now what?"

"Now you fold all the items together," Bea instructed.

Elliott nodded and looked around for something to mix the items with.

"There's a wooden spoon inside the bag," Chloe said as she tapped just below her eye socket.

Elliott found said spoon and began mixing the items within the bowl.

"That's stirring, not folding," Madeline pointed out.

Elliott looked over at her. "What's the difference?"

"Stirring is more vigorous, folding is about gently combining the ingredients."

Elliott took a breath, then slowed her pace, gently combining the items she'd added to the bowl. "There. What's the next step?" she asked Bea.

"Now we line up the thorns and coffin nails around the bowl in three unbroken concentric circles."

"Should we alternate the thorns and nails within each circle?" Madeline asked. "Or does it not matter?"

"It doesn't say," Bea replied, double-checking the book.

"We should alternate," Elliott replied. "I've read that when building out any kind of circle, you want to create variety. It seems counterintuitive, but it actually strengthens each ingredient's power if they're not clustered together."

Madeline held the baggies of thorns and nails so that Elliott could form the concentric circles around the pewter bowl, which she was forced to keep on the small side so that they could fit everything on the tray.

"Okay, and then we light the candle," Bea instructed.

Elliott pulled the purple candle from her backpack, lit it with her Zippo, moved to place it on the middle console, and then decided to just hold it.

"Okay, now what?" she asked.

Bea scanned the instructions and then looked over at Chloe, who was tapping the top of her head. "Now you channel your rage."

"Now?" Chloe stopped tapping and took a deep breath. "Okay. Now."

Bea placed the open book on the middle console.

Focus and intention, the book stated, were crucial for the spell's success. *Clear your mind and focus on precisely how the victim has harmed you. Silently gather your rage—recalling every detail of every wrong—and then channel that rage as you clench your fist over these pages.*

Chloe closed her eyes and took another deep, shaky breath. As she did so, the other girls began to chant the spell's invocation.

"Bring forth the outcome this witch seeks. Bring forth the outcome this witch seeks . . ."

Chloe *really* didn't want to go back there. She didn't want to recall every detail. But once she did this, she reasoned, she'd have *closure*. And then maybe she'd never have to think about it again . . .

It had been well after 1 a.m. when it happened, after doing shots out in the grotto, dancing on a tabletop, and playing a drunken version of Twister with Brooklyn and Mia and that other girl Chloe had never met before. She remembered that Arman came up from behind her in the living room and whispered in her ear, "Follow me."

"Where are we going?" She'd giggled as he led her by the hand through the crowd and toward the staircase—even though she knew *exactly* where they were going. As they climbed the stairs, she could hear the party down below: music thumping, a group of guys yelling "Whoa!", a girl laughing a little too loud.

"Too many questions." Arman had grinned back at her, eyes skimming her crop top and cut-offs. "You look so fucking hot."

"Shut up." She'd rolled her eyes as they reached the upstairs hall. Though truthfully the comment had made her stomach go warm.

By then, she'd hooked up with Arman a bunch of times—at Leandra's birthday and at Michael's beach house, at Dana's house and at the winter formal, and most recently at that party up in the Riviera, not that she was keeping count—but somehow this felt different. To be hooking up at *his* house during *his* party felt more official. Chloe felt singled out. Special. There were a ton of cute girls there and still he'd picked *her*.

Not that she'd expected anything *serious* to come of it. At least not right away. Which was totally fine. They could hook up and be casual and that was all cool.

But if she was honest? In her more private moments, she'd fantasized about them *eventually* being together.

Chloe remembered that when they got inside Arman's bedroom, he'd immediately pushed her up against the closed door, his mouth meeting hers. He was a good kisser, and he totally knew it.

"Come here," he'd murmured, navigating her toward his bed. He'd fallen backward, pulling her on top of him, which had made her laugh.

"Whoa." She'd paused to hold her head as it spun, realizing she was a lot drunker than she'd realized—and feeling kind of *weird*.

Arman had tucked her hair behind her ears, which at the time she'd thought was such a chivalrous action, and then pulled her face down to meet his, kissing her again, his mouth hungry as it devoured hers. Then they began making out in earnest, undressing each other, her pulling off his shirt, him unbuttoning her shorts. She sensed how much he wanted her—and she'd wanted him just as bad. They'd slept together twice before, neither of which had been Chloe's first time—she'd lost her virginity to her freshman-year boyfriend, Hunter Smith—but they'd definitely been her favorite. Arman was older and more confident, maybe even a little demanding, which she had to admit she found kind of hot.

But then she'd heard what sounded like the door opening, and when she'd looked over, her vision blurring, she was surprised to see someone standing in the doorway.

"I think we have company." She'd laughed, too drunk to actually be embarrassed, just amused that someone had wandered into the wrong room.

"Nah," Arman said, kissing her neck. "That's just my buddy Trevor."

"What?" Chloe laughed, looking back down at Arman and thinking it was obviously a joke.

"He's come to join us," Arman murmured, running a hand up under her shirt.

And still she'd thought he must be joking. Until she heard the door close, followed by the click of a lock.

"Wait . . ." She'd quickly climbed off Arman and looked back at the guy, who was standing near the bookshelf downing the last of his drink. She didn't recognize him; he definitely didn't go to her school. He was tall, with surfer-length blond hair and a humorless face that she couldn't quite focus on but that made her uneasy. "I'm not really into that kind of thing . . ."

"Come on." Arman sat up, stroking her arm. "We *talked* about this." And it was true, they had talked about it, *kind of*, but still . . .

Arman put a hand on her shoulder and gently pushed her back onto the bed, crawling on top of her, his weight pinning her down. "It'll be hot," he promised as he wound his fingers with hers and held her hands above her head, kissing her again. Above him, she could see the ceiling fan spinning.

Her vision blurred as she glanced over at his friend, who was now coming toward the bed and taking off his shirt, which sent a wave of fear through her. "I don't know, Arman," she countered between his kisses.

"But me so horny," his friend had quipped in a shockingly offensive Asian accent. "Me love you long—"

"Shut the fuck up, dude," Arman warned, looking over at his friend in irritation. "That racist shit isn't cool."

"I'm just fucking around." His friend laughed, tossing his shirt across the room. "And it's a *movie quote*, dude. Stanley Kubrick? *Full Metal Jacket*? Jesus. Lighten up. Besides, she's a cool girl, she didn't take it seriously. You know I'm just kidding, right?" he said to Chloe.

Chloe didn't know how to answer. *Was* she a cool girl? She didn't recognize his movie reference, but she did *not* like his joke, if you could even call it that, and she definitely didn't like his presence. And yet even in that moment she found herself not wanting to disappoint Arman, wanting to be whatever he expected her to be.

Arman looked back at Chloe, shaking his head apologetically. "Ignore him, he's an idiot." He kissed her neck once more. "Come on," he said, nibbling on her ear.

"Arman." She could feel a lump forming in her throat. "I really don't want to . . ."

"But it'll be *so* hot. Just do it for me," he murmured as he tugged off her shorts.

And then things began happening fast, and everything thereafter was kind of a blur—because of how drunk she was? Or had he put something in her drink? Is that why she felt so *weird*? But she could remember the strength of their hands, and the coordination of Arman's movements, like he wasn't that drunk at all. Which later would make Chloe wonder if he'd intentionally gotten her wasted. Later, she would reflect on how little she knew him; he was a totally different person than she'd originally thought.

She could remember that his friend's breath smelled, disgustingly, of salami and beer, and that he was rough—far rougher than Chloe was used to—doing things to her that she didn't like. Hurting her, actually, and ignoring her when she said so.

"You like it, don't you," he whispered to her at one point. "You're a dirty little slut."

Even in her drunkenness, Chloe was aware that she *didn't* want any of it; it wasn't something she'd signed up for.

Yet she'd felt powerless to stop it.

Though later she would begin to wonder if maybe she *had* signed up for it. After all, hadn't Arman made his desires well known? The last time they'd hooked up he'd mentioned a threesome, and in the heat of the moment she'd gone along with the fantasy. Had she made him believe she was the kind of girl who'd do whatever he wanted? Had she led him on?

And, in hindsight, had she even technically told them no?

She'd never thought of herself as a slut before . . . but she began to wonder if maybe she was. Or, at the very least, if that's how guys saw her. She'd seen social media posts about the way Asian women were often objectified and sexualized, which made Chloe want to barf.

Or . . . was it something *she'd* done? She *had* sometimes used her sexuality to get guys' attention. She'd been very aware of the hold she had over Arman. So had she in some way brought it upon herself?

She could remember, when it was over, lying on the bed and staring at the glowing fish tank across the room, watching a little blue-and-yellow-striped fish circle round and round, her head swimming, her body numb.

You're a dirty little slut.

Back inside the Lexus, Chloe squeezed her eyes shut as the memory brought on stabs of regret and pain, followed by heavy waves of shame. All of which she *hated.*

She hated that these two jerks had made her question her own experience of that night, that they'd made her question her own worth, that because of them, she felt bad about herself nearly all the time. She hated that she'd lost so much sleep—drinking a shot of vodka every night just to finally pass out—and that she'd lost so much *time*, sitting in that stupid kindergarten classroom week after week. She hated that they'd ruined *so much.*

Chloe clenched her fist over the book, so tightly that she felt her freshly manicured nails dig into her palm. All she wanted was to make them feel even a fraction of the pain that she felt nearly all the time.

The other girls inhaled sharply, which caused Chloe to open her eyes.

The pages of the book were changing, shimmering like the surface of water, reflecting the open sunroof and, beyond that, the starry night sky.

"*Take this pain,*" Chloe recited, squeezing her fist even tighter, her nails cutting into her flesh. "*Take this rage, and cast it back on its creator.*"

And then she threw her palm open.

As she did so, a bright ball of violet energy burst violently from the book and hovered before them just above Chloe's palm, as if connected to her mark. It hung there, spinning and burning, almost like the insides of one of those glass electrostatic balls you could place your hand on.

"Oh my God." Chloe leaned back against the passenger window, away from the ball of energy. Did *she* create that? She glanced at the other girls, who were equally wide-eyed, their faces lit with an eerie violet light. For a moment, the book's power felt almost scary.

And then with a *whoosh*, the ball of energy shot up through the sunroof and out into the dark night.

"Holy . . . ," Elliott breathed, quickly leaning against her window to try to see where it had flown.

Chloe glanced back at the book and saw that the shimmering pages were dulling and fading, becoming normal once more. Well, not normal, exactly—the silver script had disappeared, and the blue-black pages were now a dull ash-like gray.

Chloe's heart pounded, the blood racing in her veins as she looked back at the other girls—at her *coven.*

"Come on," Elliott urged, opening her car door.

"Wait." Chloe stopped her. "I don't know."

"What?" Elliott looked at her in surprise. "We just cast a revenge spell. You don't want to go see what happened?"

"I don't know." Chloe hesitated. "I do and I don't. I just . . . Can I have a minute? I need a minute."

She wanted the satisfaction of being present to see the damage her spell inflicted . . . but she did *not* want to get out of that car.

After a minute, Bea glanced at the clock. "If you're not sure about this, then maybe we should—should we just get out of here?"

"No," Elliott and Madeline said in unison.

"We have to *at least* find out what happened," Madeline argued.

"You could stay here, Chloe," Elliott pointed out. "We can go back and find out."

Chloe nodded. "Except . . . I mean, I *do* kind of want to see for myself." She cringed—was she being totally high-maintenance and annoying?

"Well, we can try and record it," Elliott suggested. "Or at least take some—" She cut off, her attention drifting to a noise outside the car. In the distance there were sirens.

"Is that coming this way?" Bea whispered.

The girls sat in silence, listening as the sirens grew closer. Before they knew it, two ambulances came blazing up the road, turning into Arman's driveway. The girls looked at one another.

"Okay, I want to go look," Chloe agreed in a rush, opening her door.

As they hurried toward the driveway, Chloe pulled her hat down low and turned up the collar of her coat. "But I don't want to get too close," she whispered as they half walked, half ran up the driveway.

Keeping to the shadows along the driveway's edge, they stopped a few yards from the front door and crouched down behind a black Mercedes SUV.

Kids were pouring out of the house now, gathering in the long gravel drive to bear witness to the ambulances' arrival. The party-goers crowded together in worried circles, watching as the medics pulled out their stretchers and rushed toward the house.

"I'm gonna go see if anyone knows anything," Elliott whispered to them before starting toward a group of girls standing several yards away.

Chloe watched as Elliott sidled up next to a tall blonde whom Chloe recognized from Cate International School. Elliott began chatting with her, nodding sympathetically and feigning concern.

Someone else came up to join the girls, and Chloe realized with a jolt that it was *Brooklyn*. She crouched down further, praying she wouldn't be seen. Brooklyn's arrival distracted the blonde and allowed Elliott to slip away. She rejoined her coven-mates, crouching back down behind the SUV.

"They don't know anything for sure," she whispered. "But the blond girl said they suddenly heard screaming coming from upstairs. Her friend was the one who called 911."

At that moment a stretcher came wheeling out of the house. And strapped to it, half sitting up, was Arman. He was shirtless and weeping as blood poured out of his mouth, coating his chin and bare chest and the straps of the stretcher. Walking behind him, helped by two concerned friends, was a redheaded girl in an oversized T-shirt. Her pale face was covered in blood, as were her neck and arms, though it was hard to tell if it was hers or Arman's.

A second later, another stretcher came wheeling out, this one containing Trevor. He was writhing in agony, his face twisted with pain.

Chloe covered her mouth with one hand like so many of the other onlookers—but not out of distress; she did so because she was laughing.

"Come on," she whispered to her coven-mates. "Let's get out of here before anyone spots me."

The coven crept back down the driveway and raced along the street to the Lexus, clambering back inside before the ambulances had a chance to leave. Chloe peeled out.

"Did you *see* them?" she squealed as she sped away, glancing over her shoulder at the other girls, who were still fastening their seat belts.

"I can't believe *we* did that," Bea said from the passenger seat.

"We fucking *did* that!" Elliott shouted, pounding her fist on the middle console.

"That was amazing," Madeline agreed.

"Woooooooo!" Chloe screamed, throwing one hand out the open sunroof as they sped along the dark, winding Hope Ranch road. She turned up her stereo in celebration.

"Wait, wait, wait." Elliott leaned over the center console and unplugged Chloe's phone, killing the music, and then plugged in her own. Suddenly, music blasted out of the speakers, that old '80s song "Girls Just Want to Have Fun."

Chloe laughed in appreciation, dancing in her seat as Elliott sang along. Soon, Chloe joined in, faking the lyrics she didn't know. In her rearview mirror, she saw Madeline nodding along, mouthing the words here and there. Only Bea remained quiet, shaking her head like she thought her coven-mates were crazy. But even she was bouncing one leg to the beat.

7

Chloe

"*All* of his teeth?" Madison clarified in shock.

"*Yeah.*" Brooklyn nodded from her reclined position. "According to Gia, who's friends with Aubrey, they just all of a sudden, like, started falling out of his mouth while he was hooking up with Zoey. I heard she accidentally swallowed one."

"That's *disgusting*," Chloe replied, taking a sip of her Pellegrino.

The girls were gathered poolside under a large blue-and-white-striped umbrella at the Montecito Club, lemon-tinted sunlight warming their skin, the turquoise pool sparkling before them. Beyond that stretched the emerald-green golf course, and beyond *that*, the blue-gray Pacific Ocean. Above them, palm trees swayed in the breeze. It was surreal, sitting there on a gorgeous Saturday afternoon, listening to her friends describe the very havoc that Chloe herself had wreaked the night before.

"The doctors are keeping him in the hospital for observation," Brooklyn informed them in a somber tone. "They think he might have some rare, weird fungal thing."

"God." Madison shook her head, flipping over to tan her backside. "I still can't believe it. It's just so *sad*, no?"

"*Totally,*" Brooklyn agreed, looking utterly heartbroken—even though Chloe knew for a fact she'd never thought much of Arman. "I feel so bad. I bet he's gonna need full-on dentures now. Can you imagine? At seventeen? What girl's gonna wanna kiss him *now*?"

Chloe sniffed. "Well, it's not like he was ever totally worth the hype."

"God, can you imagine if that had been *you,* Clo?" Brooklyn asked in horror. "Thank God you guys were never serious and you moved on. That could have been *super* traumatizing."

"Yeah," Chloe agreed, though all she could think was that Brooklyn knew absolutely nothing of trauma. Swallowing someone's tooth during a hookup was nothing in comparison to possibly being drugged and forced into a threesome against your will.

"So, tell us about Arman's friend, Trevor," Madison probed. "Something happened to *him*, yes?"

"Well, that's super crazy, too," Brooklyn said in a hush, like it was top secret information. "You won't even believe it, but he had a burst appendix, a ruptured gallbladder, *and* a ruptured spleen. I heard from Maggie Reynolds, who's in school with him at Providence, that they think it might have something to do with his little habit." Brooklyn pressed a finger to one nostril and pantomimed sniffing.

"It's pretty freaky, though, no?" Madison said, her head resting atop her arms. "That they both had stuff happen at the *same* time. And also totally tragic. I mean, they're not even out of *high school.*"

"I *know,*" Brooklyn agreed. "I feel like we should do something."

Chloe scratched her right palm—which had been itching ever since last night, making her wonder if that ball of light had somehow burned her—and resisted the urge to blurt out how it was absolutely *not* tragic and, in fact, completely well deserved. Because then she'd have to explain *why,* and she'd never revealed to her friends what had happened. Deep down, she wasn't sure she trusted them with that info.

"Jazmin and Taylor are organizing a big visit to the hospital to cheer them up," Brooklyn informed them. "Maybe the three of us should go and— Clo, you okay?"

Chloe had broken into a cough that rattled her chest. "Yeah, totally." She waved dismissively, taking another sip of Pellegrino.

"It's probably the Santa Ana winds," Madison said knowingly. "They always dry me out. Speaking of"—she rummaged around in her bag—"I need my lip gloss."

"You should go for a swim," Brooklyn advised Chloe, like she was an expert in such matters. "That always helps my dad."

"Good idea," Chloe replied as she pulled off her sunglasses and rose to her feet. She was grateful for any excuse to exit the conversation.

Elliott

That Monday, Elliott felt a newfound confidence as she strode through the halls of her school. Maybe nobody else knew it, she thought smugly as she plopped into her first-period English seat, but she was making a *difference*. And for the first time in a long time, she could breathe a little easier. The raging fire that so often consumed her, burning her alive from the inside out, had been channeled and unleashed. She'd taken down a couple of privileged, underserving bastards, and it was only a matter of time until she took *him* down, too.

Of course, no one at her school knew anything about what had happened in Hope Ranch. She kept an ear out for gossip but not a word was spoken about two partying rich boys being rushed to the hospital. And so, when Thursday finally arrived, it was all Elliott could do to contain her excitement; she was desperate for details from Chloe.

Grabbing yet another Uber (basically all her allowance was going to transportation these days), Elliott made a point of arriving first at Franceschi Park. She was chronically late to just about everything in life, but as their unofficial coven leader, she felt punctuality to be her duty. Madeline had offered to pick her up. "It's not a big deal," she'd assured Elliott. "It's on my way." But Elliott had declined. She didn't want to depend on Madeline too much—or anyone, for that matter.

Leaning against one of the benches, Elliott popped in yet another lozenge to calm her dry cough and turned up the volume on Tori Amos's "Cornflake Girl" as she stared out at the low bank of pinkish gold clouds laid like frosting atop the Channel Islands.

Madeline was the first to arrive, followed almost immediately by Chloe, who pulled into the parking spot just beside Madeline's Prius.

"Hey," Elliott greeted them, eagerly rising to her feet as the two girls climbed out of their cars and came over to the benches.

"Hi," Chloe said knowingly, both eyebrows raised as she adjusted the purse over her shoulder. "Oh my God, you *guys*, I have so much to—"

"Let's wait until we're somewhere more private," Madeline whispered, glancing around the empty parking lot like she thought spies might be positioned in the bushes.

"Oh—yeah, right." Chloe nodded, firmly pressing her lips together as if she needed to physically hold in the information.

"Plus, we should wait until we're *all* here," Elliott pointed out.

"Totally." Chloe nodded again, looking like she might burst.

A warm Santa Ana breeze picked up, carrying the scent of the nearby eucalyptus trees and tousling Elliott's pink hair. In one of the trees, a mockingbird was incessantly knocking.

"Did your palm get a little itchy or was that just me?" asked Chloe in a hush.

"Yeah, for a little bit," Elliott replied. "But then it stopped. I figured it was kinda like when a tattoo starts to heal."

Chloe nodded like that made sense.

Madeline checked the time on her phone. "Shouldn't Bea already be here? It's her turn, after all."

"I'm sure she'll be here soon," Elliott defended. "She made it clear that she's juggling a lot."

"We're all juggling a lot," Madeline muttered under her breath just as Bea's minivan pulled in.

"Hey," Bea called, smoothing a hand over her hair as she hurried over to join them. She was still in her running pants and track zip-up, her forehead glistening with sweat. Did the cross-country team always practice so late, Elliott wondered.

Without a word, the girls hurried down the dusky hillside to their official gathering spot just beside the mansion, and took a seat on the cracked flagstones, the lit lantern in the center of their circle.

"So?!" Elliott asked Chloe in anticipation, one arm wrapped around her bent knees. "Tell us *everything*."

Chloe launched into a full recap of all that she'd learned, detailing Arman's permanent tooth loss and Trevor's multiple organ damage and how they were both still in the hospital for close monitoring. Word had it that they weren't expected to return to their respective schools for a *very* long time.

"That's *amazing*," Elliott marveled, reveling in the details. Even though she'd seen things firsthand the night of the party, she still felt thoroughly impressed with their coven's impact.

"It still almost doesn't seem real," Bea mused.

"Well, it was real, all right," Chloe assured her. "You should see the girls at my school. They're all *pitying* Arman, it's disgusting. I mean, they're not, like, fawning over him anymore, so at least that's good, but still. Just today someone asked me if I wanted to sign *a card.*"

"Gross." Elliott grimaced.

"I was like, *Oh, I already sent one!*" Chloe made a fake, cheerful face and then rolled her eyes and gagged. "All week I just wanted to announce what a piece of shit he was and how much he deserved it, but I obviously couldn't." She let out a deep sigh, then looked around the circle. "It's so good to finally tell *you guys* this stuff. You're the only ones who actually *get* it."

Elliott nodded in solidarity. They didn't need to know the details of Chloe's story to understand what it felt like to be alone with a secret or to privately rage against a world so blind to reality.

And for the first time it felt like they were a real coven. They had a shared secret, yes, but they also had an unspoken understanding.

"But do you feel *different*?" Bea asked, still sounding skeptical.

Chloe thought a moment. "Yeah, I really do. I feel like this little weight has been lifted. Like, I'm not saying that what happened doesn't bother me, but I finally know that some justice has been served. Which feels *good.*"

Bea nodded slowly, seemingly satisfied with Chloe's answer.

"But it wasn't permanent," Madeline pointed out.

Elliott looked over at her. "What do you mean? Arman's teeth all fell out, and that other dude had to have his appendix and part of his spleen removed."

"Sure, but that's *temporary* pain," Madeline explained, sitting iron-rod straight. "Are a few days of discomfort really enough? How many of us have had to think about what happened to us *every* single day? How many of us have lost things, whether it's relationships or sleep or future dreams? Or stuff we used to love that's now tainted and totally triggers us? Are these guys going to be *haunted* by things from now on?"

Madeline wasn't wrong. Elliott had lost all of those things, and she certainly felt haunted.

Chloe played with the end of her boho scarf, looking a little dispirited. "I don't know . . . I hadn't thought about it like *that*."

"Well, but how do we even control for something like that?" asked Bea, pulling the sleeves of her track jacket down over her hands. "It's not like we get to put in an exact order with the book."

"No," Madeline agreed, running a hand through her sideswept hair. "But we *do* get to set an intention; maybe we need to go even deeper and make sure we're setting an intention for punishments that fit the crimes."

Chloe quirked her mouth to one side. "See, when I conjured, I *felt* intentional, but now I feel like I maybe messed mine up."

"No way," Elliott jumped in. "There's no messing things up with this. The book gave you what it felt you needed right now. I don't think we should question that." She glanced sideways at Madeline.

"Oh no, I didn't mean to suggest that," Madeline clarified. "I just meant that moving *forward*, maybe . . . And, you know, we can always come back to you again later once everyone's had a turn," she assured Chloe, which seemed to make her feel better.

"Speaking of turns," Elliott announced, wanting to keep things on track. She looked over at Bea, who was seated beside her, arms wrapped around her bent knees. "It's your turn next."

Bea nodded, her brow furrowed. "Yeah, though now I'm nervous. This suddenly feels like a lot of pressure to get things right."

"No, no, no," Elliott assured her as she pulled out the puzzle box from her backpack and began to slide the panels open. "The book *specifically* states that you'll conjure the spell most suited to you, so don't overthink it." She pulled the book out of the box, opened it to a new page, and set it before Bea. "Just, like, get in the zone or whatever. Isn't that what athletes do? You'll be fine. You *got* this."

Bea

Bea nodded and took a deep breath, her eyes on the blue-black pages of the book. Get in the zone, right. She could do that.

As she closed her eyes, she tried to relax her body by visualizing a wave of cool blue calming energy washing over her, a method she'd read about online while researching anxiety. But she felt self-conscious doing so while sitting there with these other girls she barely knew. Girls, whom, if she was honest with herself, she still didn't 100 percent trust.

Yes, she wanted to be part of this coven, because *yes* she wanted revenge, but that didn't mean she was entirely sold on her *coven-mates*. Madeline seemed like a control freak, Chloe was kind of flaky, and Elliott was a little too hardcore into this witch stuff.

Not that Bea didn't want to do witchcraft—she did, especially after seeing the results in Hope Ranch—but she didn't exactly see herself as a *witch*. Being obsessed with Harry Potter in elementary school was one thing; *this* was altogether different. And more dangerous. And in no small part because she was now *bonded* to these girls she barely knew and never would have hung with in real life.

Then again, it's not like she really hung with many people in real life.

Over the last few years, Bea had perfected the art of distancing herself—from her friends, from the cross-country and track teams, from the other members of the orchestra. Not that she didn't spend time with them—she did. She just didn't let anyone in. People always called her quiet or reserved, but truthfully, she was neither of those things. It's just that very few people *really* knew her. She'd managed to seal the real Bea so far away in an airtight container deep within that sometimes even *she* forgot who she was.

The only person she let in was her twin brother, Otis. She'd never distance herself from her other half. He knew *everything* about Bea, including what happened to her three years ago—but she hadn't told him about *this*. What would Otis say if he learned she'd joined a coven?

Who was she kidding; he'd probably *love* it. The kid was hell-bent on art school and would probably want to make some sort of installation piece inspired by it. The look on Aunt Clara's face when he'd rolled into Christmas dinner with his nails painted bright pink and his hair dyed green. It was enough to make Bea laugh all winter break.

Just thinking about Otis filled Bea with guilt. She'd never kept something this big from him before. But telling him wasn't an option; it was way too risky. Not for the *coven*—Otis would never say anything; he'd take Bea's secrets with him to the grave—but if things ever went sideways, she didn't want Otis in any way implicated.

Bea became aware that her mind was spinning and her body felt antsy and she was not at all in the zone.

"I'm sorry, I just need to—" She jumped up and started running in place with her knees high, then switched into jumping jacks, then switched back to high knees. She could feel the other girls watching her, probably wondering what the heck she was doing, but she didn't care, this was the only way she was going to get out of her head.

When she finally took a seat, her heart was pounding but her head felt clear.

"Okay, now I'm ready," Bea announced, taking a breath and raising her right hand over the book. She cleared her throat and began to chant, *"Bring forth that which will satisfy my—"* and then broke into a cough, which she muffled with her bent elbow.

"You okay?" Elliott asked.

"Yeah, I think it's just this weather," Bea explained, grabbing her water bottle.

"Or you could be coming down with something," Chloe said. "I feel like I am."

"Same." Elliott dug into her coat pocket. "Here, I've got a zinc lozenge."

"I better not be getting sick," Bea said. With her upcoming meet, she couldn't afford downtime.

"Well, it's going around," Madeline informed her as Bea popped Elliott's lozenge into her mouth. "You're seventy-four percent more likely to get a cold this time of year. I always have a sinus infection by mid-October."

That one, Bea thought as she extended her hand back over the open book, was already on her nerves. All self-assurance and white privilege, blind to the space she took up in this world. Which could be said for 74 percent of the kids she knew in Santa Barbara.

There was something about Madeline's pristine type-A personality that reminded Bea of her parents' most annoying colleagues. As the daughter of two UCSB professors—her dad taught in the school of Biomolecular Science and Engineering, her mom in the English department—Bea was all too familiar with that air of self-importance and elitism. She'd suffered through *way* too many mind-numbing faculty dinners.

Taking a deep, controlled breath, Bea focused herself the way she did before a cross-country meet or orchestra concert.

"Bring forth that which will satisfy my intentions," she chanted. *"Bring forth that which will satisfy my intentions. Bring forth that which will satisfy my intentions."*

A rush of cold flooded her spine as she watched the silver script begin to fade in upon the page. She'd never believed in witchcraft or magic before. Sure, she'd wished for it, especially when she and Otis were in the thick of their Hogwarts days. But she'd obviously never imagined it might be something she could *possess*.

Part of her had worried it wouldn't work a second time. What if, for some reason, she wasn't able to conjure? What if it only worked for Chloe because she was more into that kind of thing?

And yet here it was: her spell.

"'Incantation of Oblivion,'" she read aloud.

Oblivion? What did that mean? Could the simple recitation of a spell *obliviate* a person? Though hadn't they *all* been obliviated in one way or another? Bea felt equal parts horror and pleasure. No longer would she merely be the obliviated; *she'd* be the obliviator.

"A rune-carved vessel?" Madeline commented, leaning over the book to scan the spell's instructions.

Instinctively, Bea picked up the book, feeling protective of her spell. She glanced at Elliott. "Wait, is it okay if I—"

"Yeah, of course," Elliott motioned. "Why don't *you* read it to us?" she added, emphasizing *you* as if to say, *Back off, Madeline.*

Bea turned her attention toward the spell. "'The Incantation of Oblivion must be performed at sunset on the tenth day of the month,'" she read aloud. "'It requires the following items: one rune-carved vessel, ten purple candles, one small vial of distilled spirits, three wooden matchsticks, three burning bush stems, and . . .'" She trailed off and then swallowed. "'. . . three objects of significance belonging to the victim: one representing their past, one representing their present, and one representing their future.'" Bea had been praying she could skate past the personal effect thing, but apparently not. She let out a heavy breath. "Crap."

"It's okay, *we* can gather those for you," Elliott reminded her.

"No." Bea shook her head. "You don't get it. This guy . . . he's older. Like . . . married-with-kids older."

"Ohhhh," Chloe replied quietly. The way she said it, Bea could tell she had a whole slew of follow-up questions that she wasn't about to ask. Bea knew that shouldn't bother her, but it still kind of did.

"Also, he's *important*," Bea added, which felt like way too much information as it was but needed to be said. "It won't be as easy as just walking into some high school party."

Even as she spoke, Bea knew there was only one solution: Otis. She detested the idea of dragging her brother into anything . . . but who else could easily acquire the necessary objects? And who else could she trust?

"Well, I'm sure if you give us a few details, we can come up with a plan," Madeline offered.

"That's okay," Bea declined. "I'll figure it out."

"Bea, seriously," Elliott offered.

"It's fine, I'm good," Bea replied, refocusing on the book. She cleared her throat. "'Clear your mind,'" she continued. "'And focus intently and precisely on how the victim has harmed you, silently gathering your rage as you recall every detail. As you channel your rage, clench your fist over these pages, and have your coven chant the following invocation: *Bring forth the outcome this witch seeks.* Once you are ready to cast, chant the following words as you . . . ,'" Bea trailed off, her stomach curdling. "'. . . as you lay your eyes upon the victim . . .'"

"Oh my *God*, like, they have to be able to *see* you cast the spell?" Chloe asked in mild horror.

"No," Madeline corrected. "I think it means *she* has to see *him*."

Bea quickly set the book down and covered her face with both hands, feeling nauseous—and irrationally betrayed. How was *this* the most suitable spell? Forcing her to *stare* at him? A memory of his face hovering over hers flashed through her mind, and she pushed it away.

Jumping to her feet, Bea began pacing back and forth along the flagstones, arms crossed tightly against her chest. She needed to keep moving.

"Hey," Chloe comforted. "It's okay. I get it. I was freaked, too. But you can do this, Bea. I promise you."

"And you don't need to actually go *near* him," Madeline reminded her.

"Right, you just have to *see* him," Elliott agreed. "And only briefly, while you cast the spell. Then you'll never have to look at him again. Plus, we'll all be there. You won't be alone."

Bea rubbed her arms, suddenly feeling cold.

You can do this, she told herself. *You just need to survive one moment of hell.*

And one moment of hell was a fair trade for an anxiety-free future, wasn't it? Once he'd paid for what he'd done, maybe she wouldn't have to hide all the time.

And maybe she could finally stop running.

Madeline

When Madeline got home that evening, she parked in the driveway of her '90s-era Spanish-style San Roque home—which was nice, *plus*, they had a pool, but Madeline was always aware it wasn't *nearly* as nice as her *friends'* houses, or as nice as what her mom dreamed of. But with all their money now going toward Madeline's older brother's out-of-state rehab, a remodel or an upgrade was out of the question.

Climbing the lit steps past her parents' perfectly manicured front yard, Madeline unlocked the front door and let herself inside. In the living room, her mom and dad were cuddled up on the sectional, watching a documentary.

Her mom hit pause and both of her parents turned toward her. The look on their faces suggested she was fragile and might break. Madeline hated that look.

"How was group?" her mom inquired. She'd shed her corporate attire and was wearing a long cashmere cardigan and black linen pants, not a hair of her long, dark bob out of place.

"It was fine," Madeline said, peeling off her peacoat and hanging it up in the foyer closet.

"We spoke with Tom at Cyber Sleuth this evening," her dad informed her, running a hand through his sandy brown hair. "They're making great headway. Did you update your personal web—"

"Yes," she cut him off. "I published the updates yesterday."

"SEO's important." He nodded in satisfaction, taking a sip of his beer.

"Also, once you're done rewriting your personal essay, I want to proofread it," said her mom. "I really think leaning into the defamation is going to work in your favor, particularly if we move forward with the lawsuit."

"Rebecca," her dad cautioned.

"I said *if*," her mom assured him, taking a sip of her wine

Madeline knew for a fact her parents weren't on the same page about the lawsuit. She'd overheard them arguing: her dad thought it would only make things worse for Madeline, though her mom assured him they could keep it quiet from friends and family and Madeline could remain anonymous. Even so, he worried that with all their recent costs sending Caleb to rehab, they couldn't afford it. To which her mom had been notably silent.

The whole thing made Madeline feel like crap. Like she'd let her parents down; now they had not one but *two* kids they had to worry over.

"Mom, I hear you," Madeline said tactfully. "But I *really* don't want to change my personal essay. I'm proud of what I wrote. And you said yourself it was strong and demonstrated how dance has shaped my—"

"Madeline," her mother reprimanded primly, giving her a stern look. "We had a very long discussion about this. Do I really need to rehash the details?"

"No." Madeline sighed. "I'm sorry. I'm just tired."

Defamation. That's how her mother always referred to it. It was such a misleading word, so civil and scholarly sounding when the situation was so dirty and messed up. And Madeline agreed with her dad's assessment; if group had taught her anything, it was that a lawsuit wasn't going to do anything other than re-traumatize her and drag her name through the mud—not to mention further burden her family.

"You still have plenty of time before early applications are due," her mom assured her, taking another sip of her wine.

"I'm going upstairs," Madeline informed them, heading toward the staircase. "I have homework."

"I saved you some apple crisp," her mom called after her.

"I'm not hungry," she called back.

Upstairs, Madeline resisted slamming her door, quietly closing it instead. Her bedroom, like the rest of the house, was well appointed and organized, like a spread from a Pottery Barn catalogue. Harvard pennant on the wall. Photos from her ballet performances. Framed art prints—though she'd taken down the Monet and the Klimt, keeping the Georgia O'Keeffe. She no longer wanted male artists on her walls.

At her desk, Madeline sat down and opened her laptop. Her stomach churned as she brought up the browser and Googled "Madeline O'Conner."

As the results loaded, a wave of fear-spiked adrenaline coursed through her system, making the blood roar in her ears. She scrolled to the bottom of the screen, then clicked to page three.

And there, midway down the page, was the link. Madeline made sure not to click on it; she didn't even allow her mouse to hover anywhere nearby.

Cyber Sleuth was right: they *had* made progress. A month ago, the link was on page one. And Tom had said very few people ever went past page two. But that wasn't good enough. Madeline didn't just want it buried; she wanted it *gone*. And they were working on it, Tom had assured her parents, but he'd also made clear there were no guarantees.

A cough crawled its way up from her chest, and Madeline covered her mouth to muffle the sound. If her mom heard it, she'd be up there in five seconds flat, lecturing Madeline about all the things she needed to do to take care of herself, which, no thank you.

Slamming her laptop shut, Madeline consoled herself by inspecting the mark on her palm. It was a reminder of her suffering, yes, but also a promise of the suffering she'd inflict. And there was strength in its strange appearance.

Unzipping her messenger bag, Madeline pulled out a stack of books. *A History of Witchcraft*; *The Beginner's Guide to Magic and the Occult*; *Spells and Summoning: A Witch's Guide to Magic*. Secondhand books she'd purchased with cash because she didn't want a trail—digital or paper. Opening *Spells and Summoning* where she'd left off—Chapter 3, "How to Enhance Your Magical Powers"—she sat up perfectly straight in her desk chair (*Posture, Madeline*, her mother always reminded her, as if a dancer needed reminding) and, highlighter in hand, began to read.

Elliott

At school the next day, Elliott waited down near the art building between third and fourth periods, worrying the strap of her overalls as she kept an eye on the stream of students coming up the hill from the English building.

"Hey," she greeted Kaylie, falling in step beside her as she strode toward the main building.

Kaylie slid her gaze to either side, like she was worried about people seeing them together. Homecoming nominees had been announced earlier that week, and, unsurprisingly, Kaylie was among them—all the more reason for her to be on guard; people would be paying attention. "Uh, hi," she greeted, striking the perfect blend of cheerful *I'm friendly to everyone* meets perplexed *who's this random coming up to me* tone.

"Can I talk to you for a sec?" Elliott asked.

"Oh. Yeah, sure, I guess," Kaylie responded, running a hand through her wavy hair.

Elliott led Kaylie across the quad and around behind the cafeteria, where hardly anyone ever hung out and nobody would see them. She realized this was a risky move on her end as well—and one she hadn't cleared with the other girls. But it felt like the right thing to do.

"I just wanted you to know . . . ," Elliott whispered, readjusting her backpack and rattling her stack of vintage resin bracelets. "It's working. So, if you want to change your mind . . ."

Kaylie played with the tiny gold *K* delicately strung around her neck. "Well, I don't," she assured Elliott.

Elliott frowned, readjusting the bandana tied in her hair. "I'm just trying to help you."

"Look," Kaylie said in a hush, glancing to the side. "I know you mean well, and I appreciate it, but I *have* friends. And I don't need your help. What I need is to just get back to normal and move on with my life, okay?"

"But don't you want to get him back?" Elliott countered in a fierce whisper. "He *deserves* it, Kaylie. Don't you want things to change?"

Kaylie stared at Elliott like she felt sorry for her. "Whatever you're doing, it's not going to change anything."

"You don't know that," Elliott said.

"Yes"—Kaylie gave an uncharacteristic snort—"I do. Listen, I can't be late for class, I'm presenting today, so—I gotta go."

And with that, she strode off.

Elliott stood there a moment staring after Kaylie, feeling highly defensive of her coven. Kaylie was wrong; they *could* change things.

And fine, Elliott thought as she trudged off toward the main building, she wasn't going to *chase* Kaylie. If she really didn't want to do anything, that was her choice. And Elliott would respect it.

But Jesus, why *wouldn't* she want to do something? They had vengeance and control right at their fingertips—how could she pass that up?

8

Bea

Alone at home that Saturday evening, Bea did her best to distract herself—she practiced her oboe and then changed out her reed, she meticulously cleaned her sneakers, she Googled "best SNL clips of all time" and fell down a ninety-minute YouTube rabbit hole—but her mind kept wandering back to Otis and the dinner party he and her parents were, at that very moment, attending.

The dinner party was a monthly gathering put on by the chair of the English department and her spouse, and one that the faculty members and their families regularly attended. One that Bea's mom never missed, given that she was on track for tenure, an increasingly coveted and rare professorial position. Bea's Grandma Doreen had raised Bea's mom with the firm understanding that as a Black woman, she'd have to work twice as hard to get half as far as white women. A notion Bea's mother had bristled at her entire life—even as she kept attending those dinner parties without fail, smiling in public and saving the eye rolls for the ride home, aware that for *her*, there wasn't the room to take a misstep.

Bea and Otis, on the other hand, had gotten out of those dinners for the past few years, making up excuse after excuse: too much homework, there was a group project, they were both way too exhausted.

"I get it," her mom finally teased. "You're officially teenagers now and too cool for your old mom and dad. That's *fine*."

Which wasn't true at all; Bea actually *liked* spending time with her parents. Her ideal Friday night was prepping dinner all together in the kitchen, laughing over a big meal, then watching whatever weird sci-fi film her dad insisted upon. She just refused to ever return *there*. She couldn't be around *him*. And Otis, who knew everything that had happened and was unfailingly loyal to Bea, equally refused.

When Bea had asked Otis for the favor, she'd known he'd say yes. But she'd also known he'd want to know *why*.

"There's this art therapist that comes to group sometimes," she'd explained as she leaned against his desk. "And she said doing a project around our trauma could be cathartic, so I figured . . ."

He'd leaned back in his desk chair and narrowed his eyes, not buying the lie.

"I can't tell you why," she'd confessed, folding her arms against her chest. "I just need it. It's important."

"Are you gonna put a hex on this guy or something?" he'd joked as he twirled his pencil.

Bea had remained silent, unconsciously rubbing the mark on her palm. "What if I could?" she'd asked quietly.

"Wait, what?" He'd straightened. "Bea, I was *joking*."

"I know, but . . ." She'd hesitated, knowing she was treading across dangerous territory. "What if . . . What if there was someone who could actually do that for me?"

"Oh my God," he'd whispered, leaning toward her, hands flat on his desk. "Did you go see that psychic that Aurelia told us about?"

"Maybe," she'd said vaguely, not wanting to flat-out lie. "I can't tell you anything more, but I've been given this opportunity, and I . . . I need to see if it'll work."

He'd watched her a moment, then stuck the pencil behind his ear. "Okay, I'll do it. I think it's kind of *crazy*, but it's worth a try." Which was a big deal for Otis. Despite his artistic flair and gender-fluid fashion choices (which recently included thick eyeliner and a kilt), he was a total rule follower and a secret overachiever. The kind of kid who always waited patiently at an empty street corner for the light to change before crossing the road. The kind of kid who got stressed out and nervous about returning late library books. He'd joined five million clubs at school—Black Student Union, Young Feminists, Entrepreneurship Club, Photography Club, Film Club, Gender and Sexuality Alliance—partly because he wanted his college applications to stand out but mostly because he was *genuinely* interested. So, *stealing* from someone's house? That went against every fiber of Otis's being.

Flopping onto her bed, Bea picked up *The Fifth Season* from her nightstand and continued reading. Her mom was always giving Bea literature she knew Bea would love, and N. K. Jemisin's Broken Earth series was Bea's current favorite (though Otis had given her a trigger warning that child abuse and molestation were briefly mentioned). Her mom loved introducing her children to art that she thought would inspire, something Bea and Otis pretended to find annoying but both secretly adored.

Actually, what their mom really loved was steering them toward the futures she thought they both wanted. And the quickest way of winning her over was by validating her ideas. Which was why she'd been both pleasantly surprised and slightly suspicious when Otis announced at breakfast that morning that he'd like to join them at the dinner party.

"Why the change?" she'd questioned warily as she poured maple syrup on her pancakes.

"I thought about what you said and figured you're right: if I'm serious about art school, I should chat with Michael."

Just hearing *his* name had filled Bea with revulsion. But she had to admit, Otis had landed on not just a plausible excuse but a damn good one; their mom had been harassing Otis to reach out to *him* for months.

But now, as Bea sat alone in her room awaiting Otis's return, she wondered if roping him into the endeavor was a dreadful mistake. What if he got caught? What would he tell them? A Black boy getting caught was a whole lot different than a white boy getting caught—the blame always came swifter, and the punishment never actually fit the crime. Not to mention, she could only imagine her parents' deep concern and disappointment. And hadn't she promised herself with all this witchcraft stuff that she needed to make sure Otis was in no way implicated?

A wave of guilt swept through her. How could she put Otis in such a position? Maybe she should have at least tried to come up with an alternate plan.

At that moment there was a knock on her bedroom door that jolted Bea from her thoughts—one long knock, followed by two quick ones.

Bea rolled off the bed and unlocked the door. She'd gotten in the habit of keeping it locked, even though it made no sense to do so: Their house had an expensive alarm system, and besides, was a cheap lock really going to do anything? Also, did she really think *he* was going to come find her in her house? There was nothing rational about it, but it made her feel slightly better. One small protection against the world.

A wave of relief swept through her as Otis slipped inside.

"That was the worst." He dropped his backpack and flopped backward onto her bed.

"I'm sorry," she cringed, quickly shutting the door.

"No, listen, I agreed to help."

"Did you have to talk to him?" she asked quietly, playing with the zipper of her track jacket as she stopped at the foot of the bed.

"Yeah," he sighed. He ran a hand over his face. "And I had to *flat-ter* him. All the while, I just kept thinking how I wanted to *kill* him. And how I wanted to throw up."

Bea sat down beside him. "Thank you."

Otis kicked his legs forward to roll back up and grabbed his backpack, which was covered with paint spatters. Unzipping it, he reached inside.

"His past," Otis announced, laying a framed wedding photo down on Bea's bed. She did her best not to stare at the face peering up through the glass. "His present." Otis pulled out a postcard advertising a gallery showing of his latest paintings. "And his future," he said finally, pulling out a Father's Day card with a note scribbled inside it: *We love you, Daddy! Thank you for always taking us to the zoo!* For a moment, Bea recalled those two small faces and the many hours she'd spent making them snacks and creating scavenger hunts for them and tucking them in at bedtime.

"Is this all okay?" Otis asked, setting down his backpack.

"It's perfect," she said, quickly picking up the items.

"I wonder if there's any chance it might work," he said as Bea shoved the items away in the bottom drawer of her desk.

"We'll see," she said evasively, closing the drawer and turning to face him.

"Bea . . ." He scratched the back of his head. "I totally support this endeavor. Like, I think it's great to find ways of gaining some, I don't know, *control*. But . . . it doesn't erase the fact that I still think you need to tell Mom and Dad."

"*Otis.* I'm fine," she assured him, shoving her hands into the back pockets of her jeans.

"Yeah, but—I know it's lame of me, it's just I can't get over feeling that you shouldn't be keeping this big secret."

"It's not a secret," she pointed out, leaning up against her desk. "*You* know about it."

"Yeah, but . . . maybe I'm not the only one who should know?"

She frowned, watching as he fiddled with the strap of his watch.

"I don't know, never mind, it's probably not my business." He hopped up. "I don't want to mansplain. Just forget it, okay? I'm gonna go take, like, fifty hot showers."

He started toward the door, then doubled back and gave her a big hug. "Love you, Fred."

"Love you, George," she reciprocated, watching as Otis slipped out her door.

But for the first time, she couldn't help wondering how much of a burden it was for Otis to help carry her secret.

Elliott

The tenth turned out to be a Monday, which might have made getting away at sunset challenging for some kids, but not Elliott. Her dad was used to her coming and going, always with a different hobby or activity—thrift store shopping, a Santa Barbara City College poetry course, writing sessions at Dune Coffee Roasters. Things she'd done with Vi but hadn't done since.

Once upon a time, she and Vi had done everything together. Vi was three years older, but once Elliott graduated, they were going to become roommates and go to Santa Barbara City College together and travel the world together and eventually move to a big city, maybe

LA or even NYC, where they'd work as baristas and befriend artists and each pursue their writing.

But like their many hobbies and activities, those plans died along with their friendship. And these days Elliott had a hard time even imagining her future. What did she want now? Did she even *have* dreams?

"Where you off to this evening, El?" her dad asked, taking a bite of his mushroom risotto as she got up from the kitchen table.

"Poetry reading at the downtown library," she replied, pulling her leather jacket on over her Pixies T-shirt.

He nodded as he took a sip of his beer.

"Pssht." Prudence shook her head, dabbing her mouth with a napkin. "You just let her leave the house no questions asked and aren't even *concerned*, Daniel?"

"I *just* asked her where she was going," he pointed out.

And why are you here? Elliott wanted to ask her grandmother. *This isn't even your house!*

Prudence held up both hands. "In my day we just made sure we knew a bit more about what was going on in our children's lives. Not that it's my business." Which was not only not her business, but utterly inaccurate. Elliott knew for a fact that Prudence's children had done a shit-ton of crazy behind her back. She probably still didn't know the half of it. Like about Uncle Anthony's graduation day acid trip.

Her dad gave his mother-in-law a placating smile. "Thank you for your input as always, Prudence. But Elliott knows that I trust her."

Elliott swallowed her guilt as she donned her black beanie, just barely catching the stern look her grandmother threw her way. *We both know he's got a whole lot more to be concerned about than he realizes*, it said. Which made Elliott both pissed off and remorseful.

"I won't be back too late," she assured her dad, giving him a quick kiss on the head.

"'Kay. Love you, Pigeon," he called after her.

Once again, the other girls had met at Franceschi Park to leave their cars before picking up Elliott, but apparently Bea hadn't wanted to drive—perhaps worried her minivan would be recognized?— because it was Chloe who pulled up along Elliott's street. This time she was driving one of those jeep-like Mercedes-Benzes— clearly her family was just *rolling* in luxury vehicles.

Chloe waved as Elliott went round to the back door, though Chloe was far more subdued than last time. Perhaps trying to respect the cone of silence Bea apparently wanted, because when Elliott climbed into the car no music was playing. Madeline, who was also in the back seat, silently waved.

"Hey," Bea greeted from the passenger seat, jiggling one leg like she wanted to jump out of the car and start running.

Chloe took a left at Laguna Street and drove north, following the road until it dead-ended at the Mission. With its rose garden, candy-pink bell towers, and sloping view of the distant ocean, the Mission was just about one of the most beautiful places in town—you know, if you could ignore its history of rounding up Native Americans and forcing them into Christianity and servitude.

Once upon a time, Elliott had stood on those church steps in a white cotton dress and flower crown, ready to commune with God. And now here she was with her coven, ready to commune with . . . well, she wasn't sure what they were communing with. But it didn't seem like God. Then again, where had God been for her the last seven years of her life?

"Take a right," Bea instructed Chloe. "And head up Mission Canyon."

Chloe did as Bea requested, following the curving road past the Mission cemetery, where Juana Maria, the real-life Karana from *Island of the Blue Dolphins*, was buried (must have been pretty nice being on that male-free island), and then the turnoff for the Botanic Gardens. On either side of the road were aloe plants, tall oak trees, and cobblestone walls lined with jagged rocks that made them look like dragon spines.

The silence in the car was making Elliott deeply uncomfortable. Did Bea normally listen to music, she wondered. And if so, what was she into? Elliott would have picked out an entire soundtrack to get in the mood: Liz Phair, Yeah Yeah Yeahs, Tori Amos, PJ Harvey, maybe a little Bikini Kill. She glanced at Bea, who was gripping the door's grab handle as if hanging on for dear life and was once again struck by how little they knew one another. Elliott didn't even know what kind of *music* this girl was into, let alone what had led her to Tragic Kindergarten Kingdom.

"Okay, now take a right at Foothill Road. And then take a left up there," Bea instructed, pointing ahead to the fork in the road where the fire station with the Smokey the Bear cutout could be seen on the right. FIRE DANGER LOW TODAY! read Smokey's sign. "Also, can you slow down a little?" Bea asked edgily as Chloe took a sharp left.

"Sorry." Chloe cringed from behind the wheel, though she was in no way speeding.

"Hey, can I make a suggestion?" Elliott asked Bea, leaning toward the middle console as they climbed the narrow two-lane road. "Why don't you put on a song that will make you feel good, and you know, empowered? Get yourself in the right headspace."

Bea glanced at Elliott as if to argue, then blew out a breath and nodded. Plugging in her phone, she scrolled through her music and then hit play. Beyoncé's "Run the World (Girls)" blasted out of Chloe's speakers. Not necessarily what Elliott would have picked, but a solid choice.

"Yesssss," Chloe exclaimed, nodding along.

As they wound their way up the hill, past the famous, trippy-looking Whale House and a property with some kind of yurt out front, Elliott could see Bea's body language begin to change in response to the music, her grip loosening on the door, her head held with more confidence. Exactly what Elliott had hoped.

On the left, the hillside was covered in scrubby trees and shrubs and massive boulders, with long driveways that led to tucked-away homes. On the right were canyon-edge houses with impressive views, and arched trees dappled gold from the setting sun. Zero sidewalks to speak of, Elliott noted in disgust.

About a quarter mile in, Bea suddenly turned the music down. "Okay, wait, now slow down," she whispered to Chloe. "You see that house up on the left?" She pointed. "The one with the U-shaped drive-way? That's it, but don't stop, go past it, and then turn around and park behind that big shrub."

"And be sure to cut the engine," Elliott instructed as Chloe went past the house and made a U-turn to pull up along the moun-tainside.

The sun was sunk low over the ocean below, casting a pink glow on the mountain range and the many hillside homes. These houses stood at the edge of Rattlesnake Canyon, a popular hiking destination, which seemed fitting to Elliott, given what a snake this guy surely was.

Chloe cut the engine, and they rolled to a stop behind a mas-sive shrub at one edge of the U-shaped driveway. In the middle of the drive was a giant, sprawling fig tree, and beyond that, about ten yards from the road, sat a long, modern one-story house. The house was all glass and redwood, with asymmetrical roofs lined with solar panels.

Its lit-up rooms were easily visible from the street, like a dollhouse or a diorama on display.

"Do you see anyone?" Bea asked, staring straight ahead at the road.

"Yeah," replied Elliott, who was also seated on the passenger side and had the best view. Inside, behind one of the giant picture windows, sat a family eating dinner. The children—a boy and a girl—were laughing at something as the mother, a tall fortysomething white woman with curly, shoulder-length hair, cut up the younger one's food. "But I don't see—oh, wait—" A ruggedly handsome middle-aged white dude walked in to join them at the long farmhouse table. "There's a guy, too."

"Man bun?" Chloe double-checked with Bea, leaning forward to get a look.

Bea sucked in a breath. "Yeah."

Man bun. Don't even get Elliott started on the gender implications of *that.* Also, it was the kind of annoying fashion choice that made white dudes that much more annoying—they take a hairstyle worn by Japanese samurais and Sikh men for *centuries,* and suddenly everyone's supposed to find them all original? Cultural appropriation much?

Bea massaged her eye sockets with the heels of her hands, suddenly looking so wrecked that for a moment Elliott wondered if she should turn the music back up.

But then Bea suddenly sat up, fierce and determined. "Okay," she said definitively. "Let's do this."

Bea

Bea didn't exactly feel *safe* sitting at dusk inside Chloe's Mercedes— or whoever's expensive car this was—mere *feet* from *his* house, but she certainly felt safer than if she'd been sitting inside her parents' minivan, a vehicle that had once upon a time driven her to every single soccer practice and game that *he'd* coached.

She'd often wondered if the soccer field was where things took a turn for the worse—was his gaze constantly tracking her as she ran drills on the field? Or was it on one of the many occasions that she'd babysat for them that she'd first caught his eye?

Caught his eye. That made it sound like she'd been out fishing, like she'd been trying to lure something in instead of simply being a child living a child's life. Though it seemed like no matter what happened, no matter what kind of pain or violence a man inflicted, people still looked for fault in the *girl*. And it seemed like people *particularly* loved to blame a Black girl. Bea had sought out multiple articles about how Black girls were overly sexualized and seen as "less innocent" than white girls their age, and afterward she'd felt sick—because was that actually true of *her*?

Bea grabbed the canvas tote bag from the floor of her seat, which held the ingredients Chloe had procured. Chloe had offered to handle everything since she'd enjoyed the process, which had been fine with Bea; she didn't really have time, and she wasn't about to go storing weird witch items in her house.

But *preparing* the ingredients was something Bea wanted to do herself. She needed to take control of at least this one small moment.

"Okay, so first you add the burning bush stems and items of significance to the bowl," Elliott instructed, reading from the book.

Setting the large, engraved stone bowl on her lap—which, how much had that cost? And where had Chloe even found it?—Bea added the thin branches of flaming red leaves, then grabbed the paper bag she'd brought with her and quickly dumped in the stolen items, avoiding touching them as if they were toxic waste.

"Now you surround the bowl with the lit candles," Elliott continued.

Chloe held the silver tray on her lap for Bea, who set the bowl in the middle and then lit the purple candles one by one, placing them in a circle around the bowl.

"Then you sprinkle the distilled spirits inside the bowl," Elliott continued. "And drop in the lit matchsticks one at a time."

"I'm not loving the whole *light things on fire inside the car* thing," Chloe confessed as Bea doused the bowl's contents with the small bottle of vodka. "I'm just gonna"—she reached for her water bottle in the middle console—"keep this on hand in case things get out of control."

"Do *not* add that," Madeline warned Chloe as Bea grabbed the matchsticks. "The spell doesn't call for water."

"Well, then can we at least crack a window?" Chloe asked, rolling hers down a bit.

Bea struck the first match and it flared to life. When she dropped it into the bowl the objects immediately caught fire, the flames licking up into the air and casting an orange glow on Chloe's face. In the bowl, Bea could see the Father's Day card begin to blacken and curl.

"Okay, that's it," Elliott said once Bea added the final match.

Bea stared at the flames, which were already beginning to dim. She felt . . . frozen. She took a deep breath to collect herself, wishing she could hop out of the car and go for a quick run.

She didn't want to do this. She didn't want to face him. Not even from a distance, not even from the safety of a car, surrounded by other survivors—if that's even what they were. Because sometimes she didn't feel like she'd survived anything; she felt like she'd been killed off. Dead at the tender age of thirteen and now just a walking body that resembled the girl she used to be.

But then she felt a hand on her shoulder—Elliott's hand, reminding her that she could do this. And she had to admit that in some small way, it *did* help that she wasn't alone.

Slowly, Bea lifted her gaze and turned toward the window, her eyes landing on the house.

And there he was.

She felt an immediate jolt of panic. There was the man who haunted her nightmares. The man who'd shattered her world.

He didn't *look* like a monster, smiling as he leaned across the table toward his wife—Margaret, Bea's mom's boss—who was laughing at something he'd said. But that's *exactly* what he was. And, *God*, it was all so *fake*. The acclaimed career, the loving marriage, the perfect family. It wasn't the full picture.

Did the art collectors spending tens of thousands on his paintings have any clue they were collecting from a monster? What about his wife? How could she stay married to someone like that? Or did she not even suspect him of anything? And his children, did they have any idea who their father really was? More importantly, were they safe from him? Maya would be nearly eleven years old now, only a few years younger than Bea was when he . . . when it happened. Was he the kind of guy who'd do something to his own *daughter*?

That was the thing that constantly nagged at Bea, the thing that filled her with guilt: that others might get hurt because she'd failed to speak up.

But who would have believed her if she had? It would've been her word—a thirteen-year-old Black girl's, a nobody—against his—this important, prestigious, powerful white man. And what hell would that have brought down upon her family, not to mention her mom's career? Her mother, who was still paying off $100K in student loan debt. Who rose every morning at 5 a.m. so she could thoughtfully answer student emails before she hopped on her bike to clear her head, then made her family breakfast. Her mother, who didn't just like what she did but *loved* it.

Besides, whom would Bea have reported it to? The *police*? They weren't going to help her or keep her safe. They'd just as soon pull a gun on someone like her if they even *thought* she was in violation of . . . well, you *name* it.

But now she *was* speaking up in her own individual way, Bea thought as she took the open book from Elliott and raised her clenched fist over the pages. She *was* taking control. And not merely for revenge—though that was more than justified—but to stop him. How many other girls might get hurt if Bea didn't act?

As the coven began to chant, Bea channeled her rage. Did she want to focus on how he'd harmed her, reliving every detail? No, not any more than she wanted to lay eyes on his poisonous face. But for that young girl sitting at the dining room table—for some other young girl, out there just living her innocent child's life—she would do both . . .

It was a warm fall evening, and Bea was in the passenger seat of a car. And not just any car, a vintage Mustang with flames painted down the sides. A car she always admired when she arrived to babysit and saw it sitting in the open garage.

"I'll teach you to drive it one day, Beatrice," he always told her when he'd drive her home at the end of the night. He always called her Beatrice.

"You played great at last weekend's game," he was telling her now as he drove, windows down, along the 101 freeway to take her home. "That pass you made to Olivia, man, that was killer! I wish I had a video. You really took control of the situation, just like we discussed."

"Thanks." Bea smiled, half-embarrassed and half-thrilled. She'd been playing soccer on a travel team for a few years now, but this was the first year she'd had Michael as her coach. He was extremely well regarded in the league, and not merely because he'd played soccer in college—he was funny and gregarious, and as a famous artist who sold paintings to celebrities and billionaires alike, he brought, as her mom would say, *a certain je ne sais quoi* to everything he did. Fame of any sort, Bea often thought in amusement, made people just *like* you more. Moms flirted with him. Girls crushed on him. Everyone adored him.

And Bea liked him as well, though not like *that*. She liked him the way she liked her oboe instructor, seeking his approval because he was an expert in something she loved and a model of whom she wanted to be. When she'd babysit for Maya and Roman, his eight- and six-year-old kids, whom she adored, she'd peruse his many books about soccer, reading them after the kids were in bed. She didn't just want to excel at the things she loved; she wanted to be the very best.

The *actual* adoration, though? That she reserved for Maria, a girl on her team with bronze skin and an electric smile that made Bea's stomach flip every time they did warm-ups or carpooled to a game.

"I think, though," he said, as he pulled off at Patterson Avenue, a busy but desolate-feeling street lined with a cinder-block wall and evergreen trees, "that you could further improve your form by focusing on your recovery."

"Oh?" she inquired. Michael was big on recovery, often leading their team in twenty minutes of yoga at the end of practice, encouraging them to continue the work at home. He'd often give them adjustments to help deepen the stretches and loosen their tendons and muscles. Though if Bea was honest, she sometimes felt weird about how he touched her body and where he placed his hands.

But Michael was a nice guy—he was a *dad*—and Bea knew he was just trying to help. Besides, it was totally in keeping with his crunchy artist-yogi vibe. And she always dismissed it because it was something he did to all the girls.

"Yeah, I think your run is just a little off," he explained, as he turned onto Cathedral Oaks, a four-lane suburban road that was lined with a sprinkling of trees and modest two-story homes. "But I think I know what the issue is."

"Really? What?" she asked in concern. If there was an area for improvement, she wanted every detail. As much as she liked the praise, it was the criticism that she homed in on. If there was an error that could be pinpointed, she was going to correct it.

"Here, I'll show you." He pulled over just before the curve for her dark cul-de-sac, parking at the edge of a dim streetlamp so that his car sat in shadow. The wood-sided houses on Bea's street weren't fancy, but they were definitely upper-middle class, with basketball hoops in the driveways and the Santa Ynez mountain range as their backdrop. Not to mention their price tags, these days going for over a million dollars each. At this hour on a Friday, Bea's neighbors would all be ensconced in their homes, watching family movies or playing board games.

"So." He half turned in his seat. "Your hip flexors are a group of muscles at the top of your thighs, here and here." He illustrated by pointing to either side of his crotch. He was wearing loose drawstring pants that always made Bea think of hippies and stoners, though they were probably some fancy brand she'd never even heard of.

"They're key in walking and kicking and swiveling your hips," he explained. "But when those muscles tighten up, it can limit those movements. So you want to make sure you're regularly working them to loosen them back up. So, for example, here, lean your seat back." He unbuckled his seat belt and then hers, then reached across her, his arm brushing her chest, to lower her seat back.

Okaaay, she thought as she leaned back in the seat. She wasn't so much expecting to do this *now*.

"So, you want to stretch them, like we do in warm-ups, but you also want to massage them. Bend your leg," he instructed, laying a hand on her left leg. She was wearing soccer shorts, as she often did, and his hand was warm on her bare skin.

She did as he said, pulling her knee toward her chest like they did in warm-ups.

"No, like this," he corrected, pulling her leg out and toward him so that it was splayed open. He rested her ankle on his shoulder, one hand wrapped around her shin, which made her feel incredibly awkward. "You want to work in circular movements," he said, beginning to massage the inside of her thigh starting halfway up her leg. "And you really want to make sure you're working the muscles deep," he added, his hand moving farther up her leg. Which made her increasingly uncomfortable.

"Yeah, okay." She nodded quickly, her gaze darting outside the window where she could see her house half a block away, so close and yet so far. "I think I got it."

But he didn't stop massaging her. And she didn't dare move.

"You have to really work the tendons, too," he said, his hand sliding under her shorts so that he was massaging right at the line of her underwear. "That will *really* improve your form like nothing else."

Bea felt frozen in place. Was this normal or was it weird? Was she making things up? Wasn't he just trying to help? He was an adult, and she was practically still a kid, so no way was there anything more going on. Plus, he was her coach. He was Maya and Roman's *dad*. He was there to help. She didn't want to overreact and end up being rude.

But then two things happened at once: his fingers slipped just *beneath* her underwear, and Bea noticed he had an erection.

She jerked her leg away from him and quickly sat up. "I should get inside," she blurted out, scrambling to grab her bag. "I just remembered—my parents—they'll be wondering if . . ."

She threw the door open and was halfway out when he stopped her.

"Beatrice," he said, one hand wrapping around her arm. It was a commandment and not a question, and Bea's body complied even before she had a chance to think. She noticed how large his hands were, how strong. He could easily break her forearm, she thought absently as she failed to meet his eye. She was too embarrassed, too befuddled. She needed to get out of that car.

With his free hand he reached into his pants, and Bea felt a spike of terror. But then he pulled a wad of cash from his pocket and extended it toward her. "Don't forget your pay."

She took the babysitting money, numb.

"Spend some time loosening those muscles," he advised as she jammed the cash into her bag. He said it like things were totally normal. Like something awful *hadn't* just occurred. "And see you at practice," he called after her as she ran-walked to her driveway.

In the present moment, Bea squeezed her fist harder, her stomach crawling up into her throat.

She'd felt nauseous afterward for weeks, trying to decide if what she *thought* happened actually had. Maybe she'd just misinterpreted things. He wouldn't *do* something, would he? And even what she'd seen . . . That could have just been an involuntary physical reaction, right? It might not *mean* anything.

She'd stopped babysitting for them after that, though, making up excuse after excuse—she didn't feel well, she had homework, she'd promised to hang out with friends. Even the news that Maya and Roman really missed Bea, relayed by her mom, did nothing to sway her.

The soccer team came next. She didn't quit straight-out. They had two more games left in the season that she forced herself to get through, not wanting to let down the other girls on her team. But the minute the season was done she informed her parents that she wanted to quit the league. In fact, she gave up soccer entirely. She'd loved it with a passion for most of her life, but now it was utterly ruined. He'd ruined it.

And yet she didn't tell anyone. She couldn't. She felt embarrassed and ashamed, confused and . . . uncertain. If something had happened, was it *her* fault? She kept quiet with her teammates, was silent with her friends, didn't mention it to her parents, didn't even tell her own twin.

At least, not at first.

With Otis, it took over a year before Bea confessed what had happened, and even then, it was only after he questioned why she kept crawling into his bed every night like she had when they were kids, and why she kept waking up from nightmares.

It was Otis who eventually encouraged (well, practically forced) Bea to attend a support group. Otis who always checked in on her. Otis who gave her trigger warnings on films and TV shows and books. Otis who gently pointed out the PTSD poster hanging outside the guidance counselor's office. It was Otis who insisted every so often that it hadn't been too much time, that she could still report what had happened, that she could still tell their parents the truth.

But Bea . . . she just wanted to move on.

Though now she knew better. There was no moving on.

Bea could tell from the collective inhalation that the pages of the book must be changing, but she kept her gaze pinned on him, not wanting to look away and jeopardize the spell. Inside, he was getting up from the table, pretending to balance Maya's plate on one hand like a waiter.

"*Take this pain, take this rage,*" she recited as she squeezed her fist, "*and cast it back on its creator.*"

Bea threw her hand open, her fingers splayed wide. From the corner of her eye, she saw a bright ball of violet energy burst out of the book. Bea glanced over just in time to see it hovering there above the strange mark on her palm before it flew past them, through the window's tinted glass, and dissipated in the pink-golden light, heading straight toward the house.

The impact was nearly instantaneous. One moment he was standing there, joking around with the kids, the next he was slumped against the table.

It took his wife a moment to register what had occurred, then Margaret jumped up and ran to him, knocking over her chair in the process. The kids, Bea could see, were confused and then terror-struck, Maya's mouth hanging open as she slowly stood, Roman's little face crumpling as he looked from Maya to their parents, watching as their mother helped their father stand. *His* face was pale and blank as he held one hand to his forehead, and when he looked at his wife, it was as if he didn't recognize her. She pointed at Maya and said something that caused the little girl to sprint out of the room.

"We need to go," Bea urged Chloe, handing the book to Elliott and grabbing the tray from Chloe's lap. She quickly blew out the candles as Chloe started the car.

It was both a pragmatic decision—they couldn't be found there if an ambulance arrived—and an emotional one. Bea had *cared* about those kids—she'd wiped clean their jelly-covered faces and smeared sunscreen on their shoulders; she'd hugged them when they scraped their knees—and she didn't have the stomach to witness their panic and fear.

As they sped away, following the road as it curved down the hillside, the ocean and distant oil rigs visible out along the horizon, Bea waited for the relief to come. And it did, washing over her like that cool blue wave she'd used in her visualization techniques.

She'd *done* it. She'd gotten her revenge.

But with the relief came something unexpected: a stab of guilt.

Maybe it should have occurred to Bea before then, but it was only as they drove through the twilight that she had the realization: when they doled out their punishments, it wasn't merely their victims who suffered.

9

Elliott

Walking home that evening from her drop-off spot just down the block, Elliott kept her hand on her personal alarm and her eyes on the sidewalk, which was stained with the fallen olives that had been crushed into the cement by so many passing feet.

Why, she wondered, wasn't she feeling more celebratory? Why was she feeling so tender and . . . bleak?

It wasn't because of the song she was listening to—Metallica's "Nothing Else Matters" covered by Phoebe Bridgers—though the song was, in fact, tender and bleak. No, she'd chosen the song to match her mood.

Reaching her house, she paused and then kept going, passing the house with the little DIY lending library and continuing around the corner—though at this hour she was only willing to circle her block. Tilting her head back, she gazed up at the indigo-tinted sky and the faint stars overhead. She couldn't help thinking of that Oscar Wilde quote, about how some of us might be in the gutter but were still staring at the stars. Was that true of her?

The gutter part, yes, there was no doubt about that. Humanity as a whole was in the gutter. But did she have her eyes on the stars?

She'd *thought* so. She'd thought that forming a coven was creating her own celestial gathering, if that made any kind of sense. Magic and mystery and miracles and so much more. And it still *was* all of that, she reasoned. She still believed in it. She absolutely did.

But that little girl . . .

She couldn't get that little girl's panic-stricken face out of her mind. She kept seeing her slowly rise from the table, again . . . and again. The look on that girl's face, it was one Elliott had felt in her gut. One she'd *lived*. That look was the moment of awakening to a different world, one in which you didn't merely *know* that bad things could happen and shit could go down, but one in which you *felt* it in your bones. A world where your father could suddenly and inexplicably collapse at the dinner table. Or your mother could sit you down one day after school and use the words *terminal* and *cancer*.

Yeah, Elliott reasoned, but that didn't mean their actions weren't justified. What were they supposed to do, just let Man Bun get away with it? Hell no. That bastard had senselessly ruined a young girl's life. Or, you know, maybe not ruined, because Bea wasn't going to let that happen, but *he'd* created trauma. And for all Elliott knew, his family had been complicit. So why should *they* be allowed to live in peace? What made *that* young girl so special?

Really, at the end of the day it was all *his* fault. He was the one who'd brought hell down upon his entire family. If he didn't want to ruin his daughter's life, then maybe he shouldn't have done horrible shit.

Besides, that girl was more than likely a brat. Just look at that house. Why should Elliott feel sorry for her? Terrible things happened to people all the time. Why should that little girl be the exception? She'd witnessed something traumatic happen to one of her parents, so what? Spoiler alert, sweet pea: half the world experienced something that traumatic or worse.

When Elliott finally came in through the front door, her dad was asleep on the couch, his novel splayed open on his chest. She set down her backpack and quietly closed the door, but still he awoke, rousing himself to sit up.

"Hey, Pigeon," he yawned, pulling off his glasses to rub his eyes.

"Hi, Daddy," she greeted, coming over to snuggle against him on the couch, which clearly took him by pleasant surprise. He slid his glasses on and pulled back the blanket covering his legs so she could get underneath. She cuddled up against him like she used to when she was little, resting her head against his chest. Through the fabric of his T-shirt, she could hear his heart beating, a calming, steady *thump, thump, thump* that reminded her of falling asleep on his chest as a kid.

"How was the poetry reading?" he asked.

"Oh, you know." She shrugged. "Not bad."

"You still working on that poem for the workshop you want to apply to?"

"Mm-hmm," she lied. Actually, she hadn't picked up her pen in months.

"I'd love to read it when you're done."

For a moment Elliott wanted to tell her dad everything. And not just about the poetry reading, but *everything* everything.

Her dad rubbed her shoulder. "Hey, I was thinking—and feel free to say no—but you want to go to the batting cages this weekend? We haven't done that in a while."

That used to be their standard weekend activity. After her mom died, it seemed like Elliott's dad needed Elliott as much as she needed him. They barely spent time apart. He started coaching her softball team, volunteering at her school, taking her on regular camping trips. But once she became friends with Vi, she started spending all her time outside of the house and those things fell away. If she was honest with herself, she really missed doing stuff like that with him.

"Sure," she replied.

"Really?" Her dad looked down in surprise.

"Yeah." She smiled. Elliott had to admit that the batting cages had always been annoyingly fun, one of her favorite childhood memories. Besides, it would be good distraction for both of them; it was her mom's birthday that coming weekend.

Elliott muffled a cough as she got up from the couch; her chest felt kind of burny, and she had an unpleasant taste in her mouth.

"Pigeon," her dad said in concern. "That cough's sounding worse. Take some vitamins and get some extra rest, will you?"

"Yes, sir," she fake saluted, which made him roll his eyes. He'd briefly been in the Navy after high school, a fact she liked to subtly tease him about.

"Hey." He grabbed her hand before she could walk away. "Have I told you how lucky I am to be your dad?"

Another stab of guilt. "Yeah, about a million times."

"Okay, then we'll make it a million and one." He smiled.

Now Elliott was the one to roll her eyes as she tugged her hand free—and that's when she noticed something strange. Was it just her imagination, or had the mark on her palm . . . *changed*?

Chloe

The following morning, Chloe was feeling pretty bummed out—but for reasons completely unrelated to Bea's spell.

"Clo? You up, baby?" her mom asked brightly, knocking on her bedroom door first thing. And Chloe, who was sitting at her vanity doing her makeup, knew just from her mom's tone of voice exactly what had gone down.

"I'm up," she called back, smiling at her reflection as she applied blush to the apples of her cheeks. Inside, she felt a surging wave of disappointment.

"Hey," her mom greeted, cracking open her door. "Oooo, you look nice. Is that the new Fenty you got at Sephora?"

"He bailed again, didn't he?" Chloe asked calmly, grabbing her eyelash curler from her pink lacquer tray. Chloe, who was supposed to see her dad for the weekend (he'd made these big plans for the two of them to go horseback riding on the beach) should have been numb to these sorts of last-minute letdowns by now. And yet . . .

Her mom sighed and sat down behind Chloe on her bed. "I guess one of the twins has a music class he forgot about, and he says he can't miss it."

Chloe shrugged as she trapped her eyelashes in the curler and pressed down on the little clamp. "Whatever, that's fine."

"Clo."

"Seriously. I get it. It's no big deal."

Her mom leaned forward, resting her head in her hands, and muttered something under her breath. "Listen, baby," she said, coming over to stand behind Chloe and placing her hands on Chloe's shoulders. She met Chloe's eyes in the mirror. "This isn't about you. You need to know that men, *boys*—well, most men, most boys," she corrected. "They're just irresponsible, self-absorbed assholes. They do what they want when they want, and they don't stop to think about the consequences of their actions or how they impact others. Do you know what I'm saying?"

And Chloe did. Much more than she could ever tell her mom.

"Really, Mom," Chloe insisted, grabbing a bottle of perfume from the vanity. "I'm *fine*. I'm, like, immune to it by now."

Her mom watched her a moment. "Hey, I have an idea. Why don't we head down to LA this weekend? We can treat ourselves to a little shopping spree at Koreatown Plaza."

Shopping in Koreatown was one of their favorite mom-and-daughter activities. Chloe loved the stationery at Fancy House, and her mom was *obsessed* with the skin-care products at Cosmetics Plaza, and they always got bingsoo at Sul & Beans after.

Chloe smiled. "Yeah, okay. That sounds good. I could definitely use some—" She hacked out a cough.

"Ooo, are you okay, baby?" her mom asked, taking a step back. "You're not getting that nasty virus that's going around, are you? Because you know I can't handle vomit."

"Mom, it's nothing," Chloe assured her, swallowing the bitter taste in her mouth and waving her mom away. "Let me get ready already, will you?"

"Okay, okay." Her mom put up her hands. "I'm making green smoothies—I'll leave you one in the fridge."

The second her mom was out the door, Chloe wiped her mouth with a Kleenex—and then paused, feeling a twinge of concern at what she saw: the Kleenex was stained a deep, dark purple. The same dark purple her mark had turned. Her mark, which she'd also noticed had somehow doubled in size.

Bea

Fifteen miles away, Bea was walking into her kitchen totally out of breath, heart pounding, body sweaty. She'd barely slept the night before and had awoken early, her body humming with anxiety. She should have felt victorious and anxiety-free the morning after, but instead she was a mess. And in no small part because she'd discovered that the mark on her palm had *changed*. It was bigger and a different color, which made Bea feel like it was somehow . . . *alive.* She'd decided to burn off her anxiety by going for an extra-extra-long run.

Otis was at the kitchen table eating oatmeal, and their mom was standing at the counter, her back to the room as she talked on the phone. "Well, thank you so much for letting me know," she was saying, her voice edged with concern.

Bea went to the cupboard to grab some electrolyte powder, her attention on her mom.

"Yes. Yes, of *course,*" her mom said. "You too. Bye." She turned to face the twins, her phone clutched in her hand. "That was Delphine from the university. She spoke with Margaret last night. Apparently, Michael was in the hospital."

"Really?" Otis asked in surprise, glancing at Bea, who was focused on adding a scoop of powder to her bottle.

"What happened?" Bea asked evenly, screwing the lid back on and shaking the bottle to mix in the powder.

"They're not sure. He had some kind of episode and now he's experiencing memory loss. Margaret told Delphine that it came on suddenly. Apparently, he didn't recognize Margaret or the kids. They're running a bunch of tests."

"Whoa, *seriously?*" Otis said, unable to hide his pleasure. Catching himself, he quickly added, "God, that's horrible. Isn't his opening next weekend?"

"It is. I should call Margaret," their mother said, grabbing her cup of coffee. "And I need to tell your dad. You two have a good day at school," she added as an afterthought, coming over to kiss them each on the cheek before breezing out of the room, already tapping away on her phone.

Otis craned his neck to make sure their mom was gone, then leaned toward Bea, who was taking a swig of water.

"Oh my God, that's an insane coincidence," he whispered, eyebrows raised.

Bea choked on her water, then covered her mouth with her elbow as she continued to cough, which brought up an unpleasantly bitter taste.

"I mean, obviously that psychic isn't *actually* responsible, but the timing is super creepy, right?" Otis asked in a hush.

"Right," Bea agreed, swallowing away the bitterness and frowning at something on her sleeve.

"It *almost* makes you wonder . . ." Otis furrowed his brow as he assessed Bea. "You doing okay?"

"What? Yeah," she dismissed, pushing up her sleeves and taking another swig to rinse out her mouth. "I'm totally fine."

"Extra-long run this morning," he pointed out. "Also, I've noticed you've sometimes been running a second time in the late afternoons."

"That's called *training*, Otis. Anyway, I need to go get ready—unless you'd like me to—" She pretended to come at him for a big sweaty hug.

"Ew, gross. Get out of here!"

As Bea ran up the stairs, she pulled down her sleeve to take another look—and her stomach clenched. The spot where she'd coughed? It had come away *purple*.

Madeline

In San Roque, standing before her bathroom mirror, Madeline finished blow-drying her long hair, ensuring it was perfectly straight and smooth, then pushed up the sleeve of her uniform. Running a finger over the inside of her arm, she traced a tiny scar.

Since joining the coven, she hadn't felt the need to cut herself. Not that she'd cut herself a ton before. She'd tried it a few times—okay, maybe more than a few times—but she was always cautious, never going too deep. Just deep enough to actually *feel* something and release the built-up tension.

And it's not as if she was a *cutter* or anything. She was not *that* girl. She just needed a way of channeling her rage. And better to focus her rage on one small inch of flesh than burn down the entire house.

But witchcraft, Madeline was finding, was a *much* more satisfying way of channeling her rage. She kept thinking back to the way that monster who hurt Bea had just . . . *collapsed.* It felt amazing to punish those creeps, and so *good* to stand up for the girls in her coven.

At the thought, Madeline flipped her hand over and examined her palm. She was fairly certain the mark of the coven had grown, and it had definitely changed color—now it was a deep purple. Madeline couldn't help thinking that it was proof that their coven was growing stronger.

Pulling her sleeve back down to hide her scars, Madeline muffled a cough and quickly cleared her throat.

"Are you okay in there?" her mother called from the hall.

"Yes, I'm fine," Madeline snapped as she grabbed her toothbrush. Must her mother *always* be involved? Always *right* there, peering over her shoulder?

She'd noticed her mom was way more on her case ever since Caleb had entered rehab. Like she needed to keep at least one part of her family on track. But frankly, Madeline didn't need it—she knew how to keep *herself* on track, thank you very much.

Once she'd flossed and rinsed with mouthwash and thoroughly scrubbed her teeth for exactly two minutes, Madeline spit into the sink—then frowned. Her spit . . . was tinged *purple.*

Elliott

When Elliott arrived for the coven's gathering that Thursday, Madeline and Chloe had already arrived and were seated on the benches—and from the look on Chloe's face, she was eager to talk. Though obviously they needed privacy, and obviously they weren't headed down the hillside without Bea. Elliott wasn't about to make Bea walk through the dark to come find them by herself—who knew what random creep could be lying in wait? Though they all knew it wasn't necessarily the person hiding in the shadows you needed to be worried about; it was the one you'd let into your own home, the one smiling and calling you by name.

As soon as Bea arrived, though, dressed once again in her running clothes, the girls headed down the hill and took up their rightful position beside their mansion—or that's how Elliott had come to think of it, at least. Wasn't this basically *their* decrepit mansion?

"So, I had this weird thing happen to me," Chloe blurted out in a rush the moment her butt hit the flagstones. "The morning after we cast Bea's spell, I noticed that my mark had changed color and *grown*, and I coughed up something bitter and *purple*."

"Me *too*," Bea said in concern, fiddling with the zipper on her track jacket. "It tasted *terrible*. I thought it was maybe just me."

"I coughed up something," said Madeline. "But the bitterness didn't bother me too much."

"What about you, Elliott?" asked Chloe.

"Yeah, I coughed up purple stuff," Elliott confessed. She'd been walking to school when it happened. After hacking into her elbow, she'd found a dark purple spatter on her sweatshirt. "It didn't taste great, but it also hasn't happened again."

"But that ball of whatever that was that came out of the book, *that* was purple, too," Chloe pointed out. "So that can't be a coincidence, right? It all seems connected."

"So . . . what do we think is *happening*?" asked Bea.

"Well, some witches *do* believe in the Threefold Law," Madeline offered.

"Sure," Elliott replied, a little annoyed that Madeline was now offering up witchcraft knowledge on the reg. "But there's serious debate within the witch and Wiccan communities whether that's even legitimate."

"What is that, like karma or something?" asked Chloe.

"Yeah, sort of," said Elliott.

"The Threefold Law"—Madeline jumped in—"or Rule of Three, basically states that whatever you cast out into the Universe will come back to you three times over."

"I feel like it would have been good to know something like that ahead of time," Bea commented, a hint of accusation in her tone.

"Listen, there are *a lot* of different theories and misconceptions about witchcraft and witches out there," Elliott defended, twisting one of her pink braids. "Obviously, not all of them are true. You don't see us sinking to the bottom of rivers like stones and drinking blood, do you? You can't go believing every witch-related thing you hear." She glanced at Madeline. "Plus, the book didn't mention anything about the Threefold Law."

"But it *did* warn that whatever you seek is also seeking you," Bea reminded her.

"Sure," Elliott said slowly. "That's true. But there are *a lot* of ways of interpreting that line."

Bea furrowed her brow and absently rubbed her right palm, still not fully consoled. "Look, I'm not trying to cause trouble—especially after you all just helped me out. But I do feel like we should take this seriously."

"Of course," Elliott agreed. "Okay, for argument's sake, let's say that this *is* some kind of cause and effect. We cast a spell and get some blowback or whatever. First of all, it was pretty mild and short-lived. We're all fine now, right? And second, I don't know about all of you, but I'm willing to put up with a little temporary discomfort if it means punishing these creeps the way they deserve. At the end of the day, it's a pretty small price to pay."

"Yeah." Chloe nodded. "I mean, it only happened that once, and it wasn't that bad . . ."

"Also, don't you think," added Madeline, "that's why the book says it takes a quarter moon cycle in between each conjuring? To ensure the aftereffects can wear off before casting another spell?"

"Excellent point," said Elliott.

Bea tucked her shoelace ends back into her shoes. She still looked unsettled. "Yeah, but our marks didn't change back to how they were before."

"Sure, but that isn't necessarily a bad thing," countered Madeline. "Or even connected to the blowback. I took it to be a sign that our coven is growing stronger."

"Yes, *exactly*," Elliott agreed, surprised that she was siding with Madeline, of all people.

"I think it makes sense that there would be repercussions to our actions," said Madeline. "Which is what we all felt. But doesn't it also stand to reason that if we do something positive it would have the opposite impact and we could counter those effects? Maybe a counter-spell of some kind could prevent the blowback from happening next time."

"That makes sense," Chloe said optimistically. "Balance the scales or whatever."

"So should we ask the book for a counter-spell, then?" asked Bea.

"We could do that," said Elliott. "The only thing is we'd then have to wait another seven days to conjure. Which means delaying Madeline's spell. Would you be okay with that?" she asked Madeline.

"To be honest, I'm pretty eager to go next," Madeline replied.

Which didn't surprise Elliott. She hadn't expected Madeline to wait—and to be fair, she wasn't sure *she'd* want to wait. Bea, on the other hand, looked a little anxious.

"But at the same time," Madeline continued, glancing at Bea, "if it's for the good of the entire coven, then I want to do it. I mean, that's the whole point of this, right?" she asked Elliott. "To be in it together?"

"Yeah," Elliott replied, surprised and a little touched by Madeline's willingness to put the others first. "Totally. Okay, then . . ." She pulled out the puzzle box from her backpack, slid it open, and extracted the book.

"Should just one of us ask," said Bea as Elliott opened the book to a blank page, "or should we do it all together?"

"Since we'll all use the spell, I think we should do it all together," said Elliott, placing the book before them.

The other girls nodded in agreement.

"Okay." Elliott pushed up the sleeve of her leather jacket and placed her right hand above the book. The other girls extended their hands as well. "On the count of three. One . . . two . . . three."

"Bring forth that which will satisfy my intentions," they chanted in unison. *"Bring forth that which will satisfy my intentions. Bring forth that which will satisfy my intentions."*

And yet the pages of the book remained unchanged.

"Maybe we should say *our* intentions," Madeline suggested. "To clarify that we are united in our request."

"Good thinking," said Bea.

So they tried it again, making sure they were grammatically correct, in case the book cared about that kind of thing.

But once again, the pages remained blank.

"So, can we not do it as a group?" Bea asked rhetorically.

"Well." Chloe leaned back on her hands. "The book *did* make it sound like only one witch was supposed to conjure at a time."

"Or maybe this isn't this book's purpose," Madeline suggested.

"Right," considered Elliott. "Maybe that's not the path we're supposed to be headed down. Maybe this is the book's way of telling us to stay the course."

Bea quirked her mouth to one side. "But . . . so are we just not going to worry about the blowback?"

"Listen," argued Elliott. "I agree that it was creepy and kind of unpleasant. But we've *already* been living with discomfort after all that we've gone through, haven't we? And isn't a little bit more discomfort worth the payoff?"

"I think so," agreed Chloe.

"And again," offered Elliott, "I think Madeline is right about the seven days. That's probably the book's safeguard to ensure the blowback wears off before conjuring another spell."

Bea was silent, though she didn't argue.

"Okay. Then, Madeline," Elliott announced with a dose of formality as she pushed the book toward her. "You're up."

Madeline was so intense and focused as she conjured her spell—reciting the words at a near whisper, her rigid hand hovering over the book—you would have thought she was performing nuclear bomb diffusion with her mind. Elliott could practically see the *deep intention* written all over her face. But when her spell manifested, she seemed to deflate, her mouth turning into a frown.

"'Incantation of Transfiguration,'" she read aloud in a slightly disparaging tone.

"Transfiguration?" asked Bea. "As in Professor McGonagall transfiguration?"

"Maybe you'll turn him into an *actual* pig," Chloe guessed.

"That would be very Circe of you," Elliott commented.

"Yeah, but . . . I don't *want* him transfigured," Madeline stated bitterly. "I want him *ruined.*"

"Turning him into a pig would *definitely* ruin the rest of his life," Chloe pointed out.

"Sure, it's just . . ." Madeline exhaled through her nose. "I just really thought when it was my turn, I'd get something *worse.*"

"Well, you haven't even performed it yet," Elliott countered. "I think we should trust that the book delivered the exact right spell."

"What does it call for?" asked Chloe, as if ready to make a mental catalogue of necessary ingredients.

Madeline leaned over the book. "'To perform the Incantation of Transfiguration,'" she read aloud, "'gather together thirteen silver needles, one silver chain, a handful of snakeskin ashes, thirteen purple candles, and an object of importance once owned by the victim—' Well, *that* I already have," she added in relief. "'To cast the spell,'" she kept reading, "'gather your coven together under a new moon within one hundred yards of your victim.'"

"When's the next new moon?" asked Bea.

Elliott pulled out her phone. "Looks like it's two weeks from now. October twenty-eighth."

"Wait, what day of the week is that?" asked Madeline.

"A Friday. Why?"

A wicked grin slowly spread across Madeline's face. "That's *perfect,*" she replied, seeming slightly less disappointed. "I know *exactly* where we can cast the spell."

10

Chloe

"Remind me why we're back here yet *again*?" Brooklyn asked Chloe as they walked into Paradise Found one afternoon the following week. It was their second trip to the metaphysical store in less than two weeks.

"I told you, I want to get something nice for my mom," Chloe lied. Though maybe it wasn't *all* a lie; maybe she really would purchase something for her mom. A gift card for an intuitive reading, maybe, or perhaps another singing bowl. She breathed in deeply through her nose. "God, I seriously love the scent of patchouli."

Brooklyn scrunched up her nose in displeasure as she scanned the shop. "You've seriously gone more woo-woo than usual, Clo. I'm gonna go check out the books while you peruse. Maybe I'll *finally* be able to access my astral plane." She smiled wryly as she strolled away.

Chloe laughed and rolled her eyes as she picked up a long string of onyx and tourmaline beads. FEMININE WARRIOR CRYSTAL MALA, the tag read. Okay, she needed this *stat*.

With each new spell their coven conjured, Chloe found she was increasingly drawn to all things mystical. What she wanted was to own a huge ingredient cabinet, lined with glass vials of various sizes, all vaguely and mysteriously labeled. She wanted to drape herself solely in gauzy black clothes and breeze into every room like a young Stevie Nicks. What she wanted was to fully inhabit the spirit of the witch.

Across the room Chloe spotted an array of elaborate dream catchers and made a beeline for them, reaching for one with a lotus theme. Weren't dream catchers supposed to protect sleepers from evil spirits and bad dreams? *That's* what she needed stat.

Ever since casting her spell, Chloe'd been having nightmares. They differed each time but always featured Arman and Trevor. Sometimes they snuck into her room, their mouths dripping with blood, and sometimes they followed her around school like two dead-eyed zombies, and sometimes she couldn't even see them, she just heard them screaming from afar.

Wasn't casting a revenge spell supposed to make her think about them *less*? And yet, somehow she'd been haunted by them nearly every night. But *why*? It wasn't like she felt *sorry* for what she'd done.

What she needed was to banish them from her mind.

Which made her think about something she'd read in her mom's journal one time (yes, she read her mom's journal—how else was a girl supposed to track her mother's mental health?). In addition to dreading turning fifty-five and fretting over Chloe one day going away to college and the two of them growing apart (which, honestly, broke Chloe's heart), she'd written about a recurring dream in which she got back together with Chloe's dad: *As much as I love Richard, I'm not sure I'll ever get over Vincent. Try as I might, I can't seem to banish him from my heart or mind.*

Maybe, Chloe contemplated, they *both* needed dream catchers. Maybe then they could banish the boys and men plaguing their minds.

Bea

Bea was surprised to find that, despite casting her revenge spell, she'd yet to reduce her anxiety or remove *him* from her life. If anything, in a weird way, it felt as if he'd been drawn in *closer*.

Her mom now talked about him all the time, updating the family at dinner on his status, fretting over his health and what it might mean for Margaret and the kids, worrying about how this would impact the trajectory of his career, thinking up ways to help their family out. Just hearing his name was triggering enough, but to listen to all that *sympathy* made Bea want to scream at the top of her lungs.

And apparently, she wasn't the only one.

"We should really go bring Margaret and the kids a meal," her mom suggested at dinner one evening. "And just sit with them and spend some time distracting the kids. Also, I think it would be good for all of us to go visit Michael in the hospital."

"*Jesus! Mom!*" Otis finally snapped. And then caught himself when Bea kicked him under the table. He glanced at her apologetically.

"Did you have something to say, Otis?" their father inquired, one eyebrow raised.

"No, I just . . . maybe we should consider giving their family a little space right now. While they're in the middle of everything. Maybe they have enough going on already. That's all."

Their parents both frowned disapprovingly.

"Showing up for our friends in their time of need is one of our family's *values*," their mother reprimanded him. "And *Michael* is in a time of need."

Yeah, Bea thought, but so was she. And apparently so was Otis.

But their parents, of course, could never know *that*.

Had she not been intentional enough when she conjured her spell? Maybe she should follow Chloe's lead—in that week's coven gathering, she'd formally asked for another turn. Maybe once everyone else had gone, Bea should cast another spell, too.

And yet Bea couldn't help worrying about the future blowback. She knew her coven-mates weren't concerned—they'd said as much when she'd once again brought it up—but she kept thinking about how the dry coughs they'd all experienced after Chloe's spell were, in hindsight, most likely the first aftereffects. And how, after casting her own spell, those symptoms got worse.

Once they cast Madeline's spell, how much worse might the blowback get?

Madeline

Alone in her room one evening, Madeline ran through her nightly ritual of stretching out all her muscles, brushing her long chestnut hair exactly fifty times, and then ironing her school uniform for the following day. Downstairs, her parents were on the phone with her brother's rehab because he'd apparently tried to run away. But as Madeline set her uniform out on her desk, she did her best not to think about that.

Then she moved on to her *other* nightly ritual.

Opening her laptop, she pulled up Google and typed in her name.

By the time she reached the *O* in *O'Conner*, she felt nauseous. And as she hit enter and watched the page refresh, she felt a familiar spike of terror.

Madeline quickly scanned the results. Her personal website came up fourth, right after a social media account for some other girl, a website for an artist in Ohio, and an obituary for another Madeline O'Conner. Scrolling to the bottom, Madeline clicked to page three.

And it was gone.

For a moment Madeline felt a wave of relief.

And then she clicked page four, and there it was again, ranking at the top, not yet scrubbed from the internet.

Slamming her laptop shut with a curse, Madeline strode to her closet and pulled on the light, using a little too much force so the string bobbed and danced. Reaching for the shoebox on the top shelf, she pulled it down and flipped the box top open. Inside was a teddy bear in a little sweater, the name *Derrick* stitched across its front.

Madeline wasn't sure why she'd kept the bear. She'd burned or shredded everything else. Maybe because it seemed wrong to destroy a child's stuffed animal, even if it had belonged to her disgusting, pathological, pathetic-excuse-for-a-human-being ex-boyfriend.

Or maybe because some part of her still wanted to believe that the boy who'd gifted it to her—the one who'd shyly asked if it was okay to kiss her and wrote her a poem for their six-month anniversary and regularly babysat his seven-year-old brother not because he had to but because he loved to—still actually existed.

Slamming the lid back on, Madeline stowed the shoebox in her bottom desk drawer beside her growing stack of witchcraft books (which, fine, was probably a paper trail, but who said she had to follow anyone else's rules?).

Or maybe *this* was the precise reason she'd saved that stupid bear. Maybe she'd intuitively foreseen she'd one day need it for revenge.

Elliott

It was the day of the new moon, and Elliott had decided to treat herself to a little caffeine before meeting up with her coven. A large Americano was the perfect fuel for a night of dark witchcraft (or a night of anything, for that matter). And so, she took herself *not* to Dune Coffee Roasters—her favorite coffee shop, because she didn't want to risk running into *him*—but down to the Daily Grind on the corner of Mission and De La Vina. Where she walked in through the glass doors . . .

. . . and came face-to-face with Violet.

In a town the size of Santa Barbara, it was inevitable that you'd eventually run into one of your sworn enemies, Elliott consoled herself afterward. These things happened. And it could have been worse. It could have been *him*.

But in the moment, all Elliott could think was *shit, shit, shit, shit, shit* as a wave of panic flooded her bones.

Violet looked just as stunned, her ruby-painted lips parting as she stood there loosely holding her soy latte—which would have a shot of vanilla, Elliott knew. And two sugars. She always drank her coffee so damn sweet.

"Hey," Violet said automatically.

"Hey," said Elliott, too stunned for anything else.

And then they just stood there awkwardly near the cream and sugar station as the coffee grinders whirled away.

It seemed for a moment that Violet wanted to say something else, but she didn't; she just ran a nervous hand through her jet-black asymmetrical bob. Elliott knew she should walk away, or yell at Vi, or curse her out, or *something*, but she couldn't seem to do anything more than stand there worrying the zipper of her leather jacket.

"Well . . . I gotta get to work," Violet said, quickly hurrying past.

And then she was gone, pushing her way out into the parking lot and leaving Elliott with a flurry of emotions: disappointment, nostalgia, rage, despair.

Emotions that haunted Elliott as she made her way down Anapamu Street toward Santa Barbara High, listening to Nirvana's "Come As You Are," officially in a foul mood.

It was bad enough to be spending any more time than was absolutely necessary at her school, but a complete travesty to do so on a game night. And not just any game night: it was the homecoming game, *and* the Big Game, aka Santa Barbara High versus their local rivals, San Marcos. A double whammy. Which meant the turnout would be even bigger than usual.

In all her years at Santa Barbara High, Elliott had *never* attended a Dons football game. Not even ironically. Everything about it—the cheerleaders, the toxic masculinity, the overinvested adults trying to recapture their days of youth—made Elliott want to barf. And yet there she was, on the precipice of strolling into her own personal hell.

When she reached the flagpole, which stood on a little island of grass inside the roundabout just across from the detached gymnasium and the adjacent staircase down to the football field, the other girls were already there. Chloe was leaning against the flagpole, wearing a long black dress and scrolling through her phone; Bea was squatting down stretching one hamstring, attired in her usual track jacket and jeans; and Madeline was pacing back and forth, arms tightly crossed against her chest, wearing a loose hooded windbreaker, wireframe glasses, and a Harvard baseball cap, her hair uncharacteristically curly and pulled into a low ponytail. All of which gave Elliott the impression that Madeline didn't want to be recognized.

And staring at the three of them, Elliott's first thought was, *What a rando assembly of girls.*

But her *second* thought—which came quick on the heels of the first—was *Yeah, but these are the girls that keep showing up for you.*

She could count on her coven-mates, she realized, in ways she could never count on Vi.

"Finally," Madeline said tightly when she spotted Elliott, eyeing the cup of coffee she was holding as if to say, *Oh, you had time to stop for a beverage but couldn't be bothered to* show up *on time?*

Okay, someone was stressed as hell. "Nice to see you, too," Elliott greeted. "And not to criticize your choice of location, but remind me why we're doing this *here*?" She scanned the throngs filing in, arching a brow at a cluster of popular senior girls she recognized who were taking selfies up against the chain-link fence, the bright stadium lights behind them. A stupid football game was just about the most public spot you could pick. What, were they going to cast out on the field, too?

"We're doing it *here* because the rival game between the Royals and the Dons is one he looks forward to playing in all year," Madeline explained, picking up her leather messenger bag.

"Wait," Bea clarified as she straightened. "He's *playing* in the game?"

"He's quarterback for San Marcos," Madeline replied evenly as she started off.

"Oh *shit*," Chloe snorted, sliding her phone away. "I thought he was just, you know, attending."

"Come on," Madeleine urged them from over her shoulder.

Elliott tugged at her black beanie as she caught up to Madeline, who led the way down the tree-shrouded staircase—despite it being *Elliott's* school. But Madeline was in close proximity to her ex and was clearly freaking out—albeit in her type-A Madeline way. She was kind of like a duck, Elliott had decided: all smooth glide on the surface and manic paddling underneath.

"I'm sure you have a plan here," Elliott whispered to her. "But I also can't help noticing you're leading us *toward* the football field, when there's an entire campus available to us, rife with—"

"I *do* have a plan," Madeline interjected, eyes straight ahead. "And I'd really appreciate it if you'd just trust me."

Elliott started to say something, then bit back her words. "You know what." She held up both hands. "You're right—this is your night. We're here to support you, so you lead the way."

Madeline glanced at her in slight surprise and adjusted her glasses. "Thanks."

Nearing the bottom of the staircase, the sounds of the band playing a pep-'em-up ditty and the cheerleaders leading the crowd in a rousing round of "Be—aggressive! Be, be aggressive! Hey!" grew louder, feeling very much to Elliott like a personal affront.

"Ugh, like football players *really* need their aggression stoked," Chloe muttered from under her breath. A sentiment Elliott wholeheartedly agreed with. Why did people even *attend* these events? Because of *tradition*? But what good was your tradition if it upheld the patriarchy?

After paying their entrance fees to the PTA mom guarding the walkway (a complete waste of nine bucks), the coven rounded the recently renovated football stadium and field (which cost thirty-nine *million* bucks, also a complete waste—they could be fighting climate change or housing the homeless with that cash), past the field house and the parked ambulance—seemed like any sport requiring *that* was a hard pass—and the snack bar, where a group of little kids were in line to load up on sunflower seeds and Skittles.

Elliott scanned the sidelines and found the line of Santa Barbara High cheerleaders—and there, being held high by a trio of girls, her pom-poms shimmering above her head, was Kaylie.

Come halftime, Elliott knew, Kaylie would change out of that uniform and into some equally ridiculous glittery outfit so that she could be paraded out with the other homecoming nominees to stand there and smile for the crowd as they awaited the announcement of who was voted Homecoming Royalty. Like they were all still living in 1955 or something.

The trio of cheerleaders boosted Kaylie up and she flew into the air, doing a complicated twist as she fell back down into their arms.

God, didn't it bother her, Elliott wondered. Cheering for the very high school boys who did so much freaking harm?

Fortunately, Madeline angled them away from the football field and the set of concrete stairs that led up to the new stadium seating—which was packed with students and sad, grown-ass adult fans who were embarrassingly doing *the wave*—and took the coven through the lower level, weaving around a pack of freshmen (fresh*persons*) who were awkwardly laughing at someone's joke. She continued around toward the back of the stadium.

"Wait." Chloe looked around in confusion as Madeline angled toward the bathrooms. "*What* are we doing?"

"Listen, she has a plan," Elliott assured her as Madeline pushed her way into the women's restroom like she owned the place.

Inside the white-tiled bathroom, a cluster of possibly middle-school-aged girls were standing before the row of mirrors, reapplying their lip gloss as they chatted with their friend in the first stall. They looked over as Madeline strode in and quickly appraised the other five empty stalls, like she was some kind of inspector.

She glared at the girls as she strode back across the room. "Get out."

"*Excuse* me?" said one of the girls in an offended tone.

Elliott was loving this zero-fucks version of Madeline, but she could also see that her method wasn't going to work.

She approached the girls. "I'm sorry, I realize this is awkward, but I'm kind of on the verge of a psychological breakdown here, and my friend"—she nodded toward Madeline—"is trying to help me out because I'm basically gonna self-implode any second. So could you all vacate *les toilettes* and give me some personal space to openly weep?"

"*O-kayyy.*" The girl laughed uncomfortably, glancing at her friends. Then she realized Elliott wasn't joking about the personal space part, and maybe not the psychological breakdown part, either. She motioned for the other two to follow her out. "Brittney, we'll meet you outside," she called.

Two seconds later, a toilet flushed, and a short brunette came out of the stall. She avoided eye contact with the coven as she rushed to wash her hands and then hurried out of the bathroom.

"Is this really the best spot?" Bea asked as Madeline force-closed the bathroom door. "It seems pretty . . . exposed. A bunch of other people are bound to walk in any second."

"Yeah," Chloe agreed as Madeline knelt on the bathroom floor and opened her bag. "Couldn't we just do it from inside one of our—"

"*This* is where we're doing it," Madeline insisted, pulling out three bright green clamp-looking things. She proceeded to wedge them under the bathroom door. Madeline had clearly scoped out this location ahead of time and planned accordingly. Elliott couldn't help being impressed.

"This is where Madeline wants to do it," Elliott reminded the group. "So we'll just try and be quick, just in case someone gets suspicious about the bathroom door being barricaded."

"In there," Madeline ordered, pointing toward the handicap stall at the far end.

"Your wish is our command, milady," Elliott commented as they shuffled into the oversized stall.

Madeline

"No." Madeline stopped Chloe as she arranged the ring of purple candles. "The circle needs to be perfectly symmetrical, and the candles equally spaced." Why was it that no one else ever seemed to take things as seriously as her?

"I'm pretty sure that's not written *any*where in the spell," Chloe defended.

"Now what?" Madeline asked, adjusting the candles herself. She had no patience for imperfection—not tonight of all nights.

"Hey," said Bea, in a gentle tone. "I think you might be feeling a little stressed-out being so near your target."

"Yeah," agreed Elliott. "Which is totally understandable. But maybe you should take a deep breath before we keep going."

Madeline started to argue, then realized Bea and Elliott were dead-on. She was so tensed up, her shoulders were practically near her ears.

"How about you breathe with me?" Chloe suggested.

Madeline nodded, then inhaled in time with Chloe, holding her breath a few seconds before slowly exhaling.

"Better?" Elliott asked.

"Yeah. A little, actually," she admitted. "Thanks."

"Okay." Elliott nodded. "'Now place the thirteen silver needles into the object of importance,'" she read. "'And then bind it with the silver cord.'"

Madeline grabbed the pack of sewing needles and, one by one, stabbed them into the teddy bear, particularly focusing on its button eyes and insidious smile. Stupid bear. Why had she ever thought it was so sweet to receive a ratty old childhood souvenir as a nine-month anniversary present?

Taking the silver necklace chain, she wound it round and round the bear's throat, pulling it tight until it looked like the bear was choking. How many times had she fantasized about doing this very thing to Derrick? Or scooping out his eyeballs with a tablespoon? Or forcing him to eat a pile of dog crap? There were a million ways she'd imagined torturing him. Sometimes it involved making his friends and family watch.

"'Then place the object of importance in the center of the ring of candles,'" Elliott instructed. "'And sprinkle the snakeskin ashes over it in a spiral.'"

Madeline placed the bear in the circle's center, then took the baggie from Chloe and sprinkled the ashes over the bear, feeling the grit of them between her fingers.

Sometimes she'd fantasized about burning down his house. How easy would it be to just sneak in at night while he was sleeping—she still knew the alarm code—leave a lit candle near his bedroom drapes, remove the smoke detector from above his door, and sneak back out? She could be in and out in five minutes flat, and no one would even notice. Of course, in this fantasy he always perished. And would it really be a loss? Did the world really need one more good-looking, college-bound, athletic, self-centered a-hole who'd just go on to ruin more girls' lives?

"And now," Elliott announced, setting the open book before Madeline, "you cast your spell."

Madeline straightened her spine and extended her right hand over the book. It wouldn't take much to channel her rage—it was right there beneath the surface nearly all the time—just as it would not take much to recall her—

"What the hell?" a girl's voice complained as the bathroom door rattled.

"Shit," Chloe whispered.

"It's always open," said another voice. "Did somebody *lock* it?"

"No, it doesn't lock," said the first girl. "Trust me, we've tried."

"Should we stop?" asked Bea, glancing at her coven-mates. "Maybe we should stop."

"No," said Madeline and Elliott in unison.

"Come on, let's start chanting," suggested Elliott.

And just like that, they did. No stalling, no complaining. Which made Madeline so grateful for her coven-mates, she could have practically hugged them. Except there was no time for that, and so she closed her eyes . . .

It happened a week before her eighteenth birthday, three weeks before senior year. Madeline had awoken early that morning to go to a kickboxing class with her mom, but first she'd checked her email.

The first item in her inbox was from a stranger named Andrew, and the moment Madeline saw the subject line her stomach dropped through the floor. "Ex-boyfriend revenge video on NaughtyXXX . . . ?"

I'm so sorry to have to be the one to tell you this, the email read, but I found your email after Googling your name. It seems as if someone (probably your ex-boyfriend?) posted a very detailed video of you on the internet in an attempt to defile your public image. I love porn and under other circumstances, this video could have been very enjoyable, but I found it to be in extremely bad taste as he could potentially ruin your life/career. I've already reported the video, so hopefully by the time you read this it will be gone, as he's included some relatively personal information that allows anyone to easily identify you, as I have.

There was a link, too, which Madeline knew better than to click.

First, she Googled "phishing scams" to see if there was anything going around that resembled this email (spoiler alert: there was no such scam). Then she Googled the stranger to see if he was legit. What if it was yet another attempt by Derrick to get her to respond? But this Andrew, who looked to be nineteen or twenty, seemed to be a real human and had a decently established YouTube channel where he reviewed video games.

Next, she typed in the website URL, her hands shaky, her body humming.

The home screen of the amateur porn site was mildly horrifying. Not that Madeline hadn't seen porn before, but she also hadn't seen *a lot*, and she'd certainly never imagined navigating to such a site looking for images of *herself.*

All the featured thumbnails were girls in obscene and embarrassing positions, the bad lighting and backgrounds clearly indicating they were in their own homes (or *someone's* home). One particularly depressing thumbnail was of a beautiful, chubby girl with sad green eyes who was down on her hands and knees in her underwear, her nose taped to her forehead to make her look like a pig.

As Madeline searched for her own name on the site, she felt disconnected from her body, a numbing cold sweeping through her insides.

The results turned up nothing, so she went to the MOST RECENT videos tab and began clicking through each page. And there it was on page eight. For Madeline on her birthday. Madeline clicked on the black thumbnail image, feeling another sweep of numbing cold.

It started innocently enough, with a slideshow of photos of Madeline from social media and text about where she went to school and the fact that she was a dancer, a former Girl Scout, and a devout Catholic. And then it cut to black and stated, in big bold font, that she was also a full-time slut.

Then it cut to *the video.*

She hadn't been *forced* into making it, exactly. But it had taken weeks of heavy persuading, and two shots of tequila, before she caved. She'd never done something like that before—she didn't even like looking at her body in the mirror, let alone having it documented as she was being *intimate*—but she trusted Derrick (or thought she did) and he'd really wanted to, and this was her long-term boyfriend, the person she'd lost her virginity to, and so she'd said yes. At the time she'd told herself she was cool with it; she could be that kind of girl who was super chill.

Except she wasn't super chill. She was the good girl. The obedient girl. The girl who'd been told her virginity was a pearl she could only give away once and to save it for marriage, which she'd already disobeyed. The girl expected to get straight As so she could get into an Ivy League school, so she could get her master's and have a big career and live a perfect life. The girl who sat beside her parents at Catholic Mass every Sunday and knew the words to all the hymns and would never, ever, *ever* dream of talking to them about sex.

She and Derrick only filmed themselves that once, and she hadn't let Derrick use his phone—no way was she going to have someone accidentally see it—but if he wanted to use his dad's decrepit old MiniDV camera so he could watch it later in the privacy of his room, well, maybe that was okay.

Except this was far from private.

Why hadn't she stolen the camera from him before they broke up? No, why had she ever filmed that video in the first place? Hadn't she feared this very thing when Derrick lost his mind post-breakup and started stalking her?

At first, he'd called and texted her incessantly, sometimes upward of fifty times in a row. And then he began following her places and spying on her with her friends. On more than one occasion, he broke into her car to leave her flowers or love poems or other "romantic" gifts, but eventually he cut all the cables in said car and slashed all four of Cameron Miller's tires when she went out with him to one single measly party.

Madeline skipped to the end of the video—which was nearly ten minutes long—and saw there were end cards. THIS WILL BE THE END OF MADELINE'S DIGNITY, they read. THE END OF HER SELF-RESPECT. THE END OF ANY RESPECT ANYONE WILL HAVE FOR MADELINE. AND THE BEGINNING OF HER NEW LIFE AS AN EXPOSED SLUT.

Madeline hit the pause button, having the presence of mind to take screen shots. And then she calmly but frantically emailed the website. She had to get this thing down.

And within three hours she had, the website apologizing and assuring her that it was a consensual site and not a place for revenge porn—especially if she was, as she'd identified, a minor. She Googled herself obsessively all day, but it was just all the usual stuff: her social media accounts, the articles she'd written for the school paper, the announcements for her dance recitals.

But that evening she got another anonymous email: **Hey hot stuff, nice tits. Can I get some action too?** Madeline's heart sped up and she quickly Googled herself again. The video had been taken down, yes, but it had now been posted to a revenge porn site. One that also posted her full name and her social media accounts and all her personal details.

And so, the emails and direct messages kept coming, from grown men in Thailand and Poland and Ecuador and Russia. Emails that sometimes included screenshots of Madeline, or worse, dick pics of the men themselves, all of which Madeline immediately deleted while adrenaline coursed through her blood.

At least, she reasoned later, Derrick hadn't advertised what he'd done to his *friends*. How much worse would her life be if people at their *schools* found out?

And yet, how easy would it be for someone she knew to stumble upon the video one day?

Derrick had publicly violated and humiliated her and turned her into a porn star against her will, that's what he'd done. He'd taken a private moment shared between two consenting people and thrown it out into the wider world so that anyone and everyone could leer at her and objectify her naked body doing intimate things, and then hunt her down and harass her. He'd known all about her body image hang-ups and discomfort with her own sexuality, steeped as she was in Catholicism and Christian purity culture. He'd been told point-blank that she felt deeply guilty over losing her virginity. And in the end he'd turned around and used those very things *against* her.

Some people called it nonconsensual porn, but Madeline had also seen the term *image-based sexual abuse,* which felt far more accurate. She'd even read an article that went so far as to call it digital rape, which was honestly what it felt like. She hadn't been physically assaulted or harassed like most of the girls in group—and sometimes because of that she felt like she wasn't worthy of being there, like what happened to her didn't count—but the trauma they all described was exactly how she felt.

Madeline had done everything right—straight A's, AP classes, ballet classes, youth group, volunteer work, a seemingly nice boy-friend who never pressured her or treated her bad . . . that is, until he did—and she'd always made an effort to never take a misstep, aware of girls who freely shared nudes with guys they liked and then had those same nudes circulated by the entire football team or posted to a "Thots of Santa Barbara" slut page.

And yet after all of that, here she was, an internet slut.

What would Harvard think when she sent in her applica-tion? What would future employers think? Would any decent guy ever want to go out with her once he did a quick Google search?

She'd had her whole life planned out, and now that life was ruined.

Kneeling on the cold, beige-tiled bathroom floor, Madeline squeezed her fist so hard she thought she might crack the thin gold band of her ring, wishing it was Derrick's head she was squeezing. Or, better yet, his balls.

He was out there on that field right now, just living his life like always, getting all that stupid acclaim. Not impacted by what he'd done, not the least bit concerned or ashamed. Meanwhile, she was the one expected to change her college application essay by *leaning into the defamation*—like she really wanted to ruin her clean slate by announcing to the Harvard admissions committee that one of her extracurriculars was filming a sex tape.

In front of her, the pages of the book began to change, shimmering and shining like the surface of a silver lake.

"Take this pain, take this rage," Madeline recited through gritted teeth. *"And cast it back on its creator."*

When Madeline let her fist fly open, a ball of violet energy burst from the book. It hovered there, spinning and turning, burning radiant and beautiful and bright, and then, with a howling rush, it took flight through the bathroom wall.

At that moment there was a roar from the crowd.

"Come on," Madeline urged, hurrying to her feet to unlock the stall door.

It was only as she crossed the small bathroom that she became aware that someone was now pounding on the door, complaining loudly to their friends.

"Stupid janitor probably locked up even though—"

Madeline pulled out the clamps and wrenched the door open.

A group of younger girls were just outside, one blond girl with her hands on her hips. When they saw Madeline, they instinctively stepped back and then looked past her into the bathroom.

"Excuse me." Madeline impatiently pushed past them. She could tell from the shift in the crowd's tone that something was happening out on the field.

Her heart sped up in anticipation as she strode around the stadium, pulling her hood up to shield her face.

People in the stands were now rising, watching the field in concern. As Madeline neared the field, she wove through kids standing on tiptoe and craning their necks. She could see that the game had stopped. The San Marcos players were gathered near the sideline closest to where she stood, and the cheerleaders on both sides of the field had taken a knee. Madeline could hear murmurs of concern being whispered among the crowd.

"I don't know," someone said. "They hiked the ball and it just bounced right off his helmet."

"What happened?" Madeline asked a kid standing nearby.

"Don't know." The kid shook his head. "Their quarterback just stood there all of a sudden like he'd forgotten how to play. He didn't even try to catch the ball."

Madeline covered her mouth, trying to suppress the grin that was spreading across her face.

As she pushed closer, she could see that some of the San Marcos coaches were gathered around one of the players, leaning close and talking to him in concern. Someone with a medical kit was jogging over to the group from across the field, a team doctor or maybe an EMT, and when they reached the gathering, the coaches parted to make way. In the center stood Derrick, his helmet off, his black hair all sweaty.

Derrick seemed to, unfortunately, be all in one piece, and he hadn't transformed into a pig or any other kind of beast. But even from where she stood, Madeline could tell he was distressed.

The EMT asked him a question, but Derrick turned in the wrong direction to answer. One of the coaches gently took Derrick by the shoulders and turned him back. And now Madeline could hear that Derrick was repeating something to the EMT over and over again, his voice rising in both octave and volume with every utterance.

"I can't see. *I can't see.*"

11

Elliott

Madeline spun around to face her coven-mates in triumph—and then froze. Elliott followed her sightline and spotted the blond girl from outside the bathroom standing at the far edge of the field house, pointing an accusing finger at Madeline.

"That's the girl," she told the security guard standing beside her. "*She's* the one who did it."

"Oh shit," Elliott muttered under her breath as the security guard strode toward them. He was tall and burly in his khaki uniform and security cap, all self-importance and white privilege. The kind of guy you could just tell was going to be trouble. Bea and Chloe instinctively stepped closer to Elliott as Madeline rejoined their group.

"Ladies," he greeted condescendingly, stopping before them. "You want to tell me why you barricaded yourselves in the little girls' room?"

Bea glanced at Elliott uncertainly.

"Are we in trouble, sir?" Elliott asked the security guard in her most innocent white-girl voice. She instinctively hated this dude.

"I think that's all gonna depend on what you have in your possession there." The security guard eyed Elliott's backpack, which Elliott was clutching in her arms. She resisted the urge to grip it tighter.

We didn't do anything, Elliott reminded herself. Well, not anything this guy could *prove*. And, okay, so they'd barricaded themselves in the bathroom—was that a crime?

Actually, maybe it was . . . Elliott couldn't be sure.

Okay, if he searched her bag, what did she have in her possession? The book, but she could lie and say she didn't know how to open the puzzle box. Her knife and Mace, but she could claim personal protection, which was 100 percent true. A lighter and a bunch of purple candles, but so what? Teen girls burned candles all the time.

An ash covered voodoo-looking teddy bear . . . with what Elliott was fairly certain was that football player's *name* stitched on the front.

Okay, that was *not* going to look good. And taken together with the candles and the knife and the fact that they'd been locked away in the bathroom . . .

Behind them, the crowd started cheering ferociously, drawing the security guard's attention. When Elliott glanced back, she saw that Madeline's ex was now being escorted off the field—and directly *toward* them. Oh crap.

Elliott sensed Madeline stiffen beside her, pulling the brim of her cap lower under the shadows of her hood, and so Elliott readjusted her position to block Madeline from view.

"All right, step aside, step *aside*," the security guard ordered the crowd, clearing space, which forced the coven closer to the field's fence as the small nation surrounding Madeline's ex—which included a coach, several players, the EMT, and a distressed couple Elliott assumed were his parents—hurried through the gate's opening and toward the parked ambulance.

"Should we make a run for it?" Chloe whispered while the security guard was distracted.

"That's going to look suspicious," Elliott whispered back.

"But we can't let him search Elliott's backpack," Madeline hissed.

Bea hesitated a moment, then nudged Elliott. "Give me your backpack," she muttered under her breath. Elliott handed it to her, eyes wide. With a look of resolve, Bea whispered, "Meet me at the school's sign out front."

And then, just as the security guard was turning back to face them, Bea took off at a sprint.

"Hey!" he shouted after her as she darted through the crowd.

"Go!" Elliott urged the other girls, taking off in the opposite direction.

"*Hey!* Get back here!" the security guard called after them.

Elliott glanced back just in time to see him looking from them to Bea, unsure which way to run.

Racing past the crowd gathered around the ambulance, Elliott led the girls behind the field house and darted toward the service entrance near the high school's pool. Bolting up the driveway and out into the adjoining neighborhood, they took off down the sidewalk. Any moment, Elliott panicked as they raced past the line of little Spanish-style homes, they would hear the thunder of the security guard's footsteps as he chased them down.

In fact, Elliott didn't dare slow, not until they'd rounded the corner and circled all the way back to the front of the school. Only then, when it seemed that he hadn't actually given chase, did she allow her pace to slow.

Adrenaline was coursing through Elliott's body and her heart was thundering in her chest as they neared the meeting point. What if he'd gone after Bea? Was there any way he could have caught her? And if he *had*, what were they going to do?

But as they reached the high school's sign, sure enough, there was Bea, crouched down between a couple of agave plants.

"Holy *shit*." Elliott laughed, panting as she neared and bent over to catch her breath.

"That was unbelievably close," said Bea, rising to her feet. Her voice was tinged with fear but also a hint of victory.

"That was . . . oh my God, that was *amazing.*" Madeline grinned, wrenching off her baseball cap and shaking free her ponytail.

"I can't believe we just did that!" breathed Chloe, doing an excited little hop. "Bea! You're freaking *fast.*"

"We should probably get out of here," said Bea, glancing in the direction of the stadium as she handed Elliott the backpack.

"Agreed," said Elliott.

"Wait, you guys," said Chloe. "I don't want to go *home*—let's go somewhere!"

"Yes!" agreed Madeline.

Elliott nodded. "I'm in."

"Where should we go?" asked Bea.

The beach was a logical choice. And so, they headed to their respective cars—Elliott riding in Madeline's Prius, where she immediately blasted the radio—and drove straight down Garden Street, which dead-ended at the ocean, and then followed Cabrillo Boulevard over to East Beach.

After parking in the lot for the Cabrillo Boathouse and East Beach Grill, a restaurant Elliott's mom used to love, they kicked off their shoes and raced out across the cool, rippled sand.

A few yards from the shoreline Elliott plopped herself onto the beach and breathed in the salt air, burying her toes in the damp sand as the other girls sat down around her.

"Oh my God, *look,*" said Madeline, pointing toward the ocean. Before them, the crashing waves were *glowing.* Lit up bluish-green as if someone had turned on a submerged neon light.

"God, that's beautiful," breathed Bea, wrapping her arms around her knees.

"Okay, I know that's just the red tide's bioluminescent algae or whatever," said Chloe, reaching into her purse. Red tides were an annual occurrence in Santa Barbara. "But, *guys*. Doesn't it feel like we're tapped in something cosmic? Like that's a sign from the Universe?"

And the thing was, Elliott *did* sort of feel that way. They just cast a revenge spell in the most public of locations and *completely* got away with it. She felt kind of invincible.

"We're fucking *witches!*" she howled at the top of her lungs, hands raised to the new moon shining above.

Chloe and Madeline howled along, too.

"Okay, maybe don't *announce* that," cautioned Bea, laughing a little.

"I think tonight calls for celebratory drinks," Chloe declared, producing a flask from her purse and unscrewing the lid. She took a big swig and then handed it to Elliott, who took a sip—vodka, which burned its way down her throat—before handing it to Madeline, who took a huge chug. Bea was more hesitant, taking the smallest of sips. Alcohol probably *wasn't* part of her athlete manifesto.

"Not to distract from the celebration," Bea said as she handed the flask back to Chloe, "but have the rest of you noticed your marks yet? Because mine has already changed. And it's looking a little . . . creepy." She held out her right palm.

In the moonlight, Elliott could see that the dark purple mark had grown to overtake Bea's entire palm, its tendrils now extending out onto her wrist. And when the rest of them flipped over their hands, they saw that their marks had done the same.

"Okay, that *is* kinda creepy," admitted Chloe, inspecting it closer.

"But also beautiful," argued Elliott.

"They're responding to our power," commented Madeline, her eyes glowing.

Bea looked less certain. "I mean, yeah, maybe, but . . . I know you think our marks aren't connected to the blowback, but I'm still not entirely convinced. And I'm just a little worried that *this*"—she nodded toward her palm—"means the blowback is going to be even worse this time around."

"You know what?!" Madeline announced fiercely. "Even if that's true, I don't fucking care! What we did felt *so* good. Because fuck him." She grabbed the flask from Chloe. "*Fuck. Him.*" She took another huge chug, wiping her mouth with the back of her wrist before handing the flask over. "He thought he could just get *away* with it? That he could slink off into the night and never have anything traced back to him? Never suffer? Think again, shit-face! I could be doubled over and sick for *weeks* and it would be worth it."

"God, I *hope* it never gets that bad," said Bea, looking a little disturbed at the idea.

"You know what," Elliott interjected, reaching for Chloe's flask and taking another sip. "I vote we don't worry about the blowback for tonight. This is a moment to celebrate. What we just pulled off was *amazeballs*. And I think we need to honor our fearless coven-mate Madeline, who marched us straight into a frickin' *football game*, pretty much the *heart* of the patriarchy, to practice *witchcraft*." She held the flask high.

"To Madeline!" cried Chloe, clapping wildly above her head. Elliott and Bea clapped, too, though Bea was slightly less enthusiastic. Madeline raised her arms above her head in victory and then fist pumped the air.

"Wait, wait, wait," said Elliott, passing the flask to Chloe and jumping to her feet. "I just need to recreate something here." She proceeded to imitate the security guard barging up to them and then exaggeratedly fumbling to decide which way to run. Her coven-mates doubled over in laughter.

"How freaked were you when he came up to us?" said Chloe.

"That dude was a piece of work," said Elliott, falling back onto the sand. Okay, she was *definitely* feeling the alcohol now.

"I was actually pretty scared," admitted Madeline.

"The whole *thing* was pretty nuts," said Bea, shaking her head. "I honestly can't believe you had us cast at a *football game*."

"Such a badass choice," said Chloe.

"Honestly, yeah," agreed Elliott. "To do that in front of all those people? These douchebags have no *idea* what's coming for them. They're so used to thinking of themselves as the heroes, but sorry, fuckers, your plotlines have been rewritten! They *all* deserve to be punished like that in the wide open."

"Seriously," agreed Chloe, taking another sip. "I mean, they just do the shit they do and get away with it and go on to live their lives like nothing even *happened*? Don't you all feel like . . . sometimes I feel like a crazy person, like I just made the whole thing up in my head even though I *know* I didn't. I mean, after he . . ." She shook her head as if trying to shake the memory away. "*After*, he just acted like nothing even happened. Like it was all just fine and normal and we were totally cool. And we were *not* cool." She snorted.

"That"—Elliott pointed at Chloe—"is classic gaslighting, my friend. Like that old-time movie where the dude makes the woman think she's going crazy by flickering the gas lights? And yeah. Been there."

Chloe handed the flask around and they each took another sip— everyone except Bea.

"I wish," Bea said softly, running a hand over one of her braids, "that every single one of them, anyone who's ever done anything, was haunted by what they did. I wish they all thought about it even half as much as we did."

"I wish it gave them nightmares," stated Chloe.

"I wish it made them change up their routines," added Elliott. "And triple-lock their doors at night. And sleep with knives underneath their pillows."

"I wish I could escape thoughts of what happened," Chloe admitted. "I hate that it's made me second-guess myself and every choice I've ever made."

"I hate that the burden's always on *us*," Madeline interjected. "Why are *we* supposed to be *good*? Because being a good girl isn't the same thing as being a good human, you know?"

"Totally," agreed Elliott. "It's like this straitjacket that gets placed on us, and we're supposed to just smile and say, *Thanks, I just love this jacket! It's such a flattering fit and such an unassuming color!*"

The other girls chuckled in appreciation.

It was the first time any of them had ever really shared anything about how they'd each been impacted. It felt surprisingly good to be talking like this.

"I just feel like I'm hiding all the time," Bea admitted, her gaze on the glowing waves crashing before them. "My parents don't know about what happened. And I don't want them to know because I'm worried . . . I'm worried they'll think *that's* why I'm gay," she admitted. "Which they also don't know."

"Shit, Bea," Chloe replied.

"Are you out to anyone yet?" Elliott asked carefully.

"Yeah, a few friends," Bea nodded. "And my brother. I mean, I'd been *planning* on telling my parents, but then *this* happened. And, I don't know, it's not like I think they'll even *care* that I like girls. It's more just that hiding one thing makes it hard to be open and honest about anything for some reason. I mean, what am I supposed to say? *Hey, Mom, Dad, I'm gay. Oh, and by the way, I was also molested.*" She shook her head and blew out a breath. "I feel like he's just tainted *every*thing."

The other girls nodded, not trying to make it better, just sitting with Bea in her anger.

"My dad's basically abandoned me," Chloe offered. "I haven't spent any real time with him in over two years. And even before then, I barely saw him after the divorce. And I don't think he even really cares. I think all along he just wanted little kids that looked like him, and now he has them, so he doesn't even need me." She sniffed and shook her head a little as she took another sip from the flask. "And of course, I can't say any of this to my mom because she was such a mess when he left her—like stay-in-bed-for-weeks-on-end kind of mess. She told me I was the only thing that got her through, that I was her light in the darkness. I mean, if she knew what I was really going through? She'd just blame herself and then it would be awful. So . . ." Chloe shrugged. "I don't tell her. It's like she needs me to be this happy, shiny, steady presence in her life."

"God," said Madeline, reaching for the flask and taking another sip. "Sometimes I feel like that with my parents. They never talk about this with anyone, but my older brother? They had to send him to rehab."

"Shit," said Elliott. "I'm sorry."

"Thanks," Madeline sighed. "Yeah, it sucks. I really miss him. And the scary thing is I don't even think it's going to work. Like, I really worry what's going to become of him. And I don't know, I guess sometimes the whole thing makes me feel like it's up to *me* to be the good one. Especially with my mom."

Elliott's gaze was on her Doc Martens, which used to belong to her mom. As did her leather jacket . . . and her Smiths T-shirt. And basically nearly everything else she wore. All her favorite music was her mom's favorite music as a teen. All the TV shows she watched were ones her mom loved in high school. She'd done everything she could to saturate her life with elements of her mom's lost youth, as if that would somehow connect them, as if it would somehow be enough.

But it wasn't, not by a long shot.

"You know, my mom," Elliott said finally. "She died when I was ten."

"Oh, Elliott," Madeline breathed. "I didn't know."

"Yeah," Elliott nodded. "When I was nine, she found a lump in her breast. She did everything the doctors wanted, a ton of radiation and chemo and a double mastectomy, but in the end none of it mattered. She fought so hard, and yet . . . ," Elliott trailed off, the memory of learning the cancer was terminal still fresh in her mind all these years later.

Her dad had picked her up from school that day, and the moment she saw him, Elliott knew something was wrong. His eyes were glassy, and he had that forced cheer that came from being super upset but not wanting her to worry. When she'd gotten home, Prudence was busy cooking an elaborate meal in the kitchen, a telltale sign that *she* was worried, and Elliott's mom was on the couch, her bald head propped up on a pillow, a blanket over her legs. She'd smiled at Elliott and beckoned her over, running a frail hand through Elliott's hair, tracing the shape of her face. Elliott, in turn, had absently traced the pink burn scar on her mom's forearm, just the way she'd always done her whole life. And then her mom told Elliott what they'd learned: the treatments weren't working and the cancer was still spreading. The doctors had tried everything, but there was nothing more they could do. They'd given her three months to live, maybe four. But in the end, she would be dead in less than two.

"Anyway," Elliott continued, letting out a sigh. "My dad . . . It was really, really hard on him. And after, he completely dedicated himself to parenting me. I'm basically all he has. And I guess I just didn't want to break his heart. So . . . I haven't told him about what happened to me, either. He might think it's his fault, like he wasn't a good enough dad or something. Plus, I just feel like it would be one more burden in his life that he absolutely does not need."

"God, Elliott," said Bea. "That's really heavy."

"Yeah," agreed Chloe. "I'm so sorry."

Elliott felt a hand on her back and glanced over to realize it was Madeline's.

They all grew quiet and contemplative, having each opened up and revealed a vulnerable part of themselves. It felt . . . unexpectedly good.

And for a moment Elliott had the thought that there was magic in this, too. In being together and finding connection in their coven. In refusing to be alone in the dark.

But almost immediately that good feeling morphed into feeling oddly . . . *exposed*. Like a turtle without its shell. Or maybe more like a hedgehog that had unballed itself and rolled over to reveal its soft belly. Whatever the metaphor, it wasn't a sensation Elliott particularly liked. She'd done the whole vulnerability thing with Vi and look where *that* had gotten her.

"Okay, enough of all our stupid talking," she declared, pushing the feelings away. "I need another drink. And then I need to get outta here."

She reached for the vodka, and that's when she noticed that her right palm—which was *also* feeling oddly exposed—was almost faintly . . . *shimmering*. And her mark . . . it looked *rosy lavender*. But when she blinked and looked again, it was back to normal. Or, you know, not *normal*, since her mark had now spread up her wrist, which *was*, in fact, kinda creepy, but normal*ish*.

"What?" said Chloe, clearly noticing Elliott acting weird.

"I—nothing."

Had she *actually* just seen that? Had her mark magically albeit temporarily transformed?

No, it had to just be the alcohol.

"Okay, clearly I'm pretty wasted." Elliott laughed, taking the flask from Chloe. Her movements had that slightly out-of-sync feeling, like her mind and body had disconnected and were now just sort of floating near each other.

"What time is it, anyway?" asked Madeline, checking her phone. "Crap. I should probably go," she announced, attempting to stand, which failed spectacularly and resulted in her sort of plopping over onto all fours.

"Oh my God," laughed Elliott.

"Okay, you should probably *not* drive," pointed out Bea.

"Shit," Madeline agreed, sitting back on her heels and running a hand over her face. "I am *drunk*." She widened her eyes as she attempted to unlock her phone. "I should text my friend Amalia. That's who my mom thinks I'm with anyway. She can get a ride over and drive me home."

"Okay, good," said Bea. "Chloe? Is there someone who can pick you up?"

Chloe waved a dismissive hand as she replaced the flask in her bag and struggled herself to her feet. "I'll just take an Uber home and come back for my car tomorrow. No biggie."

"Same," said Elliott. "I'll grab an Ubertoo. Uber, *too*. Ubertu." She laughed, snorting a little.

"Or Amalia could drop you off," Madeline offered. "It's on the way."

Elliott hesitated a second. *Was* it on the way? "Yeah, okay, sure. Thanks."

Bea rose to her feet, offering Elliott a hand to stand. Which Elliott took, her head reeling as she rose to her feet.

Back in the parking lot, Bea waited around as Chloe and Madeline each texted for their rides.

"It's really nice of you to wait," Elliott slurred, leaning against the hood of Bea's minivan.

"It's not a big deal," said Bea.

"You're just, like, *really* nice," Elliott commented.

Bea glanced at her, amused. "And you're really drunk."

Chloe's Uber was first to arrive. "Later, witches!" she called, waving to her coven-mates as she climbed into the back seat.

Bea checked the time on her phone as Chloe's Uber pulled away. "Shoot. I should probably go. I need to be home in time for curfew." She glanced at Madeline and Elliott slumped on the curb. "Are you two gonna be okay waiting here?"

Madeline waved Bea away like it was no big deal. "Amalia'll be here in, like, two minutes. We're *fine*."

"Okay," Bea said as she unlocked her driver's-side door. "Hey. Is it cool if I text each of you later? Just to make sure you all got home safely?"

"Against the rules," Elliott declared, wagging a finger at Bea. "But I'll allow it. See you Thursday."

"See you Thursday," Bea agreed as she climbed into her minivan.

Elliott and Madeline watched as Bea's car pulled out onto Cabrillo Boulevard, the salty breeze lifting their hair and yet somehow not touching them. In the distance, Elliott could hear the crashing waves.

Madeline looked over at Elliott, an expectant look on her face.

Elliott raised her eyebrows. "Yes?"

Something about the glow in Madeline's eyes reminded Elliott of that first time they'd hung out, at Anastasia's Asylum. "We're really doing it." Madeline grinned.

Elliott smiled widely. "Fuck *yeah* we are."

"I just . . ." Madeline shook her head, then threw her arms around Elliott.

"Whoa." Elliott laughed as Madeline squeezed her tight.

"Thank you," Madeline breathed. And her words had such deep intensity and emotion that for a moment Elliott thought she might cry.

"Hey," Elliott said as Madeline relinquished her hold. "You don't have to thank *me*. Tonight was all you."

Madeline inhaled deeply and let the air out through her nose, then tilted her head back to look up at the stars. For a moment she was quiet. "We're fucking *witches*," she whispered quietly, to Elliott, to the night sky.

Elliott glanced at her, then tilted her own head back to gaze up at the stars. "Yeah," she agreed. "We *are*."

12

Madeline

That weekend Madeline was pleased to discover that her hypothesis about their marks being unrelated to the blowback seemed to be accurate, because while the marks had grown, this time around the blowback wasn't nearly as bad. In fact, Madeline would argue it was downright mild.

It certainly wasn't as bad as the hangover she woke up with Saturday morning and had to hide from her parents—whom she'd just barely slipped past Friday night, thanks to Amalia.

Her parents were too distracted that Saturday morning to really notice her hangover, because news of Derrick's "tragedy" had reached them via the local news. And while, outwardly, they were both shocked and saddened, she overheard them discussing how this might impact a possible trial. "If we press charges now," her mom worried, her voice edged in irritation, "it might be seen as insensitive." Which honestly gave Madeline mixed feelings. She by no means wanted a trial, and yet *they'd* be the insensitive ones? After what Derrick had done?

It was disgusting to think about him receiving *any* level of sympathy. In fact, at church that Sunday, Madeline almost snorted when someone had the audacity to offer up Derrick Bolton's name in prayer just before Communion. Seeing all those heads bowed in sorrow sent sparks of rage through Madeline's blood, which she channeled by squeezing her right hand around the mark of the coven. A mark she now considered a badge of honor.

During coffee hour, Bev Anderson, whose daughter went to school with Derrick, had the nerve to come up to Madeline and her mom and fill them in on all the details about Derrick's condition— which Madeline would have *relished* listening to if it weren't for Bev's mournful tone.

"That poor boy." Bev shook her head. "Mingyu and Doug were in the hospital with him *all* weekend."

"Is it permanent?" Madeline blurted out, keeping her expression even as her mother raised an eyebrow (*be polite, Madeline*).

"They don't know yet," Bev replied. "They're bringing up an ophthalmologist from UCLA to see what, if anything, can be done."

"Well, thank you for filling us in," Madeline's mother commented, clearly ready for the conversation to be over. Either because she found post-church small talk exhausting or because she was worried about what else Madeline might say.

"Of course." Bev nodded. "I know you'll all keep Derrick in your prayers."

Oh, Madeline would keep him in her prayers, all right. She'd pray that an old-school vengeful god struck him down with a bolt of lightning and finished off the job she'd begun.

In the car ride home, Madeline's mother seemed particularly irritable. "Madeline," she said halfway through the drive as she reapplied her lipstick in the visor mirror. "When we get home, I need you to print out your revised essay so I can proofread it. I'm assuming you're finished by now."

"No," Madeline answered honestly.

"*Madeline,*" her mother eyed her in the mirror. "I need to overnight your application *tomorrow.*"

"Rebecca," Madeline's dad reasoned. "We can always just wait until Harvard's normal admission period."

Her mother flipped the visor mirror back up in response.

Madeline hesitated a moment. Was she really going to do this? "Mom. I am *not* changing my essay."

"*Madeline*—"

"I'm really proud of what I wrote. And being a dancer is a huge part of my identity. Why should I let what *Derrick* did suddenly define me?"

Her mother turned in her seat to look at Madeline, momentarily at a loss for words. "We talked about this," she insisted.

"Yes, well . . . I changed my mind," Madeline responded firmly. "I'm sending Harvard admissions my original essay, and that's final."

Elliott

That Sunday afternoon Elliott was displeased but unsurprised to find Prudence whirling around their house like a white tornado, cleaning the drapes (why?), reorganizing the pantry (unnecessary), and cooking up a huge Sunday dinner. As if they were a big jolly family who just *loved* gathering around the dinner table every weekend, instead of a sad, grieving, sometimes-disgruntled trio.

Elliott's dad was locked away in his home office, finishing up a project for one of his clients—an advertisement for a podiatrist or something equally ridiculous—and so Elliott had to brave Prudence by her lonesome. Which she mostly handled by hiding out in her room. But eventually the need for sustenance won out.

As she entered the kitchen, Elliott was hit with the aroma of garlic and basil mixed with Prudence's powdery perfume—not the greatest combo. Prudence was sitting at the kitchen table, her KISS ME, I'M SICILIAN apron pulled on over her church attire, her legs crossed primly as she read the local paper. A giant vat of marinara was on the stove.

"Well, there she is," she said pleasantly, folding her newspaper.

"Hey, Grandma," Elliott greeted, opening the dishwasher to pull out a possibly dirty bowl.

"You hungry, Ellie?" Prudence asked, rising to her feet.

"Yeah, but I'm just gonna grab some cereal."

"Nonsense. How about some sfingi?" she asked, pulling a covered bowl from the fridge. "I have the dough ready to go."

"That's okay," Elliott replied, but Prudence was already pouring oil into a pan and turning up the heat. And once she got started, there was no stopping her, plus, sfingi happened to be Elliott's favorite childhood treat, so she relented and took a seat at the kitchen table. Soon the room was filled with the sizzling and pop of the oil and the pleasant aroma of fried dough.

"So," Prudence said as she used a spatula to transfer the last of the little pastries to a napkin-covered plate. "How's school going?"

"You know, okay." Elliott shrugged.

"You like your classes?" Prudence asked, dropping the cooled sfingi into a paper bag that she'd filled with sugar.

"They're okay."

Prudence shook the paper bag to coat the sfingi. "And how's that friend of yours?" she asked carefully, placing the finished sfingi on a plate. "Victoria, is it?"

"Violet."

"Right, Violet." She set the plate and a cup of coffee in front of Elliott.

"Thanks, Grandma. Yeah, we don't really talk anymore," she explained.

"Oh," Prudence replied in surprise, taking a seat across from her. "Well, I'm sorry to hear that. You two were so close."

Elliott shrugged and popped one of the sfingi into her mouth, soothed by its warm sweetness. Sfingi were essentially just small airy donuts, but for Elliott, they took her back to a simpler time. And something about having Prudence make Elliott's favorite childhood treat—one that she knew for a fact Prudence used to make for Elliott's mom—filled Elliott with tenderness.

"Yeah, well. It is what it is," she replied. "But I've made some new friends."

"Oh, you have?" Prudence arched her eyebrows, pleased, and took a sip of her coffee.

"Yeah. Actually, I met them at group," Elliott confessed, taking a sip of her own coffee.

Prudence seemed slightly uncomfortable with the mention of group. "Well, that's . . . I'm so pleased to hear that, Ellie."

Elliott traced her finger through the sugar on her plate. "And actually, Grandma, I've been thinking lately . . . maybe I *should* tell Dad."

"Oh." Prudence shifted in her seat. "Well, I don't know. I don't think he needs to hear about that unpleasantness, sweetheart," she said in a low voice. "Like you said, he's already been through so much. He'll only blame himself for whatever happened. And you *have* your group."

Elliott sat there a moment, the sweetness of the sfingi turning bitter in her mouth. Was she mad because Prudence still so clearly thought what had happened to Elliott was shameful and somehow *her* fault? Or was she mad because deep down some part of her wondered if Prudence was right?

"'*That unpleasantness*'?" Elliott repeated, pushing her plate away from her. "Actually, Grandma, it's called *sexual assault*. Actually, no. You know what it's called? It's called *rape*. And euphemisms like that only undermine its seriousness and uphold rape culture."

Prudence looked at Elliott in surprise, as if she hadn't expected her to speak so openly of *the incident that shall not be named.* Elliott stared back. It felt surprisingly good to speak her mind.

But almost immediately Elliott noticed two things: one, Prudence had what looked like tears in her eyes, and two, her gaze had moved beyond Elliott.

"Daniel," she said in surprise.

Elliott looked over to find her dad standing in the doorway. Oh crap. How long had he been standing there? How much had he heard?

"Hey," he greeted seriously, looking from Prudence to Elliott. "What's going on in here?"

He didn't seem *too* overly concerned, which Elliott hoped was a good sign. "Nothing," she said, taking a sip of her coffee.

"We were just discussing a story in the news," Prudence lied, picking up and unfolding her newspaper.

"We have a difference of opinion," Elliott explained, grabbing her plate and taking it to the sink.

"Clearly," her dad commented, tracking Elliott as she crossed the room.

"Anyway, homework calls." Elliott gave her dad a peck on the cheek before retreating to her bedroom. She only hoped he hadn't heard enough to tip him off about her own *unpleasantness.* The thought of which made her even madder at Prudence.

Bea

Across town, Bea wasn't faring well.

All weekend long she'd had a low-grade stomachache. And that Sunday night, she once again found herself lying wide awake. As she had the night prior . . . and the night before *that.* In her head, she kept replaying Friday's football game, over and over again.

I can't see. I can't see.

And she kept thinking about those boys—Arman and Trevor—who'd been carted away from the party, both of them crying and distraught. She didn't even know exactly what they'd done; she'd just convicted them without question and altered their futures. And was that okay? Was that, in fact, justice?

Yeah, but did she *really* need to know the details to know they were guilty? She believed the girls in her coven; she trusted that these guys were just as deserving of punishment as *him*.

And yet . . .

Bea kept seeing Maya's face again and again, that look of terror as she watched her father collapse at the dinner table. She couldn't get it out of her head.

Apparently, *his* show had been indefinitely postponed, and he still wasn't entirely himself: of all things, he'd forgotten how to paint. And Margaret had reported to Bea's mom that the kids were now having nightmares.

As Bea stared at the ceiling, her mind whirling, she considered waking up Otis—his mere presence was always a comfort, and he somehow always knew the exact thing to say to put her at ease.

And yet . . .

Was it unfair to always burden her twin? She thought of his words: *Maybe I'm not the only one who should know.*

Rolling on to her stomach, Bea grabbed her phone off the nightstand, hesitated, and then sent a text.

r u up?

Less than ten seconds later, Elliott texted back. yuuuup.

Can u talk?

Bea's phone rang almost instantly.

"Hey," she answered.

"Hiya," greeted Elliott.

"Sorry for the late-night text," Bea apologized as she rolled onto her back. "It's just . . . I can't sleep."

"*Ohhhh.*" Elliott half laughed. "Welcome to the club! Well, actually, I can *fall* asleep, I just consistently wake with night terrors."

"Jeez, really?"

"Yeah. *Super* fun. I bolt awake in a cold sweat at, like, three a.m. Every night. Four months and counting . . ."

"God. Well, I just end up lying in bed, my mind spinning," Bea admitted.

"That *also* sounds super fun," Elliott enthused. "Look at us, we are *really* winning in the circadian rhythm category."

Bea snorted. "Yeah."

"So . . . ," Elliott said in a quieter voice. "How are you feeling after Friday night?"

"Oh. Um. I don't know. Not too bad," Bea said vaguely, highly aware of Otis just next door. Their walls were thin, so she wasn't about to go into detail about how while the blowback had seemed surprisingly mild, her ever-changing mark was actually starting to freak her out.

"Same," Elliott agreed. "I coughed up some stuff but way less than last time. Which is kind of unexpected but a relief."

"Yeah," agreed Bea.

"Hey. On Friday night . . ." Elliott paused. "Did your mark . . . Did it ever change color?"

"What? No. At least, I don't *think* so. Why, did yours?"

"Well . . . for a second I *thought* mine looked all shimmery and almost *pink.*"

"Okay, that's strange. When was this?"

"I guess right around the time we were all sharing stuff and I talked about my mom?"

"Huh." Bea considered this, wondering if the timing had anything to do with it.

"But I think I must have just imagined it," Elliott added. "I mean, I *was* pretty drunk."

"True," said Bea. Though she couldn't help thinking, *Why wouldn't it shimmer and turn pink?* At this point anything felt possible. Which wasn't particularly comforting.

"Anyway . . . ," said Elliott, as if wanting to change the subject. "Since we're both awake, you wanna Watch Party a dumb movie together and ridicule the dialogue?"

Bea couldn't help smiling into the phone. "Sure," she agreed, getting up to find her Chromebook. "I'm also rather excellent at pointing out continuity fails."

"Perfect," declared Elliott. "Let the nocturnal film critique commence."

Chloe

At school that Monday, Chloe was feeling kind of nervous. Which had nothing to do with the blowback or the fact that her mark was now creeping up her wrist. No, it had everything to do with the fact that she was on her way to the principal's office.

Actually, when it came to the blowback, the weekend hadn't been at *all* bad. She'd had to bow out of the Montecito Club Saturday morning, claiming a migraine—but that was entirely due to her hangover. Plus, a morning of lounging in bed had been kind of nice. Though she'd spent *waaayyy* too much time scrolling through other people's posts, thinking how their lives looked so happy and uncomplicated, the opposite of hers. Which put her in a bit of a funk. Other people just seemed to have it easier, like they'd been slipped the memo of how to get life right. Chloe'd had to offset that funk by charging a new pair of black suede boots and a vast array of essential oils to her dad's credit card. *Thanks, Daddy!*

Though the retail therapy hadn't *really* helped. Chloe obviously knew that a new pair of cute boots wasn't going to fix her life. Which got her thinking about how she appeared to the outside world. Maybe *other* people thought *she* seemed so happy and uncomplicated. Maybe *other* people were hiding secrets that made *them* feel alone. And maybe . . . maybe she should try to do something about it.

As she walked through her rambling, tree-shrouded campus, with its many courtyards and winding paths that led between the cottagey tiled-roof buildings, Chloe did 4-7-8 breathing to calm her body. Though by the time she reached the Head of Office building, she still felt anxious, so she sat on the little wrought-iron bench outside and did a quick round of EFT.

Feeling as calm and composed as she was ever going to, Chloe let herself into the office.

Principal Dinaberg, a sixtysomething white woman with silver hair, was seated at her desk, wearing a classic coastal grandmother ensemble—crisp white button-down, ivory linen pants, a beige cashmere sweater draped over her shoulders—as she typed something on her computer. She looked over and sat back in her seat. "Good morning, Chloe," she greeted, taking off her tortoiseshell reading glasses.

"Hi, Mrs. Dinaberg." Chloe smiled.

"What brings you here this morning?" Mrs. Dinaberg was always reminding students about her open-door policy, but Chloe had never dreamed of actually taking her up on the offer.

"Well." Chloe sat down in one of the two mid-century modern chairs on the other side of the desk. Mrs. Dinaberg's office was a mix of modern furniture and folksy art, with plaques and diplomas and student photos on the walls. "I have a suggestion, actually."

"Wonderful." Mrs. Dinaberg sounded genuinely pleased. "I love student recommendations."

Chloe nodded, swallowing. Her throat suddenly felt very dry. "So . . . I think we need to have a school assembly. To address sexual assault."

Mrs. Dinaberg raised her eyebrows—not as if she were shocked or offended, but more like she hadn't expected that particular suggestion on a Monday morning, or from Chloe. "Okay." She nodded. "Say more."

"Well, you know that local rape trial? And the recent verdict?"

"I do," Mrs. Dinaberg said seriously.

"Well, I think a lot of people feel pretty frustrated about it . . . and like we need to be doing more. And I just thought, we've never really talked about something like that as an entire school. But . . . maybe we should? And, like, not just once. But regularly."

Principal Dinaberg nodded slowly, her hands templed on her desk. "Well, creating an impromptu school assembly—let alone an entire series—would require buy-in from the entire staff. And we'd need to reallocate part of our budget."

"Right." Chloe nodded, already preparing herself for disappointment.

"We'd also likely want to notify parents ahead of time, as a courtesy," she added, thinking aloud. She was quiet a moment, as if running numbers through her head. And then she nodded once. "Okay."

"What?" said Chloe. "Okay . . . as in you'll do it?"

"Well, I can't guarantee anything quite yet, but I'm going to mention it in our staff meeting later today," said Principal Dinaberg. "A few of us have discussed introducing something of the sort, but having the voice of our students behind it creates a deeper sense of urgency. You're right to feel that we should be doing more, Chloe. Some of our student organizations discuss these matters on a one-off basis, but that trial impacted our entire community, and as such we should discuss it as a community. Thank you for bringing this idea to my attention."

"Oh, yeah. Of course," Chloe said, surprised that she'd had such an immediate impact. She felt surprisingly emboldened. And as she got up from her seat, she couldn't help glancing down at her mark.

Elliott

At school on Monday, the fact that it was Halloween was practically a footnote at Santa Barbara High; everyone wanted to discuss the San Marcos football game and the quarterback who'd suddenly gone blind. A point of discussion that made Elliott proud. Though some other drama must have been afoot, because Elliott noticed a cluster of seniors in the main hall looking at their phones in shock and had to wonder what *that* was all about.

"I heard he's still in the hospital," Elliott overheard Sarah Martinez, who sat in front of her in first period, whisper to Annabelle Walker, who sat one row over.

Like many students, Sarah and Annabelle had come dressed in their Halloween costumes: Sarah, a sexy superhero; Annabelle, a sexy . . . Renaissance fair participant? Normally, Elliott *loved* Halloween—she and Vi always DIYed their costumes (Thelma and Louise had been her personal favorite) and then streamed cheesy horror films and binged on candy.

This year, however, Elliott's mood was about as dark and deflated as Sarah's reject-bin superhero cape. There was no point in lying to herself: Elliott really missed Vi.

"I guess he was being scouted to play basketball for different colleges, too," Sarah was commenting.

"Wait, *basketball*? Don't you mean football?"

"No, apparently he *also* played basketball and was really good. But now his chances of being recruited are, like, zero."

"Oh my God, that is *so* sad," Annabelle responded, twirling a strand of her long dark hair. "Can you imagine? One second he has his whole future ahead of him and then, just like that, it's totally— Oh my God, Elliott," Annabelle cut off.

Elliott looked up from doodling in her notebook. "What's up?"

Annabelle had a weirded-out look on her face. "There's something coming out of your nose."

Elliott put a hand to her face and felt something slippery near her nostril.

"Where are we going, Miss Brandt?" Mr. Trudeau asked as Elliott strode out of the classroom, one hand covering her nose.

"*D'Angelo*-Brandt," she corrected, not slowing down. "And the bathroom."

When she reached the girls' bathroom, she pushed her way through the swinging door and went straight to one of the stalls, locking herself inside. Pulling her hand away, she braced herself, ready to see dark purple.

But to her relief, her fingers came away red. It wasn't blowback; it was just a good old-fashioned nosebleed.

Which made Elliott realize that some part of her had still been anticipating the blowback would return and be even worse. Was she just paranoid? Or did she somehow unconsciously feel that she deserved to be further punished?

At that moment her phone buzzed as a text came through.

It was from Bea to the entire group, and it sent a chill down Elliott's spine. Just two letters: FP. Their code to meet at the park that night.

Was *her* blowback getting worse?

Or maybe one of their victims had *died*? Bea's target? Or one of the kids from the party?

Or what if someone had discovered what they'd done? Elliott's stomach tightened.

No, that was ridiculous. Surely, Bea would have sent an even more urgent text.

But *something* had happened. And Elliott had a sinking feeling it was *not* good.

13

Elliott

By the time Elliott Ubered to Franceschi Park that evening—passing front porches glowing with jack-o'-lanterns and trails of costumed kids out trick-or-treating with their parents, all of which filled Elliott with a homesick ache—she knew *exactly* why Bea must have sent that text. Because by the end of first period, the gossip mill at Santa Barbara High had swiftly transitioned from the blind football player to a new topic, one that filled Elliott with burning rage.

When she arrived at the park, the other girls were already near the benches—even Bea, who had her arms crossed over her chest and was wearing an enraged expression that mirrored Elliott's.

Bea met Elliott's gaze. "I'm guessing you heard."

"Oh, I heard, all right," Elliott confirmed in disgust, adjusting her backpack strap. "Except, how did *you* hear?"

"Kaylie's parents go to the same church as my parents," Bea explained. "My mom got a call from the church phone tree this morning because her parents wanted support."

Elliott hadn't known Bea and Kaylie were in any way connected, let alone that their parents went to the same church. It had just never come up. Then again, she'd never mentioned her own childhood connection to Kaylie.

"Wait." Chloe held up a hand. "*What's* going on?"

"Yeah, would one of you like to *please* fill us in?" Madeline said in thinly veiled irritation.

Elliott took a breath as she looked from Madeline to Chloe. "Kaylie got doxxed."

"*What?*" Chloe's lips parted in shock.

"Oh shit," Madeline breathed.

Bea nodded toward the mansion. "We should talk down there . . ."

Once they were seated down beside the mansion, Elliott filled the coven in on the details she'd gleaned over the course of the day.

Friday night, just hours after Kaylie was crowned homecoming royalty, someone posted a bunch of Craigslist sex ads to Santa Barbara and the surrounding Central Coast towns, impersonating Kaylie. She had a "rape fantasy," the ads claimed, and she wanted men to come find her and "not take no for an answer." The ad included her email, phone number, and home address.

Almost immediately Kaylie began receiving a barrage of lewd and abusive emails and texts. And that weekend two different men showed up at her house, which was just beyond freaky. Kaylie was at the homecoming dance at the time and her parents were home to deal with the situation, but they obviously weren't taking any further chances. By Sunday night they'd packed up their family and left town. They hadn't even told anyone where they were going or if or when they'd be back.

"I can't believe it," Madeline muttered, her face twisted in disgust.

"Except that's not all," Elliott informed them.

As if the ads weren't terrible enough, someone had *also* posted a video to social media that weekend. The *same* video filmed by Kaylie's rapist. Except this time it had a photo of Kaylie's face pasted onto her body, along with her full name and the words "LYING SLUT" pointing toward her, along with dubbed-in porny-sounding female moans.

The video's title was "How well do you really know your Homecoming Queen?"

"That's just . . ." Chloe shook her head. "I can't even . . . I mean, *fuck.*"

For a moment, the coven sat in silence. There was just the quiet of the evening—dogs barking, the distant laughter of trick-or-treaters, the wind whispering through the trees—and the weight of their collective rage.

All this time, Kaylie had just been trying to get on with her life, trying to manage things in her own way, trying to get back to some semblance of normal, whatever that looked like now. And after everything she'd been through, didn't she *deserve* a little fucking normalcy?

Except now someone had gone and done *this.*

Elliott remembered the first time she heard Kaylie share in group. It was the first time the group had learned that *Kaylie* was Emily Doe. She'd raised her hand and then hesitated when called upon.

"This is a lot harder than I thought," she'd admitted out loud.

"You're doing fine," Mary had assured her.

"So . . . the guy who hurt me," Kaylie had started. ". . . what I've never said in here is that my parents . . . we actually pressed charges against him. And I'm going to have to take the stand. And I . . . I'm a little scared to be saying any of this in here, because . . . because no one knows it's me, that *I'm* the victim. I mean, you've probably all heard about the case in the news?"

The other girls had nodded, registering exactly what Kaylie was talking about. The way Mary had nodded, Elliott got the distinct impression that she'd known all along, like she'd had a conversation with Kaylie and her parents when Kaylie first joined or something.

"Anyway," Kaylie continued. "I'm pretty freaked out about court, and I just needed to say that out loud. I know I need to do this—I *want* to do this, so that I can tell my story, and so justice can be served. But also, another part of me just wants to get back to normal, or you know, like you said, Mary, a *new* normal—and I want my parents to get back to their lives, too. They've been so supportive and amazing, but their lives have been *so* disrupted and they've spent *so* much money on attorney fees. Anyway . . . that's all. I just . . . I needed to say that. Thanks for listening and being here for me."

Of course, in the end there was no real justice—not even for a girl like Kaylie. Her rapist had gotten off with a slap on the wrist and a lament that he'd "made a mistake," which was no reason to "ruin his future." And Kaylie was left to pick up the pieces of her old life and try to construct a new one.

Except how the hell was a person supposed to do that when the world kept smacking you down?

Elliott looked up at the Franceschi mansion, nearly swallowed up by the darkness, once so grand and beautiful and now a complete ruin. Its windows smashed out and boarded up, its plaster crumbling. Didn't anyone fucking *care*?

"I never really liked her," Elliott admitted out of nowhere. "I mean, don't get me wrong, I always thought she was really nice. We went to elementary school together, actually. I never told you all that. Though we were never friends. But I don't know, she always seemed so cheerful and girly and *basic*. And to be honest, I think I kind of judged her? For not joining our coven, for wanting to just get on with her life. But now . . . I mean, now I feel like she really *is* a fucking badass. For hauling his ass to court, yeah. But also, for just continuing to hold her head high."

"I know," Chloe agreed. "I always think about what it must have been like for her, sitting in that courtroom, having to tell her story with him sitting right there. Having to relive her worst moments with him staring at her. And then to basically be told that none of it mattered, that her *rapist's* future was more important than hers. I mean, three months in juvie, one hundred hours of community service, and a year of *probation*? Do you know how long someone gets for being caught with an illegal controlled substance? One *year* in *jail*. And *still* she somehow managed to keep going."

"And she had to hear all that *talk*," added Madeline. "I mean, even when she was anonymous, her story was still public. She still had to hear all those opinions about Emily Doe and whether she 'asked for it.' She still had to hear people question her experience and call her a slut."

Bea hugged her knees to her chest. "But do you ever wonder . . . I know I'm probably not supposed to say this, but do you ever feel in some ways that reporting it just made it worse for her? I mean, if a girl like *Kaylie* can't even get justice and then ends up totally targeted, then what chance do the rest of us have? What's the point in putting yourself out there if you're either not believed or you're just dragged through the mud? I keep wondering if she wouldn't have been better off just *not* saying anything."

"No," Elliott interjected adamantly. "That's not the problem, *we're* not the problem. Whether we report it or we don't, whether we press charges or not. Everyone's got a fucking opinion about what we're supposed to do and how we're supposed to handle the shit that happens to us. But that's all beside the point, and it's no one's fucking business! The *problem* is these assholes, and that they *keep* being assholes, and that they never admit to a fucking thing they've done, and the system enables it!"

"We have to take action," Madeline declared, her face bent into fiery determination.

Which wasn't even a question; *of course* they had to take action.

"Yes." Elliott nodded. "If there's going to be *any* justice, then it's up to us."

"So, we cast a spell on Kaylie's rapist," Chloe agreed. "*And* on the judge—"

"And on whoever did *this* shit," Madeline cut in. "We just need to figure out who."

"Oh, I *know* who," Elliott informed them.

"You *do*?" Chloe asked.

"Yeah." Elliott nodded again. "And, actually, it makes the whole thing even worse."

That afternoon Elliott had tracked down Kaylie's best friend and fellow cheerleader, Breanna Hernandez, in the senior parking lot. Breanna had been reluctant to talk—that is, until Elliott confided that she and Kaylie were both in group.

Apparently, Kaylie's rapist had dated someone in their year—Amber Tuffalo, an honors student and member of the tennis team. They'd been on-again, off-again last year and, at the time of Kaylie's rape, were on the outs. But Breanna had heard they'd gotten back together during the trial, which was just *beyond*. Apparently, Amber was adamant that the whole thing was a lie, that whichever "slut" accused him was just mad that he didn't want to be with her. And Breanna was pretty sure Amber must have found out that Kaylie was Emily Doe, because about a month ago Kaylie got an anonymous text basically saying, *You're just jealous he's not yours*. Plus, Breanna knew for a fact that Amber had a copy of the video; she'd overheard her talking about it.

"A fucking *girl* did this?" Chloe said in disgust when Elliott finished filling them in. "Like, I don't know why I'm surprised. It's not like girls don't slut-shame other girls all the time, but *still*, this is just so . . . I mean, this is *terrible*."

"Well, she's going down," Madeline said definitively.

"The only thing," said Bea, and Elliott prepared herself for an argument. Bea, as the cautious one, would likely reject the plan. "Is that it's Elliott's turn next." She looked at Elliott. "If we do this, you'll have to wait another seven days to conjure your spell. Are you sure you don't want to go first, and then we can come back to Kaylie?"

On the one hand, Elliott had waited far too long—not just within the coven, but during all those soul-crushing days prior. She was *more* than ready to take her pain and rage and cast it back on the one who'd created it.

But on the other hand, Kaylie deserved vengeance. And it felt incredibly urgent that the people responsible for hurting her pay for what they'd done.

If Elliott's coven had the means, that meant they had the responsibility. It was up to them to take a stand and deliver a response that was not only forceful but *swift*.

"No, I've waited this long," Elliott assured her coven. "I can wait a little longer. Let's do this. Let's get revenge for Kaylie."

14

Elliott

"Who's going to summon the spell?" asked Chloe as Elliott pulled the puzzle box from her backpack and extracted the book.

"I think we should try and summon as a group," suggested Madeline.

"That didn't work the last time we tried," pointed out Bea.

"True," said Madeline. "But I feel like the counter-spells just weren't the right path."

"Well, I for sure think the book will be in support of *this*," said Chloe.

"Agreed," said Elliott.

"Also, if we summon as a group," continued Madeline, "maybe it will even strengthen the spell we receive"

"It's at least worth a try," agreed Elliott, opening the book and laying it in the center of their circle.

One by one, each girl extended her right arm, four hands splayed like starfish over the blank page.

"Bring forth that which will satisfy our intentions," they recited as a group, and Elliott was surprised to hear their voices so unified in both rhythm and timbre. *"Bring forth that which will satisfy our intentions."* An image of Kaylie cheering at the game flashed through

Elliott's mind. *"Bring forth that which will satisfy our intentions,"* they declared, Elliott's heart breaking, the shattered pieces bursting into flame.

And just like that, the silver text rose from the depths of the book and surfaced on the blue-black page. A silver thread of hope amid a storm of darkness.

Except when Elliott saw the title, she felt . . . confused.

"'Incantation of Estimation,'" she read aloud.

Bea frowned. "What does that even mean?"

"I don't know," Chloe responded, craning her head to look, as if she might be able to interpret it if she saw it right-side up. "But that doesn't sound any worse than the other spells we've received. That sounds . . . not that bad."

"Well, if this is the spell we manifested," Madeline reminded them with the conviction of a born-again preacher, "then we just need to trust the book. It's leading us in the direction of our higher purpose."

A statement Elliott agreed with—though she couldn't help thinking that Madeline sounded less like someone in a coven and more like someone in a cult.

Bea

In addition to a bat's heart, a cow's tongue, and bloodstone, among other ingredients, the spell called for a personal object from each victim—more specifically, one that had touched their lips.

An object from the rapist's girlfriend was easy enough to collect—at that Thursday's coven gathering, Elliott reported that she'd successfully stalked the girl during lunch and stolen her empty iced tea bottle. But the coven-mates agreed they would divide and conquer to gather the remaining objects: Elliott and Chloe would take Kaylie's perpetrator, and Madeline and Bea would take the judge.

Which is how Bea and Madeline found themselves together early one morning the following weekend, sitting in Madeline's Prius across the street from the judge's large Victorian-style home.

Bea hadn't watched a lot of detective shows—true crime always creeped her out—but she'd seen enough to know that this was them officially trailing their target. According to Madeline, it hadn't been hard to track down the judge's address—while her mother was a divorce attorney, she was apparently very well connected in the larger Santa Barbara legal community. A quick swipe through her contacts led to the defense attorney in Kaylie's case—whom, Madeline suggested, they might want to add to their target list—and a quick email to the defense attorney, under the guise of being her mother, led to a home address for Judge Ramos.

"I told the attorney I wanted to send the judge a fruit basket as a token of sympathy and solidarity over all the *recall nonsense*." Madeline snorted, referring to the "Recall Judge Ramos" movement taken up by a collection of local feminists who were outraged over his lenient sentencing. In the wake of Kaylie's doxxing, their outrage had only intensified. "Also, like *recalling* him is even enough." Madeline sipped her coffee, her gaze never wavering from the judge's home.

Bea took a sip of her own coffee—which Madeline had been thoughtful enough to bring, along with two raspberry scones. Bea wasn't usually that big on caffeine, but today she needed it. She'd had trouble sleeping all week.

"Did you delete those emails from your mom's account?" she double-checked.

"Yeah, of course," Madeline replied. "Don't worry. I'd never do anything to jeopardize the sanctity of the coven."

Bea glanced at Madeline. *Sanctity?*

Judge Ramos lived over on the Mesa, just off of Shoreline Drive. From where they were parked, Bea could see Shoreline Park—a long, grassy area that ran along the ocean bluff, filled with picnic benches and a playground and steps down to the beach—and beyond that, the Pacific Ocean, gray and flat under the misty, overcast sky.

Bea and Otis had their seventh birthday party at Shoreline Park. It had been so windy that Bea had to lie on top of the tablecloth as her mom attempted to tape it down, large palm fronds raining down around them, one of which had crashed into Otis's head. In the end, they'd abandoned the beach in favor of La Mesa Park, all the seven-year-olds running around on the playground pretending to be pirates. Her mother, Bea reflected, was always good at taking a near disaster and flipping it around. A thought that made Bea feel sad for some reason.

"There he is," Madeline whispered, sitting up straight in her seat.

Bea glanced out the window and saw a tall Latino man in expensive-looking loungewear exiting the house with a little girl in a puffy pink coat and a bike helmet. The girl couldn't have been more than four years old. The man was older, maybe in his early seventies, with gray hair, a salt-and-pepper beard, and a prominent nose. The little girl skipped ahead of him as he followed behind her, a kids' scooter in one hand, a tall thermos in the other.

"Come on," Madeline urged as the judge and the girl started for Shoreline Drive.

Madeline and Bea slipped out of the car and trailed them down the sidewalk, being sure to stay several yards behind. The morning was cool and breezy, the tall palm trees above them swaying in the wind. Bea shivered and pulled her coat close.

When the judge and the girl reached the corner, the judge took the little girl's hand, carefully looking both ways before crossing at the crosswalk.

"Come *on*, Abuelito," the little girl said, trying to pull him faster through the intersection.

"Hold your horses, Rosie," he laughed. "Abuelito's got a bad knee."

Once across the street, the judge set the scooter down on the sidewalk, and the little girl took off on it, headed toward the playground.

"Not too fast!" he called after her, shaking his head and laughing.

"I can't believe he's *laughing*," Madeline whispered as she and Bea trailed him down the sidewalk, "when he's definitely heard about what happened to Kaylie by now."

"Well, but we don't know how he's *feeling*," Bea pointed out. "How many times have we both acted like everything was fine, when inside it totally was not?"

Madeline seemed reluctant to admit they could share any similarities with the judge. "We need to steal that thermos," she whispered as the judge took a sip.

Bea nodded in agreement, her gaze on the little girl, who was yelling something indecipherable back to her grandpa.

The judge was a friendly man, Bea noted; he kept waving to every single passerby. And he clearly loved his granddaughter; when they reached the playground—an open, sandy area surrounded by a circle of wood posts resembling a rising wave—he chased after her to the dolphin statue and climbed on behind her.

"Do you ever feel guilty?" Bea whispered to Madeline as they neared the playground.

"Over what?" Madeline replied.

"I don't know. Any of it. All of it."

Madeline slowed her steps and turned to look at Bea. Dark purple circles stood out under her eyes. "No. Because you know what I remind myself of? *They* don't feel bad. They probably don't even *think* about us. Not a single one of them. Did the guy *you* targeted *ever* stop to feel guilty? Because my ex certainly didn't. And take this asshole." She nodded toward the playground. "Just because he's *friendly* and *affectionate* with his grandchild doesn't mean he's a good person."

"Yeah, I know," Bea replied. She was all too aware that just because someone loved and respected their granddaughter—or their wife, or their daughter, for that matter—didn't mean that love and respect extended to anyone else. You could be a loving father or husband, or a doting grandfather, and still be capable of tremendous harm.

And yet . . .

"It's just . . . I thought getting revenge would make things better," Bea admitted. "And instead, I keep feeling . . . just really *bad*."

"Listen," Madeline said earnestly. "I really don't think you have anything to feel bad about. What you're doing is justice. Think about all the other girls out there that you've protected simply by taking down the guys we've targeted. And think about the guts it took for you to show up at your target's home, *especially* someone that much older, and stare him down after what he did." Madeline looked her straight in the eyes. "That was so brave. You should feel proud of yourself, Bea. You are an avenging angel, a goddess warrior. You are a goddamn *witch*," she whispered. "Besides"—Madeline turned back toward the playground, where the little girl was now jumping off the dolphin and racing toward the swings—"the Bible says an eye for an eye, so even God knows sometimes revenge is justified."

The thing was, the Bible said a lot of things, and Bea, who'd grown up going to church with her parents, didn't believe all of it. Just as she didn't believe all of what Madeline was saying. On the one hand, it felt good to have Madeline in her corner. But Bea was pretty sure the situation was more complicated than she made it seem.

"Come push me, Abuelito!" the little girl was yelling.

"One second, mi amor," the judge called back, jogging over to grab her scooter from where she'd abandoned it at the entrance. He brought it over to the bench seating that ran along one edge of the playground and placed his thermos down beside it.

"Okay, you go distract him," Madeline whispered to Bea. "I'll grab the thermos."

Bea hesitated, then made her way over to the swing set, sitting down on the open seat next to the girl. The judge was standing in front of the girl, instructing her on how to swing on her own. Bea felt awkward being this close to him—both because of his ruling and what the coven had planned.

"Wow, you're really good at that," Bea commented as the little girl tried to pump her legs.

"I know!" the girl replied. "And I'm really good at my scooter."

For some reason the little girl's confidence brought tears to Bea's eyes. She blinked them away as she began to swing. From the corner of her eye, Bea saw Madeline reaching for the thermos.

"*Hey*," the girl called out indignantly. "You're too big for swinging."

"Rosie," the judge cautioned.

"Well, she *is*." The girl frowned, completely unrepentant.

"Yeah, you're probably right," Bea agreed with her. "But I'm really good at jumping off. Wanna see?"

The girl's eyes lit up. "Yeah."

Bea swung herself back and forth a few times, adjusting her hold on the chains as she gained height. And then, swinging forward, she launched herself off and landed gracefully in the sand.

"Whoa," the girl enthused as Bea strolled off to meet Madeline. "I'm going to do that, too!"

Elliott

On the other side of town, Elliott was camped out with Chloe in her Beemer just across the street from a tiny bungalow off Milpas, only a few blocks from Santa Barbara Junior High, Elliott's old school.

A chain-link fence surrounded the bungalow's front yard—which was cluttered with broken furniture and old ladders, a pile of dirty mops and grungy buckets—and two mangy dogs were asleep on the front porch.

This part of Santa Barbara was one of the few areas that remained industrial and non-picture-perfect pristine, occupied by auto repair shops and large supply warehouses sprinkled in among the apartment complexes and small homes, the streets lined with work trucks and delivery vans.

"Ugh," Chloe commented from behind her sunglasses as she stared at the bungalow. "Isn't it disturbing knowing who lives here? Like, how many houses do you think we pass every single day that *actually* have assailants living in them?"

"Way too many," Elliott replied, glancing over from the shadows of her David Bowie hoodie. She, too, had sunglasses on, huge Jackie O's. "And he's probably in there just sleeping in all cozy, or making himself goddamn eggs and toast." All this time, he'd just been living his life.

"Piece of shit," Chloe muttered, adjusting the collar of her Lululemon jacket.

Kaylie's assailant, Brett Hunt, still lived with his mom and stepdad even though he'd graduated last year. According to Caitlyn Espinoza—a junior with questionable taste in guys who was dating Brett's best friend—he'd been set to attend UCSB, but the attorney fees had drained his family's finances and ruled out that option, so now he was at Ventura Community College—a good forty-minute drive south, on a campus where people might not know his deal. But, come on, was Elliott supposed to feel *sorry* for him just because he couldn't attend his college of choice? Kaylie'd had her *entire life* disrupted, and here this dude was still walking around, taking Intro Biology or some shit, serving his weak-ass community service. Please.

Chloe shifted in her seat. "I know it's probably not fair of me, but I truly feel suspicious of *all* guys now."

"Umm, no, that's one thousand percent justified, my friend," Elliott retorted.

Chloe snorted, then sighed. "You know, this whole experience has also made me realize how focused I've always been on guys. Like, talking about them, and thinking about them, and dressing in ways I think they would like. *Is this flattering? Do I look cute? Does it accentuate my boobs?* Ugh." She shook her head. "And I realize I do it, like, *all* the time. Even when I don't mean to. It's kind of exhausting."

"The male gaze is fucking *pervasive*," Elliott agreed. "And, listen, we live in a patriarchy. So it's not like it's some failure on *your* part. Everything around you has *pushed* you in that direction and asked you to think that way."

"Yeah," Chloe agreed. "But still. I just feel like . . . I want to do my *own* thing, you know? Live outside of these expectations and give zero fucks." She hesitated a moment. "Kind of like you."

"Me?" Elliott said in genuine surprise.

"Yeah. I mean, *look* at you. Sporting pink hair and retro clothes, barging into rich kids' parties like you own the place, starting *covens*."

All of which was *true*, except Elliott wasn't sure she'd *fully* rejected outside expectations. She still cared about what people thought, despite her best intentions. "I think you might be giving me a little too much credit," she admitted.

"I don't know. You're pretty badass." Chloe was quietly reflective. "Sometimes . . . you know, sometimes I just really wish I wasn't *into* guys."

Elliott glanced over at her. The way Chloe had said it was so earnest and so incredibly haunted that it broke Elliott's heart.

"Like, not that I'm saying it's easier being gay or bi or anything like that," Chloe clarified. "It's just . . . I wish I could just turn off that part of myself that likes the opposite sex. I just want to be *done* with guys, you know?"

"Oh, yeah, I know," Elliott agreed.

"I mean, can you imagine ever wanting to *kiss* another guy again?"

"Umm, negatory."

"Exactly. Let alone wanting to— Oh God, is that him?" Chloe whispered, sliding down in the driver's seat as someone stepped out the front door.

Elliott narrowed her eyes behind her sunglasses. "Yeah. That's him, all right."

Brett was broad-shouldered, white, and blond, with the kind of forgettable face worn by basically every former-varsity baseball player Elliott had ever seen. She shot daggers at him as he strolled down his porch steps and unlocked the red truck out front.

"Okay, tail him, but don't get too close," Elliott instructed as Brett's truck pulled out. But he immediately did a three-point turn, bringing the nose of his truck perilously close to Chloe's car. Both girls instinctively slid down in their seats—like that was any more inconspicuous.

Chloe waited for his truck to pass and then pulled out and followed him as he turned right onto Gutierrez, which ran one way. At this hour he was probably hitting the gym, Elliott thought in annoyance. Or maybe he was going for a run. He'd definitely be one of those people who'd waste gas by driving a long distance just to go running someplace else. She doubted he was headed surfing; he didn't have a board in the truck bed, and he also wasn't that cool.

But they only went a few blocks before he took a right onto Santa Barbara Street.

"Are you shitting me?" Elliott asked as he flipped on his blinker to turn left into a busy parking lot near downtown.

Sure enough, he pulled into the lot for the Saturday farmer's market. Chloe waited for the elderly woman in the neon green vest to wave them the okay, then pulled in after, parking at the far end of the lot a few cars down from Brett's red truck.

Brett was already strolling through the lot, and Elliott and Chloe quickly climbed from the Beemer and casually began walking behind him.

The Saturday farmer's market took up a large open-air parking lot encompassed by a stucco wall and was filled with lines of booths selling everything from tangerines to fresh strawberries to garlic roasted pistachios, tie-dye T-shirts, and artisanal honey. Elliott's mother used to take her there every weekend to buy ranunculus, plum jam, and the sweetest carrots Elliott had ever tasted. She always let Elliott get a flower-shaped balloon from the man who handed them out, passing him a few dollars in return.

"Is he seriously here to buy organic food?" Chloe muttered to Elliott as they navigated around a woman with a cart full of sunflowers. To their right, an older white woman in what appeared to be a deerskin dress was playing a didgeridoo. Brett was at a booth just up ahead, sniffing an avocado like a complete prick.

"It would appear so," she replied as Brett paid the dreadlocked hippie farmer behind the booth and put his avocados in a knit bag he produced from his pocket.

As they trailed him, he purchased some cilantro-flavored hummus, a carton of organic eggs, and a cherimoya. Plus, he stopped to pet every frickin' dog that passed his way, often asking the owner about the breed and where they'd gotten it. So, what, he was Mr. Humane Society now? Was that it? Because Elliott wasn't buying it.

"If he doesn't eat something soon, we're going to have to find a plan B," Elliott whispered, pretending to be interested in a dried flower wreath as she watched him from the corner of her eye. He'd stopped at a honey stand where he was eyeing a beeswax candle shaped like a pine tree, then picked out five honey sticks, paid the woman, and moved on.

But as they started after him, Chloe grabbed Elliott's arm. "Look," she whispered.

He was biting open one of the honey sticks and proceeded to suck the amber liquid from the plastic tube. When he was finished, he dropped the empty tube on the ground, even though there was a small trash can nearby. Which felt entirely indicative of this dude's entitlement: just take what you want when you want it, and then toss it without care when you're done.

Elliott quickened her pace and stooped down to snatch up the empty tube, feeling like an FBI agent surreptitiously gathering a DNA sample to put some mofo behind bars. Except *this* mofo had way worse things coming to him than jail.

15

Elliott

That Sunday evening, Elliott met up with her coven-mates at Franceschi Park, where they immediately piled into Chloe's car before driving off into the dark.

The spell stipulated that it had to be performed at night over a grave. And so they drove across town to Calvary Cemetery, where Elliott's mom was buried.

The cemetery was totally nondescript, just a large rectangle of grass about a quarter mile long with flat headstones, a scattering of tall palm trees, and two large bland community mausoleums. Even the entrance was boring, with its cluster of tall narrow evergreens and its wall made from cinder-block-like bricks. Elliott always wished her mother were buried somewhere gothic and gorgeous, with weeping angel statues, old-fashioned headstones, and creepy mausoleums. Instead, her mom was eternally resting beside a mobile home estate.

The cemetery was surrounded by a chain-link fence covered in overgrown vines, which was incredibly easy to scale. And even in the dark, and coming from the remote northeast corner, Elliott had no problem locating her mom. She'd been there so many times and in so many circumstances that she was pretty sure that, like opening the puzzle box, she could find her blindfolded.

When they reached her mom's grave near the statue of St. Francis, Elliott knelt, quickly kissed her hand, and pressed it to the flat, black granite headstone like she always did, while the other girls stood quietly behind her. Then they got down to business.

Seated in a circle, Chloe retrieved the ingredients from her canvas bag while Elliott pulled out the book and Madeline extracted the objects of importance, all while Bea used her phone as a flashlight. They'd done this enough times that their coven was now starting to operate like a well-oiled machine.

Madeline laid out the cow's tongue and bat's heart at the foot of the grave and sprinkled them with the ocean water and iron filings while Bea circled the grave with the bloodstones and Chloe lit the purple candles. Elliott placed the objects of importance in the center of the grave beside the open book. Like all the other spells, this one required a conjuring of rage, and since Kaylie wasn't there to conjure her own rage, they'd agreed to collectively conjure rage on her behalf.

As Elliott pushed up the sleeve of her mom's old flannel shirt and raised her right hand above the book, she thought about Kaylie. Where was she now? Would she ever be back?

"Bring forth the outcome this witch seeks," the girls began chanting. *"Bring forth the outcome this witch seeks . . ."*

Kaylie had worked so hard to have this perfect albeit conventional life: cheer captain, National Honors Society, highly ranked in all her gymnastics competitions, voted into homecoming royalty, and on her way to the UC school of her choice. She'd done everything right. She'd checked every box. She'd lived up to every ridiculous female standard and been the center of high school life.

And in the end, none of it mattered.

She'd still been violated and then dismissed. She'd still been targeted and blamed. And Bea was right, if someone like *Kaylie* couldn't get justice—a cisgender, white, upper-middle class, sparkly, straight-A gymnastics champion and cheerleader—then what did that mean for the rest of them?

These boys and men, they just charged through the world crushing everything in their way, taking what they wanted, discarding what they didn't. Elliott thought of that rotten excuse of a human at the farmer's market, sucking out the nectar and discarding the plastic straw. He'd never looked back. He'd never even truly *apologized*. Elliott had read all the articles about Kaylie's case, seething at how in his statement to the judge, Brett had blamed his actions on too much alcohol and a "momentary lapse in judgment"—and then Elliott had felt bad that she'd read those articles, as if she'd somehow violated Kaylie's privacy.

Did Kaylie ever think back on that party and wonder how her life might have been different if she'd just stayed home? Or if she'd gone but never gotten drunk? Or if she'd gone but decided to leave early? Elliott wasn't trying to victim blame; she was genuinely curious—because that's where *her* mind went when she thought about what happened to *her*. Hadn't they all wondered about the people they might have been and the lives they might have led if only they'd had the chance?

Elliott's mind flashed to her mom, buried six feet beneath her in the ground. Sometimes—Elliott felt bad even admitting this—but sometimes she felt like if her mom had only lived, none of this would have happened. If her mom had lived, maybe Elliott would have kept her old friends, which meant she wouldn't have needed Vi, which meant she never would have met *him*.

If her mom had lived, maybe everything would be different.

But her mom *hadn't* lived. She'd been robbed.

Just like Kaylie had been robbed, just like Elliott had been robbed—of a normal adolescence, of a trajectory she might have had, of the girl she might have become.

But that girl was gone, lost to the flames of the hell she'd walked through. And this girl—the one sitting there in the dark atop her mother's grave, her right hand clenched tightly in rage—was, for good or bad, the one left standing.

"Ready?" Elliott whispered to the other girls, who were all staring intently at the book, shimmering before them like a miniature ocean. "On the count of three," Elliott instructed. "One . . . two . . . three."

"*Take this pain, take this rage,*" the coven recited in unison, their fists raised over the book. Elliott could feel not only the rage coursing through her body, but the unbearable brokenness of her own heart. "*And cast it back on its creator.*"

The girls let their hands fly open and the violet ball of energy burst from the book, bigger and brighter than anything they'd conjured thus far. It hovered there before their marked palms, electrified and terrible. But also darkly beautiful.

And then, with a whoosh, it zoomed out into the pitch-black night.

16

Chloe

The following morning Chloe was still wondering about the spell's impact as she pulled into school.

The first thing they'd done after casting it was drive straight to Judge Ramos's house over on the Mesa. But when they'd pulled up on the dark street, which was misty with ocean air, the palm trees swaying in the night breeze, all the lights in the judge's home were off.

"Maybe he's out of town?" Chloe had commented, leaning over the steering wheel to get a better look.

"He was there yesterday," Bea pointed out from the passenger seat.

"Also, where does *this* guy have to be at this hour on a Sunday night?" Madeline asked offendedly, as if his absence was a personal attack.

They'd waited another ten minutes before Elliott had finally announced, "Screw it. Let's drive over to Brett's."

At least the lights were on in *his* small bungalow, but once again the girls waited just down the street for nearly fifteen minutes with zero evidence. No screams, no ambulances, no panicked shouts for help.

"Maybe it hasn't taken effect yet," Elliott suggested.

"Or did it just not work?" Chloe worried as she played with her scarf.

"No," Bea said in concern, shining her phone's light on her right forearm. "I think it definitely worked."

Her sleeve was pushed up, and her mark had now spread halfway toward her elbow, a few dark curving tendrils reaching even farther. The others had quickly pushed their sleeves up only to find the same.

Frankly, Chloe had felt alarmed. She'd thought their marks were so cool at the start, a symbol of their empowerment, but now . . . now they were beginning to look sinister.

As she climbed the staircase that curved up the hill from the parking lot toward her campus, Chloe passed seniors Ruby Montgomery and Lilly Rosenberg and heard Ruby murmur, ". . . and *she's* the same one who was homecoming queen?" Chloe's ears perked up as a jolt of adrenaline flooded her system. Were they talking about Kaylie?

It wasn't until Chloe was sitting in the outdoor U-shaped Greek theater for an impromptu school assembly, however, that she got full confirmation and the full story.

"And *she* was Emily Doe, yes?" Madison was whispering to Brooklyn as Chloe slid into the empty space beside them on one of the stadium bench seats.

"Yeah," Brooklyn whispered back as Mrs. Dinaberg walked up to the podium, checking a message on her phone. "The same girl we were talking about last week. And I guess he said in his note that he couldn't forgive himself for what he did. That he finally understood her pain and anguish."

"What are you guys talking about?" Chloe asked casually, adjusting her transition lens frames, which had darkened in the dappled sunlight. She rarely wore her glasses because they never fully lightened when inside—a bonus today, seeing how the tiny blood vessels in her eyes had turned a disturbing shade of purple, the same color the world was now slightly tinted, and that she'd been retching up since last night.

Chloe hadn't been surprised by the blowback, but given how inexplicably mild it was last time around, she *had* been surprised at how miserable she felt now. She hadn't slept at all and was feeling particularly sensitive to the light, plus she was incredibly nauseous and couldn't get this horrible taste out of her mouth: a mix of rotten onions and spoiled milk, as if she were going bad inside. Also, had someone cranked up the AC, she'd wondered in homeroom as she shivered through her sweater, or was it just her?

"You know that guy from Santa Barbara High who went to trial and got convicted of rape?" Brooklyn asked, applying a layer of lip balm. "It turns out his victim got doxxed last week and had to leave town, and in the wake of the doxxing he suddenly felt so guilty that, get this, he tried to *kill himself* just last night. I guess his mom found him in the bathtub with his wrists slit."

A chill ran down Chloe's spine. "Jesus," she breathed, not sure how she felt about the information. Was she unsettled because of his suicide attempt, or because he was still alive?

"Good morning, students," Mrs. Dinaberg greeted from the podium. "We're going to get started in just a moment. Thank you for your patience while we wait for our guest speaker."

"But that's not even the craziest part," Brooklyn added, enjoying her role as dramaturge, which Chloe found slightly annoying. This wasn't some teen drama; this was real life. "It turns out the rapist's *girlfriend* is the one who doxxed his victim."

"No way," Madison exclaimed.

"Yes way. She uploaded this crazy video to social media late last night, sobbing and confessing to all of it, and, like, going into *detail* about how she made this fucked-up video and then posted all these fake ads, all because she couldn't accept the idea that her boyfriend actually did something like that, because then what would it mean about *her*? Plus, she proceeded to confess to all these *other* times that she slut-shamed girls. And *also* also?" Brooklyn held up her hand, indicating the story got even wilder. "The judge from that case? I heard from Sofia, whose mom is friends with the judge's ex-wife, that *he* had a full-on mental breakdown last night, too. He actually drove himself to the police station and asked that he be arrested because he felt responsible for ruining a young girl's life."

"All right, quiet, please," Mrs. Dinaberg announced, glancing over at a Latina woman in a white linen dress and a big, bright necklace who was strolling toward her from one of the side paths before stopping beside her.

The students settled down.

"We have a guest speaker this morning who was kind enough to come in very last minute," Mrs. Dinaberg announced. "We'd had this planned for later this month, but due to recent developments, I felt it important to bring you together for an essential conversation. I don't want things whispered about in the hallways. I want them discussed out in the open."

Chloe's throat had suddenly gone tight, though she wasn't sure why.

"It's my pleasure to introduce Celia Muñoz." Mrs. Dinaberg motioned to the woman. "A UCSB professor, adolescent counselor, and trauma expert. I've been friends with Celia for several decades, and she is one of the most brilliant and kindest women I know. I'll let her address you directly, but I first wanted to say that this is just the first in several planned discussions. And my door is always open. Celia?"

"Thank you for that kind introduction, Elizabeth," the woman said from behind the podium. She was tall and regal, and when she looked out at the students there was a stillness about her that reminded Chloe of Mary Yoshida. "Before we really get into things—and I assure you there will be time for questions as well as small group discussions this morning—I want to begin by telling you my story."

Chloe listened as the woman shared the story of her rape in honest, unflinching detail. Chloe had obviously heard many firsthand accounts in group, including Mary's, but somehow this felt different. In fact, she was having a hard time holding back her tears.

Was it because she was listening to these same details in a normal setting, surrounded by both male and female classmates? Or was it because *she'd* made this happen? Or was it knowing that somewhere out there was Kaylie, forced to abandon her old life?

Maybe it was all of the above.

But as Chloe sat there listening to Celia Muñoz talk about sexual violence and women being believed, the "me too." Movement started by Tarana Burke, the importance of consent, and the disproportionate violence against women and girls of color and trans people, Chloe couldn't help thinking that schools should be having these discussions all the time. It should be baked into their curriculum from the very start. Growing up, girls got lectures that basically amounted to *how to not get raped*; maybe boys should get weekly trainings on *how not to be a rapist.*

If Arman had been forced into something like that, would he have behaved differently?

But it shouldn't take a coven of witches, Chloe thought morosely, and some dark magic to force a true reckoning.

Bea

At Bea's school, what had happened that weekend was all anyone could talk about. There were murmurs of Kaylie's doxxing the week prior—not because people knew her, but because a local scandal like that was a big deal—but now that Kaylie's rapist and his girlfriend *and* the judge had apparently all come forward to take accountability for harming her, the halls were really buzzing.

Of course, there were conflicting stories about what had actually occurred, like a morbid game of telephone, several of which Bea overheard as she stopped at her outdoor locker between classes, the November breeze sending shivers down her spine. Some people reported that the rapist tried to kill himself and was in the ICU; others said he was actually *dead*. Some people said the *judge* tried to kill himself, while others said he'd cracked up and was in a mental health facility for observation. Other rumors reported that the girlfriend had officially dropped out of school, or that she'd actually left town. But everyone agreed on one thing: all three had been crushed under the weight of their guilt and had completely and utterly broken down.

Bea knew she should feel proud—she and her coven-mates had forced them to reckon with how their actions impacted Kaylie—but as she sat in orchestra practice that afternoon, all she could think was that someone had almost *died* because of her, which made her sick.

She *wanted* revenge, but when it came down to it, maybe she just didn't have the stomach for the results. Which felt like a personal failure. She wanted to *harden* herself. Why *should* she care? Had anyone cared about Kaylie? Had anyone cared about *her*?

Bea and Otis didn't have classes together, and he was meeting with the Entrepreneurship Club at lunch, so it wasn't until they were in the car on the drive home that he had the chance to bring things up.

"Didn't you say that Emily Doe—I mean, Kaylie," he corrected now that the truth was out there, "was in your group?" Otis glanced over at her from behind the wheel.

She shouldn't have shared that detail—group was supposed to be anonymous, and what was said there was supposed to stay there—but . . . it was *Otis*. "Yeah," she confirmed, turning to stare out the window at an orchard they were passing.

"*God*. So, did you know her well?" They'd both gone to church with Kaylie, but they hadn't been friends.

"No, not really," she replied truthfully.

"The whole thing is so horrible." Otis let out a deep sigh. "Also, I can't believe that rapist's *girlfriend*. As if Kaylie didn't have enough to deal with already. And, God, her poor *family* . . . ," he trailed off.

Bea looked over at him and noticed how tightly he was clenching the wheel.

"I hope," he added, "that the three of *them* feel traumatized for the rest of their lives."

Bea closed her eyes and breathed in the cool air rushing through her cracked window. She was *not* feeling well. Everything was a little too loud, a little too bright. And she couldn't get this awful taste out of her mouth. Or this rotten smell out of her nostrils. She hadn't slept well in days, and her joints and muscles were starting to ache. Her *teeth* ached. Plus, she'd been retching up purple since the night before.

"I'm sorry," Otis apologized. "I know this has gotta be triggering for you. I shouldn't— Let's change the subject."

Which he did, launching into a funny story about how he and his friend Priya had tried and spectacularly failed to do an art piece using resin. But even as Bea chuckled along, her mind roamed elsewhere.

All day, despite her best efforts, *he'd* been on her mind. That morning she'd overheard her mom on the phone with Margaret, and afterward her mom reported that while his health was restored, his spirits were low. He was still unable to paint, despite doctors' assurance that there was no neurological damage, and his confidence was completely rattled. Maya was faring poorly as well, still having night terrors, and Roman was now wetting the bed. Margaret was at her wits' end, worried about both her husband and children and unable to focus at work. Basically, the entire family was traumatized.

Which was exactly what Bea wanted to avoid in her *own* family. She could just imagine her parents' faces if she broke the news, their expressions falling as she shattered their world. They didn't need that kind of pain. It was bad enough that *she* had to live with the knowledge, she didn't need to pass it along to anyone else.

Except, of course, she already had, hadn't she? Otis carried that burden right alongside her. Which made her wonder how traumatized *he* felt.

Trauma seemed to have this way of rippling out and taking down everyone in its path. Bea thought of Maya and Roman watching their father. And she thought of Kaylie's family. And she imagined Brett's mother coming into the bathroom to find her son in a puddle of blood. And she pictured the judge's granddaughter, sitting somewhere worried about her abuelito. She wondered about the parents of those boys from the party. How had they felt when they got the calls? Were they terrified as they rushed to the hospital? Did they stand over their sons later that day, their hearts constricting at the thought of ever losing them?

And what if Brett really *had* died? What if his mom hadn't found him in time? What if the judge or Brett's girlfriend ended up hurting themselves, too? Is *that* what they deserved? Bea wasn't sure anymore. What *was* the appropriate punishment? Was it death? Was it banishment? Was it even for Bea to decide?

She wanted a reckoning. She wanted repercussions—and not just for them, but for every person out there who'd violated someone. But she didn't want it to be up to *her* to decide. It was too much. She could barely carry her own trauma, let alone hold someone else's future in her hands.

Madeline

All day Madeline absolutely *reveled* as the gossip flew around her school. Yes, she hadn't slept. And yes, she was nauseous and had been throwing up purple since last night. And yes, there was a bitter taste in her mouth and a terrible stench in her nostrils, and things were starting to look tinted—but even that didn't bother her. It was as if the world couldn't touch her.

There were only two things she wished as she pretended to pray during Mass—Father Gutierrez was leading them in a prayer for those in need of redemption—the first was that she'd been able to witness the moment of impact, and the second was that people knew *she* was involved.

Not that she needed the credit, exactly. But she wanted people to understand that this wasn't mere coincidence, it was part of a calculated effort; the judge and that rapist and the rapist's stupid girlfriend had all been in the sight lines of people with the power to take them down, and that same power could easily be pointed toward any one of them.

When school wrapped up that afternoon, Madeline texted her parents that she had a few errands to run, and then she got in her car and drove farther into Goleta, making a pit stop at In-N-Out—where she picked up a Double-Double, animal style, a large fry, and a vanilla shake—before taking Turnpike over to Cathedral Oaks. She passed Tucker's Grove, where she and Derrick had celebrated their first anniversary with a romantic picnic dinner (ugh), and then turned onto a side street, pulling up in front of a modest, Spanish-style ranch home. Out front there were three cars in the driveway. Good, everyone was home.

"Madeline," Mrs. Bolton said in surprise when she opened the front door. "This is—wow, I don't know what to say. I wasn't—oh my goodness, sweetie, it's so good of you to come." She pulled Madeline into a hug.

"How are you doing, Mrs. Bolton?" Madeline asked as she extricated herself from the embrace, her face creased in worry. Frankly, Mingyu Bolton looked like crap, her normally glossy black hair unwashed, no makeup to speak of, and, of all things, she was wearing a sweatsuit. Good, that was the least of what she deserved.

Mrs. Bolton let out a long, weary sigh. "We've all been better. But I'm doing okay."

"And how's Derrick?" Madeline asked in concern.

"Well, doctors are hopeful that once the swelling goes down around the optic nerves, he'll eventually regain his vision. It was only a partial vision loss, you know. People keep saying he's blind, but he can still vaguely make out shapes and—" Her voice hitched, and she put one hand over her mouth, collecting herself. She forced out a smile. "Doug and I are just so grateful that it wasn't more serious. But Derrick's been feeling pretty low."

"I'm sure." Madeline nodded seriously.

"It really is so good of you to come," Mrs. Bolton repeated. "I know things ended badly between you two kids—which I've always felt was such a shame," she added, as if their breakup had been some routine heartbreak filled with a string of tear-filled conversations instead of months of one-way stalking and, ultimately, an act of revenge porn. All of which Mrs. Bolton fucking *knew*. She knew it, she'd just completely minimized it, making up excuse after excuse. Her son wasn't an *offender*; he was simply *heartbroken*. And he couldn't *possibly* be the one who'd made and posted that video. Someone must have hacked into his computer. Now Madeline's presence seemed to confirm for her what she'd always wanted to believe: it was all just a misunderstanding over hurt feelings, and *no big deal.*

"I brought him something," Madeline offered, holding up the In-N-Out bag. "Do you think it'd be okay if I gave it to him in person?"

"Oh, sweetie. You were always so thoughtful. Yes. I think he'd like that." Mrs. Bolton smiled.

She led Madeline down the carpeted hallway, toward a back bedroom—one Madeline had been in many times. Memories flooded Madeline's brain. How often had she come over to this house and stayed for dinner, sitting with the entire family around the knicked-up farm table as they ate takeout from Ca'Dario or Los Agaves and played a round of Monopoly? But she steeled herself against the cascade of emotions, willing them all away.

"Baby?" Mrs. Bolton called as she gently knocked on the door. There was a UCLA poster taped to it.

"Yeah?" came a downbeat voice.

"Derrick, honey. There's someone here to see you. Someone I think you'll really want to—want to visit with." She opened the door and nodded at Madeline to go in.

Derrick was sitting propped up in his bed, still wearing his pajamas even though it was well after three. His black hair was messy, and his muscled body seemed somehow smaller and deflated. The air was stuffy and stale, tinged with the heavy scent of roses, which came from the bouquets that covered nearly every available surface. There were get-well cards everywhere, too (not that he could read any of them). On the dresser the TV was on, playing *Ghostbusters*, a film he'd seen about a million times and could probably mentally recreate by sound alone.

"Hey," Madeline said from the doorway.

Derrick's face morphed into an expression of apprehensive shock as he registered her voice. "Hey."

Madeline closed the door and dragged his desk chair over to his bedside. "I brought you something," she said, opening the In-N-Out bag and holding it up for him to smell.

"You brought me my favorite meal?" he asked in surprise.

"Yeah, of course," she said as she sat down. This was the meal Derrick turned to in times of both celebration and distress. The one he claimed he'd want as his last meal on earth. "Here." She handed him the milk shake, which was beginning to sweat in her hand, being careful not to let their fingers touch.

He brought the straw to his lips, taking a tentative sip, which made him close his eyes and groan in pleasure. A noise that reminded Madeline of other things she'd rather forget.

"Here's the fries," she offered. "I'm going to set them right beside you. You want the Double-Double, too?"

"Yeah, thanks." He nodded, accepting the huge paper-wrapped burger. He took a big bite, getting special sauce on the corner of his mouth and spilling the lettuce and pickles onto the blanket, then took a big sip of the milk shake. The way he was acting, you'd think he hadn't eaten in days.

"Good?" she asked him.

"Yeah," he answered through his food, swallowing it down. He set the burger on his lap. "Mad, I can't believe you *came* here. God. I really can't believe this."

"How are you *doing*?" she asked.

"I'm not really—" Tears began to leak down his cheeks. "I'm gonna lose *everything*, Mad," he confessed, his voice wavering with emotion. "The whole future I worked toward. All those summers at basketball camps, all those late-night training sessions, all those weekends spent on the road for tournaments, all the money my parents spent. It's all gonna mean nothing. I mean, even if the doctors are right about my recovery, it'll take too long and be too late. And without a full ride, I don't know if I can even . . ." He started crying in earnest, pinching the bridge of his nose. "I don't know what I'm going to do, Mad," he cried, his body wracked with sobs. "I don't know what I'm going to do."

Madeline stayed silent, watching as Derrick fell apart. He'd always been so charismatic and confident, so sure of his place in the world. And now here he was, a shell of his former self, his life burned down around him, his future a pile of ashes.

"And I've been thinking about what I did, Mad," he said suddenly, his voice urgent.

"Oh yeah?" she asked evenly as her heartbeat quickened. She swiftly brought up the voice memo app on her phone and tapped record. "What do you mean?"

"I was *so* fucked up. I *really* loved you, Mad—I *still* love you—and when you broke up with me . . . I mean, maybe you were right that we needed to do it before college anyway, but I was so hurt and in such a dark place, and I just wanted you to hurt as much as I did. I just wanted you to stop and see—but that's not an excuse. I know that, too. And I just wanted you to know . . . ," he trailed off.

"Yes?" Madeline gently encouraged.

He looked up, appearing much younger than his years. "I just wanted you to know, I've been thinking about it a lot."

Madeline tapped the stop button on her app, quite aware that he still hadn't *really* taken accountability or actually *apologized.*

"Derrick," she said softly, leaning in close. "No matter what happens to either one of us moving forward, no matter where our lives go or who we become, I just want you to remember one thing."

"Yeah?" he sniffled, his eyes seeking out the shape of her face.

When she spoke, her voice was a saccharine-sweet whisper. *"I'm* the one who ruined your future."

Derrick's face bent in confusion. "What?"

"This tragic accident that made you lose your vision out on the field and knocked you off course?" she said lightly. "It was *not* tragic. And it was *no* accident. It happened because *I* commanded it."

"*What?*" A mix of shock and betrayal washed over his face. "You—What are you saying? I don't under—how could *you*—you can't—"

"Oh, but I can." She smiled, relishing his expression of horror. "I can. And I did. And I can do *worse*, Derrick. Much worse. And also, Derrick?" Madeline added sweetly as she stood up from her chair. "You'll never be able to prove it, and no one will ever believe you. Enjoy your favorite meal," she added brightly as she headed to the door. "I hope that when you eat it from now on, you'll always think of me."

Elliott

That Monday, Elliott felt terrible.

Not terrible as in she was *remorseful*, mind you. But terrible like the one time she got sick from eating bad fish tacos. Her body ached, and everything was too bright; she had a horrible taste in her mouth that she attributed to the purple stuff she'd been consistently coughing up and a rotten stench in her nostrils that she attributed to the purple junk that was now leaking from her nose. And she'd awoken that morning to everything looking as if she were viewing the world through light purple glasses. When she peered closely at her reflection, she spotted a ring of purple around her eyes.

These new developments filled Elliott with the same level of unease she felt when she now looked at the mark that was creeping up her arm.

Their blowback had never been *this* bad. Was it because their spell had taken down *three* people this time around?

Or was it possible that their revenge had a cumulative effect? What if each time they cast a spell they experienced a wave of blowback that wasn't merely from the most recent spell, but from every spell they'd ever cast?

Except if that were the case, why hadn't it been worse after Madeline's spell? It just didn't make sense. What was so different that time around that it tempered the blowback?

For a moment Elliott recalled her mark magically shimmering and turning pink as she sat on the beach . . . right after they'd each opened up to one another. In the wake of her confession, she remembered feeling good . . . and then exposed. And her *mark* feeling exposed.

Was there any way . . . Had connecting and being vulnerable made a difference? Was it possible that something about their interaction had counteracted the blowback?

Elliott's dad had taken one look at her that morning, wearing her sunglasses indoors as she poured herself a cup of coffee, and asked her point-blank if she was hungover. If only it were that simple.

"If by hungover you mean surfing the crimson wave, then yes," she'd lied, taking a big sip of her coffee.

"Nice *Clueless* reference." He'd smirked as he drank his own coffee. "Hey, Pigeon . . . can we talk a minute?" he said seriously.

Elliott leaned on the counter and closed her eyes against her rising nausea. "Dad, can it wait? I'm really not"—she put one hand to her mouth, afraid she might retch up purple—"feeling great."

"Of course. Hey." He rubbed her back in sympathy. "If your period's that bad, you can always skip school, hon."

"No, that's okay." Elliott shook her head. She didn't want him worrying about her, and more importantly, she *wanted* to go to school and hear what, if anything, people were saying.

And there were *plenty* of rumors. Especially because Brett had apparently fully blamed himself in his suicide note, making it clear that he had, in fact, raped Kaylie and that he'd known exactly what he was doing at the time. Which was a *huge* revelation among the halls of Santa Barbara High.

At first, it felt good to hear people talk about things and grapple with the facts out loud—even if some were complete asshats about it, more invested in Brett's pain than Kaylie's. Case in point, in History class, Elliott overheard Quintana Royce say to Isabella Dominquez, "That court case must have *really* gotten to him. I mean, it's terrible that he tried to *kill* himself."

"Oh really?" Elliott spun around in her seat, glaring at them through her sunglasses, which she'd worn through all her classes without comment from her teachers. "And what about Kaylie, who was *raped* and had to literally *skip town*?" She pointed at Quintana. "*Himpathy*, that's what that's called." She'd read about it in an article about philosopher Kate Manne, who'd coined the term. "People always overempathize with the perpetrator instead of the victim, which is total bullshit."

"No!" Quintana defended, going pale. "I'm not saying that; what happened to Kaylie is *tragic*. I'm just saying that *anyone* trying to *kill* themselves is also terrible."

But was that really true when it came to someone like Brett?

For the briefest of moments, Elliott allowed herself to wonder if there was any chance the punishment had gone too far.

Except Brett deserved *some*thing more severe than three months of juvie, a few weekends of doing community service, and a year of probation, and Elliott didn't see anyone else coming up with a solid plan. In fact, she resented that she even had to *think* about the question of justice and what was deserved—had Brett thought about anyone else when he'd raped Kaylie? No! He'd just wreaked havoc and then skated off.

But as the day wore on, Elliott found herself becoming kind of . . . well, the only word for it was *depressed*.

Walking along State Street that afternoon as a much-needed distraction before heading home, Elliott put on Radiohead's "Karma

Police." Above her, a murder of crows swooped across the sky before circling one of the many treetops they dominated. Passing the Fiesta 5 Theatre, where she and her mom used to see Pixar films together, and Paseo Nuevo, the now nearly empty outdoor mall where her mom used to go shopping as a teen, Elliott couldn't shake the feeling that even after casting Kaylie's spell and forcing Brett and Amber and the judge into a reckoning . . . it still wasn't *enough*.

Was she feeling depressed simply because she'd yet to have her turn at exacting revenge? Or was it something else?

Kaylie's comment came back to her then. *It won't change anything.*

At the time Elliott had thought Kaylie was—well, not *crazy* for passing up the coven, because she'd never want to call another girl *that*—but . . . *misguided.*

But now, in some ways, she realized Kaylie was right.

Their spell hadn't really changed things because it hadn't undone the past. It couldn't prevent Kaylie from being raped or doxxed.

Except *not* casting the spell wouldn't have done that, either, Elliott reasoned.

And if "girls like her" had to live with so much pain, wasn't it better to also make their perpetrators suffer? Yes, maybe that meant creating a ripple effect, impacting their families and friends and wider community. But there were ripple effects to what *they'd* done.

No, that wasn't quite right. It wasn't a stone dropped in the water; it was more like a long winding path of dominos. And it was those bastards who'd tipped the first one by acting so inhumane, but what they didn't realize was that they themselves were in the path and were now getting knocked down, too.

But still . . . Elliott couldn't shake this haunted feeling.

A dry cough rose up in her throat, and she stopped where she was to hack into the elbow of her oversized cheetah-print cardigan, nearly doubling over on the sidewalk. Glancing around, she spotted

Dune Coffee Roasters, hesitated—she'd sworn she'd never go there again—then veered inside, making a beeline past the wall of skateboards and hip baristas behind the glassed-in pastry display. In the back of the bright and airy café, she quickly punched in the bathroom code, which she knew by heart, locked herself inside the small white room, and leaned over the porcelain sink, where she spit out a stream of purple.

After rinsing out the sink and guzzling some water, Elliott straightened and stared at her reflection in the mirror. She really did look *terrible.* And, she had to admit, it wasn't someone-who'd-eaten-bad-fish-tacos terrible, but more like someone-burning-in-the-flames-of-hell terrible. She pushed up the sleeve of her sweater and traced the curving lines of her mark, now spreading up her forearm. She was beginning to have her doubts that their marks were disconnected from the blowback. If they kept casting spells, would it eventually overtake her body?

Except it was *worth* it, she argued with herself as she grabbed some Kleenex and exited the bathroom. Besides, what else was she supposed to do?

The revenge was *justified.* It was a refrain Elliott repeated to herself over and over as she made her way up State Street, headed for home—*revenge is justified, revenge is justified, revenge is justified.* No, not just a refrain, a guiding mantra. In fact, by the time she turned onto Olive Street, she'd repeated it so many times that the individual words had lost their meanings—sort of like when she used to repeat words like *butter* and *pencil* over and over as a kid.

When she got inside, her dad was seated on the sofa working on his laptop. He glanced up at Elliott and she got the distinct feeling he'd been waiting for her.

"Hey," she greeted, setting down her backpack.

"Hi, Pigeon." He placed his laptop on the coffee table and patted the spot next to him.

Elliott pulled off her sunglasses, trying not to squint against the sunlight, and went over to sit down next to him.

"So, listen." He ran a hand through his hair. "With all the stuff in the news about that trial, and the recall campaign against the judge, and now hearing from the Petersons about what happened to Kaylie Meyers . . . which, I mean, I can't even imagine what that's been like for Beth and Phil . . ."

He paused, shaking his head. Elliott noted that her dad remembered Kaylie's parents' names. He'd driven her to that birthday party once upon a time, but she didn't think he remembered. It was the kind of small detail that made her love her dad all the more.

"Anyway, I've been doing a lot of thinking," he sighed. "And I wanted to apologize because I realize I haven't been doing a good enough job as your dad."

Elliott's stomach went cold. Where exactly was this going? "What? No, that's not true."

"Yes it is," he countered. "Because *I* should have been the one to tell you about your mom, not your grandmother."

Elliott went still. Her *mom*? Wait, what was he talking about?

"The other day when I overheard the two of you . . . I obviously knew what you were discussing. And it woke me up. I need to be better about this stuff. I guess I just never know the right age to bring up difficult topics. And your mom, she didn't like to talk about what happened to her. But I *know* she would have shared it with you. And I feel bad that you had to hear about it from Prudence first instead of me."

Elliott nodded, slowly processing.

"But I'm going to be better," her dad assured her. "I want us to share things with one another. I feel like we don't talk the way we used to. And I know you don't hang out with Vi anymore—and I'm not asking you in this moment to tell me why," he quickly added. "But I just . . . I want to really know you, El. I want us to be close."

Elliott looked up at her dad and saw tears in the corners of his eyes, which broke her heart. She felt like she should say something—she wanted to tell him the truth.

"I want that, too, Dad," she replied. Which was also the truth.

He wrapped an arm around her shoulders and pulled her close. Elliott buried her head in his shirt as she hugged him back, feeling so loved that she could cry.

"Okay," he said after a minute, kissing the top of her head. "I should probably get back to work."

"Yeah," she inhaled. "I have homework anyway, so . . . get outta here."

Her dad laughed as he picked up his laptop.

After he'd gone back into his home office, Elliott sat there a moment, thinking.

Your mom didn't like to talk about what happened to her.

Pulling out her phone, she made a call.

"Hey," she greeted. "It's Elliott. Can we talk?"

Half an hour later, Elliott's Uber pulled up in front of a modest '70s-style track home over in Hidden Valley.

As she made her way up the front walk, she could feel something beginning to drip from her nose, and she quickly wiped it away with a balled-up Kleenex, double-checking with her phone's camera that she looked normal. Well, not *normal*—she had uncombed hair that was beginning to resemble a pile of day-old pink party streamers, a purplish paranormal substance dripping from her body, and a magically invisible, possibly sentient mark creeping up her arm—but normal-*ish*. Then she knocked on the front door.

When it swung open, Mary Yoshida was standing there, composed as always in her cheerful turquoise silk top, long prayer bead necklace, and cat-eye frames. For some reason, *astonishingly*, Elliott found herself hoping that Mary would hug her.

Instead, Mary spoke. And when she did, her voice was warm but firm, her words a statement, not a question.

"You have the book, don't you?"

17

Elliott

Never in a million years would Elliott have imagined finding herself in the home of Mary Yoshida, fearless leader of Tragic Kindergarten Kingdom. And yet there she was, settled into Mary's comfy breakfast nook in her cheerful kitchen, in her artsy Hidden Valley home.

From the outside, her house was nothing special—just a boxy mix of brick and siding—but when Elliott walked through the front door, she'd been surprised at the creative vibe. There was a large Buddha statue and a fountain in the foyer (which was filled with actual fish), a mix of photography and Basquiat-style oil paintings on the walls, and an eclectic array of furniture, including a vintage sewing machine table and a swing hanging from the living room ceiling. It wasn't exactly the kind of interior design Elliott would have picked, but she admired Mary for so clearly shaping her own world.

"Here we go," Mary said, bringing Elliott a mug of coffee and sitting down across from her. Mary had put on some folksy harp music—Joanna Newsom, maybe?—and Elliott could smell the last hazy trails of smoky incense. Sun streamed through the leaves outside the window, creating dappled light that made the room feel underwater.

"So," Mary said, stirring cream into her own coffee and leveling Elliott with her gaze. "It seems we have a lot to discuss."

Elliott nodded in agreement. She'd started piecing things together—her mom's friendship with Mary; her mom's ownership of the book; the fact that something apparently happened to her mother, too—but Elliott wanted to hear it all straight from Mary. "I want you to tell me everything," she insisted. "I want to know all about your friendship with my mom."

Mary studied Elliott over her mug, then nodded. "Your mother and I met in the dorms freshman year, and we quickly became good friends. So much so that we moved into an apartment together with our friend Suzanne during sophomore year. We were roommates for three years. I considered Ronnie one of my best friends." She smiled. "In some ways, I still do."

And yet in all the conversations Elliott had had with her mom about her own youth, Mary's and Suzanne's names never came up. Then again, was that so surprising? Friendships ended all the time. Just look at her and Vi.

"We did everything together back then," Mary reminisced. "We took the same gender studies courses, we went to the same indie rock shows, we stayed up late smoking cloves and having heated debates with our friends. And it was in our junior year that we became intrigued by witchcraft."

Witchcraft. Elliott could feel the hairs standing up on the back of her neck.

"We took a class about the Sacred Feminine Divine, and our professor focused a good portion of the course on witches. Ronnie became particularly interested in how feminism and the history of witches intersected. But it was more of a casual interest at that point, in the same way I was interested in the history of independent cinema, or Suzanne was interested in the history of rock and roll."

Typical '90s-era college student interests, Elliott thought with both envy and a slight internal eye roll.

"And then senior year ... well, something happened to your mom ..." Mary hesitated, carefully turning her mug around on the table. "Did she ever talk to you about any of this?"

"No," said Elliott. "My dad hinted at it, but he didn't tell me the details." Elliott and her mom never had the chance to discuss the types of intimate things that would have been disclosed in Elliott's teen years, one of many things she mourned. Though for some reason she felt nervous about whatever Mary might say.

Mary nodded, considering her words. "I don't usually feel it's my place to speak for someone else's trauma, but I think it's important that you know. Ronnie—your mom—she was raped by a friend of hers."

The information settled into the pit of Elliott's stomach like a rock.

"She went out with him one weekend," Mary continued, "and he slipped something into her drink. It was only the next morning when she woke up in a strange room that she realized she'd been raped. Though she didn't call it that right away. It was only once she told Suzanne and I what happened that we helped her see what he'd done."

Rage flared within Elliott. She wanted to do something right then and there to protect her mom, even though the damage was done, and her mom was already dead.

"That's when Suzanne and I each admitted we'd had something happen to us, too," Mary explained. "Suzanne, as it turned out, had been molested by her youth pastor, and I, as you know, was raped by my high school prom date."

Elliott nodded; Mary had often shared her own story in group. But there was something different in hearing about it now: it wasn't just the experience of the Tragic Kindergarten Kingdom leader, it was the experience of her mom's old best friend, an experience her mom had shared.

"We didn't talk about our experiences in detail, and we certainly didn't get into how we were each impacted or feeling. Back then almost everyone we knew seemed to have been 'taken advantage of' by a guy or had the guy *attempt* to take advantage of them," Mary explained. "It was considered normal, boys will be boys and all that crap. We didn't even *know* to call it sexual harassment or sexual assault, even though that's exactly what it was. But we *did* know we were sick of it, and that we wanted to do something—and that no one was going to do a damn thing for us."

That, Elliott thought, sounded all too familiar.

"And right around that time was when Ronnie came across the book. She'd been hunting down literature about the history of witchcraft, and one day in the UCSB library she discovered a book with an unusual binding, one that she knew she hadn't seen the day before. There wasn't an author listed, and when she opened the book there wasn't a library card. But after reading the introduction she was incredibly intrigued. She took it to the front desk, but instead of allowing her to check it out, the librarian on duty determined it must be someone's personal journal and put it in the lost and found.

"Your mom came home and told us about it that evening, lamenting the fact that she hadn't simply taken it. So I offered to go back the next day and pretend it was mine. When I did, I'll never forget what the librarian on duty told me: *Be careful with that one,* she warned. Which felt both eerie and meaningful. But then she added, *It really is a lovely cover and binding. They don't make books like that anymore.*

"Of course, we were skeptical about the book at first, but, as you know, we quickly saw that it was real. And so, we decided to form a coven and get revenge on those who'd wronged us."

Elliott's lips parted at the revelation. She'd known this was where the story was leading—of course she had—but hearing it out loud, knowing for sure that Mary and her mom had been in a *coven*, that her own mother had practiced *witchcraft* in order to get *revenge*, was astonishing nonetheless. It simultaneously made Elliott feel distanced from her mom—how much did she not know about her? Could never know?—and incredibly close—in so many ways their stories were mirrored.

"What spells did you each conjure?" Elliott asked. "And what happened to your targets?"

"Well," Mary recalled, "Suzanne conjured the Incantation of Renunciation, and her youth pastor lost his faith. In God, in his family, in himself. We found out he just walked out in the middle of a youth group sermon one day. He left the church, he left his wife, he lost everything in the end. He wound up homeless and despondent on the streets."

Which seemed about right to Elliott. Why *should* he have anything good left in his life after what he'd done?

"And your mother," Mary continued, "conjured the Incantation of Degradation. Her target lost control over his own body. Not *everything*; he could still walk and talk and was functional in many ways. But he could no longer control his bowels or bladder, and both his eyes began to wander. When he walked it was with minute, shuffling steps, and when he spoke all his words came out backward."

Again, that seemed right to Elliott. Was he still alive, she wondered. Could she find him and revel in his backward babbling and tiny steps?

"And my spell"—Mary paused, pressing her lips together—"I conjured the Incantation of Enervation. And when I cast it . . . my target wound up dead."

Elliott stared at Mary, unsure what to say. She tried to absorb the information. Her mother's coven had cast a spell and *killed* someone. Her mother had been responsible for someone's death.

No, not just anyone, she reminded herself. Mary's attacker. Someone who deserved what he got, who deserved to be destroyed.

"How did it happen?" Elliott asked.

"He jumped off Stearns Wharf and swam out into the ocean until his body gave way and he drowned. A boat five miles out from shore came across his body."

A disturbing image of a man floating facedown in the abyss that was the Pacific Ocean flashed through Elliott's mind.

"I thought his destruction was the very thing I wanted," Mary said, her gaze on the table. "But once we'd manifested it, I felt a huge weight of guilt over what we had done."

"And how did my mom feel?" asked Elliott. Had she felt that they'd evened the scales? Or was she conflicted, too, questioning if it was even her place to touch the scales to begin with?

"Your mother was haunted," Mary confirmed. "We all were."

Elliott thought of how melancholy her mom often was, drawn to sad music and dark art and books about grief and death. She'd named Elliott after Elliott Smith, for God's sake—a musician who wrote beautiful, sad songs about his struggles with depression. Was all of that her mom's way of trying to cope and work through what they'd done? Or was she melancholy because of her trauma? Or would she have *always* been drawn to stuff like that?

Yeah, but casting that spell clearly hadn't ruined her mom's life, right? She'd gone on to get married and have a film editing career and start a family. She was mostly happy.

Also, who else was going to make sure that guy was punished? What recourse did she have? What recourse did any of them have? Were they supposed to just take what was dished out and quietly put up with it like good little girls?

"And, as I'm sure you know, there were other consequences to our actions, too," Mary continued. "After all, what we were seeking was also seeking us. Suzanne became particularly concerned about the aftereffects and the way our marks were spreading across our palms."

Across their palms, Elliott noted; *her* coven's marks had already spread much farther, a detail she didn't share. "What kind of blowback did you each experience?" asked Elliott.

"At first it wasn't noticeable, but after the second spell we began coughing up a strange purple substance. And after the third time, it grew worse. We began to feel ill . . . almost *poisoned* by what we were doing."

Elliott hadn't put it into those words, but that's exactly how she felt. Though the blowback Mary had described was only half of what Elliott was suffering—which filled her with additional alarm.

But she immediately pushed the fear away. Perhaps her mom's coven just wasn't dedicated enough. Elliott could put up with some temporary discomfort if it was on a path toward justice.

"And strangely enough," Mary went on, "I found that in pursuing revenge I was centering all my energy on *him*. My assailant. In some ways, I found myself focusing on him more than ever."

But wasn't that to be expected, Elliott reasoned. You *had* to focus on your target if you were getting revenge.

"After my target died, the coven broke apart," Mary continued. "Suzanne was worried, and I felt guilty. I think your mom *might* have agreed to keep going if *we'd* really wanted to, but she wasn't confident in continuing, and of course even if she'd wanted to, she couldn't conjure or cast without us. We debated what to do with the book. Suzanne actually tried to burn it but couldn't."

"Why, what happened?" asked Elliott.

Mary responded by pulling up her shirtsleeve. Licking up the inside of her forearm was an angry pink scar, the same one Elliott had caught a glimpse of outside of group.

"Wait—my mom had a burn scar *just* like that," Elliott said, an inadvertent shiver running down her spine.

"I know. We all ended up with these," Mary confirmed as she pulled her sleeve back down. "So, we knew we couldn't destroy the book, and we didn't feel comfortable getting rid of it in case it wound up in the wrong hands—"

Wrong hands. Was Elliott's coven "in the wrong hands"? But how was it wrong to use the book for the very thing it promised: *A means to control your path . . . a resolution to your darkest tribulations*? The book *stated* it was a *most special device*; devices were *meant* to be used, right?

"—so your mom agreed to lock it away for safekeeping," Mary went on. "After the coven disbanded, Suzanne moved to Colorado and pretended none of it ever happened, and I never heard from her again. But your mom actually reached out to me years later. By then so much time had gone by, and I was slow to reply. When I finally did, I learned she'd already passed away."

Elliott wondered what her mom had wanted to tell Mary. What if she was hoping to gather the old coven together to help in her time of need? For a moment Elliott felt enraged at Mary for being so slow to respond.

At the same time, a logical part of Elliott knew that attempting to use the book for something like her mom's cancer wouldn't have necessarily worked. Was that even the book's purpose? Also, it's not like the book was a direct line into the metaphysical plane where you could just order up the precise outcome you wanted.

Thinking of her mom's cancer, though, Elliott had a horrifying thought: What if *that's* why she got sick? Because of the book.

But then Elliott realized that line of thinking didn't hold up. If that were true, Mary and Suzanne would have gotten sick, too. No, her mom's cancer wasn't karmic bad luck; it was just your average the-Universe-can-randomly-screw-you-over-whenever-it-wants kind of bad luck.

But, in the end, how *had* her mom felt about the coven? Was she filled with regret over the harm they'd caused? Or had some part of her missed being a witch? Is *that* why she kept the book? She could have chucked it into a landfill somewhere, which wouldn't have been foolproof but a pretty safe bet. And yet she hadn't.

It was overwhelmingly sad and frustrating that Elliott could never fully know her mom. She was literally standing in her mom's old shoes, and yet she couldn't know her heart or mind.

"And what about you?" Elliott asked genuinely. "Did you just . . . move on?"

Mary smiled kindly. "Not exactly. I went through a very dark time that landed me in rehab, actually. Once I got sober, I determined that the only way to truly make amends was to use what I'd gone through to help others. So I became a counselor. But then I realized I didn't *just* want to help people with their trauma; I wanted to have a positive impact earlier in life. So I became a kindergarten teacher and decided to use my counseling background to start a support group."

Mary unexpectedly rose from the table and went over to retrieve something from a shelf on the wall. When she came back, Elliott saw that she was holding a small cobalt blue bowl. It was delicate and beautiful but clearly had been broken in a dozen pieces and then put back together, the cracks filled in with gold.

"Are you familiar with kintsugi?" she asked Elliott.

"No." Elliott shook her head. She could feel a lesson coming on.

"It's the ancient Japanese art of repairing broken pottery," Mary explained. "But instead of trying to camouflage the cracks, the artist calls attention to the imperfections. The object is considered more beautiful and precious for having withstood its breaks."

"Okay," Elliott said slowly.

"These experiences that we go through, Elliott, they break us. Make no mistake about that. But *we* get to decide how we piece ourselves back together. There are some things you simply can't *move on* from. Like grief. Like trauma. Like the guilt of knowing someone's death is on your hands. But that doesn't mean you have to remain shattered. Here, this is for you." She handed the bowl to Elliott.

"Oh. No. I don't really—"

"I want you to have it," Mary assured her, holding the bowl out farther.

"Okay." Elliott took the bowl. "Thank you."

It was a nice gesture, but Elliott couldn't help thinking that it was always the same with Mary, all kindness and light and kumbaya shit. She and her bowl metaphor were about as useful as her support group and all that talk. Just sit with your pain and accept it, and then what? Meditate on a mountain somewhere and be all Zen for the rest of your life? Was that it? Because if so, no thank you.

"But of course, my history with the book isn't why you're *really* here, is it," said Mary.

Elliott stared at Mary. It wasn't? No, Elliott was pretty sure it was.

"Judge Ramos, Brett Hunt, and Amber Tuffalo," Mary added. "I know that was you."

Elliott took a sip of her coffee, unwilling to confirm, not wanting to deny.

"I'm not asking for a confession," Mary assured her. "And I'm not going to out you and your coven."

Not that anyone would believe an accusation like that if she tried. This wasn't the 1700s. Mary would look bonkers trying to report a bunch of teenage girls using *witchcraft*.

"But I know how it feels to bear the weight of your actions," Mary said gently. "How it can eat at your soul. How you can find yourself becoming the very thing you hate."

Elliott shifted in her seat. "That's not how I feel," she said reflexively.

"Hmmm." Mary nodded, like she didn't quite buy that. She looked down at her mug, which she was slowly turning around in her hands on the table. "You know, I've thought about that book quite a lot over the years, and I've come to realize something. The book was never inherently bad or good. I think it was merely a reflection. It gave us whatever we sought. And in hindsight, what we sought was such a *waste.*"

She gave Elliott a meaningful look. Elliott silently stared back, just like she did in group.

"Whether or not you continue down your current path, Elliott, is ultimately up to you. Some people would think it wrong that I don't try to stop you, given the book's power, but I firmly believe we must all make our own choices and forge our own paths. And then live with the consequences, whatever they might be. Besides, I'm not convinced I *could* stop you. Even if I found a way to steal the book from you, somehow I think you'd find a way to get it back."

Which was absolutely 100 percent dead-on.

"But I will say this: that book is *extraordinarily* special, and I often wish we'd given more thought to what we *truly* sought."

Elliott nodded, as if she were actually considering Mary's words.

"Well, it's getting kind of late," Elliott said awkwardly, standing up from the table. "I should probably go. Thank you for letting me come here—and for the bowl."

"I'm here any time you'd like to talk," Mary reminded her. "And I'd be happy to drive you—"

"No, that's okay," Elliott assured her. "I'll get myself home."

And with that, she saw herself out the front door.

But as she strode down the front walkway and out to the sidewalk, she had to admit that there was something about what Mary had said that rattled her. *I often wish we'd given more thought to what we truly sought.* For some reason it made her once again think of Kaylie's words: *It won't change anything.*

Except *no*, Elliott rejected as she ordered her Uber. She *knew* what she truly sought. She'd known from day one.

The problem, she decided as she chucked the bowl inside her backpack and crossed the street toward the church at the corner, was Mary's generation. They just weren't *ready* for the kind of power the book offered. They didn't have the backbone for it, or the determination to see things through.

But *Elliott's* generation was different. Her coven had already gone further than her mother's coven ever had—their marks were proof enough of that. They had both the backbone *and* the determination. And *Elliott* was absolutely going to see things through.

18

Elliott

That Thursday afternoon, Elliott was holed up in her room attempting to catch up on all of her overdue homework, which seemed like a losing battle.

Over the past few days, the worst of her symptoms had dissipated—she wasn't nauseous or expelling weird purple stuff, and the faint purple tint to the world had faded—but the blowback wasn't *entirely* gone. She still wasn't sleeping well, her dreams strange and restless or flat-out nightmares. And the rancid taste and stench had lingered. Plus, her body felt constantly cold. All of which had Elliott concerned. This was the worst the blowback had ever been and the longest it had lingered.

It made her think of what Mary had said. *We felt poisoned by what we were doing.* What if that was true? What if with each new spell, they were being poisoned? And did that mean they were building up a tolerance, or slowly destroying themselves?

But none of that was what drove Elliott to be alone.

It was because, despite her best efforts—which included rewatching *Beetlejuice*, dancing full-out to New Order's "Age of Consent," and drinking copious amounts of coffee—she'd been unable to shake her funk.

Maybe it was because so many people at her school had swiftly moved on and were no longer talking about Kaylie, obsessed with the next drama, the next juicy gossip. Kaylie's story, only a few days old, had already lost its shine.

Which made Elliott feel as if their spell hadn't impacted anyone—at least, not in a lasting way.

Except the judge and Brett and Amber would never be the same, she reminded herself. And *that* was something. More than something.

Plus, she'd feel better once she cast her *own* spell. Certainly, her coven-mates must feel better, even if they didn't always seem outwardly different. Hadn't Chloe said she felt better directly after?

Revenge. *That* was what she truly sought, Elliott repeated to herself again and again. And when Kaylie's words whispered in her head, *It won't change anything,* Elliott mentally shouted back, *Yes it fucking will.*

A knock on her bedroom door pulled Elliott from her homework—which she'd been more staring at versus actually doing.

"Pigeon?" her dad called.

"You can come in," she called back over the sounds of Siouxsie and the Banshees.

He cracked the door open, smiling when he heard what was playing: a cover of the Beatles' "Dear Prudence." "Your mom loved this song."

"I know." Elliott smiled as she rummaged through her desk for a highlighter.

"You need a snack before you head out to your SAT class?"

"Nah, I'm good," she replied, swallowing her guilt over lying to her dad. SAT course. She hadn't even *registered* for the SAT. "Actually, Dad?" she said before he could close the door. "Can I ask you something?"

"Of course." He leaned against the doorframe.

Elliott fiddled with the cap to her highlighter. "When Mom told you about what happened to her . . ." She uncapped and recapped her pen. "Did it make you see her differently?"

Her dad was quiet, reflecting on the question. "Yes."

Elliott looked up at him in surprise. It wasn't the answer she'd expected.

He came over and sat against the edge of her desk. "It made me realize how incredibly *strong* she was, Elliott."

Elliott looked back down at her homework. Her throat felt very tight. "But you never, you know . . . thought less of her?"

"No, *never*," he said earnestly. "Not for one single moment. What happened to your mom was in no way her fault. And I loved her exactly as she was. I hated that she suffered, just the way I hate it when you suffer. But every single one of us has our struggles, Elliott. And those struggles don't define us; it's how we choose to handle them and move forward that does."

Elliott nodded.

"Hey, Pigeon." He put a hand on her shoulder. "Look at me."

Elliott met her dad's gaze, which was so full of love, she wanted to cry.

"You know, the thing I didn't say to you the other day, maybe one of the most important things I could ever tell you, is that if something ever happens to you—if something *happened* to you," he added carefully, "I would want you to know that nothing you could ever tell me would lessen my love for you. Not a thing. You understand?"

Elliott nodded, swallowing away the lump in her throat.

"I'm a rain-or-shine kind of guy. Especially for you." He ruffled her hair. "Even when you leave dirty cereal bowls stacked on your desk like a total barbarian." He side-eyed the dishes piled near her books.

"Okay, *Prudence*," Elliott teased.

"Oooof, harsh." He squeezed her shoulder. "I love you, kid. Always have. Always will."

"I love you, too, Daddy," Elliott managed.

"Okay." He pushed himself off her desk. "I'm going to let you study. I'll save you a plate of lasagna for when you get home. Speaking of your grandmother, she actually made it vegetarian this time."

And with that, he went out, leaving Elliott to sit with his words as she listened to his footsteps fade away.

Elliott left fifteen minutes early for Franceschi Park that evening, but when she arrived, Madeline was already there.

"Hey," Elliott greeted in surprise, hoisting up her backpack.

Madeline looked wired as she paced back and forth in front of the benches, one arm wrapped around her torso, an extra-large coffee in her free hand. Her already-thin frame looked especially sharp and angular under her cashmere sweater, and her normally sleek hair was surprisingly wild and curly.

"Hi," she greeted excitedly. "I have something *really* important I want to discuss with the group once we're all here. Which, speaking of, where is everyone? We should really probably stick to the schedule."

"It's only five forty-five," Elliott reminded her, sitting down on one of the benches, which was cold through her ripped black jeans. The air was cool and crisp, which somehow reached her even through her vintage faux-fur leopard-print coat. "You feeling okay?" Elliott asked Madeline, watching her in concern as she took a chug of her coffee, still pacing back and forth.

"What? Yeah. I'm great."

"Because you seem kind of on edge," Elliott observed.

"I just didn't sleep at all last night," Madeline dismissed, like it was no big deal. "I stayed up researching—well, I'll save that for when everyone's here."

Maybe it really was just the lack of sleep, but Madeline . . . God, she looked like the Bride of Frankenstein. Or the before picture in a sad makeover show. Or the after picture in a sad cautionary tale. Had her parents or friends said anything? Is that how *Elliott* appeared? If so, no wonder her dad felt compelled to ask how she was.

Chloe was next to arrive, pulling up in her Beemer and trudging over to the benches.

"Hey," she greeted, rubbing her gloved hands together as she plopped down onto the bench beside Elliott. "God, I can't seem to warm up," she confessed as she pulled her black wool coat around her. "And I can't get rid of this weird taste and bad smell. Do you guys have that, too?"

"Yeah," replied Madeline. "But I'm actually feeling *great*."

"Well, *I've* been better," admitted Elliott.

Bea arrived only five minutes late, wearing her running clothes and a puffy Patagonia coat that looked better suited for the cold harsh winters of Minnesota than the midfifties-range winters in Santa Barbara. Her skin lacked its usual luster, and for some reason Elliott sensed that she was not only exhausted but hesitant to be there. The moment they were down the hill and beside the mansion, Elliott learned why.

"Before we begin," Bea announced, "I have something I need to tell all of you."

"Me too," Madeline said enthusiastically. "But, Bea—you go first."

Bea nodded as she sat down cross-legged. "Well, it's awkward to say this, but I wanted to tell you all . . ." She ran a hand over one of her braids. "I think I want out."

"What?" Madeline jutted her chin out in surprise.

"I'm not going to bail on you," Bea assured Elliott. "But after this . . . I don't know that I want to do this anymore."

"Bea, no!" Chloe pleaded. "We need you."

"Why do you want out?" asked Elliott.

"I don't feel great about what we're doing," Bea admitted quietly, shoving her hands into her coat pockets. "Maybe I should be fine with it, I *want* to be fine with it, but . . . it turns out I'm not. And I also don't feel any *better*, you know? If anything, I'm feeling worse. I mean, do either of you feel better?" she asked, looking at Madeline and then Chloe.

"Well . . . I don't know," Chloe admitted, which was a change of tune from what she'd previously said. "But doing this, it's special. I don't really have anyone else who gets it, like you all do. And being in a coven . . . it makes me feel powerful, and a little less alone. I really don't want to lose that. Or all of you. I mean, maybe it's cheesy of me, but you've all become my *friends*. Plus, I don't want to lose the magic. I *like* having magic."

"Honestly?" said Madeline. "I'm feeling amazing. And I think the reason you're not feeling better, Bea, is because we haven't gone far enough."

Bea quirked her mouth to one side, like she doubted that.

"I'm serious," Madeline insisted. "What I wanted to tell the group is that I realized, what we did for Kaylie? We should be doing that for others. And I've already started a list."

"A list?" asked Elliott. "Who's on it?"

"I began with the names of boys I'd heard about from girls I know," Madeline explained. "Guys who hurt someone, or took advantage of someone, or shared nudes, or just generally made girls feel like crap—though this can definitely be expanded to include boys from a wider variety of schools. And then I used the online family court records to research the names of anyone who'd been accused of or charged with sexual abuse or assault, sexual harassment, or domestic violence within the last five years. And that led me to a list of local sex offenders, all of whom should *absolutely* be punished, whether or not they've served time—because obviously we can do a *much* better job of making them suffer.

"And so far, I have 846 names," Madeline informed them proudly. "Which is obviously only a partial list. And that's *just* Santa Barbara. Think about how many names we'll have if we extend to Oxnard or Ventura. Or if we go up to Santa Maria or Lompoc. We could take down the entire Central Coast. Not to mention Los Angeles, which is just the mecca of creepdom."

"But we never agreed to go full-on vigilante," Bea pointed out.

"True," said Madeline. "But maybe we should. When we started this, we were thinking small, we were being selfish—and that was *fine*. That was where we needed to begin. But now that we've seen what we can do, how can we stop at just ourselves?"

"Because *look* at us," Bea countered.

Elliott glanced at each of her coven-mates—their exhausted eyes, their hunched frames. They pretty much all looked like crap.

"And what about *this*." Bea pushed up her sleeve to reveal her mark. "*This* is not normal. We don't know what we're dealing with here. Or if we'll all stay this way if we just keep going, or if we'll get *worse*."

"Yes, *look* at us," Madeleine agreed enthusiastically. "We're having an *impact*. Is anyone else holding these people accountable? Has anyone else done *any*thing like what we've done?"

Elliott's mom and her coven flashed through Elliott's mind, but for some reason she kept her mouth shut.

"How can we sit here and worry about *ourselves*?" Madeline continued, looking each girl in the eye. "Think about all those girls out there who have been in our exact situations, but don't have access to something like the book. They're out there in pain with *no* recourse."

Bea flinched and looked down. Clearly Madeline had struck a chord.

"This is no longer about us," Madeline argued. "This is about being on the right side of justice. About *manifesting* justice. And not just for us, but for every person who's ever been made to feel afraid, or ashamed, or like they're relegated to the shadows. And I don't want to simply target victims' assailants. We can *start* there, but I want to go after every last asshole involved. The ones who enable the assailants or fail to hold them accountable for their actions. The ones who don't believe us when we speak up, or turn around and make us believe that *we're* the problem, or that somehow *we* asked for what happened to us or could have done something to prevent it. I want to punish the creepy men who send me dick pics with messages like, 'Hey, hottie, will you suck me off?' and the random guys downtown who think they can whistle at me and call me 'sweet cheeks' as I'm crossing the street. I want to punish the mother of the jerk who—who did what he did to me, for being so in denial about her child and raising an asshole of a son. I don't want to just punish rapists and molesters and stalkers and abusers, I want to burn the whole fucking misogynistic system to the *ground*. The world used to set fire to witches, but now it's time that we witches set fire to the world."

Elliott stared at Madeline, a little bit shocked, and a little bit impressed, but also a little bit frightened. Who *was* this person? When had the old Madeline disappeared? This Madeline wasn't just a rebel or a revolutionary; she was entering into anarchist, guerilla warfare territory.

"Whoa," said Chloe, looking intrigued but also a little conflicted. "That was . . . wow."

"But when does it *end*?" asked Bea. Which was a valid question.

"It *doesn't* end," Madeline declared. "Why should it end? They went out into the world and wreaked havoc—and some of them did it on *purpose* because they *wanted* us to suffer. So it will end once each and every assailant and accomplice is punished, and the *abuse* fucking *stops*. In the meantime, they should just be glad that all I want is an eye for an eye, and not the rest of them, too."

Bea leaned backward, looking concerned. She glanced at Elliott, her eyebrows raised in question. "Elliott, what about you? You've been quiet, but *you* started this coven. What do *you* want?"

The question reminded her of Mary's words: *I often wish we'd given more thought to what we truly sought.*

The thing is, Madeline wasn't *wrong*. There was a huge part of Elliott that wanted to burn the system to the ground, too. And she *cared* about all those nameless girls out there, suffering without recourse.

And yet . . . it wasn't the *exact* vision she'd had when starting this coven.

For good or bad, Elliott was mostly thinking about herself and the girls in her immediate vicinity at group. And did that mean that Madeline's plan was the wrong path, or did Elliott simply need to revise her vision? And was she willing to give over her entire life to the cause?

She wasn't sure. She didn't know. And she felt disappointed in herself that her immediate reaction wasn't *hell yeah*.

She'd started this coven with such absolute clarity, but now . . . now she felt unstable, like the floor had tipped sideways. It was disorienting to suddenly be filled with doubts.

"What I want," she finally told the group, "is to have my turn."

Madeline pressed her lips together, like she was disappointed in the answer. But in that moment, it was the only honest reply Elliott could provide—and one that couldn't be argued with; after all, that's why they were there.

"That's fair." Chloe nodded.

Madeline blew out a breath. "Well, we can revisit this conversation after we cast Elliott's spell," she assured the group, to which Bea was notably silent.

Elliott pulled the puzzle box from her backpack, retrieved the book, and opened it, flipping through the dull ash-gray pages. Pages that once held the promise of untold magic and were now a quiet reminder of her coven-mates' spells.

This was it, Elliott breathed. The reason she'd started this coven. The moment she'd fantasized about for so long.

She set the open book before her, the fresh blue-black pages both a question mark and an invitation. What spell might she conjure to satisfy her desires?

Extending her right hand, Elliott took in a deep breath and began to chant.

"Bring forth that which will satisfy my desires," she whispered, closing her eyes in concentration. *"Bring forth that which will satisfy my desires."* She trusted this book. It would deliver exactly what she sought. *"Bring forth that which will satisfy my desires."*

She opened her eyes just in time to see the silver script rise from its unknown depths, manifesting on the page. Even now, after so many spells, the sight filled her with awe.

"What does it say?" whispered Chloe.

Elliott picked up the book, a shiver running down her spine at the title. Her mind immediately flashed to Mary. "'Incantation of Destruction,'" she read aloud.

"Damn," Chloe exhaled.

"That's really . . . ," Bea trailed off.

"Badass," Madeline finished, her eyes gleaming with fervor.

"No," argued Bea. "That's not . . . I don't like the sound of it."

"Well, we don't know if it means *destruction* destruction," Chloe countered. "It could be like getting the Death tarot card, which is rarely about a literal death and more about endings and spiritual transformation."

"Yeah. But this isn't tarot, Chloe," Bea quietly pointed out.

"Let's see what the spell says," Elliott stated, setting the book in her lap. "'To perform the Incantation of Destruction,'" she read aloud, "'first gather together the following items: one ounce dead sea salt, one ounce sulfur, one spoonful of belladonna seeds, a handful of shattered glass, a pinch of graveyard dirt, three broken eggshells, four purple candles, and an image of your victim.'" *Not a personal effect,* Elliott thought in relief. *Thank God.*

"'To cast the spell,'" she continued reading, "'gather your coven together in the location of your choosing at midnight on a full moon—'"

"Wait," Madeline interrupted. "But that's tonight."

"Are you sure?" Elliott craned her head to look up at the moon, which was hidden behind the clouds.

"I'm positive," Madeline replied.

Madeline had memorized the moon cycle? Of course she had. "Shit," said Elliott. "Well, I don't think we can—"

"Let me see those ingredients again?" Chloe asked, reaching for the book. She scanned the text and then nodded, handing the book back. "Yep, I have everything."

"Really?" Elliott said in surprise. Since when did Chloe have a full stock of witchy ingredients? "Okay . . . so, we're good?"

"Wait . . . so, we're actually doing this, then?" Bea double-checked, clearly troubled by the spell's title.

"Of course we're doing this," Madeline dismissed. "*This* is the spell the book provided."

"I think Madeline's right," Elliott agreed. "If this is the spell most suited to me, it's the one I need to cast."

"And I say we do it tonight," Madeline added. "Otherwise, you'll have to wait another twenty-nine days."

Which, needless to say, Elliott did *not* want. "Right. Okay. So, we do it tonight," Elliott confirmed. "Does that work for everyone?"

"Yep," said Chloe.

Bea hesitated, though eventually she nodded her consent.

"And as far as location," Elliott suggested, "let's keep it simple and come back here."

"It's supposed to rain late tonight," Chloe reminded her. The first, and probably last, rain of the season.

"Okay." Elliott looked around, then pointed toward a set of splintered double doors on the backside of the decrepit mansion. "Then let's meet inside there."

Of course, once she was back at home and alone, Elliott allowed herself to admit that the title of the spell had *her* concerned, too. What if it really did mean *destruction* destruction, she worried as she picked at her grandma's lasagna, Tori Amos's "Precious Things" blaring through her earbuds. Was she okay with that?

She must be, though, she realized. Why else would the book provide such a spell?

And yet, it provided something similar to Mary, Elliott considered as she pulled a photo book from the top shelf of her closet. And look how *that* had gone.

But she was different, Elliott reminded herself as she blasted Smashing Pumpkins' "Bullet with Butterfly Wings" and flipped through the book's pages. It was one Vi had gone to great trouble to make, printing a copy for herself and one for Elliott. She located the photo in question, cut it out from the page, making every effort not to look at it, and shoved it into her back pocket.

She had the backbone and the determination. She was going to see things through.

And why should she be worried about destroying *him*? Had he worried about destroying *her*?

No, he abso-fucking-lutely had not.

So maybe he deserved destruction.

And maybe Elliott wasn't going to care.

19

Elliott

By quarter to midnight, it wasn't just raining, as Chloe had predicted; it was flat out pouring. The trees outside Elliott's window lashed in the wind, which was blowing the rain sideways, pelting it against the window's glass. Any kind of rain was infrequent in Santa Barbara, but a storm like this was a rarity—the kind of deluge that overwhelmed the parched, often-fire-scorched earth and resulted in mudslides. Not exactly the kind of weather that made one want to sneak out said window to catch the Uber they'd ordered. But Elliott did so nonetheless.

At Franceschi Park, Elliott's driver pulled up beside Madeline's Prius—of course she was the first one there. The driver turned in her seat to say something to Elliott, one arm holding the passenger seat, her head craned.

"I'm sorry?" Elliott asked, pulling out her earbuds and pausing Hole's "Violet."

"I said, you sure you're okay to be here, hon?" the driver asked.

Elliott registered the genuine concern in the woman's eyes—this stranger was looking out for her—which flooded Elliott with surprising gratitude and made her own eyes fill with tears. "Yeah, I'm good," she assured her, blinking rapidly and tucking her phone away.

There was no point in using the clear umbrella she'd brought; the wind just immediately whipped it inside out, so Elliott ran through the downpour in her black trench coat and bright orange beanie, water soaking in through the eyelets of her Docs. By the time she reached the mansion and climbed through the double doors, she was soaked, her pink hair hanging in stringy clumps when she took off her hat.

"Hey," Elliott greeted Madeline, who was seated rigidly on the floor of what appeared to be a wood-paneled library, a lit candle before her and a book in her hands. Water was dripping through the dilapidated roof and collecting in the corners of the room, but the center, where Madeline was seated, was dry.

"Did you know that in the nineteenth century, Madame Zuifraine led a coven of witches in an expedition to burn down the Capitol building in Charlotte in protest against the abuse toward women?" Madeline asked.

"I did not," Elliott replied as she shrugged off her coat.

"Actually, you probably already know this, but there's a *whole* connection between feminism and witches," she informed Elliott. "And I was just reading something this evening that further connected feminists and witches with labeling women *sluts*."

"Are you not concerned about someone finding that book?" Elliott asked, folding her coat and setting it to the side before taking a seat on the dusty wood floor.

"This is a *historical* text," Madeline justified.

Which was technically speaking still a paper trail. But Elliott decided to let it go.

Chloe was the next to arrive, holding on to the hood of her raincoat as she rushed through the doors.

"Jesus." She unzipped her coat, which was dripping everywhere. "It's crazy out there." She tossed it onto the floor beside Elliott's and slung off her canvas ingredients bag. "Wait, Bea's not down here yet?"

"No," replied Elliott. "Why?"

"Her car was already in the parking lot when I got here," Chloe said. "I assumed she'd be here."

"That's weird," Elliott replied, trying not to feel too alarmed.

"Should we call her?" Madeline asked.

"Maybe we should go outside and check for her," Elliott suggested, rising to her feet. "What if she slipped and fell on the way down?" Or what if something else had happened?

"I think I would have seen her, though," Chloe pointed out.

"True," Elliott said, her unease growing.

"You don't think she's backing out, do you?" Madeline asked in concern.

"I'm not backing out," Bea replied as she walked through the doors. She pulled down the hood of her raincoat, water running off it in rivulets. "I just needed time to think. But I'm *not* backing out." Her gaze met Elliott's.

Elliott understood that it must have taken quite a lot for Bea to show up, given all her reservations. And yet here she was anyway, choosing her coven-mates over herself. Which really meant something.

"Okay." Madeline clapped her hands. "Then let's do this."

The girls swiftly transitioned into spell-casting mode. Chloe formed a three-foot-wide circle on the floor with the powdered sulfur, dead sea salt, and belladonna seeds, while Bea lit the purple candles, and Madeline arranged the shattered glass and broken eggshells in the center of the circle, sprinkling it all with graveyard dirt.

As they worked, Elliott pulled the photo from her pocket, pressing it facedown against her damp jeans so she didn't have to see it, then opened the puzzle box and retrieved the book. At the last second, she flipped the photo faceup and placed it atop the eggshells and glass.

Once all the coven-mates were seated around the circle, Elliott opened the book before her and took a deep breath, the spell's title shining up from the page below: *Incantation of Destruction.*

Was she really going to do this?

Yes, Elliott determined. She absolutely was.

"I'm ready," she announced to the other girls, her voice slightly more confident than she felt.

In response, Madeline, Chloe, and Bea began to chant the incantation in unison. *"Bring forth the outcome this witch seeks . . ."*

As they did so, Elliott raised her right hand above the book . . .

It had all started because Elliott didn't fit in at school.

Her mom always said she was an old soul, which might have been true, but it was also true that her mom's death rapidly aged her. You don't go through the fires of hell and come out the other side unchanged. In the wake of her mom's death, Elliott felt decades older than the other kids her age and quickly became a loner.

In fact, she'd started high school already praying it would fly by, dreaming of the day she could attend college and meet mature people to whom she *actually* related.

Which is why Violet was such a godsend.

They'd met at a Santa Barbara film fest documentary screening over at the Arlington theater during the middle of Elliott's freshman year, and even though Violet was a senior, the two hit it off right away. Violet was into vintage punk bands, French new-wave cinema, and Russian literature. She liked thrifting and baking and had a penchant for anything David Lynch. And because she had a single mom— her dad died when she was a baby—the two immediately bonded and soon became inseparable.

The first time Elliott met Violet's older brother, Oliver, who also still lived at home and was nearly five years older than Elliott, he'd seemed super nice and chill as he kicked back on the sofa drinking his beer. Though Elliott could tell it was far from his first drink of the night. Vi had said Oliver was a little troubled, and now Elliott understood. He wasn't merely troubled; he was an alcoholic. But, like, a nice one. One that grew quieter as his blood alcohol level ticked up.

The first time something happened, Elliott wasn't even sure it *had* happened. Maybe it was *nothing*, she told herself afterward. Vi was helping her mom bring in a Costco haul and Elliott was washing dishes when Oliver came up beside her at the kitchen sink.

"I'll dry," he offered.

"Cool." She smiled, even though she felt like he was standing a little too close.

But then . . . nothing. And afterward Elliott felt stupid for being so on edge when he was obviously just trying to be nice. He'd been raised with two women and was doing *dishes*, for God's sake. Wasn't that a sign that he wasn't some misogynistic toxic-male douche?

Over time, however, she often felt like maybe he was being a little *too* nice. Like when he'd come up and give her a shoulder massage out of nowhere. Or like when he'd greet her with a hug that lasted a little too long. Or like how he'd do an over-the-top old-fashioned whistle whenever she wore a vintage baby doll dress, which she *knew* was just good-natured and jokey but still made her feel kind of weird.

And then one day she was at their house and Violet got a call from her sobbing, heartbroken cousin and excused herself to the backyard.

"Hey, give me some of that," Oliver said, plopping down on the couch next to Elliott and tugging on the afghan. He pulled it over himself as well, settling in to watch *Blue Velvet*, a film Elliott could never bring herself to watch again.

"You're a cool chick, you know that?" he said after a moment, as on-screen Isabella Rossellini cowered in fear from Dennis Hopper. Under the blanket, he gave Elliott's leg a pat . . . and then just kept his hand there, which made her body tense. "It's awesome Vi found such a cool friend."

She kept waiting for him to remove his hand. But he didn't. He just kept it there resting on her thigh. Elliott felt frozen, unsure whether she should say something, unsure if this was weird.

And then he just all of a sudden got up. "I'm gonna get a drink. You want anything?" he offered.

"I'm good," she replied, even though she felt anything but good.

Had that been something? Had he been *hitting* on her? Even though, at the time, she was sixteen and he was nearly twenty-one? Elliott knew girls who dated guys that were way older, and she certainly felt well beyond her peers. But she'd never given Oliver any indication that she was into him—because she was *not*.

But maybe her lack of response had sent him a clear enough message. Yes, he'd tried something questionable, but he wouldn't *actually* do something again.

So, on the night a little over five months ago when Elliott slept over at Violet's and they both fell asleep in the living room while rewatching *Wild at Heart*—Elliott on the sofa, Violet in the La-Z-Boy—it was a complete shock to awaken to Vi's brother putting his hand up her shirt . . . except also not.

Elliott opened her mouth to object, and he immediately covered it with his free hand, which sent a spike of fear through her body as he pressed himself onto her, his beer-heavy breath in her face. She tried to let out a muffled scream, but somehow her voice came out too small, and the TV's volume drowned out any noise. She could feel him reaching down into her pajama pants, which she absolutely *did not want*, and tried to push him off but couldn't. And then she could feel his hand in her underwear, his fingers painfully shoving inside her. And just like that, her mind went numb and detached from her body. Just floated away. This wasn't happening. It couldn't be happening. She didn't want to believe this was *actually* happening.

In the La-Z-Boy, Vi stirred in her sleep—and just like that, Oliver sprang off of Elliott and casually strolled to his bedroom, leaving her frozen and shaky on the living room couch. She just barely had the presence of mind to leap up and race into the bathroom, where she locked herself inside. She should have sprinted out the front door, but somehow in that moment it didn't feel like an option.

But the worst part—worse than being assaulted in her sleep, worse than sitting in the cold bathtub all night long, terrified that he would try to unlock the door—was what happened when she brought it up with Vi.

Elliott could still remember standing before Violet, Vi's face gone pale as she stared back at Elliott with shock and disgust, and—

No. That part was too painful to revisit. Elliott couldn't go there.

Because it was one thing to be attacked by Oliver, but quite another to have Violet, her best friend in the world, not believe her.

Elliott opened her eyes and gazed upon the dreaded photo sitting atop the broken eggshells and shattered glass: a selfie Violet had taken of herself, Elliott, and Oliver.

It was the only picture Elliott had of him, taken one Halloween right before she and Vi handed out candy to trick-or-treaters. Elliott and Violet were dressed as the twins from *The Shining*, and Oliver was wearing a black skeleton hoodie, a bottle of beer in one hand. He was objectively good-looking, that bastard, with crinkly green eyes and shaggy black hair. He'd had plenty of girlfriends. So why had he assaulted *her*?

And the thing is, Oliver hadn't simply assaulted and traumatized her—as if there were anything simple about any of that—he'd taken away the one person who mattered. The only person who *got* her. The only person since her mom's death who'd made Elliott feel less alone.

That more than anything else was why she loathed him.

She stared at his disgusting, hateful piece-of-shit face, her fist clenching tighter and tighter.

And then her gaze slid across the photo to Violet.

They never hung out after that. Violet stopped inviting Elliott over and didn't return her calls or texts. She just flat-out ghosted her.

Violet ghosted *her*.

Like somehow *Elliott* was the one who'd done something wrong or caused offense, when all she'd tried to do was tell Vi how Oliver—

And how could Vi just *abandon* her? Elliott had been wounded and broken and in desperate need of her best friend. She'd stood there sobbing her heart out, and all Violet could do was stare back at her and say—

I mean, hadn't they talked about practically being sisters? Hadn't they said they were chosen *family*? Hadn't Violet told her that she trusted Elliott above everyone else? And yet, in the end, she'd gone and sided with *him*?

And had Elliott ever given Violet any reason to doubt her? Had she ever done anything besides treat Vi like the most important person in the world?

So how could Violet allow their friendship, this thing that had been so vitally important to both of them, to just fizzle out and *die*? Didn't Elliott mean *anything* to her?

Pressure was building up behind Elliott's eyes, and it suddenly gave way as an involuntary cry escaped her throat. Sobs wracked her body, and she crumpled over the book, angry tears streaking down her cheeks. Her throat felt raw and choked up with all the words she'd never told Violet—how much she missed her, how much she loved her, how much she hated her for walking away.

After all they'd been through, Violet chose *him*. Even though he was a rapist. Even though he was a monster. Even though he'd assaulted Elliott in her sleep. She'd chosen *him*. And it made Elliott so fucking torn up and ragey and heartbroken and betrayed that all she could do was scream out at the top of her lungs into the once beautiful and now broken down and neglected mansion as she beat her clenched fist against the book.

She was so *tired* of feeling broken. She was so tired of burning alive with rage. She didn't want to be the living embodiment of pain and suffering. She didn't want to carry this shit around with her for the rest of her life.

She wanted to be *done* with it.

She wanted to drop it off the top of the highest mountain.

She wanted to make like Elsa and fucking *let it go.*

"Wait."

Elliott became aware of someone speaking. It was Madeline's voice. She'd nearly forgotten the other girls were there.

"Wait—what's *happening*?" Madeline asked in concern.

For a moment, Elliott thought Madeline was referencing *her*, but when she straightened—her sobs subsiding, her fist still clenched tight—she became aware that *something* was happening with the *book.*

The pages, which were now glowing and shimmering, had clouded over, just as they had when the coven first formed. A deep magenta blossomed out from the center of it, changing the pages to a rosy lavender and transforming the silver text.

"Did the spell just *change*?" Bea whispered.

Elliott reached for the book—she could see that the spell's title was still the same—but in doing so, she momentarily forgot herself and allowed her fist to relax.

Immediately, a ball of energy arose from the book, the same rosy lavender as the pages. It was bigger than anything they'd conjured thus far, and it wasn't spinning or burning; it simply hovered there before them, softly glowing.

"It's beautiful," Chloe whispered.

And it was, all iridescent tinted light. The same rosy lavender, Elliott now realized, as her mark, which had changed color and was shimmering, just as it had that night at the beach.

For some reason, Mary's words came back to Elliott: *The book was never inherently bad or good. It was merely a reflection. It gave us whatever we sought.*

Elliott looked from the ball of energy to each of her coven-mates, their faces lit pink by the glow—girls who'd gone through different kinds of hell than her, but who'd walked through fire all the same; girls who'd shown up for her and one another time and time again; girls, Elliott realized, she'd not only grown to respect, she'd actually grown to *love*.

I often wish we'd given more thought to what we truly sought.

Elliott looked back at the glowing pink orb. Did she know what she *truly* sought? Yes, maybe she *did*.

Maybe she wanted revenge—and maybe that was even justified—but maybe there was something else she wanted more.

"It isn't *going* anywhere," Madeline commented. Which was true, the ball of energy just continued to float there. "Why isn't it shooting off somewhere?"

As if in response, the ball suddenly flared brighter, like someone had turned up the wattage, which forced Elliott to half turn her head away as she squinted her eyes.

And then, before Elliott knew what was happening—before any of them could even react—the ball of energy rapidly expanded outward, like the glowing equivalent of a shock wave, and swallowed the room and the coven in blinding pink light.

Suddenly Elliott was lying on a bed.

No, that wasn't quite right; she was both lying on the bed and *observing* the bed. None of which looked or felt entirely real. As if she were in a dream world, and not the real world, the colors oversaturated, the lighting—a tinted rosy lavender—somehow both too dark and too bright.

Actually, it wasn't even *her* lying on the bed. It was *Chloe*.

Her gaze was on a bright, glowing fish tank across the room. Inside, an electric blue and yellow fish was circling round and round. Beneath Chloe, the dark blue sheets were twisted and warm, but her body felt cold and numb.

"Come on." Arman laughed, and his levity reverberated through the room and sent a complicated wave of rage and humiliation and shame through Elliott's body. Except she was aware that it wasn't just *her* humiliation and shame—it was *Chloe's*, and somehow also Bea's and Madeline's. She could feel her coven-mates invisibly floating beside her, separate and yet connected, as if they were four strands woven into a single braid.

Arman grabbed Chloe's wrist a little too roughly—Elliott could feel his calluses on the inside of her *own* wrist—and pulled her upright so she was in a seated position.

"Here." He tossed over her shirt, which landed on her lap.

Chloe picked up the crop top, fumbling to pull it on, and glanced over at the open bathroom door, where Trevor was peeing.

Seeing him, a rush of urgency descended upon Elliott—she needed to get out of that room.

But when Chloe tried to get up, she lost her balance and plopped back onto the bed.

"Whoa," said Arman, putting out a hand. "Jesus, you're wasted. Whatever you do, don't go hurling in my room."

His words sank into Chloe like stones sinking into a river. Elliott could feel them weighing her down.

Because he was acting as if being wasted was entirely *her* fault.

As if the only thing worth concern was keeping his room pristine.

As if Chloe was completely disposable.

Which, Elliott realized, was exactly how Chloe felt.

And the feeling wasn't new. Hadn't Chloe's dad treated her essentially the same way? Just casting her aside and moving on with his life as if she were *nothing*.

For Chloe, the moment confirmed something she already suspected was true—something she cringed away from as she realized the entire coven would now know: she wasn't deserving of anything more than drunken hookups and being used however guys wanted, because she wasn't deserving of anything that too closely resembled love.

But that wasn't true, Elliott wanted to scream; Chloe wasn't disposable *or* nothing, and this awful moment was in no way a reflection on *her*.

And then all of a sudden Elliott was in a car.

Except it wasn't really her in the car, she realized, it was Bea. But a younger version of Bea. And sitting in the driver's seat was Man Bun.

"Here, lean your seat back," he commanded, unbuckling himself and then reaching across Bea for her seat belt.

As he leaned Bea's seat back, Elliott felt a wave of anxiety wash through her body—as well as Bea's body, and, Elliott sensed, Chloe's and Madeline's.

"So, you want to stretch them like we do in warm-ups," he was instructing. "But you also want to massage them. Bend your leg—no, like this," and Elliott could feel his strong hands on Bea's leg as he positioned it so that her ankle was up on his shoulder. Except, as he began to massage Bea's inner thigh, it was also somehow Elliott's thigh, which filled Elliott with further anxiety, along with a heavy wave of shame.

The moment froze, and began to reverse itself, like a video scrubbed backward, until Man Bun had buckled Bea back into her seat and then rebuckled himself.

And then it started up again.

"Here, lean your seat back . . ."

Elliott became aware that they weren't simply *reliving* this moment; they were retracing Bea's steps. Playing and replaying a pivotal moment to answer her fundamental questions.

Except the questions, Elliott realized, weren't really questions at all. Bea had phrased them that way inside her head for years, but in her heart they were already conclusions:

Did I put out a signal that somehow attracted this into my life?
Did I somehow bring this moment upon myself?
Am I fundamentally bad inside?

Elliott felt Bea inhale sharply as her deepest, darkest, most shameful beliefs about herself were suddenly revealed. And at the same time Elliott inhaled sharply, because the answer to all three questions was so very clearly NO.

And then Elliott was sitting at a desk.

A desk that was *definitely* not her desk, it was far too orderly: books perfectly lined up between white marble bookends, a stack of highlighted papers resting in a clear acrylic organizer, an open, smudge-free laptop before her.

Madeline's desk, she realized.

And on the bright screen in front of her, a slideshow of Madeline was playing. Images of her posing with her dance friends, and touring Harvard with her parents, and volunteering at a Toys for Tots drive. Below the images were lines of innocuous text narrating Madeline's life—where she went to school, and the fact that she was a dancer, a former Girl Scout, and a devout Catholic—but for some reason the words filled Elliott with dread. Elliott could feel the same dread crawling up into Madeline's throat.

The slideshow cut to a black screen with a single line of bold white text—MADELINE GRACE O'CONNER IS ALSO A FULL-TIME SLUT—which sent a cold spike of adrenaline rippling out through all four coven-mates.

And then the slideshow cut again, but this time it went to a video of Madeline kneeling on a—

"No!" Madeline screamed.

And suddenly the video vanished as the world froze.

Elliott had a moment's awareness that it wasn't the Madeline in the desk chair who'd screamed; it was the Madeline enveloped with her in this dreamlike space—which was now flickering before her, surging bright and dark, like a strobe light had been turned on.

Elliott could feel Madeline's anger burning inside her, threatening to scorch the entire earth, but alongside it was something else. A deep, dark, humiliating shame—because in all moments, Madeline believed there was a right choice and the possibility for perfection, and yet she'd failed and taken a single misstep, and that misstep had led to—

And then suddenly Madeline was *gone*.

Both the Madeline seated at the desk, but also the one somehow connected to Elliott and her other coven-mates. One moment Elliott sensed her there, and the next moment she felt her pull away, as if they'd all been holding hands and Madeline yanked hers free.

In Madeline's absence, the empty room fractured like a shattered mirror, and the rosy lavender light began to drain away, traveling inward toward the laptop's screen, like an old-school TV being turned off in slow motion. At the same time, Elliott's connection to Chloe and Bea began to slip away, the magic binding the coven together now unraveling and allowing them to drift apart. If it had felt like the girls were holding hands, it now felt like their hands were loosening as all three coven-mates were pulled in different directions, the dream-space beginning to vanish.

But Elliott didn't want to lose their connection.

She didn't want to drift apart.

She didn't want to be left bearing her pain alone.

Something within her reached out to them. And at the same time, she sensed Chloe and Bea reach out, too, all three girls fumbling for and seeking one another in the dark, arms extended, hands splayed, fingers stretched so taut it felt as if they might burst into flame.

And then they found one another. And held on. And they did not let go.

The light, which had dwindled down to the tiniest pale pinprick, suddenly reversed itself, brightening as it traveled outward.

And then Elliott was standing before Violet.

"What are you saying?" Violet asked, her face gone pale as she stared back at Elliott with a mix of shock and disgust. "That my brother *raped* you?"

"I . . ." Elliott hadn't used that word. She didn't want to use that word. Even thinking it felt huge and scary. Rape was what happened in dark alleys to girls walking home alone at night.

Though, even as Elliott had the thought, she knew that wasn't true. *Yes*, her mind flickered. *No*, her mind rejected.

"He forced himself on me," Elliott repeated, choking on her own tears. And she could feel Chloe and Bea invisibly beside her, their throats also clogged with tears. "Vi, he . . . I was *sleeping*, and he . . . he put his *hand* over my mouth and he . . ." She couldn't even get the words out.

"My brother would never do something like that," Violet defended stiffly, her expression turning stony. "I think *I*, of all people, would know."

Which made Elliott suddenly question herself and feel crazy. Was she misremembering things? Did she make it up? Had it all just been a dream?

Except she *wasn't* misremembering—she could still recall the feel of his hand clamping over her mouth, his heavy stomach pressing into hers, his sharp fingers stabbing into her body.

And she *wasn't* making it up.

And it wasn't a dream; it was a nightmare.

"It happened," Elliott insisted, barely able to speak the words. "He . . . he *assaulted* me, Vi."

"No." Violet shook her head. "He's not like that. I can't *believe* you would even say that. You expect me to believe that Oliver—*my* brother—is a rapist? How could you even *say* that to me?"

In that moment, Elliott felt small and broken. And like she'd somehow failed at her friendship with Vi.

Even though *she* was the one standing there sobbing.

Even though *she* was the one in pain.

Was there something about Elliott that was fundamentally unlovable? Because why else would Vi be standing there staring back at her like she was suddenly this incredible burden?

And yet even as she had the thought, another thought pushed back, one that didn't come from her—one that came from Chloe and Bea: Elliott wasn't unworthy *or* a burden, and *she* hadn't failed *Violet*; *Violet* had failed *her*.

Suddenly, everything went bright, a brilliant rosy glow that forced Elliott to close her eyes.

"You know what you have to do," a voice whispered. A voice Elliott recognized but couldn't place.

And then suddenly the light faded, and Elliott opened her eyes.

She was no longer in the dream-space. And she was no longer sitting inside the mansion.

Somehow, she'd been transported and was standing outside a bedroom window. And not just any bedroom window, she realized as the rain plunked down on her head and soaked through her shirt—*Violet's* bedroom window.

Which she must have knocked on without realizing, because suddenly the curtains parted, and there, on the other side of the pane of glass, was Vi.

"You know what you have to do," the voice repeated.

And this time Elliott recognized it. Because the voice was *hers*.

Bea

Across town in Goleta, Bea suddenly found herself standing in Otis's bedroom door, the overhead light switched on.

He rolled over, his sleepy face squinting up at her from the comfort of his bed.

"Bea?" he asked in confusion. And then, seeing her standing there in her dripping wet clothes, he sat up in concern: "Bea? What's going on?"

It was as if Bea had finally stopped running, and all the pain she'd attempted to escape for so long suddenly caught up to her and came crashing down. Her legs buckled and she collapsed right there, standing in the doorway, as her tears came pouring out.

"Oh, *Fred.*" Otis was suddenly beside her, his arms wrapped tightly around her.

She couldn't speak, she couldn't acknowledge him. All she could do was cry and cry.

"Honey?" a voice came from behind her.

Bea lifted her head and half turned to see her parents standing in the lit hallway. Her dad had flicked on the light.

"Baby?" Her mom stepped forward and knelt beside the twins, one hand on Bea's back. "What's going on?" she asked Bea, who couldn't seem to stop crying.

"Hey," her dad said gently, kneeling beside her mom and placing a comforting hand on the nape of Bea's neck. "Whatever it is, you can tell us."

This was the moment she'd always feared. The one in which she tore her family apart. Her parents were looking at her with such love and concern, and she knew their faces were about to crumple as she destroyed their world.

But she choked out the words anyway. "I need to tell you something . . ."

And she did. She told them all of it. Everything she'd been holding back.

And when all was said and done, when she'd done the thing she'd been dreading for years, her parents didn't crumple or fall apart. Instead, they wrapped their arms around her and held her close.

"I'm so sorry this happened to you," they whispered. Over and over and over again. "We believe you, sweetheart. We believe you. We believe you and this is not your fault."

Chloe

Out in Montecito, Chloe was standing in her bedroom before her vanity mirror, her phone in one hand. It was on speaker, and it was ringing, though she didn't recall dialing anyone.

"This is Vincent," her dad's voicemail picked up. "Leave me a message and I'll get back to you. Thanks."

At the sound of the beep, Chloe started to hang up—and then reconsidered. She brought the phone closer, swallowed, then spoke straight into the phone's mic.

"Dad . . . ," she said, her voice wobbling at first and then growing stronger with each new word. "Dad, I just want you to know . . . you can't treat me like this. I'm not disposable. You don't get to act like I'm your daughter only when it's convenient for you. And actually? I don't think I want to see you or talk to you for a while. So . . . bye."

She hung up, feeling shocked at her own gall. And kind of empty, because leaving that message had *hurt*. But Chloe also felt, surprisingly, relieved. Like she'd put down a heavy boulder she hadn't even realized she'd been carrying.

Which made it easier to open her bedroom door and head down the dark hallway to her mom's room.

When she reached the closed door she hesitated, then knocked. Tentative at first, then louder.

"Clo?" her mom asked when she opened the door, her sleep mask pushed up onto her forehead. "What time is it?"

"Mommy," Chloe swallowed, her voice cracking.

"Sweetie." Her mom put a hand on the side of Chloe's face, like she used to when Chloe was little. "What is it? Did something happen?"

Chloe nodded, the tears beginning to stream down her face. "I need to talk to you about something," she confessed.

All along Chloe had worried that her mom might be too weak to hear the truth, that she might buckle under Chloe's words, but as Chloe told her story, she saw her mother transform before her very eyes, growing taller and stronger, turning full-on mama bear.

"Oh, baby, I am *so* glad you told me," her mom whispered when Chloe was done, pulling her into a fierce hug. "This is not your fault. Do you understand me? This is *not* your fault. And we're going to deal with this together."

Madeline

Madeline suddenly found herself back inside the Franceschi mansion, sitting on the cold and dusty floor. Four candles flickered from inside the circle, but outside the circle sat only one coven-mate.

"Hello?" Madeline called, her voice echoing through the dilapidated library and falling into silence. Where was everyone? Were they even there? Or were they still inside that—whatever that thing had been? Either way, had they *abandoned* her?

She stood up and went to the double doors, throwing them open to peer out into the night. The rain was still falling, though the storm had subsided, broken branches and eucalyptus bark splayed across the wet flagstones.

"Elliott?" she shouted into the dark. But her call went unanswered. "Chloe? Bea?"

There was no sign of her coven-mates, just the rush of cold wind.

Stepping back into the mansion, Madeline looked around the empty room, her jaw clenching as the truth slowly sank in. She didn't know where the others had gone, but one thing was clear: she was on her own.

Madeline wanted to scream. She wanted to kick over the candles and burn down the house. Not that she even *could* after that torrential downpour.

And then something caught her eye.

Walking back over to the circle, she bent down and picked up the open book.

Elliott's spell had disappeared, though the pages hadn't turned ash gray; they'd transformed and were once again ivory. The same color they'd been before the coven ever formed. Instinctively, Madeline pushed up her sleeve, only to discover that her mark had disappeared, too.

What did it mean? Was their coven *over*? Had it somehow been dissolved? And was that even possible? Didn't the book say that, once formed, the coven could be abandoned but never broken?

Madeline didn't know for sure. But she *did* know one thing: she was taking that goddamn book.

Elliott

"What are you *doing* here?" Violet asked as she cranked open her window.

"Vi . . ." Elliott's teeth chattered, though whether from the freezing rain soaking her clothes or the anxious adrenaline coursing through her body was hard to know. "Vi . . . ," she began again. And swallowed. "What you did . . . what you did was so fucked up."

"*Excuse* me?" Violet blinked, like she hadn't heard Elliott correctly.

"You were my *best* friend and I fucking loved you. I still love you, even though I don't want to. But what you did, the way you treated me . . . Your brother *raped* me—"

Violet flinched at the words.

"He *did*. And I can't *believe* you'd take his side and not *mine*. I deserved *better* than that, Vi." Elliott could feel the tears coming, but she didn't try to hold them back.

Violet stared back at her, face pale, lips parted like she was searching for the right words. And then she pressed her lips together and said nothing.

Which hurt like hell. Elliott hadn't *really* expected Vi to speak, but still. The silence was crushing.

"I don't want to be your friend anymore, Vi," Elliott said softly, which broke her heart to say out loud. It was the painful reality she was already living—after all, they hadn't actually been friends for months—but still, to say it to Vi felt so . . . final. "If this is what friendship is to you . . . I don't want it. I deserve *better*."

And with that, Elliott turned her back on Violet and walked away.

As she did so, she wondered if Vi was still watching her. If anything in Vi wanted to call out, *Wait*. But even if she did, it wouldn't change things. Violet couldn't take back what she'd done. And Elliott hadn't come there to win her over; she'd shown up to do the very thing that hurt most: be vulnerable and admit her pain. And now that she had, she could feel something within her begin to loosen and let go.

Besides, Elliott realized as she headed toward home, tiny raindrops falling on her shoulders and soaking through to her skin, these days she had more important people to rely on, and more important things to do than stand around waiting for an apology that would never come. She needed to go home and talk to her dad.

20

Elliott—*one month later*

Actually, Elliott could not only imagine *a lot* of things more depressing than attending a sexual abuse and assault support group for Santa Barbara County teen girls housed in a kindergarten classroom, she was kind of, shockingly, finding said classroom . . . (gasp) *not that bad.*

Well, okay, the chairs left something to be desired. And the artwork was amateur-hour, even for five-year-olds (were those white blobs supposed to be geographically inappropriate winter *snow-flakes*?). And why did it always have to smell like a mixture of hand sanitizer and tempera paint with a faint undertone of pee?

But all in all, the Tragic Kindergarten Kingdom wasn't nearly as awful as Elliott remembered.

Her dad had driven her to group that evening, parking in one of the open spots in the elementary school lot, a travel mug of Earl Grey tea in the cup holder, an aspirational winter scarf wrapped around his neck even though Santa Barbara in December was eternally temperate.

A lot of things had changed between Elliott and her dad since the night of her spell. They now had a standing date at the batting cages every weekend and were planning a big national parks road trip for that summer. And Elliott found herself confiding in him in ways she hadn't for years.

It also didn't hurt that her dad had asked Prudence to keep her distance. Not that he'd phrased it that way. *You've done so much for us over the years*, he'd assured her, *but it's time El and I learn to stand on our own.* Though he *had* directly informed Prudence that he didn't appreciate her withholding vital information about Elliott—or making Elliott think that he'd be upset to know. Elliott's and Ronnie's histories, he was adamant, were nothing to be ashamed of.

Apparently, this had prompted Prudence to admit that perhaps she *hadn't* always handled things the best way—which was a small thing, yes, but kind of *huge* for Prudence. And it made Elliott wonder if there was the possibility for even someone like her grandmother to change.

Prudence had agreed to give them some space, but she still insisted on dropping off weekly vegetarian lasagnas. And neither Elliott nor her dad could be annoyed by that; after all, food was Prudence's love language.

"You don't have to wait for me," Elliott had told her dad as she'd opened the passenger door when they reached the elementary school parking lot.

"I know," he'd replied, cracking open detective novel #758.

"It's going to be, like, ninety minutes, Dad."

"That's fine," he'd assured her.

"I mean, if you want to go and come back, I'll totally—"

"El, I really don't mind. Now, will you get out of here so I can lose myself in chapter thirteen and ignore the improbability of so many innocent bystanders getting murdered in this quaint English seaside town?"

Elliott had rolled her eyes as she stepped out of the car.

"Hey, El?" he'd called after her.

She'd bent down to look at him, one hand on the doorframe. "Yeah?"

The way he'd been smiling made her feel like she was his most important person in the world—which she knew she was. "I'm really proud of you." His eyes had glittered in the overhead light. "Also? You're a fucking *badass*."

"Daddy!" She'd laughed in faux shock and embarrassment, shaking her head as she closed the door. "God, I can't take you *anywhere*."

But truthfully his words had made her heart sing.

It had been over a month since Elliott cast her spell, and a week since she'd seen her coven-mates. Well, most of her coven-mates.

Madeline, she hadn't seen since the night of the spell.

And not for lack of trying.

When Elliott returned to the Franceschi mansion the following day to retrieve the items she'd left behind (after, you know, she and the other girls were *magically transported*, an event she still couldn't believe actually happened and which had somehow reversed all of her lingering blowback symptoms and changed her now-rosy-lavender mark back to its original size), she'd found her coat and her backpack and the empty puzzle box. But the book was missing.

She'd already been texting with Chloe and Bea and knew they didn't have it. So she'd immediately texted Madeline. **Hey, did you happen to grab something of mine?** When Madeline failed to respond, Elliott tried calling. Multiple times, in fact. But the weekend came and went, and Madeline never answered. Which worried Elliott. What was going on with her?

It wasn't hard to find Madeline's address online, and so that Monday Elliott had Ubered over to San Roque after school to talk face-to-face.

Madeline's mother was the one who answered the door, and something about the way she'd stood there in her white pantsuit and heels made Elliott feel really bad for Madeline. She remembered what Madeline had said about being all too familiar with overbearing maternal types.

"Can I help you?" Mrs. O'Conner asked, eyeing Elliott's choice of fashion. She clearly didn't appreciate the acid-washed jeans or vintage Hole T-shirt, and the pink hair and nose ring probably weren't doing it for her, either.

"Um, yeah, I need to talk to Madeline?" Elliott had informed her.

"I'm sorry, but she's not here right now."

Elliott could see Mrs. O'Conner trying to figure out where in the world her daughter met someone like *Elliott*, and then something clicked into place.

"Are you in group together?" she'd asked.

"Uh, yeah," Elliott had replied, surprised that Mrs. O'Conner knew about group.

At that, her demeanor had shifted, her expression softening. "Well, I can certainly give her a message," she'd assured Elliott gently, like Elliott was delicate and might possibly break.

"Oh no, that's okay," Elliott declined. Though she knew that when Madeline's mother told her that a pink-haired girl had stopped by, she'd obviously know who it was. Which, good. Maybe that would prompt Madeline to get in touch.

Except she hadn't.

Elliott tried again a few days later, but still with no luck.

"I'm so sorry, but she's studying at a friend's house," Mrs. O'Conner said that time around. "It's Elliott, right?"

"Yeah," Elliott replied. Okay, so, they'd talked about her. Interesting.

"I'll be sure to let her know." Mrs. O'Conner smiled. And then added, "You take care."

But by the third time Elliott had stopped by at the end of that week, now feeling deeply concerned—partly because Madeline had the book, but mostly because she was isolating herself—it was clear Madeline had made up some kind of lie; Mrs. O'Conner's demeanor was markedly different. When she opened the door and saw it was Elliott, her face hardened.

"I'm sorry, but she isn't available," she informed Elliott crisply. "And I think you should go."

"Okay." Elliott hedged. "Well, the thing is, she actually has something of mine."

"Yes. I was told you might say something of the sort. I'm not sure what you think my daughter took from you, but I assure you it's not the case."

"Can I at least speak with her for just a minute?" Elliott asked.

"No, you cannot," Mrs. O'Conner said icily. "I'm sure that whatever you've gone through has been very troubling, and I wish you well"—she did *not* sound like she wished anyone well—"but you need to leave my daughter alone. And you need to stop showing up like this."

Elliott had reared back a little. *Jesus, lady.* "I'm not sure what Madeline told you—"

"My daughter told me *everything*," Mrs. O'Conner cut in, eyes narrowed. "And I have to say, I was extremely tempted to reach out to your family. I'm not going to, only at my daughter's behest, but if I hear that you've attempted to contact or approach her ever again, even *once*, you can be sure that I'll take action."

Elliott had been dumbstruck. What the hell had Madeline said? But Elliott also wasn't an idiot, and this lady was kind of freaky, so she'd turned around and gone home.

Afterward, she'd texted Bea and Chloe and asked them to meet her that weekend at the breakwater, a long jetty leading out into the ocean, where their conversation would be covered by the sounds of crashing waves.

When she'd filled them in, they were equally dumbstruck and disturbed.

"Do you think she told her mom all about the witchcraft?" Chloe had asked in horror.

"No, I kind of doubt it," Elliott replied. "But I do think she could have told her I tried to recruit her to be in a coven. Or maybe she made up something even more extreme, that I was obsessed with her and stalking her or something. Who knows?"

"And now *she* has the book." Bea shook her head. "Do you think Chloe or I should try and talk to her?"

"I'm pretty sure Madeline's already thought that far ahead," Elliott replied, leaning against the metal railing. "I'm betting she's fabricated stories about the two of you as well."

"Okay, but there's definitely a way of getting through to her, not to mention getting the book back," Chloe said with determination, chewing on a strand of hair. "Let's think about this."

But once they'd talked everything through and run through all the options—including breaking into Madeline's house while she was sleeping, or kidnapping her at her school, which was tempting— what they'd *actually* decided was that the best course of action was to just . . . let it all go. The book, for starters—which wasn't what Elliott would have ever in a million years thought she'd be cool with—but also Madeline.

And that was the hardest, most heartbreaking part. After all, Madeline was their *coven-mate*. And without her, their coven just wasn't the same. Besides, they wanted for her what they'd started gaining for themselves the night of Elliott's spell: healing.

But they couldn't *force* her. They could only hope. And never stop hoping. Maybe one day Madeline would find her way back to them.

In the meantime, when it came to the book, they knew Madeline couldn't form another coven—she was forever bound to them—or conjure or cast on her own. And even if she attempted to recruit a group of girls to form a coven to carry out her burn-it-all-down plans, she'd have no control over what they conjured, and no real authority over the coven's direction. And Madeline relinquishing control and authority seemed highly unlikely.

No, the only thing Madeline would be able to do on her own with the book was call up the hologram image of her imagined future self. Which, honestly, just made them feel really sad.

"So, that's it, then," Chloe had said in disappointment, her gaze on the boats in the harbor, the flags lining the breakwater flapping in the wind. "Madeline's gone. The book's gone. I guess that means the coven's over."

"I guess so," Bea sighed, tucking her hands into the pockets of her zip-up.

"Well, actually," Elliott said, brushing away a strand of her pink windswept hair. "That's something I wanted to discuss . . ." Because she'd already been formulating an alternative plan.

Back in group, Mary Yoshida, fearless defender of Tragic Kindergarten Kingdom, took her seat at one end of the circle, wearing a long, indigo cotton dress, a geometric wood necklace, and a warm expression.

"Greetings to all of you lovely people. I see we have at least one new face here today." She nodded at a nervous girl four seats over. "And many old faces as well. Welcome. As always, I want to remind you of a few ground rules. There is no pressure to speak, you may share if and when you are ready to do so, and you can choose what it is you disclose. First names only, though if you want to identify your school, you may do so. Also, we are here to listen without judgment, and we never offer our opinions or advice unless directly asked for them. Also, as you all know, this is a safe and sacred space. Anything said here remains within the confines of this circle.

"So." Mary calmly surveyed the girls. "With that said, who would like to share?"

The group remained silent, the squeak of people shifting in their chairs. Even Chatty Charlotte was quiet today.

Mary's gaze moved clockwise around the circle, past Church-Mouse Maritza and Never Have I Ever Raya, and landed on Elliott.

Elliott stared back. Hesitated a moment. And then, swallowing away the lump in her throat, she raised her hand.

Elliott—*five months later*

Sitting on a swing at Kids World playground one warm Saturday spring evening, Elliott checked the time on her phone. Five minutes to eight. She slipped her phone into the pocket of her leather jacket, turned up the volume on Alanis Morissette's "Thank U," and pumped her legs back and forth, rising higher and higher.

Kids World was a sprawling wooden play structure within Alameda Park, originally built by the community back in the '90s with input from elementary school kids—which explained its many hiding cubbies, the handprints on the ceramic tile posts out front, and its immense and undying popularity among Santa Barbara's kindergarten set. Elliott and her mom had spent many weekends there, racing across the high bridges and feeding woodchips to the life-size shark. But Elliott had picked it for that evening's meetup because it was easy to get to, be it by car, bus, bicycle, or on foot.

There were only six more weeks left of senior year—and God, those six weeks were draaaaagging on—but that meant soon enough Elliott could peace out on Santa Barbara High and never look back. Nostalgic post-graduation visits? Ten-year high school reunions? God no, and *hell* no. She wasn't going to *pine* for high school. These were absolutely *not* the best years of her life.

Of course, that made her think about Kaylie, who'd *loved* high school but had peaced out on Santa Barbara High *and* Santa Barbara itself—except not of her own volition. Kaylie and her family hadn't returned, and from speaking with Breanna Hernandez, Elliott knew they weren't going to. Which still filled Elliott with righteous anger, but she also knew from Breanna that Kaylie was doing okay, all things considered. She had her family, and she was still in touch with her closest friends, and Kaylie would make new friends wherever she landed.

Of course, unlike Kaylie, Elliott would be hanging around Santa Barbara for a little while longer. Sadly, she'd for some ungodly reason— and only after confirming via some light cyber-stalking that Vi had transferred to UCSB—agreed to go to Santa Barbara City College in the fall.

Which, by the way, she was *only* committing to for one year. One year, and then she and her dad would talk. *Maybe* she'd continue.

Or *maybe* she'd transfer somewhere else.

Or maybe she'd move off and become a barista in LA or NYC, or pack up a week's worth of stuff and go backpacking across Southeast Asia. Dreams she'd once shared with Vi and had let die but which she'd started to rekindle. Who knew? Her future sort of felt like the pages of the book: empty and open, waiting for her to set an intention.

The new girl from group—her name was Samira—was the first one to show. She'd ridden there on her bike, which she walked over across the grass. Samira was a sophomore at the Anacapa School, with shoulder-length black hair, olive skin, and a quiet, sad demeanor. Elliott had added her to the List right away.

"Hey." Elliott smiled, pulling out her earbuds as she climbed off the swing and met Samira at the picnic tables. "We're just waiting for a few more people. I'm really glad you came."

Church-Mouse Maritza was next, followed by Never Have I Ever Raya, and then Chatty Charlotte, who was already looking weirded out. The last to show were Chloe and Bea.

"Let's talk over here," Elliott said, nodding toward the castle-like play structure.

She led the group under one of the playground's many bridges and toward the center of the structure where, tucked away from view, was a small wooden stage half encircled with several small rows of stadium seating. She motioned for them to sit and remained standing on the stage with Chloe and Bea.

"So . . . what is this?" Charlotte asked, looking up at Elliott.

"We gathered you here this evening," said Bea, "because we have a proposition."

"We sit together in that group, week after week," Chloe added, her long, black skirt billowing in the breeze. "And that's great, that's a real start. But also? There's a whole lot more we could be doing."

"And if you're interested," said Elliott, "we can show you how to really do something about stuff."

Raya frowned. "Like what?"

Elliott looked at each of them, seated tentatively before her. "How much do you know about witchcraft?"

Charlotte laughed. "You can't be serious."

Elliott's gaze didn't waver.

"Is this a joke?" Raya added.

"No," said Chloe firmly. "It's not a joke."

"It's *real*," added Bea.

"Prove it," the new girl, Samira, piped up. Elliott already liked the hint of steel in her voice.

Chloe and Bea looked over at Elliott, eyebrows raised in question.

When they'd met up all those months ago to discuss Madeline and the book, Elliott had confessed something to her coven-mates.

"I had something . . . strange happen to me. I woke from a dream the other day and had this weird, tingling sensation running down my arms and into my fingers. And not like I'd slept on my arms weird, but like something *else* was happening."

"Wait, I had something vaguely like that, too," Chloe said, as the salt air blew her hair around her shoulders. "I just thought my arms had fallen asleep."

"That happened to me, too," Bea added. "And same."

"No." Elliott had shook her head. "I think it was something else. Because when I sat up, I noticed . . ." She'd glanced to either side, ensuring no one could hear. "Sparks."

"Sparks?" Bea had frowned. "What do you mean, *sparks*?"

"Just what I said. *Sparks.* Coming from my *fingertips.*"

"Wait, whaaaat?" Chloe had leaned forward, eyes wide. "Are you serious?!"

"It happened two mornings in a row," Elliott informed them. "At first, I thought I was hallucinating. But then I remembered—"

"'*Your magic, now unlocked, will radiate from your skin and spark from your fingertips,*'" Chloe had quoted from the book.

"Exactly."

"Oh my God," Chloe had gasped. "Do you think that means . . . And is that why our marks now look like *this*?" She raised her right hand, where her mark, like Elliott's, had turned rosy lavender and returned to its original size.

"I don't know." Elliott shook her head. "But I think we should test it out."

"Okay, but how?" Bea asked. "We don't even have the book."

"That's the thing," Elliott said. "We might not *need* the book. And I was thinking—Mary said the book was merely a reflection—"

"Wait, Mary?" Bea frowned.

"Oh." Elliott realized then that she'd yet to mention her conversation with Mary. "I may have failed to share some pertinent details."

And so, she'd told them everything, all about Mary and her mom and the coven they'd formed.

"Mary was a *witch*?" Bea said in shock.

"Your *mom* was a witch?!" Chloe had been delighted. "Elliott! That is so badass!"

"But they never got this far," Elliott continued. "Their coven fell apart before they could ever unlock their own magic."

Chloe had chewed on her bottom lip. "So, if the book is a mirror of sorts . . . I mean, that makes sense. It's like it was tapping into our unconscious desires and reflecting them back to us through the spells."

"Right," Elliott agreed. "So maybe what we need to do now, in order to test things out, is tap into our desires *ourselves* and create our *own* spells."

The girls had grown quiet, thinking.

"Okay, but I don't want to hurt anyone," Bea said adamantly. Chloe and Elliott nodded their agreement. They'd already seen where that path led.

"And I want it to be for more than just us," Chloe said, leaning back against the breakwater's railing.

Bea tilted her head in thought. "What if we cast a spell upon ourselves so we can recognize abusers? That way we could warn people."

"I like the *spirit* of that," Elliott said. "But think about the reality. Do we really want to spend all our days thinking about and being alerted to every single creepy man around us?"

"Ugh, no." Chloe shivered. "Also, isn't that still centering our magic on *them* somehow?'

"True." Bea nodded.

"What if . . ." Chloe thought aloud. "What if we place a spell upon ourselves and other girls so we're untouchable and invulnerable?"

"Yeah, but I feel like that could go really wrong," Bea pointed out. "And is that what we *really* want?"

Elliott agreed. She was beginning to suspect that vulnerability, while incredibly uncomfortable, was actually the thing to move *toward*. "Also, something about making ourselves invulnerable is still in relation to the person who could harm us," she'd added. "And I don't want to cast any spell that's about them. This is about *us* and what *we* want."

"Okay," Bea said. "So . . . I guess the question is, what do we want?"

They all thought a moment.

"I want to be a badass," Chloe declared. "I want to walk into any room and just, like, *own* it. I want to do my thing and be a leader of sorts, and not even *care* what people think. And I want to completely ignore the male gaze."

"Love it," Elliott replied, beaming at Chloe.

Bea had been quiet a moment. "I want to shine."

Elliott could feel her heart breaking, because from her perspective Bea *already* shone. But Elliott also understood; after hiding herself for so long, why wouldn't Bea want to shine?

"No, wait, that's not exactly right," Bea said. "I don't *just* want to shine—it's not about showing off. I want to be a beacon and attract the people I'm meant to have in my life."

"I love that." Elliott smiled. And she couldn't help thinking that Bea was onto something; maybe that's what their coven could become.

"What about you?" Chloe had asked her.

There were so many things Elliott wanted. She wanted to walk down the street without fear. She wanted to stop curating her life, constantly thinking about where she was and wasn't allowed to be. She wanted strength, but, she'd been surprised to discover, she also wanted vulnerability.

"I want my dreams back," she'd said at last. "After everything I went through, I just kind of gave up on my future self. But . . . I don't want to."

The girls had looked at one another, a feeling of promise in the air.

It was decided that they'd test things out by each casting a spell. It was at their discretion to make their spell as simple or as elaborate as they wanted. They'd cast that same night, and then reconvene the following week to report the results.

And the following week, when they met up at Elliott's house (which her dad was *thrilled* about, offering to bake cookies as the girls headed to Elliott's room), all three girls were buzzing.

Because it had *worked*.

Bea informed them that she'd cast a simple spell, lighting a candle alone in her room, and that very week she'd found out that she'd been selected as her cross-country team's athlete of the year and would get to attend a black-tie student athlete award ceremony, *and* that her orchestra had been selected to play an exclusive performance at Carnegie Hall in NYC—and *she'd* get to play a solo.

Chloe, unsurprisingly, had done a much more elaborate spell, smudging her room, dabbing clary sage oil on her temples and eyelids, sprinkling geranium petals around her altar, lighting a series of candles, and holding her crystals. And that same week she'd been approached by her principal to be the student leader for a new sexual assault advocacy group starting at her school. Chloe wasn't even nervous about the leadership opportunity; she'd leapt at the chance. She'd get a voice in defining the curriculum *and* she'd get to lead student meetings.

Elliott had done her spell alone in her backyard. She'd lit a candle, burned some incense, held a photo of her mom—it felt right to have her mom's memory near—and quietly chanted, *Bring forth that which will satisfy my intentions.* And the very next *day* she learned she'd won a competitive online poetry contest. One that she'd entered months ago and had all but forgotten. The prize was a writing workshop with a poet Elliott admired, and the whole thing had inspired her enough that she'd sat down for the first time in months and written a new poem.

"Also, you guys, there's something else," Chloe had whispered, as if Elliott's dad might be listening through the wall. "That thing about sparks from your fingertips? *I had that, too.*"

"No way," Bea said.

"*Yes.* Right when I first woke up, same as Elliott. So I decided to try meditating on it, and—here, I need to show you guys something."

Chloe sat very still, eyes closed, hands palm up on her knees as she concentrated on breathing. And pretty soon, Elliott noticed something—the palms of Chloe's hands were very faintly *glowing.*

"Holy crap," Bea breathed.

Chloe reopened her eyes, and the glowing subsided. "You guys. I think it's official. Elliott's spell really did *change* us . . . It unlocked our magic."

Which, of course, begged the question: What were they going to *do* with such magic?

"I think," Elliott suggested, twisting one of her rings around her finger, "we should start a new coven." One that was bigger. One that wasn't reliant on any book and had a very different mission. "And I think we should recruit from Mary's group."

Neither Chloe nor Bea had been back to Tragic Kindergarten Kingdom yet, though Elliott knew they were each handling things in their own ways.

Chloe's mom had found her an energy worker and a therapist, both of whom Chloe *loved*, and her mom had started planning a trip to South Korea for just the two of them. Maybe it wouldn't be the family trip they'd once envisioned, but perhaps it could be good in a new and different way. Chloe still hadn't spoken with her dad, and she wasn't sure when she'd ever feel ready. But she *had* confessed her trauma to Madison and Brooklyn. Madison had been *nice* about it but almost *condescendingly* pitying, which annoyed Chloe and told her that perhaps their friendship wasn't meant to be. Brooklyn, on the other hand, had been 100 percent empathetic and sensitive, and being honest with her had really brought them closer. Which probably would have been true from the start if Chloe had given her the chance.

Bea's parents had also found her a therapist, who was help-ing Bea navigate the emotional terrain of pressing charges against Michael. Something Bea had been incredibly nervous about when her parents suggested it, but she'd decided that, as hard as it might be, was important for her to do. What if coming forward helped some other girl find the courage to come forward, too? Plus, she knew her entire family was fiercely behind her. It felt good, she'd reported to Chloe and Elliott, to no longer be hiding. Her parents now knew that Bea was gay and were unsurprisingly supportive. And Bea had even started toying with the idea of returning to soccer. After all, she *really* did love it. Why should she allow someone like Michael to steal her passion?

Elliott's dad had also asked if *she* wanted to go to the police, which she'd thought long and hard about. But in the end, she'd decided she really didn't want to. And maybe that was cowardly of her. Maybe she was weak. Maybe she was letting Oliver off the hook. She wasn't certain. She just knew she didn't want to give him any more energy. She needed to focus on herself for a little while.

Which included going back to group.

"Also," she'd told Bea and Chloe, "I think I know what we should name our coven."

"A *coven name*," Chloe had said excitedly. "Except, wait, I thought you said coven names were passé?"

"I know, I know, but I was wrong. We just hadn't settled on our coven's identity yet." Elliott smiled. But now they had. Which made her think about the poem she'd just written: "For Girls Who Walk through Fire."

Because that's what they were.

Elliott had spent a lot of time thinking about the experiences they'd each gone through. How they'd feared they were now damaged and ruined, that they'd always be isolated, that their lives would never be the same again.

And on that last part, they were correct. Their lives never *would* be the same.

But in some ways, their experiences had actually made them *stronger*, and had, surprisingly, brought *connection*.

Which wasn't to give their experiences a silver lining. Like, they didn't need to be *traumatized* just to find strength and connection. That sort of "everything happens for a reason" thinking was utter horseshit.

But what came *after* the trauma, Elliott was realizing, didn't have to be completely dismal and dark.

Because here was the truth of walking through fire: It was excruciating, and it burned, and it turned you to ash. But flames did more than burn. Flames also brought light. And witches, Elliott had decided, were like the mystical Phoenix bird. Witches *might* burn, but eventually witches *rise*.

Standing there now before their recruits, Elliott gave Chloe and Bea a small nod. Prove it, Samira had asked? Yes, they could absolutely prove it.

In unison, the three coven-mates closed their eyes.

With spines iron-rod straight, they tipped their heads back so that their throats were exposed. *You need to allow your heart to crack wide open*, Chloe had instructed both Elliott and Bea in one of their countless practice sessions in Elliott's bedroom. Which at first had sounded like woo-woo granola shit to Elliott . . . until it hadn't.

Slowly, the three girls lifted their arms before them, hands open, palms facing the starry evening sky.

Elliott could only imagine their recruits' confusion as they sat on the wooden steps, watching this display. Confusion maybe even tinged with embarrassment. "This is crazy," she heard Samira mutter under her breath.

Which was a natural reaction when you didn't believe in girls with magic.

Which was understandable when you thought magic impossible, and *certainly* impossible in *you*.

And then their recruits let out a collective gasp.

Even with her eyes closed, Elliott knew small balls of iridescent light were forming in her coven-mates' hands, swirling and glowing in the center of their open palms. She could feel them in her own palms, as sparks of magic radiated out from her fingertips. The first time they'd all managed to do this at Elliott's house, after months of diligent but fruitless practice, Elliott had gasped, too.

But it was their feet that Elliott knew their future coven-mates would be staring at.

Because their feet, the ones that allowed them to run free as children, the ones that carried them through every heartache and misery, the ones that walked them through fire and clear out the other side . . . their feet no longer touched the ground.

ACKNOWLEDGMENTS

First, thank you to each and every reader of this book. Becoming a published author was my childhood dream but it took a lot to get here—years of writing and seeking and excavating. All of which is to say: buckle up, because this is going to be a long list.

Thank you to my amazing and steadfast agent, Kathy Green. You've believed in me and my stories every step of the way, and never gave up. I am incredibly grateful for our partnership.

Thank you to my magical editor, Laura Schreiber. You've understood this story and loved these girls from the start, and are the smart, insightful, thoughtful collaborator I always hoped for. Thanks also to the amazing team at Union Square Kids, including Stefanie Chin, Diane João, Marinda Valenti, Grace House, Marcie Lawrence, Melissa Farris, Chris Vaccari, Daniel Denning, Jenny Lu, and all the fantastic folks in design, sales, marketing, and publicity. I am thrilled to have landed with your team.

Thank you to early readers Shirley Liou and Michele Debreceni, for your insight and ongoing friendship, and sensitivity readers Molly Geisinger and Amber Williams, for your thoughtful feedback.

Thank you to my dearest friend, Yoshie Suzuki, for reading the first *and* the last draft, and being someone with whom I can exist in the messy middle—both in art and in life. I'm so grateful for you and our friendship.

Thank you to the therapists I've been blessed to work with. To Evans, who saw me through some of the most painful moments in my life. To Maria, who helped me stay afloat during years of grueling infertility treatments. And most of all, to Lauren. For seeing me, for believing in me, and for helping me see, believe in, and heal myself. Our work together is what freed me to write this book. I am so immensely grateful for your ongoing insight, wisdom, and guidance.

Thank you to all the teachers I had who instilled in me a love of art and literature, especially Mrs. Adams, Mrs. Schmulowitz, Mrs. Robertson, Mrs. Wilson, Mrs. Dovgin, Mr. McEachen, Mrs. Lorber, and Mrs. Taylor.

Thank you to UCLA's MFA Film Directing program, where I rediscovered my creative voice, and to the individuals I studied under while I was there, particularly Marina Goldovskaya.

Thank you to Vivian Umino, for your ongoing mentorship and friendship.

Thank you to all of my wonderful friends, especially Lucy Anderson Mueller, Katie Middleton, Liz Smith, Justin Mabardi, Sarah McIver, Jaya Nolt, Lindsay Evans, Heather Miller, Kelly Lisy, Cheryl Burkowitz, Michelle Hinebrook, Abby Specht, Drew Sample, Hannah Losman, Bonnie Pipkin, Brittany Moffatt, and Gabriel Peters-Lazaro (whom I dearly miss).

Thank you to my mom and dad, Sue and Jerry DeRose, for your ongoing love and support. And thanks, Mom, for the many library visits, buying me books at every book fair, and signing me up for the third grade after-school writer's workshop. Thanks also to my brother, Geoff DeRose, who put up with an authoritative older sister for oh so many years; your artistic talent is only second to your ability to forge new paths.

Thank you to my in-laws, Pam and Sam Sample (in whose kitchen I wrote the first draft of this book) for your ongoing love and support, for raising the outstanding human I married, and for taking us in during Covid and providing much-needed childcare, amongst so much more. We will never be able to repay your kindness, only pay it forward.

Thank you to my entire extended family, on both the DeRose and Sample sides, particularly those of you who have been so invested in this journey.

Thank you to Sarah Huck, Allon Azulai, and the entire staff at Kos, whose Americanos and granola bowls have fueled endless hours of writing. And thank you to Halle Becker and Philip Urso, whose yoga instruction and wisdom have kept me grounded and in my body.

Thank you to every survivor, especially those of you who have shared your stories in art and activism. You didn't owe the world a thing, but your work and bravery are deeply inspiring and a much-needed shining light. Special thanks to Chanel Miller, Dr. Christine Blasey Ford, Roxane Gay, Ashley C. Ford, V (formerly Eve Ensler), Lacy M. Johnson, Emma Sulkowicz, the entire USA Women's Gymnastics team, Michaela Coel, and Evan Rachel Wood. And a very special thank you to Tarana Burke, who founded the "me too." Movement and whose art and activism are so profoundly impactful. (Also, attribution for the words, "nothing you could ever tell me would lessen my love for you," which I first heard spoken by Tarana Burke and which I now tell my own children.)

Thank you to all the bold, authentic women out there, whose work and existence continually teach and inspire me, especially Glennon Doyle, Amanda Doyle, Abby Wambach, Pamela Adlon, Samantha Irby, Nora McInerny, Alex Elle, Brené Brown, Rachel Elizabeth Cargle, Anne Lamott, Brittany Packnett Cunningham, and Elizabeth Gilbert.

Thank you to Beth Pickens, whose work helped me understand and value myself as an artist.

Thank you to my two beautiful and miraculous children, Graham and Frankie. You teach and inspire me every day and make my life so much more fulfilling. I am incredibly lucky to know you, love you, and be your mother.

Thank you to my husband, co-parent, creative partner, co-conspirator, travel buddy, and co-pilot (though who are we kidding, I'm always asleep in the passenger seat), Brad Sample. My art and my life would not be the same without you. Thank you for seeing me, believing in me, always telling the truth, never putting up with bullshit, holding my hand when I'm scared, wanting me to take up space, and loving me and our kids so well. Simply put, you're the top.

Lastly, to anyone in my life reading these words right now: if I haven't mentioned you by name, please know that you've played a role all the same, so one last overarching *thank you.*

ABOUT THE AUTHOR

Kim DeRose grew up in Santa Barbara, California, where she spent childhood summers reading books and writing stories (which she was convinced her local bookstore would publish). She now lives in New York City, where she spends all seasons reading books and writing stories. She earned her MFA in film directing from UCLA, and she currently works in digital media. When she's not reading or writing she can be found listening to podcasts on long walks, drinking endless cups of coffee, and spending time with her family. *For Girls Who Walk through Fire* is her debut novel. You can visit her at kimderose.com.